KAT ⎯⎯ ⎯RS

One Good Thing

Number
Forty.

For all the people I've loved, whether they knew it or not.

Thank you for giving me the words.

Contents

1

Everything is Fine

When Simon proposed to her, Rae Logan was ordering a sandwich.

It was a quite unremarkable Tuesday; neither sunny nor rainy, with a light wind and the mildness of early spring beginning to creep into the air. Rae didn't find it strange at first that she had captured the meteorological features of the day so clearly in her mind, and yet she couldn't for the life of her remember perhaps the more pertinent details, like the look on Simon's face, or even the words that he'd said.

Did he use her full name? Take her face in his hands? Did he go for a traditional w*ill you marry me?* or something a little more personal? Did he do a little speech beforehand, a declaration that he couldn't possibly imagine life without the warmth of her quiet touch, the very spirit of her, their two souls joining as one on the path of life's great adventure?

She couldn't be sure.

What she was sure of was that it was a perfectly clement Tuesday, and the sandwich that she was ordering was pastrami and pickle with English mustard and a half portion of sauerkraut.

It wasn't until some time later that Rae would begin to question how it happened that her brain had prioritised weather and food over what should have been the most important question in her life.

It was in fact, rather inconveniently, at the exact moment that she dropped their wedding invitations into the postbox. She felt fine as she released the bundle, and yet when she heard the dull thump of the two dozen envelopes landing inside, she was struck with the sudden and overwhelming urge to vomit.

Nerves, she told herself. Nothing more.

She took the test print of the invitation card out of her coat pocket and studied it. It was thumbed and worn now, the edges softly creased from days of this, of her running it between her fingers, trying to pinpoint in her mind what it was that didn't sit well with her.

The font, she'd thought at first. Too modern somehow. Too blocky. Something about the uncomfortable slant of the descenders.

Or the colours, perhaps? They'd gone for classic mid grey text with paler green detailing. Classic. Or, as Rae had described it, dull. They'd fought about it, of course, but it ended, as their arguments so often did, with Rae swallowing her feelings and agreeing.

'Fine.' She'd said, stuffing the test print into her pocket. 'It's fine. Classic is fine.'

Fine. What a sentiment to build your entire future on. And yet with Simon, things *were* fine. He was a reasonably pleasant man, handsome, sometimes funny. He was a middle manager for an investment company in the city, and Rae, in all their years together, had never figured out what that actually meant. He sat in a lot of meetings, occasionally darted away from the dinner table to join an unexpected conference call, and used phrases in everyday speech like 'I'll jump on that right now' and 'let's flesh out that idea'. Rae had generally found people who used those kinds of phrases to be insufferable arseholes, but she'd learned over time to hide her reactions. Because life with Simon was fine. He was the one good thing in her life, after all.

And yet, looking back at the test print, as the real invitations had barely settled into the postbox, she was suddenly struck by what had been wrong the whole time, and it felt like everything and nothing all at once. It wasn't the font, or the colours, and it wasn't the slightly obnoxious sheen of the luxury card stock that Simon had absolutely insisted on. It was the names themselves.

And Rae had absolutely no idea what that meant, and even less of an idea of what to do about it.

She took a deep breath and started back on the path to their house - a mediocre two-bedroom end terrace with a paved front yard and a granite planter which they'd picked up from the garden centre months ago but never quite got around to planting anything in. It annoyed her every time she passed it, but never to the extent that she'd actually get in the car and drive back to the garden centre to buy plants. Like a lot of things in her life, it was good enough.

Rae Logan was not a master of many things, but settling was definitely something she excelled at.

She wasn't unhappy. Far from it. She was just living, she told herself, taking each new day as it came and focusing all her energy on getting by.

She could almost have believed it when she told herself that this was just how she was. Almost. There was just a tiny nagging voice at the back of her mind, a memory of times when she'd really come alive. The faint, dulling traces of perfect summers in Blackston.

But that was half her life ago now, and adult Rae was absolutely sure that she would never experience anything like it again.

She latched the front door behind her and kicked off her heavy boots. The year was just beginning to wind down, and the first frosts had started to creep in. It was Rae's most and also her least favourite time of year.

Simon looked up from his seat at the breakfast bar as she padded into the galley kitchen.

'Your mum says she'll go straight to the cemetery.' His voice was hesitant. '11 o'clock.' He handed her a mug of tea. 'Want me to come with?'

It was the first Sunday in November, the date of the annual procession at the cemetery for All Souls' Day. It was never a question for Rae whether she would attend or not, but she could hear the reluctance in Simon's voice even as he asked.

'It's ok.' She smiled tightly. 'I'll be ok.' She cradled the hot mug in her hands and took a sip, marvelling as she always did how Simon could have spent four years with her and still not know how she took her tea. She grimaced.

'Milk, no sugar... cause you're sweet enough.' It was a statement, but he phrased it like a question. 'Right?'

Rae's smile didn't quite reach her eyes. 'Milk, two sugars.' She heaped a couple of sugars in and stirred. 'Cause I'm not nearly as sweet as I should be.'

4

'Oh,' Simon laughed. 'Sorry, babe.' He hopped off the bar stool, kissing her lightly on the forehead as he passed. 'What am I like?'

She nodded after him and settled on the stool where he'd been sitting, stirring her hot tea absentmindedly and letting her thoughts drift.

Should she have asked Simon to come to the cemetery with her? He had never made a secret of his disdain for family events, not least with Rae's mother who, though she was essentially a good person, was adept at hiding it. Her unconventionality and general brashness had never gone over particularly well with Simon. His family was overwhelmingly sensible, always looking at Rae and her mother as if they were problems which needed to be fixed.

The child of an immigrant mother and novelist father, Rae had always felt herself a sharp contrast to the clean lines of the Collins household. They'd never been anything but cordial with her, but there was something about the way they talked to her that made her feel out of place.

'You're so *artsy*,' Simon's mother would say, smiling politely, and dragging out the first syllable of artsy in a way that made it feel like it wasn't a compliment, the unspoken judgement buzzing in her ears for days afterwards.

Rae had learned, over the past four years, to make herself smaller, quieter - less like herself. She'd become so used to trying to please Simon that she had now all but forgotten who she really was. But, as she always told herself, wasn't that how love worked once the lust had burned away? And Simon was a good man.

She shook her head and gulped down the last of her tea, yelled a quick goodbye and pulled on her boots and winter coat, wrapping the wool tightly around herself. She steadied herself, took one last deep breath and headed out.

2

A Single Sunbeam

I t was a bright morning, the cold bitter and biting as Rae
Logan trudged up the path through the cemetery, passing
graves which had become so familiar to her that she used
them as wayfinders.

Left at Elizabeth Earnshaw, then straight on past Henry
Carnforth. Through the gap in the snarl of winter-worn trees
and onwards to the smaller Polish section of the cemetery,
where there was already a small crowd gathering.

She heard her mother before she saw her, talking to one
of her old friends, slipping seamlessly between Polish and
English with the ease of someone who had spoken both
languages for a lifetime. They'd stopped in front of a fresh
gravestone, the clean marble sharp against the mossy edges
of the older stones, and they gesticulated wildly towards the
grave and each other as they spoke.

Didn't know he'd died... Rae heard as she approached *...no,
only our age...*

'*Kochanie!*' Zosia crowed as she spied her daughter approaching, and she rushed over in a cloud of cheap perfume

and cigarette smoke to kiss her dramatically on both cheeks. 'Pan Jurek,' she said motioning to the fresh stone. 'Only my age, can you believe it?'

'I can't.' Rae shook her head. 'Hi, Mama,' She hugged her mother lightly, forcing a smile.

Zosia extracted herself from the embrace and gripped her daughter's shoulders lightly, holding her at arms' length to assess her. 'You look thin,' she said, her cerise lips twisting. 'Are you eating?'

'Yes, Mama.'

'Come for food after.' Zosia smiled broadly. 'Don's making lunch for us.' She lowered her voice, as if she were sharing a secret. 'Oh, he's such a wonderful cook.'

Rae smiled a *yes, thank you* and snapped her gaze away from her mother's. Dinner with Don. What a treat.

It wasn't so much that she didn't like Don. In fairness there was not a thing wrong with him. But the dirt had barely settled on her father's grave before Zosia had moved him in, leaving Rae with the uncomfortable feeling that perhaps he had been waiting in the wings the whole time.

It was a feeling that seemed like both the simple truth and a dirty secret she didn't know what to do with.

She crouched down in front of the grave she had gravitated towards, a conspicuously English-sounding name among the rows of Poles. With the price of a final resting place surprisingly high, it had seemed only prudent to Zosia to buy a double plot, but from the way she spoke about it, Rae had always wondered if the identity of the second resident didn't seem to really matter too much to her mother, just so long as she didn't spend eternity alone.

Raymond Joseph Logan

14th September 1949 - 6th August 2011
Loving husband, father and friend

'Hi, Dad,' she whispered, trailing her fingers down the smooth marble of the stone.

In the four years since Ray had died, the loss had dulled some, and the slicing grief had slowly given way to a quiet thump, a drumbeat of pain which caught Rae off guard less often now. Yet still she carried her grief like a penance, a whispered prayer of repentance which followed her around.

She hadn't been there when he slipped away. She was on her way to the hospital when she got the call, but she was running behind. She was tired that morning, and she'd stopped to buy a coffee.

Just that.

Just a simple, everyday action, but it had meant the difference between being able to see her father awake for the last time and sobbing her apology into his stilling body.

Time had helped though, and the regret which initially had her in a chokehold settled over the years into a vow to make her namesake proud.

Like her, Ray had been a writer, but unlike his daughter he'd actually made a success of his craft, publishing a dozen novels in the latter years of his life and becoming quite the celebrated figure in crime fiction circles.

In contrast, Rae had been writing the same book for the last seven years and she'd only ever got as far as chapter five before unceremoniously deleting the entire thing. She'd landed a job writing for a marketing company with little regard for literature and a love affair with bullshit salespeak and it didn't make her feel much except tired.

It pays the bills though, she'd always say to herself. *It'll keep me going until I finish this book. It's enough for now.*

The low hum of the procession approaching pulled her from her thoughts, and she re-lit a wick which had blown out with one of the other candles, nodded towards her father's grave and clambered back to her feet.

The sweet smell of incense filled the air and the people about her began to mutter prayers along with the priest. Rae bowed her head and twisted her fingers together awkwardly while her mother frowned. She'd never managed to be quite as Catholic nor as Polish as Zosia would have liked.

Rae could almost feel her mother still tutting as the procession moved off. The crowd thinned out to only the relatives of the row they stood on, and she returned to Ray's grave to neaten the flowers which had been laid across the dirt.

She was just straightening the lid of one of the candles when she heard Zosia's shrill shriek from the next row down. Snapping her head up, she saw her mother gripping Jurek, the man whose grave they'd met in front of, by the shoulder, while she berated him animatedly in Polish. Rae could only pick out a few words... *Jesus... Oh Jesus... IDIOT.*

She nodded a farewell to Ray's grave and jogged lightly back over to Zosia.

'Not dead, then?' Rae couldn't fight her smile.

Zosia was visibly shaken. She laughed, but it was hollow. Almost a mockery. 'I knew he'd bought the plot of course.' Her painted-on brows furrowed. *'Jezus Maria!* Didn't know he'd go and engrave his own headstone!' She smoothed her dyed red hair back into place. *'Idiota!'*

She muttered barely concealed obscenities all the way back down the hill as Rae fell into step beside her, chuckling to herself and silently thanking Jurek Lewandowski for bringing her a single sunbeam on an otherwise oppressively grey day.

They sat around Zosia's laminate table later that day, chasing the first hint of heartburn from Don's enthusiastically seasoned Spanish chicken with poppy seed cake and coffee. The conversation turned, as Rae knew it would, to the wedding.

'So...' Zosia began cautiously, with a saccharine-sweet tone to her voice that told Rae immediately that she wasn't going to like the next thing to come out of her mother's mouth.

'So...?'

The older woman smiled. 'So, about the wedding.'

Of course.

'Have you thought any more about Don walking you down the aisle?'

Rae pressed her lips together and took a deep breath. 'I thought about it. I decided against it.' Her eyes darted to Don, a flash of apology in them.

Don coughed awkwardly. 'Oh, I... um. I'll just leave you two lovely ladies to this conversation.' He smiled quickly at Rae, grabbed his coffee cup and pushed through the decorative glass door which separated the kitchen from the rest of the house.

Zosia looked back to Rae and her mouth opened hesitantly.

'No,' Rae said, simply. 'No. To whatever you're about to say, just no.'

'He's very fond of you.'

Rae held her mother's eye contact. 'He's not my dad.'

'Give him a chance.'

'I do, in most things.' Rae felt her mouth twist to the side. A nervous twitch. 'Not in this.'

'Kochanie, be reasonable.' Zosia sat up straighter in her

chair, smoothing her blue corduroy skirt down over her knees. 'If not Don, then who?' She took a long, deliberate sip of her coffee. 'You cannot walk *yourself* down the aisle.'

Rae's eye narrowed. *I could, if I wanted to, I could.* She teased her cake crumbs between her forefinger and thumb. 'I'll worry about that nearer the time.'

Her mother's eyes widened. 'But the wedding is in three months!'

Three months, Rae thought. Three months of this conversation. Three months of seating plans and menus and colour choices and arguments about music and favours and whether she wore a damn veil or not. And just for a second, there was nothing Rae would have liked more than to burn the whole thing to the ground and run far, far away.

But Simon was a good man.

Rae popped the last of the cake crumbs into her mouth and turned back to her mother. 'Three months is a long time, Mama.' She smiled lightly, a peace offering. 'I'll figure something out.'

She kissed Zosia lightly on the cheek and headed out, yelling towards the living room as she went. 'Bye, Don. Thanks for lunch!'

'Anytime, sweetheart,' came his muffled reply, above the sounds of whatever antique-based weekend TV fluff he was watching.

The thing was, she had no problem with Don. He was pale and portly with a brush of short ginger hair and a permanently damp brow, and absolutely not a worthy replacement for Ray in any conceivable way. But, however abrupt his entry into their lives, Rae had to admit that he had never shown anything but kindness toward any of them, her father's memory included.

She also noted with some discomfort that she had never seen her mother so happy. She'd tried to explain it away - the first flush of a new relationship, some kind of rebound effect tied in with the grief. But when all was said and done, it was as if that short, sweaty man was Zosia's whole world, and it wasn't a feeling that Rae liked, although she couldn't even begin to say why.

She sighed and picked up her phone, tapping out a text to Simon.

RACHEL: *I've eaten. Want me to bring you anything?*

He didn't reply immediately, and Rae tossed her phone onto the passenger seat of her ageing Ford Fiesta and climbed in. She gripped the steering wheel for a few moments, resting her head against it and breathing away the conversation with her mother, before starting the car and setting off.

She was almost all the way home before her phone beeped with a message. She pulled onto the drive and grabbed it.

SIMON: *Actually, babe, could you grab some bread? We're all out. Thnx.*

Rae sighed. For someone who seemed permanently attached to his phone, Simon always knew how to time his texts in the worst possible way.

She briefly considered telling him to walk his lazy backside to the shop and buy his own damn bread, but, as if it already knew she wouldn't, her hand brought the key back to the ignition and restarted the car.

Rae Logan was a lot of things, but she was not a ruffler of feathers.

Simon was just getting out of the shower when she returned, and he wrapped his arms around her from behind, kissing the side of her head lightly as she set the loaf on the table. 'Thanks, babe.'

The 'babe' always made her shrink a little, distancing herself from the term of endearment. It seemed so generic as to almost be an insult. As if he couldn't think of a single personal thing to call her. No pet name, no in-jokes. But she shrugged the thought away and smiled, leaning back into him.

Simon always smelled good. Freshly-washed and with his towel riding low on his hips, she breathed him in and remembered all the things that she liked about him. He was undeniably attractive, with dark hair, sharp blue eyes and the kind of cocky smirk which allowed a man to get away with murder.

His hands dropped to her hips and he pulled her body back harder against his, nipping lightly at the nape of her neck with his teeth. 'I missed you.'

Rae huffed a soundless laugh through her teeth. 'My mum was asking about the wedding again. She wants Don to walk me down the aisle.'

Simon hummed a response, moving his mouth down to kiss the top of her shoulders. 'And what do you want?'

Space, thought Rae. *Silence. My dad back. An idea for a novel which forces me to write it or a job which makes me feel alive. And most importantly, love. The real, electric, eviscerating kind of love which hollows you out and fills you up all at the same time. That kind of overwhelming want for another person which grips you so tightly that you can't even breathe. Just that.*

But she didn't say any of that. Because she knew that wasn't the question Simon was asking.

Turning in his arms, what she actually said was: *I want you.*

And as he brought his mouth to hers she almost believed it.

Sex with Simon was always an energetic affair. He knew what he was doing, there was little doubt about that, but there was no quiet intimacy, no making love.

Simon Collins fucked like he had a point to prove.

Most of the time Rae appreciated that about him. There was no subtext to his touch. He knew what he wanted, and he took it, and though she found the endless position changes and Hollywood grunts wearing at times, she felt a certain comfort from the routine these days. Granted there was a certain amount of just going through the motions, but Simon made sure never to forget about her, and in turn she played her part with good humour and was rewarded with an orgasm or two and a fleeting sense of satisfaction.

Afterwards she curled against him, her back to his front, and tried to remember all the reasons why marrying Simon was the right thing to do.

'Love you, babe,' he whispered against her, tightening his grip and pulling her in.

'Love you too,' Rae replied softly.

And in that moment, it was the truth.

3

The Mill

" **B**uilt in the late 18th century, Blackston Mill was used to grind the corn harvest from the northernmost fields of Blackston Farm until the end of World War II, and thereafter was used primarily for animal feed until its closure in 1959.

It is positioned in the heart of the village, where the River Stam flows down to meet the North Sea. The river, named for the large rock which has shaped the landscape of Blackston for millennia, is also the namesake of the Stamford family, who for generations have owned the land by the ford crossing of the Stam.

It's not just established residents who enjoy the many charms of the village, either, as Blackston prides itself on the quiet magic which hangs unseen in the sea air of the village, making it the kind of place visitors happen upon and immediately want to set about making their home.

In fact, one such visitor was Ms. Danusia Nowak, who bought the mill in 1981 after falling in love with it whilst on a visit to the coast. Ms. Nowak has poured herself into converting the mill into a residential dwelling for decades, and these days it stands proud, *restored to its eminent former glory as the jewel in Blackston's crown."*

- F. W. Merryfield, *A Brief History of Blackston Bay*

4

Pierogi and Denial

The drive out to Blackston Bay had always filled Rae Logan with a strange kind of peace. Almost a homecoming.

Her aunt had lived out on the wilds of the Yorkshire coast for as long as she could remember, and over the years she'd spent many happy days running up and down the coarse sand of the beach, climbing the shallow parts of the cliffs, and feeling nothing less than absolutely alive.

It was the second Sunday of November which for Rae meant only one thing - it was Pierogi Day. For at least the last decade, she'd made the drive out to the coast and together the two of them would make dozens of the little dumplings ready for Christmas Eve.

Outside her window, the scenery turned from farmland to scrubland, and once she saw the densely wooded area in the near distance, Rae let out the breath she hadn't realised she'd been holding and felt all the tension in her body pool in her feet and then drain away. By the time the car dipped over the hill and began the steep climb down into Blackston, she was smiling and humming along to the radio, which was playing a song she didn't even know that she recognised.

Blackston Mill sat proudly in the very heart of the community, set just back from the bridge over the river. Danusia Nowak - she went by Nush - had bought the former water mill just after Rae was born and had poured her heart and soul into renovating it. Her dedication was like an energy, bright and alive right there in the very bones of the place.

Nush was sitting at the table when Rae's tyres crunched a welcome on the gravel of the driveway, and through the large window Rae saw her quickly jump up at the noise.

'Kochanie!' Nush squealed, flinging open the heavy front door and kissing Rae warmly on both cheeks. 'Come, come, it's so cold out.' She ushered the younger woman into the kitchen, where the heat from the Aga warmed the whole room.

She held Rae gently at arms' length, one hand on each cheek, then softly muttered something to herself in Polish and kissed her cheeks again. 'It's good to see you.'

'Hey, Ciocia,' Rae said through a smile.

There was an easy affection between the two women. Rae had never doubted that her mother loved her, but it was not an easy thing for either of them to be together. They each had rough edges which grated on the other.

With Nush, it was effortless.

The two sisters weren't close. They'd grown up together in a resettlement camp after the war, bonded in a way which should have been lifelong, and yet these days they could barely stand to be near each other. Neither of them had ever seemed to have a reason, but the only contact Rae could remember was the yearly ritual of her parents dropping her at the end of

Nush's driveway at the start of the school holidays with her small suitcase and a kiss on the cheek.

Because of this, or maybe because they seemed to be two halves of a single soul, Nush and Rae had always got on like a house on fire.

When she was younger and particularly furious with Zosia, Rae would often tell Nush that she wished she were her mother instead, which would make Nush's grey-green eyes crinkle at the corners as she hugged her niece gently and told her what a lucky girl she was to have two mothers. Rae always felt a pang of guilt then, although she knew that wasn't Nush's intention. Hollowed out by the horrors of war, their mother, Rae's grandmother, had succumbed to tuberculosis in her forties, leaving the two girls to be raised by the community, bouncing from family to family.

Their father was long gone by then. Broken beyond repair by his years in occupied Poland, he'd taken the bus to town one day and thrown himself in front of a train.

To this day, Zosia blamed her father for taking his own life, for choosing to leave his family when her mother was taken without choice.

Nush, the elder of the two, never had. *It was too much*, she'd once said to Rae, simply. *He did the best he could. That's all any of us can do.*

Nush put a hot cup of tea down in front of her niece. 'How is your mama?'

'She's good.' Rae took a long sip and smiled. A routine. They did this every time.

'And Simon?'

'Yep, he's good too.' Rae rarely went into more detail. There was no need, when her aunt could read her like an open book.

Any of the times in the past when she'd arrived at the mill with news, Nush had seemed to already know.

'Dobra.' She slipped an apron over her head, tied the strings and tossed a second one gently towards Rae. Like Zosia, her English could have been flawless had she wanted it to be, but she often liked to speak in the same curious mix of languages. The sisters had barely even visited Poland, but their speech was laced with its memory, the language of the people who had raised them.

'I hope you have warm fingers, Kotku, we have a lot of work to be done here.'

Rae chuckled. Nush never liked to settle on just one term of endearment. 'Tea first.' She wrapped both hands around the stoneware mug, feeling the heat spread all the way to her fingertips. 'What's happening in the big old world of Blackston? Tell me something I don't know.'

At that, Nush's eyes widened with delight. Local gossip was her very favourite thing in the world. 'Oh M*yszko*, let me tell you a few stories.'

The funny thing about a small village is that no one ever thinks not to know everyone else's business, and Blackston was not the kind of place you could easily keep a secret. Nush didn't miss a thing.

'Well, you remember Penny who had the art gallery on the seafront?'

'Penny with the husband who died?'

'No... that's Pauline, and her husband was Geoff, God rest his soul. Penny's the other one. The *single* lady.' She drew out the emphasis on *single*, which made Rae chuckle again.

'You mean she's a lesbian?'

'Lesbian?!' Nush hooted, the soothing song of her laughter

warming the whole room. 'Słoneczko, no. She's not a lesbian. If only she were, *o Boże!*' She adjusted her apron and pulled up a chair next to Rae. 'I've seen her go to church every night this week, six o'clock, sometimes six thirty, and she stays for half an hour and then goes home. Every night, always for half an hour, and then she walks back to the gallery. She does those workshop classes at the gallery now, you know the ones I mean. Flower arranging and all those kinds of things. She has to get back for those.'

'Right,' Rae began slowly, '...and you think she is...'

'Sleeping with the priest, obviously!' Nush threw up her arms as if it were a punchline.

'Wow.' Rae's voice had an edge of sarcasm to it. 'And what does God think about that?'

'I think he has bigger fish to fry,' Nush adjusted her wire-framed glasses on her face in punctuation. 'Don't you?'

Rae smiled at the idiom. 'Careful, Nush, your English is showing.'

'I'll show you my English, *Podjudzaczka!*' She enunciated each syllable, her accent growing thick as the slightest hint of a smile crept into the corner of her eyes.

Rae's smile grew. 'I love you.' She downed the last of her tea. 'You're completely ridiculous.'

Nush shrugged a half smile - a *we'll see*. 'And you will not guess who I saw in the pub last night.' She paused for maximum dramatic effect. 'Jamie... ah, what was his name?' She raked her fingers through her wild salt-and-pepper curls as she thought. 'Stamford! Yes, young Jamie Stamford.'

Rae stiffened, a whisper of something she couldn't quite put her finger on snaking its way down her spine. That name had meant something to her a long time ago.

22

'Ah, well he is not so young now.' Nush continued. 'I haven't seen him since he left with his fancy wife, oh it was a good few years ago now.'

'And his fancy wife...' Rae began, the question heavy in her voice.

'Was not with him!' Nush brought her palms together as she spoke. 'He was with the other one - that brother of his. Ah, what was his name now?'

'Joe.'

'Yes! Joe, of course he is.' She met Rae's gaze and held it lightly for a second. 'I forget that you and Jamie were friends.'

Rae's lip quirked up in a lopsided smile. 'That was a long time ago.' She coughed and stood, taking the apron Nush had thrown her and easing it over her head. 'Anyway, let's get on with it. You can talk while you roll.' She joke winked. 'It'll make the batch taste better - chock full of juicy gossip.'

The look Nush gave her was laced with knowing. 'You're right.' She gave Rae one last glance and stood, moving to the worktop where her big stoneware mixing bowl sat, covered by a dampened tea towel. 'These pierogi are not going to make themselves. Get the board, Myszko!'

Rae padded across to the small pantry and grabbed Nush's prized pastry board. She'd had a local craftsman put it together from some of the wood which had been reclaimed from the mill when she'd first bought it, and she would have sworn till her dying day that now she'd experienced it, it was not possible to make quality pierogi on any other surface.

Together they laid it down on the worktop, adjusting until the position was just so. It was an easy routine at this point, a well-practiced dance that they'd been rehearsing since Rae was a child, and both women played their part without even needing to think.

Rae grabbed the flour packet, which lifted far too easily in her hands. 'You're almost out of flour. We might need a restock at some point.'

Nush nodded, dusting her clean hands on her hips. 'Ah, I should have checked. We will make this batch and then you can get more while I make food.'

They fell into their roles effortlessly, Rae flouring the board, Nush rolling and cutting and Rae laying out the little circles until the whole of the batch of dough had been cut.

Nush fetched a big bowl filled with the cheese and potato mixture they'd fill the dumplings with and handed Rae one of the two spoons she was carrying. They each tasted a spoonful.

Rae chewed the mouthful and swallowed it carefully. 'More salt?'

Nush shook her head. 'No, the salt is good.'

They each thought for a split second and then spoke at once. 'More pepper!'

Nush chuckled to herself, grabbing the pepper grinder from behind her and adding a few firm twists of pepper before mixing it through the big bowl. They had another taste.

'Perfect,' Nush declared with a smile and Rae nodded her agreement.

They sat together then, falling into a rhythm of picking a circle of pastry, adding a spoonful of filling and crimping the edges together to make a half moon. They each had a distinctive style - Rae pressed the whole edge together first and then nipped back along to make a wave pattern, while Nush's nimble fingers twisted tiny pinches down in turn so the edges ended up looking almost as if they had been braided.

While they worked, they talked. At first it was more stories from the village, and Nush had her niece laughing so hard at times that she had to stop what she was doing and take a couple of deep breaths.

Rae had always loved Nush's stories. From torrid affairs to family feuds with the occasional mystery thrown in, she thought she could listen to the outlandish speculations forever.

After an energetic interpretation of a conversation she had overhead in the grocers about Molly Spink and her blossoming romance with the pub owner's eldest son, Nush stopped abruptly and looked Rae straight in the eye.

'How are you getting on with the wedding plans?'

Rae blew out a breath. 'I posted the invitations last week.'

'You have a dress?'

Rae shook her head.

'Ah, you have three months,' Nush sing-songed. 'There is time.'

'It doesn't feel like it.' Rae thought of her to-do list - it had exactly two things crossed out and seemed to gain at least one extra item each day. 'Simon can be pretty specific about what he wants, so it's not easy getting him to agree on things.'

'He has good taste!'

Rae knew Nush meant it only as a compliment to her, and her mouth quirked at the corners at the very idea that Simon's taste was anything but basic.

'He doesn't, but I'm marrying him anyway.' There was humour in her voice. Deflecting.

'Because you love him.'

Rae wasn't sure if it was a statement or a question. 'Because I love him.' Her reply sounded practiced. 'He's a good man.'

Nush smiled but said nothing, her eyes sweeping over Rae's

face lightly, studying the younger woman for a moment before laughing lightly and nodding her response.

They sat in silence for a few beats, each picking up a new circle of pastry at the same time and falling into their practiced routine. They had made four each before the silence was broken.

'Did you never want to get married, Ciocia?' Rae asked, pinching her dumpling closed.

Nush's answer made her sit up a little taller.

'Of course!'

'But you never did?'

'I would marry only for love, Kochanie, and love arrives on its own timetable.' Nush's eyes crinkled at the corners, her smile at once wistful and longing, an expression that Rae was not sure she'd even seen on her aunt before. 'Sometimes you simply do not meet the people you are supposed to meet at the time you are supposed to meet them.' Her smile dropped a little. 'Sometimes you do, and it still doesn't work out.'

'So, there was someone?'

The older woman nodded almost imperceptibly. 'There was someone. It was a long time ago. Things were not simple and then there was never anyone else.' She spoke simply, as if holding tightly to whatever emotion was tied to the memory, and set her completed dumpling down.

Rae added her dumpling to the pile and gave her aunt her full attention, wondering how she had never heard this story before.

Why had she never thought to ask?

'You've never told me about him.'

'Ah, Kurczaczku,' Nush's smile twisted as she spoke. 'He is just a ghost story now.' She brushed her floured hands down her apron. 'I am happy, just me. I have had a good life.'

Rae's mouth opened, but before she could get the words out, Nush spoke again. 'So you will buy some flour before the shop closes, yes?' She smiled warmly, but there was a lingering trace of sorrow etched in her expression.

Rae knew better than to press the matter, although the clock was showing a little past two and she knew for a fact that the shop stayed open until five even on Sundays.

It was an unspoken plea. End of subject. Nush lived for her stories, and spoke openly and colourfully to her niece about any subject under the sun. If there was something she didn't want to share, it would be either for Rae's protection, or for her own.

Rae stood, washing her hands in the large Belfast sink, and drying them on the corner of her apron before untying it and draping it over the back of the chair she'd been sitting on. 'I will. Won't be long.'

Nush didn't smile, but her expression was softened by gratitude.

Rae grabbed her coat from the hallway and pulled on her heavy winter boots. The start of winter by the coast was at the mercy of the direction of the sea breeze, and today it was bracing. Rae looped her scarf around her neck, pulling it up around her face for the short walk to the village shop.

The bell over the door of Mr Cramer's shop was unreasonably loud for the purpose it was being used, and it often shocked newcomers to the village to such a degree that they'd drop full armfuls of their shopping. Rae was used to the clatter now, of course, although it still made her smile as the welcome warmth of the small shop hit her, stinging her icy cheeks.

Mr Cramer himself was a wiry little man with a kindly face and the kind of moustache which fell out of fashion in the forties. In the winter time he wore the same fair isle sweater vest every day but Monday, when he would wash and dry it ready to start the cycle over again on Tuesday.

He looked up at the sound of the bell. 'Rachel!' He threw his arms up in greeting - he had known her almost her entire life and, like most of the more established residents of Blackston, always insisted on using her full name. 'How's tha' been, lass?'

His Yorkshire accent had always been much thicker than the other villagers, and Rae had often wondered if it was something that he did on purpose, to round him out into the perfect caricature of a village shopkeeper.

'Hey, Mr Cramer.' She smiled brightly at the small man. 'Really good, thank you.'

He motioned for her to come closer, and when she did he took both of her hands in his, stroking them lightly with the affection of a grandfather, although he was closer to Nush's age. 'Aye, yer looking bonny as ever, lovely girl. Tha'll be a married woman b'time I see thee next, ey?'

Rae nodded politely.

Mr Cramer released her hands and tapped her gently on one cheek as he spoke - a gesture of affection. 'Ah, I've heard a lot about the lucky fella. I hope he knows what a gem he'll be gettin'.'

Of course. *Nush.* Just as Rae knew every last detail of life in the village, her aunt's most trusted neighbours would get a blow-by-blow account of every last happening of life back in the city, too. Rae often felt as though Blackston knew what was happening in her life before she did.

'He does,' she said with a wink, and Mr Cramer's laugh filled the shop. He had such a great laugh that a younger Rae would go into the shop with a repertoire of silly jokes just to hear it. It was warm and robust with a timbre which hit you right in the heart - the kind of laugh Santa Claus would have.

They chatted over the shelves as Rae grabbed the things she needed - flour, a couple of lemons, black tea. Mr Cramer made easy small talk, although even as they spoke, Rae suspected that he already knew the answers to all the questions.

They talked about the wedding, her job, the weather, and as Mr Cramer rang up the total, he asked Rae the same question he always asked as they parted. 'How is Nush?'

Rae answered the way she always did. 'Nush is Nush.' And they smiled knowingly at each other as if sharing a secret before Rae gathered up her shopping and headed out.

She left the shop and promptly collided with something solid. Rather - *someone* solid. She swore lightly under her breath, managing to catch the flour, but losing her grip on the lemons and the box of tea, which hit the cold stone of the pavement in a short series of thuds.

The man in her path swore too, and bent to help her gather her things. 'Oh God. I'm so sorry, I wasn't watching where I was going at all. Here, let me help you.'

She watched the man's large hands gather the lemons as she grabbed the tea, and by the time she began to stand her annoyance had eased to only a mild irritation.

'Don't worry about it, I was...' She looked up, straight into a pair of honey-coloured eyes which hit her straight in the gut, sucking all the air out of her lungs in a whoosh.

They were the kind of eyes which you didn't forget. Eyes you *couldn't* forget.

29

'Jamie.' It was simple statement, yet laden somehow with meaning.

He paused for a beat, brow furrowed, and then exhaled sharply in recognition, offering a tentative smile. 'Rachel.'

The sound of her name on his lips hadn't lost its edge over time. It sent a flash of heat down her spine and she shivered slightly as he carefully balanced the lemons in her already gathered arms.

'I...um...' The corner of his mouth pulled into a lopsided smile, laced with an expression she couldn't quite decipher. 'You're here?'

Was it awkwardness? Nervousness? She thought to herself that it wasn't like Jamie Stamford to be nervous, before quickly realising that the person standing in front of her was not the person she'd once known. This man may as well have been a stranger.

He was broader now than the younger man she remembered, and she could see the time which had passed in the sharper angles of his face and the greying threat of old age loitering at his temples. His hair was longer now, long enough to fall into loose curls on top of his head, with the shorter sides waving about his ears, and a dark scruff of beard softening his jawline.

'I'm here. I mean...' Rae stumbled over her words, her tongue suddenly feeling much too big in her mouth. 'Visiting Nush.' She smiled awkwardly. 'Just visiting.'

He nodded, still wearing the half smile. 'How've you been?' His eyes searched hers earnestly. 'God, it's been years.'

'I'm ok...' She defaulted to honesty before she even realised it and quickly corrected herself. '...I mean, I'm good. Getting married soon.'

There was a hesitancy to her voice, although she didn't know why, and she flashed her ring finger as best she could with her armful of supplies.

It was her go-to gesture when talking about the wedding. Simon had chosen an impressive diamond, and though Rae thought it almost a little vulgar, it had turned out to be the perfect distraction. People would spend so long marvelling at the honest-to-God rock on her finger that they completely forgot to ask her any *real* questions about the wedding.

Jamie, on the other hand, didn't even glance towards her finger. In that moment the mood felt completely transformed, as if someone had flipped a switch.

He held her gaze, his brow quirking into a frown.

'Congratulations.' It felt like a challenge.

Rae rose to it. 'How is your wife?'

'Ex-wife.' He didn't miss a beat.

Neither did she. 'Sorry to hear that.'

'I'm not.' His stare was unwavering.

'So, you're back?' She wanted to look away, to retreat from the intensity of his eyes boring into hers, but she couldn't.

'I'm back.'

His tongue slid out to touch his top lip. It was the smallest of actions, but one that sparked a chain reaction in Rae's body. First at the top - the parting of her lips, a breath which hitched in her throat, and then down lower, to her arms tightening around her shopping and her legs feeling a sudden, almost irresistible urge to run, a symphony set to the quickening beat of her heart, which now thundered against her rib cage.

She didn't run, of course. She was polite to a fault.

'Anyway, I've got to get back. Nush will be wondering where I've got to.'

He took a half step back, releasing her, and she almost felt the air rush in between them. 'Of course.'

A second's hesitation, then: 'It's good to see you, Rae.'

She didn't know what to say, so she said, 'You too,' and by the time it reached her lips it sounded like a surrender. Her arms relaxed slightly around her shopping and she nodded a goodbye. 'See you around, Jamie.'

She felt the lingering heat of his eyes on her back as she hurried away, and when she reached the bridge and dipped back down to the mill, she turned to find him still watching her. He raised a hand in a simple farewell and she felt something knot tightly somewhere in her chest as she watched him turn and walk away.

He is just a ghost story now.

The words Nush had spoken earlier pushed to the front of her thoughts, connecting. Only seeing him before her he'd seemed anything but - more a living, breathing reminder of a time in her life which she'd thought was long gone.

She took a deep breath, then another, steeling herself, and used one shoulder to knock on the heavy, hardwood door of the mill. She needn't have bothered, though, of course Nush was right there, swinging the door open and gathering the lemons and tea into her arms. She'd probably seen the whole thing.

Rae followed her into the kitchen, setting the flour down with a soft thump.

'I ran into Jamie Stamford.' The words which she'd felt catch in her throat suddenly tumbled out of her all at once and she was powerless to stop them. 'I mean I literally ran into him - BANG - just as I was coming out of the shop.' She barely took a breath. 'You might want to check the lemons, they fell.

I think they're ok though. I hope they're ok. I thought we could have tea?'

Nush smiled, but she didn't speak, not as she watched Rae pull off her boots and outer layers, nor as she filled a kettle and cut a couple of slices from one of the lemons.

She said nothing at all until she'd set two hot cups of lemon tea down on the kitchen table and gestured to Rae to sit. '*Siadaj.*'

Rae knew relatively few words in Polish, mostly instructions. *Sit down, come here, hurry up, be quiet.* What she did know, though, was that if Nush was telling her what to do in Polish, one of two things was about to happen. Either she was about to be bestowed with Nush's worldly wisdom, usually of a somewhat cryptic nature, or she was about to be told off.

This time it was the former, and Nush adjusted her glasses on her nose as she handed Rae the sugar bowl.

'When the universe takes our breath from us,' she started slowly, in the careful tone she used when she felt like she was saying something important, 'it is usually because it would like us to slow down and notice something.' She took a moment to blow steam from her hot tea.

Nush much preferred to put her faith in the universe than in God, and although Rae had caught her praying once or twice in particularly difficult times, she had occasionally even claimed she didn't believe in Him at all. *How could I?* she'd say. *When I have seen what He allowed to happen.*

Rae took a deep breath. 'We've been through this before.' She stirred two spoonfuls of sugar into her tea, preferring it sweeter than her aunt did. 'What if the universe doesn't have a plan? What if we're all just people making choices and then living as best we can with those choices?' She took a sip, although it was still far too hot, and she snatched her lip back from the mug quickly. 'You think the universe wanted my dad to die?'

'I'm not talking about your father.'

'And I'm not talking about the universe!' Rae was a shade off indignant, betrayed only by the subtle shake in her voice. 'Or about Jamie Stamford.'

Nush, who had been lifting her mug to take another sip, lowered it back to the table. Her eyes, normally the colour of old slate, warmed as she studied her niece.

'You loved him.' It wasn't a question.

'We were friends,' Rae stated, simply. Firmly. 'I'm getting married.'

Nush wasn't the only one who could shut down a conversation.

Nush nodded, standing from her chair and bringing plates of food to the table. 'You're getting married.'

It was a peace offering. They wouldn't talk any more about it.

They ate together in easy silence, filling their plates with sliced meat and kabanos and soft cheese, with fresh tomatoes and thick slices of the caraway bread that Mr Cramer ordered in specially.

Nush didn't ask any more questions about Jamie, and Rae didn't ask any more questions about the ghost, and when Nush broke the silence later in the meal it was as if none of it had even been said in the first place. They each appreciated that from the other.

Rae cleared the plates into a small heap in the sink and turned to Nush, her smile soft. 'Come on, Ciocia.' She grabbed her apron from where it lay over the back of the chair and pulled it over her head. 'These pierogi are not going to make themselves.'

5

Fire and Ice

J amie Stamford was a man of few words, unless he was held up in slow-moving traffic, whereupon he swore often, and furiously.

Moving back from London to Blackston had been a real punch in the gut, not just because his marriage to the beautiful Romilly that everyone had warned him would end in tears had, in fact, ended in tears, but also because he now found himself frequently at the mercy of the curious whims of countryside traffic.

Today Ted Garratt was moving his dairy herd from the farm's east field to the west field and it was causing a traffic jam the likes of which he had previously only ever seen on Tottenham Court Road at the very peak of rush hour.

'FUCKSSAKE,' he exhaled through gritted teeth, lightly punching the side of the steering wheel with a loosely clenched fist. 'Cross the road faster, you COW BASTARDS!'

He slammed his head back against his head rest and looked to the sky, as if invoking God himself might make the cows move faster.

Jamie was usually not the kind of man to partake in this kind of unbridled outpouring of rage, but there was something about traffic jams which really got under his skin. That and the two months of speculation he'd endured from the residents of Blackston when they thought he couldn't hear them.

He's divorcing that fancy wife, it would always start.

Always *that fancy wife*, he noted, never *that fancy Jamie*, as if Mills were always just too good for him and it was an inevitability that she would eventually realise it. He huffed at the thought.

'Oh, CHRIST ALMIGHTY!' He shouted at no one in particular, as his car failed to move forwards for the twentieth or thirtieth minute in a row.

He had heard the more elaborate rumours too, of course. The whisperings of betrayal and adultery and one including murder which he couldn't quite fathom. In truth the drama of it all amused him as much as it annoyed him.

He wondered what they would think if they knew the truth - that the fit simply wasn't right. That they were just two people who thought that the sum total of what they would have was more than they ended up having. That he had loved Mills, and she him, but it had always left them wanting somehow, an unspoken longing for something greater.

Though he did almost like the idea of drama, there had been none. Perhaps disappointingly so. There had just been a quiet admission from his wife one day that things just weren't working out, a sentiment he couldn't help but agree with, as they began the strangely impersonal dividing of their possessions.

Mills took over the lease on the flat in Highbury, God help

her, while Jamie made the decision to move back to the old cottage in Blackston that they'd been trying to rent out for almost the whole time they'd been together. They'd never even put Milly's name on the deeds, such had been the brevity of their marriage, and while Jamie imagined that he'd feel a certain sense of failure about that eventually, he was currently struggling to feel anything at all other than relief.

He'd known they weren't right for each other, of course he'd known. As he'd looked up into her eyes after slipping the ring onto her finger and found, not for the first time, the jarring sensation that he was not looking into the *right* pair of eyes, he'd known.

He knew he shouldn't marry Romilly and he married her anyway. Because if there was one thing Jamie Stamford was good at, it was making a terrible decision.

'Oh, you've got to be FUCKING KIDDING ME,' he bellowed, as one of the cows broke loose from the herd and started weaving down through the traffic, prompting a comical chase as Ted and his farmhand tried to get her back up and through the open gate. 'I am going to GROW OLD and FRIGGING DIE in this car!'

The truth was that he actually had nowhere to be. This hold up was nothing more than a minor inconvenience, really, as he'd taken some time off from his job to tie up all the loose ends of the divorce, and his plan for this particular week involved little more than driving around a few local furniture shops to see if he could make the old cottage feel a little less like a place where an elderly relative might have died and a little more like home.

The problem was that something else had got under his skin. Or rather, *someone* else had got under his skin. Since he'd run into Rae Logan outside Mr Cramer's shop the previous week he couldn't keep the thought of her out of his head, and it ruffled his feathers.

There'd always been something between them, through the years, some kind of strange energy which had pulled them together time after time and then pushed them apart with equal force. He'd spent the best years of his life tied to her by the fierce and unwavering devotion of unrequited love, watching from the sidelines as she blossomed from a girl into a woman and believing with all his heart that she would always be in his life.

Why had they lost touch? He couldn't even remember. Life, like the runaway cow who was now being manhandled through the field gates, seemed to have its own plan.

'JUST PUSH HER IN, TED - JESUS WEPT!' He wound the driver's side window down angrily, for no reason at all, then wound it immediately back up. It didn't help calm him, not that he'd thought it would.

Fuck, Rae Logan. He couldn't stop thinking about her. She was so different from how he remembered her and yet so familiar, all at the same time.

Her dirty blonde hair had always had a wild quality about it, and time hadn't tamed it any, with the brisk sea air whipping at the waves from under her scarf.

And those eyes. Hazel, he was sure of it. Warm, like the first changes of autumn. Eyes which, in past times, had cut him off at the knees and made him whole in relatively equal measure. They were beginning to crinkle at the corner now, slightly, just a whisper of the woman that she'd grown into, and he wondered for a moment about the other ways that her body might be different now.

If it weren't for the fucking cows he might have thought more about whether the slope of her breasts was a little sadder now, the curve of her hips rounder. How different she'd be from the young slip of a thing he'd admired lounging on the beach in her swimsuit on one of the handful of hot days that Blackston had, and the thought did very little to ease the burning heat rising through his body.

'SHIT this SHITTING… argh!' He dropped his head to the steering wheel, huffing a deep breath which didn't help him feel any better at all.

All these thoughts weren't helping anything though, not with the way she had all but run from him the other day. It was like she couldn't get away fast enough. He sighed, betting that wherever Rae Logan was at that exact second, she sure as hell wasn't wondering about all the ways his body might be different now.

He squeezed his eyes shut. 'DAMMIT!'

He was cursing now for a different reason. He'd sworn to himself that he wasn't going to fall for any of that love nonsense after the first time a young Rae had unknowingly stolen his heart clean out of his chest, and yet here he was again, a grown man turned inside out by little more than a memory.

There was only one thing for it, he thought to himself. He was going to find another woman to wash away the bitter taste of his failed romances. A new woman. Something of a palate cleanser. Someone who could obliterate every last trace of Rae's fire and Romilly's ice from his mind.

Definitely someone whose name didn't begin with an R, he thought, and as he congratulated himself on making such a sound decision, the cow bottleneck seemed to ease and the last of the beasts slipped through the gate, thudding a staccato trot up into the empty field and shaking their heads and haunches in delight.

The traffic dissipated, and the road ahead freed up without seemingly any warning at all, leaving Jamie with what seemed like hours' worth of accumulated fury and not the slightest idea what to do with it.

And as he drove down the winding road, headed inland, he settled for singing along to the most obnoxious 80s music he could possibly find at the very top of his lungs.

6

Good Luck With That

She wasn't sure if it was the bright office lighting searing her retinas, the perpetual drone of the girls in finance or the constant churning thoughts about her wedding, but something was giving Rae Logan a migraine.

She blew a low, shaky breath out as her head hummed and pulsed with a beat of pain that she in no way had time for. She necked a couple of painkillers and rubbed her temples, praying that she could stave it off long enough to get to lunch time and sneak off for a power nap in her car, but even before eleven the pain had swelled into a raging beast which made it difficult to even open her eyes.

Health & Safety Gary offered to run her home. It wasn't a good idea to drive in her current state, he said, and as he was a Health & Safety guy, Rae thought it reasonable that she listen to him on a health matter. Gary had a daughter about Rae's age and a protective streak a mile wide, and Rae smiled weakly at him as she concentrated very hard on not vomiting in his Panther Black Ford Mondeo on the three-mile ride home.

He walked her to her door, gently cupping her elbow, and she thanked him in a whisper, before grabbing the washing up bowl and gingerly pulling herself up the stairs. She set the bowl at her bedside and crawled in, thankful for the soothing coolness of the cotton against her burning face.

She wasn't sure how long she laid there for - an hour, maybe two? She only vaguely heard the sound of the door being unlocked followed by the thump of Simon kicking off his shoes, muttering something she couldn't make out and then the click of the kettle going on.

If she had been less consumed by the unbearable noise tearing through her skull, she might have paid more attention to the second, female voice. The one which said *milk no sugar, I'm sweet enough.*

But as it was, it was all she could do to lift the palm of her hand to her forehead and press hard until everything started to go black.

Rae woke with a start, and for a second she didn't know where she was. Then she caught a glimpse of the bright red bowl she'd left by her bed, and when she pushed down the covers to find she was still wearing her clothes it all came back to her in a rush. She didn't know how long it'd been, but though she was still fuzzy and disoriented from sleep, the migraine had faded to a low hum at the base of her skull.

She grabbed the bowl and started for the kitchen to grab some more painkillers, making a mental note to thank Health & Safety Gary in the morning, and she didn't notice the knocking until she was almost all the way down the stairs.

Thud, thud, thud.

She paused on the stairs, trying to shake the haze of sleep

from her brain.

Thud, thud, thud.

What *was* that?

Was it the door? She turned to look through the frosted glass panes of the front door. She couldn't see anything.

The thudding stopped, a few seconds passed, and then it started again with a different pitch and tempo.

Thud, thud, thud, thud, thud.

It was coming from the kitchen.

All of a sudden Rae felt a prickle of fear grab her, and as adrenaline flooded her body she was struck with the inevitability that something bad, *really bad*, was happening in her kitchen. Her brain, fully lost to its fight-or-flight response now, began to flick through scenarios, each increasingly terrifying and ridiculous. A wild animal? A burglar? A wild animal burglar?

She didn't know what to expect as her hand gripped the door handle and time seemed to slow to a stutter as she began to turn it.

She definitely didn't expect that she would open her kitchen door to find Simon vigorously fucking their next-door-but-one neighbour, Carla Bates, against the American-style fridge freezer.

Carla Bates, all edgy blonde hair and fashion magazine eyeliner.

Carla Bates, with tits that could sink a battleship.

And Simon, who, as it turned out, was not a good man. Not at all.

Rae watched for a second, rooted to the spot and completely unable to tear her eyes away from the queasy pallor of Simon's buttocks as they jackhammered away. As she watched, a wave of realisation washed over her like puzzle pieces shifting and falling into place. She knew at once why she had never been quite at ease with the idea of spending a lifetime with Simon. In a curious moment of clarity she could pinpoint all the times when he was with her but so obviously not *with* her.

And she found, to her surprise, that she felt not so much sadness as defeat. And not really anger, but instead a cold resignation which sank like a stone in her stomach.

She pulled herself up to her full height, loosening her grip on the red washing up bowl so that it slipped from her fingers and hit the hard slate of the kitchen floor with a clatter. A clatter which made both Simon and Carla jump apart in shock, snapping around to meet Rae's hard stare, as panic all at once clouded the lust in their eyes.

She held Simon's gaze for a second, unmoving, watching guilt begin to seep into his panicked expression, and then about-turned herself and marched out of the kitchen, slamming the door behind her and racing back up the stairs.

She pulled the small suitcase out from under the bed and began to throw in her essentials as she heard the sound of Simon rushing up the stairs after her.

'Babe...' he started, his voice breathy with shock and exertion. '... Babe, wait.'

But Rae didn't wait. She moved to their small ensuite, assessing the vast assortment of hair products for only a moment before deciding to leave it all.

'I didn't know you were home.' There was a strange quality to his voice that she didn't think she'd ever heard before. It almost made her wonder if she actually knew him at all. 'Your car wasn't in the... where's your car?' He dragged a hand raggedly through his hair. 'Where's your car?'

Rae didn't turn around. 'I had a migraine at work. Someone drove me home.'

'I didn't think you'd be here.' She could hear him zipping his fly, breathing hard. 'I didn't know...'

'Careful Simon,' she snapped, cutting him off. 'It sounds a lot like you're blaming me for being unexpectedly home rather than blaming yourself for fucking another woman in our kitchen.' She spun to face him finally, meeting his steel gaze with fire.

'I'm not...' he stuttered. She'd never spoken to him like that even once in the whole time they'd been together. 'I don't know why...'

'No, you don't.' Rae threw the last of her things into the case and zipped it with a flourish. 'You don't know why, and that's the problem, isn't it?'

Simon stood, speechless, his beautiful face blurring and distorting the way faces do once an ugly truth about the people behind them is revealed.

Rae hauled her case up in one hand, pushing past him and racing down the stairs to the kitchen. Carla was still there, fixing her clothes. She met Rae's eyes with guilty tears, whispering a single phrase over and over.

'I'm sorry.'

Rae noted that Simon hadn't actually said that he was sorry even once during the whole conversation upstairs, and she assumed that the main reason for that was that he actually wasn't sorry at all.

She looked at Carla without anger, without malice. 'You're welcome to him.' She opened the freezer which they'd been fucking against, grabbing a big bag of frozen pierogi - the last thing she absolutely needed - and lifting it slightly towards

Carla as a farewell. 'Good luck with that.'

And Rae turned swiftly, throwing her car keys and phone charger into her handbag and hauling it on to her shoulder.

She saw Simon leaning in the doorway, jeans riding low on his hips, his chest bare, looking every inch the smouldering villain. And she was finally, completely and absolutely done with it.

Meeting his eyes, she slowly slid the showstopper diamond off her left ring finger and set it carefully on the work surface. 'Do what you want with this.'

He nodded, resigned. 'The wedding...?'

Rae laughed humourlessly. 'I think it's pretty reasonable to say that's not going to happen now, isn't it?'

He blew a breath out. 'I'll let everyone know.' His voice was small, but he made no move to stop her. As his panic had died away, so had his drive to explain. He stood quietly now, accepting his fate. Perhaps even welcoming it.

'Yeah, you do that.'

Rae picked up all of her things and left, in long and determined strides, and she didn't stop until she'd rounded two corners and was far enough away from the house that she could finally breathe. And once she had reached that place, she exhaled with a long sigh, breathing out all the words she'd wanted to say but thought better of and freeing them, freeing *herself*, from the crushing chains of giving a single shit about Simon Collins.

It was almost an hour later when Rae found herself on her mother's doorstep, and though Zosia seemed confused at the unexpected sight of her daughter, her suitcase and a bag of pierogi, she didn't ask any questions. Not at first.

She ushered Rae in with a quick check of the neighbours' houses - probably to see if any of them had clocked the arrival and took the plastic bag from her hands to return it to the freezer. Then she put the kettle on.

Rae had never had the same easy relationship with her mother as she did with Nush, but they were family, after all, and family looked after each other in the best way they knew how. What Zosia lacked in understanding she made up for in intent, and like Nush, she firmly believed that food cured all ills.

'Put your things in your room,' Zosia said gently, her eyes following Rae up the narrow staircase as she climbed it. 'We'll eat.'

Rae pushed the door to her childhood bedroom open and set her case and handbag down next to the single bed, collapsing down onto the ageing mattress with a sigh. The room hadn't been decorated since she'd moved out as a student, and was now home to towers of cardboard boxes piled on every spare surface.

Don described himself as an entrepreneur, but what that actually meant in practice was that he bought job lots of sub-par products from his dodgy mate Baz who worked for an import business, and then sold them as and where he could. Everyone Rae had ever known had bought one of Don's neon alarm clocks. She had three herself and none of them had successfully kept time for longer than a few days.

Rae could smell the distinctive scent of frying onions and garlic in the air as she walked back down the stairs. Zosia started every dish in this way and so it was almost impossible to guess what meal would be served until it was set on the table. She cooked with enthusiasm if not finesse, paying little heed to the traditional use of ingredients, which made meal times at her house interesting, if not always enjoyable.

'Turkey curry,' Zosia yelled from the kitchen, as if she'd read Rae's thoughts. 'We'll have to have it with pasta though, we finished off the rice yesterday.'

Curious, Rae thought. *But ok.*

It wasn't until the food was actually on her plate that she remembered that Zosia believed adding curry powder to any food was the only step required to make it into a curry, and she pushed the gritty chunks around her plate for a while before she committed to eating one or two. She crunched through the texture with a grimace which she disguised as a smile, making polite conversation with Don and her mother about what her Big Plan was now.

The truth was, she had absolutely no idea.

That night, Rae excused herself early and snuck off to the relative comfort of her bedroom, pulling her laptop out of her case and booting it up.

She started, as she had so many times before, with the same two words.

Chapter one.

It always felt like such a thrill at that point, the blank pages filled with possibility, with the chance of great literary success which had eluded her so many times.

She didn't have a plan, instead letting the words pour out of her, filling page after page with colourful scenes of heartbreak and betrayal, but never feeling she was quite heartbroken enough to adequately capture the agony in words.

There was always something missing from her writing, a depth she couldn't quite tap into, and she had just reached the end of the fifth page when she slammed the lid of her laptop down with contempt.

'Why am I no good at this?' She spoke to no-one in particular, just out into the open space of the room. And the room, as expected, gave her nothing at all in return.

She grumbled to herself and dressed for bed, finding some comfort in the routine, some strange peace from being free from the monotony of her life with Simon.

And that night, curled up in a small single bed with the sting of ageing bedsprings poking into her back, she slept better than she had for months.

7

THEN – December 1959

'Tell me again,' Zosia squealed in clumsy Polish as she spun and wove around her sister's legs, caught completely in the excitement of the day.

Danusia stepped around her with a small smile, one that made her look older than her nine years. 'We have to wait for the star, Zosieńka.' She laid another plate out on Pani Krysia's rustic tablecloth. 'When you see the first star appear in the sky, then the meal can begin.'

It was Wigilia – the main festive celebration in Poland, and though they had lived their whole lives in a post-war resettlement camp in England, the sisters thought themselves Polish to the bone.

Zosia darted over to the small window at the front of the hut, peering through the murk of the glass into the evening sky. 'I can't see it, Nusia.'

Danusia laughed lightly. 'It's still light! You need to be patient.'

Zosia harrumphed, stomping the few strides back over to the table. It was cramped in the Nissen huts, but Pani Krysia had made hers homely enough, the sparse furniture decorated with hand-stitched doilies and cloths, a carved crucifix hanging proudly under the curve of the roof, and a small picture of the Pope taking pride of place in the centre of the side wall.

A curtain separated the sleeping quarters from the main room, and Danusia and Zosia had slept together in the small bed pushed to the back-right wall of the hut since Krysia and her husband had been kind enough to take them in. Pani Krysia took the other bed, along with Pan Kazik, when he was well enough, but he seemed to be rarely out of hospital these days. Zosia wondered if he would die soon, as her mother had, earlier that year, and she felt her body start to tighten and shake as it filled with the sadness that she had become almost used to.

Danusia, as if she could sense her sister's grief from across the room, came to her then, grabbing her hand and pulling her to the other side of the hut, where Pani Krysia was sitting by the stove, a pot of barszcz simmering and bubbling beside her as she prayed silently.

'Who else is coming?' Zosia asked, noticing the settings at the table. 'One, two, three, *four* people? Who else?'

'For unexpected visitors,' Pani Krysia said sternly, not looking up from her rosary beads as she worked them rhythmically between finger and thumb.

Pani Krysia was not an unkind woman, but there was no softness to her, none of the warmth that Zosia remembered from her mother, and she was much too young to understand the reasons for that.

Magdalena Nowak had told her daughters precious little about the war while she was alive, and Zosia would not understand the extent of the atrocities her people had faced until very much later in her life. So Zosia could not have known that Krysia Wiśniewska had lost all four of her children on the month-long journey from her family's farm to the labour camp in Siberia.

Born as she was into a world of albeit fragile peace, a five-year-old Zosia could not have comprehended then the desperation the older woman must have felt as she cradled each of her youngest three children, feeling hunger and disease grip them with such a ferocity that their tiny bodies, in turn, grew cold and limp in her arms.

She could not have imagined Krysia's horror at being ordered to throw each of her daughters' bodies from the train, nor understood the depth of silent grief which overcame her as she watched her eldest child, a boy of fifteen, die from a single bayonet wound to the chest.

Had she have known, perhaps she may have had a little more patience as the older woman thumbed prayers for her fallen family on a worn set of wooden rosary beads when all Zosia wanted to do was to start the celebrations.

Zosia was too young to read much into the hushed whispers of the adults as her sister did. She heard the singing, saw the steely will of the people around her as they boldly went about reclaiming their traditions, and she took it all at face value. She was much too young to see the subtext, feel the underlying weight of loss which followed the older people around, the ghosts of lives lost heavy in their hearts.

Even then they were so different, the sisters. Growing up in the camp would make Zosia strong, and it would make her proud, determined, as she grew, to stay as true as she could to her homeland. But for Danusia, four years her elder, there was something more to be gained from the strange community in which they found themselves; the ability to really understand people, to feel their happiness and their sadness as they did.

All in all, there was a lot that Zosia didn't understand about people. Maybe it was because she was younger, maybe because she simply couldn't *see* people the way Nusia could. She couldn't be sure. But still, she could feel them then, the first small shoots of jealousy, or maybe it was bitterness, as she watched the ease with which her elder sister navigated relationships with the people around her. And the young Zosia felt separate somehow, as if she were behind glass, like an outsider peering into a different world.

She felt it flare as she watched Pani Krysia look up at Nusia and some kind of silent agreement passed between them, as Nusia took her hand again and led Zosia out into the icy air of the December night to collect some greenery for the centre of the table.

Zosia stomped the frozen earth petulantly, impatient for the start of her Wigilia celebrations, and frustrated that the unspoken agreement her sister had made was making her wait. An agreement, obviously, that she was not party to.

She pouted at her sister as Danusia smiled softly back at her.

There wasn't a lot that Zosia understood about people, but she made a decision there and then that she would do whatever it took to not feel like an outsider ever again.

8

Wigilia

Danusia Nowak had never quite got used to living alone.

She'd lived by herself for the best part of forty years now, but she never seemed to feel any better about it. Her loneliness seemed particularly acute on Christmas Eve, intensified by the memories of past celebrations she'd shared with Zosia.

But that was in the before, and she had learnt through the years that dwelling on the before was fruitless. And that the very best way to stave off loneliness was by not being alone.

Rae had always described her aunt as a collector of waifs and strays and she was quite right. Nush knew the desperate grip of isolation only too well, and wanting to repay the kindnesses which had been shown to her as a girl, she had now appointed herself the unofficial guardian angel of Blackston's needy.

Of course, not all of Blackston's needy thought themselves to be needy, but that, Nush thought to herself, was no good reason not to take care of them anyway.

And as darkness fell over the still waters of Blackston Bay,

Nush set her table for five.

Bill Cramer had lost his wife early in the year, and though he had two grown up children who would be driving up to spend Christmas Day with him, Nush simply couldn't bear the thought of him spending the evening before alone. They'd been good friends for years, the three of them, and when Sue Cramer passed away, Nush had felt it as deeply as if she'd lost a family member. She'd absolutely insisted that Bill join her for the evening.

Her second lost cause was Penny Beaumont, Penny-from-the-gallery, who Nush thought needed saving more than most, but she had still felt a pang upon hearing that she didn't have anyone to spend the day with. Not even family, which broke Nush's heart clean down the middle.

No man in your life? She had enquired in what she'd believed was quite a subtle tone. *Or woman? I don't judge!*

But Penny had shaken her head with a curious sadness which connected with Nush in a way she couldn't pinpoint. Scandalous mistress as she may have been, any lonely soul was worthy of kindness. And so it was that she offered Penny the third seat at her table.

Young Jamie Stamford was her final project. Oh, he was such a handsome boy, all dark curls and eyes the colour of a fine whiskey. She could quite see why her niece burned a flame for him. Rae had completely denied it, of course, but Nush could read her like a book, and with the flames in her eyes after that day they ran into each other, Nush could see no other option than making sure they ran into each other more often.

She'd half-engineered a meeting at the old pub in the village, sweetly dropping off one of her famous walnut cakes for

Roy in The White House one afternoon in return for his unwavering ongoing loyalty and a very discreet phone call the next time young Jamie popped down for a drink. Roy had kept his end of the bargain, of course. They went back a long time, he and Nush, and he was well acquainted with her endeavours.

And so it was *ever* such a coincidence, two evenings later, when Nush had popped into The White House for a nightcap to find Jamie sitting at the bar, spinning a single scotch in thoughtful fingers.

'Miss Nowak,' he'd said, with a genuine smile. 'It's good to see you.'

She'd chuckled softly. She'd taught in Blackston's infant school almost as long as she'd lived in the village, and her adult former pupils often defaulted to the formality of their youth by habit. 'You must call me Nush. You're not a boy now.'

Once the conversation had started, it flowed easily. He'd told Nush about his new job, his plans for the old cottage and the culture shock of being back in Blackston after his life in the big city.

'Your wife?' Nush had asked gently. She hadn't meant to pry, but curiosity got the better of her and the words spilled out before she had the chance to stop them.

He'd simply smiled wistfully and shrugged. 'Things just didn't work out.'

Nush knew a few things about that. She patted his forearm. 'Love can be like that,' she'd said, her voice thick with empathy and with regret.

And then she'd ordered him another scotch, and a brandy for herself and when Roy set them both down on the bar she'd raised her glass in a toast. 'To New Beginnings.'

And he'd chuckled as he clinked his glass to hers. He'd always had a soft spot for Nush. 'To new beginnings,' he'd echoed, and when Nush had asked him what his plans were for Christmas Eve he'd admitted that he actually didn't have any at all.

Nush had been horrified. She'd told him he simply must join her for her meal. 'Rae won't be there,' she'd said. 'But I have other guests. And you won't go hungry, of course.'

'I'd love to,' he'd answered honestly, and Nush hadn't missed the gratefulness in his eyes, nor the slight shift in his energy at the mere mention of her niece.

'Dobra!' She'd smiled triumphantly and finished the rest of her brandy in a single gulp. 'Be at the mill for 5 o'clock. Don't be late!'

And she'd swept off in a cloud of sweet lilac perfume, humming lightly and feeling very pleased with herself indeed.

She was still humming as she laid the last of the silverware out, some four days later. Christmas Eve was a sacred event for her, and she liked things to be done just so - steeped in tradition and focused around the food of her childhood. In past times she would have spent this night with her family, with Ray and Zosia and she still felt a pang of loss when she thought about it. Rae had offered in recent years to make the drive up to see her, but Nush would have none of it.

'You spend it with your mama,' she'd always insist. 'This is a night for family.'

'But you're my family too.' Rae would plead. 'Mama has my dad. But you don't have anyone.'

And though her words would slice a white-hot blade clean into Nush's chest, she never let it show, and would instead smile gently at her niece. 'I always have people.'

Rae had never asked her why she stayed away, nor what could possibly have happened between her and Zosia to put such a distance between them, and Nush was grateful for that. She shared almost everything with her niece, but this was too big, too consuming to burden her with.

She laid small plates on top of larger ones, enough cutlery for everyone, and set her cut crystal shot glasses next to wine glasses, finishing with a sprig of winter greens from the garden as a centrepiece. She stepped back, admiring her handiwork and clapped with glee just as she heard the first knock on the door.

Bill Cramer stood on her doorstep, his moustache neatly combed and a bottle of wine nestling under his arm. Nush rarely saw him without his sweater vest, but he had worn a smart shirt and tie with a tan-coloured v-neck cardigan for the occasion.

She reached up to kiss him lightly on each cheek. '*Wesołych Świąt*. Merry Christmas.' She took the wine he offered her and smiled brightly. 'Come in, come in. Can I pour you a glass?'

He beamed, his expression laced with a faint undertone of sadness but his heart thankful for his good friend. 'Merry Christmas, lass. Aye, ah'll 'ave a glass, please.' He caught her hand lightly, his expression turning serious. ''Ow can ah thank thee for invitin' me t'neet?'

Nush gave his hand a gentle squeeze. 'By eating with me.' And he nodded in understanding, hanging his coat by the door and following her into the kitchen.

The second knock, only a few moments later, was Jamie, who held a bottle under one arm and a paper package in his hand. He smiled at Nush as she kissed his cheeks in turn, patting each side very gently with her hands afterwards and muttering to herself in Polish as she did so. 'Merry Christmas,

Jamie.'

'Merry Christmas, Nush.' His smile was so devastating she wished there was a way she could have captured it somehow to show Rae later. 'Thank you for inviting me.'

'Thank you for coming!' She chuckled to herself happily, leading him down into the kitchen where he greeted Bill Cramer with a handshake before turning back to Nush.

'Here.' He handed her the paper parcel he was carrying. 'This was always Rae's favourite, but I seem to remember maybe it was yours, too?' He watched as she peeled back the paper, suddenly hesitant.

Inside was a braided challah loaf, the kind with poppy seeds on, and its rich smell had always reminded Nush of her childhood, of living in the resettlement camp, and of the women who had helped raise her.

'Oh, my boy,' she said, touched beyond words that he remembered. 'Where did you find this?'

Jamie shrugged, as if it weren't a big deal. 'I passed a Jewish bakery a couple of towns over when I was doing some work there. I saw those in the window and they made me think of you.' *You* was soft, the *both of you* implied. 'When you invited me here tonight I knew I had to go back and get some.'

The corners of his lips quirked up in a soft smile and Nush's heart clenched with a strange combination of longing for a different time and place, and absolute joy at the small kindness from this beautiful man, who she was now quite sure was an angel.

'My family was Catholic,' she started, looking at the loaf in her hands, and not at Jamie, nor at Bill who had been quietly watching the whole exchange. 'But my mama always said there was a little magic baked into Jewish bread.'

Her eyes filled up a little at the memory. Her mother had died when Nush was nine, and she had only fleeting moments of memory left - the sweet sound of her singing Polish hymns as she cooked, habits, small things that she said, sometimes without thinking. The look on her face as she lay on her deathbed, her thin hands cool and smooth as they'd touched young Nush's face.

Take care of Zosia, she'd said, through the thick rattle of her breathing. *Jesteś dla niej teraz najważniejsza. You are her everything now.* And as the rattle had slowly stuttered to a stop, Nush had sobbed into the bedsheets and sworn on her own life that she would.

A sharp knock saved Nush from her thoughts and she rushed off to answer the door to her final guest. Penny was a vision in wine-coloured chiffon and gold costume jewellery, the sweet scent of her perfume entering the house before she did. She was a little younger than Nush, somewhere in her fifties, maybe, and she radiated an energy that Nush had always found quite charming. Her natural red hair had lightened over the years and was peppered here and there with strands of silver which made it appear almost golden in a certain light.

'Nush!' The lyrical tone of Penny's voice lit up her whole face as she spoke. 'It's so lovely to see you.' She held a potted poinsettia towards Nush. 'A gift. To say thank you for inviting me to your beautiful home.'

Nush clapped her hands together in delight and kissed Penny on each cheek. How could she be unwilling to forgive the odd indiscretion with a man of the cloth for someone who had such beautiful manners?

She ushered Penny into the house and down into the

kitchen, where Penny greeted the two men equally as enthusiastically. The thing about a village is that there are few strangers, and the four of them wasted no time getting more thoroughly acquainted, with Bill pouring Penny a glass of wine while she introduced herself to Jamie, delighting at Bill and Nush's tales of him as a youngster.

'Who else are we waiting for?' Penny asked, noticing the five place settings at the table.

'For unexpected visitors,' Nush said, shrugging and tilting her head slightly in the way that she always did when she explained her traditions. She rather thought the gesture enhanced her Polishness. 'This day is for family,' she said with a smile, 'Whether they are by blood or by design. We set an extra space at the table in case someone should call by.'

'Na zdrowie!' Bill Cramer had spent many an evening in Nush's company and he couldn't help but pick up a few useful phrases along the way. 'Cheers' was the one he used by far the most, and his awkward pronunciation made Nush swell with joy.

'Tak, tak!' She beamed. 'Yes!' She looked at each of them quickly. 'You all have a drink, yes? Now we will toast!'

And the haphazard group each raised their glasses and toasted to health, to the host, to the coming year, and then they sat down to eat around the solid oak table in Nush's kitchen.

They tucked into the feast with enthusiasm - Nush had made traditional barszcz and they ate it with pickled herrings, fresh salad and the bread Jamie had brought, plus a whole baked trout that she'd sourced from the market in the nearest town, scouring her old Polish recipe books for the perfect way to prepare it. And a generous batch of the pierogi that

Nush had made with Rae, of course, fried with onions and a little butter.

They finished the last on their plates, adjusted waistbands and sat back in their chairs, completely stuffed and feeling very festive indeed. Bill loosened his tie, while Jamie removed his completely. Penny politely dabbed at her mouth with a napkin, breathing out with a satisfied sigh.

Nush rose from the table, returning with a small bottle of light golden liquid and a glint in her eye. She filled each cut crystal glass with a shot and raised hers. 'Cytrynówka,' she said, by way of explanation, although of course it was no explanation at all. 'Special Polish drink. It will help your meal to settle.'

'We should toast something.' Bill grabbed his glass and swirled the contents thoughtfully.

Penny laughed. 'Haven't we already toasted everything it's possible to toast?'

'To Absent Friends,' Jamie said, his eyes shifting to meet Nush's as he spoke.

Nush nodded, not quite managing to keep the smile from her face. He was talking about Rae, she knew it. 'To absent friends,' she agreed.

'To absent friends.' Bill smiled, but his eyes were lined with sadness, his words for his lost love.

They all fell silent for a beat, a small token of respect, before Penny lifted her glass. 'To absent friends.'

They clinked their glasses together and each downed the shot in one.

Jamie coughed in shock, his eyes reddening. 'Holy shit, Nush!' He grabbed for his water glass.

Penny cleared her throat as politely as she was able.

'It's maybe a little strong,' Nush laughed, shrugging a little.

Bill laughed with her, the tears in his eyes now from the pure alcohol slicing a burning trail down his oesophagus. 'For good health,' Nush added, now coughing a little herself, and before long they were all howling with laughter.

Nush sat back slightly, a familiar warmth rising through her body. This was the joy of taking in strays, she thought to herself. This unlikely group would each otherwise have been home alone tonight, but were instead fed, happy and maybe a little drunk.

She watched as Bill recounted one Christmas when he and Sue were newly married, when they'd each forgotten to buy a turkey for Christmas dinner and so late on Christmas Eve, after a bottle and a half of wine, Sue had insisted he go out and try to find a wild goose for them to cook. He'd failed, of course, even as a young man Bill Cramer had the build of a string bean, but he had the others in stitches with his tales of chasing a pigeon from one end of Blackston to the other and all the way back, believing the whole time that it was a goose.

They laughed so loudly that Nush didn't hear the sound of tyres on her gravel driveway, although she couldn't miss the knock on the door that came just after, and she sprang from her seat to answer it. She would know that knock anywhere.

'Ciocia.' Rae's voice was almost a whisper, her face pale and drawn, with a ghosting of old tears on her cheeks.

'Oh Kochanie.' She gathered her niece into her arms, pulling her out of the cold night and into the welcoming warmth of the house. 'What is it?'

Rae shook her head slightly and Nush could sense that she wouldn't get the full story tonight. 'I need to stay with you for a while.' She blew a breath out. 'Mama... we fought. It's a long story.'

'Good job I have a long time to hear it then,' Nush said with a kind smile, grabbing tissues from the box she kept in the hall and gently wiping the tears from Rae's cheeks. 'But not tonight.' She smoothed Rae's hair back into place. 'Your Babcia always used to tell me that if I ended Wigilia in tears, I would cry all year.' She held her niece away from her, assessing her handiwork. 'Beautiful.'

She took Rae's hand, leading her towards the laughter in the kitchen. 'Tomorrow we talk. Tonight we spend with friends. Have you eaten?'

Rae didn't have time to answer before she stiffened beside Nush, catching sight of Jamie through the open door, carefree and beautiful, leaning in to share a joke with Penny as if they were old friends.

The visitors all looked up as the women stepped into the kitchen.

'To Unexpected Visitors!' Nush declared, squeezing Rae's hand gently before grabbing her drink from the table and raising it.

'To unexpected visitors!' Bill and Penny crowed in unison, clinking their glasses.

Jamie said nothing, but he raised his glass slowly, deliberately, smiling at Rae with the warmth of his whole heart, and perhaps just a little vodka.

Nush motioned to Rae to sit in the empty chair and busied herself with gathering a plate of leftovers, warming it in the microwave and putting the hot plate in front of her niece. 'Eat.'

Nush was a firm believer in fate, and as she set a glass of wine and a generous shot of cytrynówka in front of Rae with a wink, she had a strong feeling that the universe had meant to bring her here on this night all along.

9

The Hangover

It was already light when Rae Logan woke, her head thumping a heartbeat, with the faint taste of vodka in her mouth and the familiar sound of Nush singing to herself downstairs.

For a few moments she couldn't remember how she'd ended up in her old bedroom at the mill, and then it came back to her. With a stutter at first, and then all in a rush.

Zosia's house. Their fight. What was it that had set it off? She remembered Zosia's laugh when Rae had told them about the new book she was writing over dinner, her own defensive comment, God, it all sounded like absolutely nothing of any importance now. And yet somehow it felt like everything.

'Kochanie,' Zosia had said, curling her Crayola-bright hair around a finger, her voice cloying. *'There are some people who have what it takes, and there are some people who don't. Maybe you are destined for more modest achievements.'*

And she remembered very clearly the look on her mother's face. It had been a kind look, yet her condescension was lurking, thinly concealed, underneath.

'Your dad, he had something special.'

'And I don't.' Rae had said, the hurt turning to anger in her voice. It wasn't even a question. She was already backing away, running away, losing her grip.

'That's not what I said.' Zosia had risen to the bait, the two so often rubbing each other up the wrong way it was almost like muscle memory now.

'Was it what you meant?'

The roll of Zosia's eyes would have been answer enough, but that hadn't stopped her opening her mouth and removing all doubt.

'You don't finish things, Rachel! You don't stick with them. You run away from everything that could be good in your life - your books, your marriage...'

'What!?' Rae had been indignant. 'You wanted me to stick with Simon after I walked in on him balls deep in Carla Bates?!' Her eyes had been alight with rage. 'You have that little regard for me that you think the best I can do is someone who couldn't even keep it in his pants until we were married?'

Zosia had scoffed. 'Oh, for God's sake, you are making me sound like a terrible mother.'

Rae's laugh had been humourless. 'You're doing that all by yourself.'

'Come on now, ladies,' Don had said firmly, laying a hand on each of their shoulders. It wasn't the first time he'd had to referee. 'It's Christmas.'

Rae had blown a long breath out, nodding slowly. 'You're right. It's Christmas.' And she'd put her knife and fork down carefully and stood. 'You two enjoy your Christmas together. I need to go.'

And though there had been a sadness in Don's eyes as she'd pushed back from the table and gone to throw her barely unpacked things back in her case, neither of them had made even the slightest move to stop her.

She'd made the ninety-minute drive to Blackston with her heart in her throat and her breath coming in light sobs, as the remnants of her tattered ego pooled somewhere around her feet.

And there wasn't a single thing that could have prepared her for the sight of Jamie Stamford sitting at Nush's dining table with a smile that turned her inside out. Rae had been as furious with him as she was aching to touch him and she didn't know what to do with either feeling.

She took what she believed to be the only reasonable course of action at that point and drank Nush's ridiculous lemon vodka until her head spun.

The morning after, it didn't seem like a reasonable course of action at all, and Rae wailed a little as she hauled herself upright. She grabbed the huge, fluffy dressing gown that Nush must have hung on the back of her door at some point after she'd gone to bed and wrapped it around herself, padding down the stairs gingerly.

Nush stopped singing as she saw Rae on the stairs and smiled broadly. 'Merry Christmas, Żabciu.' She flung her arms wide and Rae rushed gratefully into them. 'I have something for you, when you come round a little.'

Rae groaned. 'Oh God, I didn't get you anything.' She stepped out of Nush's embrace, looking at her earnestly. 'I'm so sorry. Let's go out shopping one day while I'm here.'

'Myszko, you being here is gift enough for me,' Nush said with a smile.

And Rae had no doubt that was the truth. But it wasn't going to stop her from repaying Nush in some way.

'But first,' Nush began, studying her niece closely. 'Let's fix all of this.' She waved a hand vaguely across Rae's body.

Rae started to laugh, but the action sliced pain through her head. She nodded instead, following Nush through to the living room where she curled up on the sofa, nestling under a huge wool blanket that Nush had crocheted once after Rae had shown her how she could learn from videos on the internet. It was the cosiest spot in the house, and Rae had almost fallen back to sleep when Nush reappeared with a tray of black tea, paracetamol and homemade poppy seed cake. She set the tray down on the footstool in front of Rae and took a seat on the other side of the sofa.

They sat in an easy silence, Rae making short work of the cake while Nush sipped her own tea thoughtfully. Rae knew she was desperate to talk about last night, but she wouldn't start to pry until she was sure Rae was ready.

It was half an hour or more before Rae spoke. 'We were talking about my writing, at first.' She sipped her tea. 'She doesn't think I've got what it takes.'

Nush nodded. 'And what do you think?'

'I'm scared she's right.' Rae's voice was small. She had never spoken about this feeling to anyone except Nush, but her father's success had cast a shadow over her that she'd struggled to get out of almost her entire life. He hadn't always been a writer - when Rae was small he'd taught English at the local high school. He'd got into it when Rae, at eight or nine, declared that she wanted to be an author when she grew up, and Ray had started writing in solidarity, quickly getting caught up in the stories which came flooding out of him. By the time Rae had left school he was hitting the bestseller lists, and she had always felt the pressure of living up to the legacy, the *name*, that he had left her.

Nush laid a hand on Rae's knee. 'You are amazing, Rachel-ciu.' She rarely called Rae by her name, only in matters of great importance. 'You are amazing and you are not your father.'

Rae laughed a little, always awkward in the face of a compliment, especially one she believed to be genuine. 'Tell Mama that, she was telling me in great detail how distinctly average I am.' She paused to take a sip, the robust blend warming her. 'She's still trying to marry me off to Simon! Says I always run away from good things.'

Nush laughed lightly through her teeth. 'Your mama, she means well. And you know she loves you with her whole heart.' She smiled, setting her empty mug back on the tray. 'But she can be an arsehole sometimes.'

Rae snorted with laughter. She rarely heard Nush use bad language and it always felt like some sort of illicit treat when she did.

'Don't laugh, Kotku, I'm serious!' Nush furrowed her brow. 'And as for Simon, *o mój Boże!*' She pushed her glasses up her nose. 'It is better to be with no one than to be with someone who does not give you the whole of themselves. And I say that to you as someone who has been alone for most of my life.' Her expression darkened then, her face drawn with something that Rae rarely saw in Nush.

Regret.

Rae nodded at her aunt kindly, sensing that this was no time to question that look. 'Well, you'll be glad to know that I am spurning Mama's advice and swearing off men completely.'

'Completely?' Nush eyes narrowed questioningly. 'You won't even make time for a handsome neighbour boy who has eyes for you like you're the only woman on Earth?'

Rae snorted, although she couldn't ignore the twist of her guts at the very thought. 'He does not look at me like that.'

'Kluseczko, trust me. That boy looks at you like he's lost in the desert and you are a tall glass of ice water.'

'He's hardly a boy these days,' Rae laughed, downing the last of her tea and marvelling at the magic it had worked on her pounding head. 'And you're completely insane. He's just being polite.'

Nush's eyes widened in mock hurt. 'You would talk to your poor old Ciocia like that?' She laid a hand on her niece's knee, her expression sobering. 'You don't have to believe me, but one day you will see that I'm right. I just hope I'm around to see it.'

Rae's head tilted to the side, one eyebrow rising. 'Oh please, Nush, you're sixty-something, not ninety-something. If you weren't around to see it then I'd be too old to do the wild thing anyway.'

Nush frowned. 'I'm just going to pretend you didn't say that.' She straightened her fading nightgown. 'I'll have you know that us people of a certain age are still plenty able to do this 'wild thing' that you speak of.' She mimed the inverted commas awkwardly with her fingers.

'Noooo,' Rae covered her ears. 'No, no, nope. We're not having this conversation.'

'You started it.' The lightness in Nush's voice was back. 'Maybe you will think twice before you write off all us old farts again?'

And the two women laughed together, forgetting everything in that moment except for how glad they were that they had each other.

It was later in the day that Nush suggested calling Zosia, an idea that Rae was very much against.

'It's Christmas,' Nush said simply.

Rae huffed. 'It was Christmas yesterday when she destroyed my life's dream.'

Nush considered her for a second, before tilting her head slightly to the side, a sure sign that Polish Nush was on the way. 'Kurczaczku, she acted like an arsehole, but you don't have to. She's your mama.' She picked up Rae's phone from where it sat on the arm of the sofa and plopped it down in front of her. 'Call her, wish her a Wesołych Świąt and then you don't have to speak to her again until next Christmas if you don't want to.'

Rae rolled her eyes like a teenager. 'FINE,' she said sullenly, but even as she dialled the number she knew that Nush was right.

Nush shuffled off into the kitchen as Rae sorted things out with her mother. They both apologised and wished each other well for the season, and Zosia did not sound a bit surprised when Rae told her that she was going to stay at the mill for the foreseeable future.

'Well good luck,' Zosia said, as genuinely as she could muster. 'I hope you find what you're looking for.'

And Rae nodded to herself and said goodbye, genuinely hoping that too.

Nush came back in a moment later with two warm cups of lemon tea. 'There. Doesn't that feel better?'

'No,' Rae lied.

But of course Nush saw right through her. Her face lit up with a smile and she rushed off to the next room, returning with a small box tied with shiny, red ribbon.

'Merry Christmas,' Nush chirped, setting the small gift on the table in front of her niece.

Rae smiled, kissing her aunt lightly on the cheek and carefully opening the box. In a nest of midnight blue tissue paper lay an expensive-looking pen, rose gold plated with an inscription on the barrel.

Rae picked it up with a gasp, turning it in her hands until she could read the words.

By Rachel Logan.

She looked up at Nush, who was beaming. 'It's for your writing. So all your masterpieces will be by Rachel Logan.'

Rae smiled, speechless. It was just like Nush to give a small present with a big meaning.

'Rachel Logan?' Rae muttered to herself, turning the pen over and over in her hands. 'Not Rae?'

'You were named after your father, but you're not him.' Nush picked up her tea carefully, blowing at the steam which was still forming. 'And you shouldn't try to be. You're something very special in your own right.' She took a sip, testing. 'You just need to find your voice. '

Rae frowned, suddenly unsure of herself. 'What if I can't?'

But Nush only nodded sagely, looking up from her mug. 'I believe in you.'

And Rae smiled. Nush had always been her biggest fan. Her most avid supporter.

When she'd written stories as a child, Nush would take great delight in reading through them with her, reacting theatrically to all the clumsy plot twists and overblown dialogue. She should have known that Nush would be her lone voice of support now.

Rae put her pen carefully back in the box and picked up her

mug of tea, raising it in the air and smiling broadly.

'Merry Christmas, Ciocia.'

10

The Church

"St. Teresa's church was built in 1529 on the site of the old Anglo-Saxon chapel, and the south wall of the original chapel structure can still be observed today along the northernmost edge of the gardens. The building underwent restoration in 1793, and more recently in 1929, when, notably, the adjacent church hall was built to accommodate the village's growing fondness for social events.

The tradition of St Teresa's has always been to open its doors to any and all of God's children, and in local history the priests of the parish have notably been involved in various schemes to help the needy. It is known in the local area as a force for good, a central, unifying point which uses its standing in the community to bring the people of Blackston together."

- F.W. Merryfield, *A Brief History of Blackston Bay*

11

One Good Thing

J amie Stamford was a man of small kindnesses, feeling himself crippled by the ostentation of a grand gesture. When he went the extra mile, which he was certainly capable of walking, it was always a few steps at a time.

It was the small houseplant he'd left in Nush's porch, along with a note thanking her for her hospitality the other night. Or the uncomfortable Christmas Day visit to see his parents, who had moved a few miles out of Blackston, having come into a little money and now thinking themselves far too important for the trivial happenings of village life.

And today, the day after Boxing Day, it was forcing himself to go see his brother when all he really wanted to do was back-to-back stream trashy action films while he sat in his pyjamas and ate leftovers.

Joe was two years his younger, and Jamie had been rescuing him for as long as he could remember. Joe Stamford had a charm to him, a cheek that could find him in a series of increasingly deep troubles just as easily as it could rescue him from them, and when the former happened the only person he knew he could count on was Jamie.

Joe had appeared back in Blackston only a few weeks later than Jamie, after hopping from one live-in relationship to the other, sometimes with barely a break between. He was like the world's worst scam artist - charming his way into a series of women lives, beds and then homes, until each one ultimately bled him dry.

His last streak had come to an untimely end when his latest interest, Leanne, had brought him to the point where he would have done absolutely anything for her before she drained the last reserves of his bank account under cover of darkness and left him, penniless and alone, with only the belongings she didn't think she could sell and two months of rent arrears.

Needless to say, Joe found himself on the receiving end of an eviction order. He'd hitchhiked back to Blackston with nothing but a rucksack and the clothes on his back, walking the last few miles on foot.

Jamie had been only vaguely surprised by the knock on his door that evening. He'd been on the receiving end of a unexpected knock on the door too many times to count, and on almost all of those occasions the knocker had turned out to be Joe.

He'd stood with his head bowed and his curly hair slick with rain. A beaten man. And what else could Jamie to do except let him in?

He was angry with Joe, of course he was. Joe's problems were almost exclusively of his own making. But they were brothers, and brothers stood by each other. Jamie had learned by his third or fourth time rescuing Joe that giving him money was fruitless. He'd fritter it away as fast as anyone could give it to him. But Jamie could provide food and a warm bed, and when the time was right he'd find work for him and help him find his own place, hoping that it would be the last time he'd have to sort these things for Joe, but always knowing that it wouldn't be.

Something about Joe was different, though, today. He stood a little straighter when he answered the door of the shared house which Jamie had helped him find. There was a cool air of confidence about him that Jamie hadn't seen in a long time. He hoped that it wasn't the influence of a woman bringing these changes about, God knows he'd been there before. But there was definitely something.

He greeted Joe with a friendly slap on the shoulder. 'You all right, mate?'

Joe grinned, his energy filling the whole room. 'Yeah, I'm good. I'm really good, actually. What about you?'

'Same old.' Jamie unwound his scarf and grabbed it awkwardly, not altogether sure what the etiquette was for hanging coats in a shared house. 'You weren't at Mum and Dad's the other day.'

Joe shrugged. 'I rang in the morning. Just to say Merry Christmas, you know.' The corner of his mouth lifted in a half-smile. 'You think they really wanted me there? I was giving them the gift of my absence.'

Jamie struggled to argue. Of course their parents loved both boys, but he didn't doubt that they found Joe to be a constant disappointment. Their mother, Patricia, was terribly concerned with keeping up appearances, and Joe's endless string of dramas mortified her. She'd told Jamie she'd mustered every last scrap of courage to tell the ladies at the social club about his divorce, so he couldn't imagine how she would deal with telling them the latest update in the Joe chronicles.

'You know they only want the best for you.' Even as it left his mouth it sounded like a lie.

Joe must have known it, but his face lit in a grin anyway. 'Yeah. Anyway though.' He pressed his hands together and then touched the tips of his fingers lightly to his lips, suppressing joy about whatever this was.

Jamie braced himself.

'I've met someone!' Joe said, the words tumbling out in a rush of excitement. 'She's not like the others, I swear to God, Jamie. And I know I say that every time, but it's really true this time.'

Jamie fought with every scrap of willpower he had not to roll his eyes, smiling instead. 'Ok...' He took his heavy coat off, holding it along with his scarf. 'Tell me about her.'

Joe's face softened, his eyes darting to the ceiling as his face cracked into the widest smile Jamie thought he had ever seen. This was the Joe who could get himself out of trouble. 'Ok, so her name is Allie, she's my age, I think. Pretty much my age. And I swear down she is the most beautiful girl I have ever seen.' He bit his lip, his eyes alive. 'I want you to meet her.'

This is new, thought Jamie. He tended to only meet Joe's ladies as they were hotfooting it out of his life. 'Yeah, that sounds good.'

He would do this for his brother, the way he would do anything for his brother.

Joe squeezed his shoulder, touched. 'Jamie, look,' he began, his voice hesitant.

Here comes the bit where he tells me he's changed, thought Jamie, desperate to be proven wrong.

'...I'm not going to tell you that I've changed, cause I've said that a million times before, and it always turns out that I haven't.'

Jamie couldn't argue with that.

Joe went on. 'I'm actually just the same old Joe who makes shit choices and disappoints you all. Only this time I'm making a good choice.' He beamed.

In the moment Jamie found it difficult to be sceptical, so he smiled too. 'I really hope so, mate.'

Joe nodded lightly. 'Ok, so let's go out for some food in the week. Nowhere fancy though, I'm not made of money.' He chuckled. 'Anyway, Allie's not like that.'

They never are, at first, Jamie thought, but he didn't say anything.

'Anyway, Allie's got a friend who we think you'll like so we thought maybe we could all go out together.' Joe clapped his hands together, clearly pleased with his masterplan. 'She's called Nina. Tall, smart, long, dark hair, *fitasfuck*, man. I swear to God.'

Jamie ignored the plummet of his heart. He had, after all, told himself that he needed a palate cleanser, and Nina sounded like just that.

'You're not interested in anyone at the moment are you?

'No,' Jamie lied.

Joe grinned. 'Then it's a date.'

'It's a date.' Jamie feigned excitement, changing the subject quickly. 'I know that's not the only reason you asked me round here tonight, though.'

'You're right, it wasn't,' Joe said with a mysterious smile. 'We've got a job to do.'

It was a short walk into the heart of Blackston from the shared house, and Jamie was surprised when Joe stopped just after the peak of the hill at the entrance to the churchyard. Joe turned, raising an eyebrow at his brother.

'Confession?' Jamie asked, amusement dancing in his voice. Their family wasn't Catholic, but as St. Teresa's was the only church in the village, it had adopted a curious mix of traditions from various denominations over the years. There weren't many children in Blackston with Christian parents of any variety who hadn't occasionally been dragged in to confess something to Father Kevin.

Joe's mouth edged into a half smile. 'Not as such.' He nodded his head towards the small church hall. 'Come on.'

Jamie noticed then that the lights were on, and his interest was piqued. Joe led him through the heavy double doors and into the familiar scent of the hall, casting him back to a multitude of birthday parties and christenings and at least one wedding.

Behind a small table stacked with box files and loose sheets of paper, Father Kevin and Penny Beaumont sat, drinking coffee and talking animatedly.

Penny looked up as they walked in and smiled widely at Jamie, then at Joe. 'Good evening, boys!' She stood up, walking around the side of the table to greet them both with a small hug. 'You know,' she said, holding Joe lightly by the shoulders, 'it actually didn't occur to me until just a moment ago that the two of you are brothers.' She laughed lightly. 'Silly, really, you look just the same. Your mother must be very proud of creating *two* such handsome boys.'

Jamie's brow furrowed in confusion. 'I didn't realise that you two knew each other.' Penny hadn't lived in the village long, and Jamie couldn't think where they would have met.

She smiled, patting Jamie's cheek gently, then tuning to Joe. 'I met this one when he walked through those doors a few weeks ago.' She nodded back towards the door they'd come in. 'He'd heard about Father Kevin's project, and he thought it would help him.'

'I call it One Good Thing.' Father Kevin rose from his seat for the first time, walking over with a smile on his face. 'It's an idea I've had for a while.' He was a tall man, slight but with a presence which felt significant. 'When people are troubled, when their life has taken them somewhere dark, they come to confession and they are crippled by all the bad thoughts they're having.'

His eyes darted to meet Joe's, only for a split second, but it didn't escape Jamie's attention. 'They're so overwhelmed by the bad that they can't think of a single good thing about themselves. I used to tell them that they should do a small kindness for someone, not for anything in return, just for the sake of helping another person. And then the next time they question themselves, the next time they can't fathom what good can they bring the world, that can be the one good thing.'

Joe looked up at his brother, a strange vulnerability in his eyes. 'The first good thing I did was pick up some shopping for Mr Winters. It was just after his wife had the stroke, and he didn't want to leave her to go all the way into town. He gave me money and a shopping list, and I went for him. It wasn't even a big thing, he gave me money for the bus and everything.' Joe paused, blinking away emotion. 'When I got back, I helped him put his shopping away. It didn't take long. When I went to go, he shook my hand and he had tears in his eyes. That's when I realised how much it meant to him. That time with his wife. Not having to worry about her.' His voice was thick, and he coughed a little to clear it. 'The next time I felt bad about myself, I remembered that I'd given him that gift. And it made me feel like it mattered whether I was here or not.'

Father Kevin smiled gently at him, then turned his gaze to Jamie. 'It's really as simple as that.'

Jamie's heart dropped with a dull thud. He'd known Joe was having a hard time, of course he'd known. But he never realised he'd been feeling so down on himself. The guilt thumped like a heartbeat in his throat.

Could he have done more?

The priest spoke again, shaking Jamie from his thoughts. 'Joe's done a few good things for us now. When we asked him to come in tonight, we told him it was a job which required an extra set of hands. Someone strong.' He peered at the two of them over his half-moon glasses, his kindly face softening with a smile. 'He said he knew just the fellow.'

Jamie smiled in return. 'And here I am.'

'Here you are.' Penny clapped in delight. 'Now, let's get the two of you to work.'

It wasn't long before the boys were opening the door to Norma Grey's stone-fronted cottage. She'd had a fall earlier in the week, tumbled straight down the stone steps which led from the lower part of the village up to the cliff top, and broken her leg in three places. She was lucky to be alive, the doctors had said, but that wasn't of any practical use to her.

What would be of practical use to her was if a bed could be moved from her upper floor down to the living room, to save her having to worry about climbing the stairs while she was healing. In advance of her being discharged from hospital the following day, that was exactly what Jamie and Joe would do.

They assessed the living room first. It was unusually spacious for one of Blackston's cottages, which made their job much easier. Between them they moved the TV unit up into the space below the front windows and pushed the sofa and the wingback chair against the near wall, leaving plenty of space for a bed to go against the back wall.

The staircase posed more of a problem. Narrow and steep, with a sharp corner right at the top, it took a good half hour of puffing, panting, and furious swearing before they managed to manoeuvre the small single divan base down from the spare room. The mattress was a piece of cake in comparison, bending around the corners with little fuss, and they pushed both parts of the bed into place in the living room.

Jamie brought down extra bedding, making the bed up neatly, while Joe ducked out of the front door, reappearing a few moments later with a small handful of snowdrops from Maggie's garden. He arranged them in some water in a cut-glass tumbler and left it on the kitchen table.

'Who even are you?' Jamie asked, his eyes wide.

Joe smirked. 'I told you, I'm a better man now.'

Jamie's smile twisted, a stab of some emotion or other catching at the pit of his stomach. This was not at all what he had expected when Joe had told him they had a job to do, and he took an uncharacteristic amount of satisfaction in being wrong.

He looked up at his little brother, a man he wasn't even sure he recognised now, the only thing he could think of to say on his lips. 'I'm proud of you, mate.'

They walked back up the hill to drop Norma's spare key off

with Father Kevin, Joe tapping a rhythm on his phone.

'New Year's Eve.' Joe looked up, the light from the screen making his face glow.

Jamie's brow creased. 'Is that a question?'

Joe rolled his eyes with a grin. 'Are you free? For the date.'

The date, thought Jamie, with a strange sinking feeling in his guts. But he pushed it away. He'd promised himself he was going to date, and he would, regardless of the roar in his chest whenever he thought of Rae at Nush's party.

She'd been so pale, so broken, and his heart had leapt and knocked against his ribcage as he watched her over the table. Her pain was palpable, and every muscle and sinew in his body screamed at him to go to her, to gather her up and to hold her pieces together so tightly that she would never come undone again.

But she was separate, guarding herself from him, and although she was never anything less than polite, she'd put distance between them at every turn. With every pull, she'd push, and the message she was sending out to him could not have been clearer. She didn't want him near her.

So he looked back up at Joe and said the only thing that felt like it made sense.

'Yeah. I'm free.'

The night of the date came altogether quicker than Jamie hoped it would, and before he knew it he was waiting awkwardly at the bar of The White House, his mind running a loop of all the reasons this was a good idea, quickly followed by all the reasons it wasn't.

He wanted to meet new people. Blackston's gene pool was limited, and his strongest chance for some semblance of a normal relationship was meeting someone from somewhere else. That had been his intention with Milly all along, really. He'd just wanted to get out, and if he were being really honest with himself even he would agree that he took up with the first pretty face who made it seem like she could make it happen.

That wouldn't happen again, though, he thought, tracing a finger down the droplets gathering on the outside of his pint. Not this time. This time he would make sure he did things for all the right reasons.

The warmth of the pub felt stifling after the icy sting of the December wind, and he quickly took his jacket off and was rolling up the sleeves of his dress shirt when the door opened again and he heard the distinctive timbre of Joe's laugh.

'Jamie!' Joe strode straight over, pulling him into a light hug and clapping him firmly on the back as if it'd been years since the brothers had seen each other, and not just a few days. 'Good to see you, man.'

Jamie laughed, pulling back from his brother and slapping him amicably on the shoulder. Joe had scrubbed up for tonight, too, looking every inch the charming rogue in a v-neck jumper and smart shirt. 'You too, you idiot.' He ruffled Joe's lighter brown curls jokingly. 'It's been what... two days?'

Joe snorted a laugh, then stepped aside as a small, blonde woman moved up next to him, smiling timidly up at Jamie. She was the kind of pretty which you don't even realise at first, with a dimpled smile and soft creases at the corners of her eyes. 'This is Allie.'

'Hey, Jamie.' Her voice was warm, but tentative, like she was holding a part of herself back. She held a small hand out to shake his. 'I know everyone says this when they meet people but I've heard a lot about you.' Her handshake was warm, and firm.

Honest, Jamie thought, although he couldn't say precisely why.

'Don't believe a word this joker says about me, or anything else.' Jamie grinned at her, noticing the faint stain of a blush colour her cheeks. Joe had been right, she wasn't his usual type at all, and Jamie felt himself warm to her immediately.

'And this,' Joe continued dramatically, '...is Nina.'

Jamie turned to the taller woman on Joe's other side and immediately felt as if all the blood in his body had fallen southwards at once, then started to rise in surges, rushing to his chest and his ears.

Fitasfuck had been an understatement. Nina was the kind of beautiful which punches you clean in the gut.

She was tall, but not awkwardly so, and supermodel tiny with a perfectly proportioned face and an alluring air of confidence. Her long, dark hair fell in perfect waves, framing bee stung lips and clear blue eyes.

Fuck, she was stunning.

'Hey,' Jamie heard himself say in what seemed to be a surprisingly collected voice considering the riot of activity happening beneath his skin. 'I'm Jamie.' He held out his hand.

'Hi, Jamie,' Nina said, slipping her hand into his. Her skin was soft, her grip firm, and he imagined her hands on his body for a second, before she spoke again. 'It's nice to meet you.' Her mouth quirked into a smile, her eyes dancing.

She's flirting, he thought to himself, feeling a rush of pride but with light panic at its heels. Shit, what if he'd forgotten how?

He shook the fear off and nodded. 'Nice to meet you too, Nina.' His mouth pulled into a smile in return. He could do this. 'Now, can I get anyone a drink?'

The girls found a table while Jamie and Joe stood at the bar, waiting for Roy to get the drink orders together.

'Sooo...' Joe began, drawing out the vowel dramatically. 'Was I right, or was I right, man? Fit, isn't she?'

Jamie blew out a short breath. 'You were so right. The rightest. Sir Right moving home to Right Hall.'

Joe laughed.

'She is shit-your-pants gorgeous,' Jamie clarified, eyes comically wide. It had been a while since the brothers had shared such easy conversation, and it felt good. Too much of the last few years had been taken up by Joe's endless need to be rescued, and Jamie's subsequent need to bite his tongue.

Joe grinned triumphantly. 'You're welcome.' He turned to grab the G&T and glass of Sauvignon Blanc that Roy was handing over, setting them on the bar next to the pint and reaching into his pocket.

'Don't you dare,' Jamie's voice had a warning tone, and he grabbed his wallet quickly, passing Roy a note before Joe could react. 'I'm paying. No arguments.'

Joe shrugged, before nodding and slipping his wallet away. There was no pride to maintain here. Jamie had seen him at rock bottom more times than he could count.

'Thanks, Roy,' they chimed in unison, and he nodded, *you're welcome.*

Joe picked up his drink and held it up to clink Jamie's in a subtle *cheers.* 'Let's have ourselves a date!'

The conversation flowed, and the hours passed easily. With a little wine in her, Allie wasted no time coming out of her shell, and Jamie was pleasantly surprised by the quick-witted, easygoing woman who was exactly the right kind of person for Joe and exactly the opposite of the girls he'd gone for up until this point. He still wasn't completely convinced that Joe wouldn't fuck it up, but right at that moment he rather fancied that she might be the one for his little brother, and that thought made him feel prouder than he'd expected he might.

And Nina. Well.

Nina was an A-class flirt. Obvious enough so that Jamie knew she was interested, but with just enough subtlety to maintain an appropriate air of mystery. She laughed believably at his jokes, her manicured fingernails lightly grazing his forearm as she did. She had a depth to her, too, an obvious intelligence which brought an intriguing edge to her conversation skills. They talked about art and travel and books, finding common ground in many areas with just enough conflict for friendly debate.

If Jamie had been asked, abstractly, to describe his ideal woman, the person he would have described would probably have been a lot like Nina.

She laughed at something Joe had said, and hunched over in a giggling fit, clasping Jamie's arm and leaning in to him while she laughed. Her perfume smelled sweet and sultry and Jamie breathed it in gladly. Emboldened by the three pints of beer running through his veins, he looked down at her, smoothing a rogue strand of hair away from her face as her pupils dilated almost imperceptibly. He inhaled slowly, catching his lower lip in his teeth, caught in this moment, this spell that she was casting over him.

The moment, that split second, hung heavy in the air, their company forgotten, the space between them alive with want, and possibility, and the heady surge of excitement.

The door opened and closed in his periphery, and the gust of cold air shook them from their perfect moment. Nina smiled, almost shyly.

Jamie smiled too, but something had shifted. He didn't have to look up to know who had just walked into the pub, and when he looked back into Nina's eyes, the spark that he'd felt a moment ago had ignited into a boiling rage which clawed at his stomach.

Nina looked down coyly, oblivious to the sudden flip of Jamie's mood, and when she turned to whisper in his ear, Jamie could feel the burn of fiery hazel eyes on him from across the room.

So he did the only thing he could think of, and catching Nina's velvet-soft chin in his fingers, he brought his lips to hers.

The kiss was light, little more than a chaste brushing of lips, but with the dark promise of more written into it. It was everything a decent first kiss should be, and for a second Jamie lost himself to it.

And when he broke away and looked back up, the hazel eyes were gone.

12

Happy New Year

Rae Logan had never been a big fan of New Year's Eve. It was almost ten when Nush decided that she wanted to go out for the chimes of midnight. At first Rae huffed at the idea, but Nush's energy eventually had her plodding up the stairs to her room, half-heartedly making the most of the outfit she was wearing. God forbid Roy or Mr Cramer might see her in her current, perfectly reasonable state. She rolled her eyes at no one in particular.

She came back down the stairs five minutes later wearing a slightly nicer top and a reluctant smudge of eyeliner and Nush clapped her hands together in delight.

'A new year is coming,' she said, with a knowing smile. 'It's another chance. A new beginning.'

'Listen to yourself,' Rae grumbled. 'You sound like the Dalai Lama.' She pulled her boots on and grabbed her coat off its hook. 'Have you ever said anything in your life which wasn't ridiculously positive?'

Nush held out a scarf for Rae as she stood, fully dressed. 'Positivity saves lives, *Gołąbeczku*. We would not have made it out of the Old Country if we had not thought positively.'

Rae scoffed, although her lips were beginning to edge into a genuine smile. 'Oh please.' She took the scarf and wound it loosely around her neck with her free hand. 'The closest you've been to the Old Country is that day they started stocking krokiety in the world foods aisle.'

Nush blinked slowly, her smile unchanging. 'One day you will be my age.' She turned to check her reflection in the oak-framed mirror by the front door. 'And when you are, you will want to pass your hard-won wisdom on to the next generation.' She fluffed her greying curls with a flourish and turned back to consider Rae over the top of her glasses. 'Now will you stop giving me hassle and put your damn coat on.'

By the time they reached The White House, Rae had perked up a little, and her initial grumpiness had eased into a genuine desire to ring in the new year with the good people of Blackston. She'd known Roy, the owner, since she was a little girl, and he was as good as Nush for the odd juicy tidbit of gossip.

Mr Cramer would likely also be there, and maybe Penny, too. She thought of the night she'd turned up on Nush's doorstep and they'd both known exactly what to say to make her feel better, and the smallest smile edged at the corners of her mouth.

'Ah, smiling now, I see,' Nush quipped, her smirk under-scored with a hint of smugness, and Rae was just working up to a smart-arse response when she swung open the heavy pub door and all the breath left her body.

Not ten feet in front of her, practically coiled around the most beautiful woman Rae had ever seen in her entire life, was Jamie Stamford.

He was looking into the woman's eyes, falling into her, the look on his face equal parts longing and uncertainty. It made Rae's whole body tighten, starting at the throat and ending with the clench of her fists.

The woman looked back at him, her desire posted like a flag, and the jealousy which Rae had not even realised that she felt crashed over her like a wave and pulled her down. She felt the sharp flare of loss as her ownership of this man was snatched out of her hands while she could do nothing but watch. It didn't matter that she barely knew him anymore. It didn't even matter that he had never been hers to claim. She couldn't explain the small cracks beginning to show along the surface of her heart at the sight, but she felt every one.

And, as she watched, Jamie took the woman's chin gently in his hand and leaned in to kiss her. Rae's feet were rooted to the spot as the small cracks grew to fractures along the fault lines of her heart, keeping a beat through the magnitude of the shocks as it ached and heaved in her chest.

She ducked towards the bar, leaving Nush chatting to someone just inside the door. She didn't even notice who it was.

Rae chanced a glance backwards as she reached the bar. Jamie hadn't seen her. He'd been too wrapped up in his mysterious beauty to notice anyone else in the room.

'Rachel,' said Roy as she turned back around, with the slight nod which had become their standard greeting over the years.

'Roy.' She returned the nod, slowly, ignoring the thundering of her heart against her rib cage.

'What'll it be, love?' His voice had roughened over the years, but always maintained a soft edge, a quality which felt welcoming.

'Something strong.'

Roy laughed, his face creasing and crinkling, a road map of decades well enjoyed. 'Scotch?'

'Something less strong.' Her heart rate was slowing, her breath easing. 'Surprise me.'

Roy nodded again with a smile and set about shovelling ice into a tall glass, while Rae grabbed a beer mat off the top of the bar and spun it in her hands, the pads of her fingers finding the smooth edges, soothing her.

Nush had appeared back beside her by the time Roy set the drink on the bar, and she nudged Rae's arm gently as she slid into the space next to her. Rae didn't need to look at Nush's face to know what the nudge meant. Nush didn't miss a thing.

Rae took a long sip of the golden drink Roy had made her, the liquid warming her throat as she swallowed. 'Mmmm, oh that's nice.' She wiped the beads of condensation off her lower lip. 'Rum, right? Is it... spiced?'

Roy nodded. 'With ginger ale.' He waved away her money as she tried to hand it over. 'Sweet and spicy.' He winked jokingly. 'Like you.'

Rae pursed her lips. 'Take my money, Roy.'

The older man shook his head with a lopsided grin.

'Come on now, none of this silliness,' she chided. This too was a routine. Rae would offer to pay three times, and if Roy refused all three times she would accept gratefully. She often wondered how he made any money at all. 'It's New Year's Eve.'

'Exactly!' Roy chuckled. 'And that's my gift to you. You can pay for the next one.'

Rae's smile was genuine that time. 'Well, thank you.' She

95

lifted the glass in a *cheers*, and Ray clinked it with his pint glass of tap water.

'Come on Roy,' Nush piped up from next to her. 'What does an old lady have to do to get a drink in a place like this?'

'I don't know,' Roy shot back, 'But all *you* have to do is ask!'

They both giggled as Roy poured Nush's drink without her having to ask at all. A double brandy, neat, and the good stuff too, although he only ever charged her the price of the cheap stuff.

'Na zdrowie!' Roy offered, holding up his glass again, and Nush clinked it with a wide smile.

Her smile dropped the moment Roy turned to serve someone down the bar.

'Słoneczko, who is *she*?'

Rae didn't need to ask who. She shrugged. 'You mean Miss World over there?' She took another sip of her drink, steadying herself. 'Well, good luck to him. She looks nice.'

Nush snorted. 'She looks difficult to maintain.'

'You mean high maintenance?' Rae stirred her drink with her straw. 'Well, maybe that's his type now.'

Nush's judgement came as a low whistle through her teeth. 'It didn't work with the fancy wife and it won't work with her.'

'Who's tha gossipin' about now, Nush?' Mr Cramer's familiar drawl cut through the noise of the pub, and both women turned to welcome him.

As she turned, Rae caught Jamie looking straight at her, with a look on his face she couldn't place. Her stomach leapt back up into her throat and she snapped her gaze away quickly, her heart picking up its pace again.

'Mr Cramer!' Her voice was high, fake, and although the

creasing of Nush's brow meant she wasn't fooled, Bill Cramer didn't seem to notice anything amiss. He kissed both women lightly on their cheeks and pulled up a bar stool next to them, patting it for Nush to sit. She did, with a smile of thanks.

They talked then about the village and the weather and about the coming year, and about all the things that had happened in the year just gone. And though Rae smiled and nodded at what she hoped were all the right places, her mind was anywhere but on the curious and varied fortunes of Blackston.

She looked up at the large old clock keeping time above the bar. Twenty minutes to midnight.

It had been a funny old year. Until a few weeks ago she had thought she would end the year almost a married woman, and she thought back to the day she'd posted the invitations, wondering why she hadn't recognised the alarm bells clanging in her subconscious.

And then there had been her writing, God. She had written twenty chapters of her book this year, of which seventeen had been chapter one. She'd abandoned a twenty-first idea only that morning, backspacing fourteen pages so hard it had turned her finger white. She was beginning to sense the end of her dream, and Zosia's words popped into her head.

There are some people who have what it takes, and there are some people who don't.

Rae had never in her life thought that she was one of those people who didn't have what it takes, but she was beginning now to think that was the only reasonable explanation for her complete inability to make anything of herself. When she'd handed her notice in at the company the other week they'd wished her well, but no one seemed in any particular rush to convince her to stay.

No one ever seemed in any particular rush to convince her to stay. Not her mother, not Simon, not any job she'd ever had, and she suddenly felt very small, and insignificant in a way too subtle to put into words.

She felt the warmth of a hand on her shoulder, just then, and it made her jump.

'Rachel!' She looked up, slamming straight into a pair of whiskey-coloured eyes which almost made her heart skid to a stop in her chest until she looked closer at the man behind them.

She steadied herself with a breath. 'Joe Stamford, as I live and breathe.'

The boy she had known was long gone. The man standing in front of her was tall and strapping, with lighter, curlier hair than his brother, but the same striking eyes, in a shade of amber which bore deep down into her.

The relationship between Rae and Joe had never been an easy one. He'd been so jealous of her friendship with Jamie, so spiteful at times that it had been difficult for them to repair things in later years. And then he'd up and left Blackston, always chasing some woman or another, and she hadn't seen him since.

Not until now.

'How's things?' His smile was easy, only a hint of awkwardness creasing around his eyes as he spoke. 'You're back in Blackston, eh?'

'For a bit.' If he was going to extend the olive branch, she would take it. 'I'm staying with Nush for a while.' Her face softened, almost into a smile. 'What about you? Are you living here now?'

'Yeah, back in the village. I wanted to be near my girlfriend,' he beamed, nodding his head towards the table where they were all sitting, a subtle, proud emphasis on the word *girlfriend*.

Rae followed his gaze against her better judgement. Jamie and the mysterious beauty had put each other down now and were laughing with the pretty blonde girl who she assumed must be Joe's girl.

'She's called Allie.'

Rae's breath caught like a hard lump in her throat. 'Who is?' Her voice was barely audible over the hum of the busy room.

'My girlfriend. She's the blonde.'

Rae's throat relaxed a notch and she smiled at Joe. 'She's pretty.'

His face erupted in pride. 'She is. And that's her friend Nina, who seems to be making quite the impression on our Jamie.'

As if he'd heard, Jamie looked up at that point, looking quickly between Rae and his little brother. His brows creased in a question and Rae darted her gaze away.

Joe continued, and Rae wasn't sure if he was trying to make a point, although there was no edge to his voice. 'She's pretty perfect for him, I've got to say.' He downed the last dregs of his pint, as if it were a statement. 'I don't think I've ever seen him so happy.'

'Yeah, well. Good for him.' Rae spoke too quickly, unable to hold back the defensiveness in her voice.

Joe smiled, oblivious. 'Anyway, it was good talking to you. I've got to get some drinks in.' He held up his empty glass. 'Fifteen minutes to midnight!'

And in a second he was gone. And Rae was alone, her gaze

accidentally wandering back to Jamie.

What if this flawless specimen of womanhood *was* perfect for him, Rae thought. After all, she had no claim on him. He'd never even been hers. And here she was, all hung up on all the could haves and would haves of her past while her present passed her by.

What if she'd just never been good enough for Jamie, just like she'd never really been good enough for anything?

Fuck.

She looked over at Nush, now entangled in a very deep conversation with Mr Cramer about the intricacies of modern European politics. Nush was gesticulating wildly as Rae patted her gently on the shoulder to let her know she was going somewhere, and she rushed down the side corridor towards the toilets.

She'd barely locked the cubicle door as the sob bubbled up and out of her. Her sadness came in waves then, and she let it, all at once feeling the loss of her dad, her engagement, her dream. All at once trying to forget the last year, and the one before it, trying to get back something of herself from a long time ago, the last time she remembered feeling whole.

She put the toilet seat down and sat on it, leaning lightly against the cold brick of the walls. She stayed for a while, gathering the pieces of herself, wiping her eyes, trying to quieten her thoughts enough to go back inside and celebrate with the others.

At not quite thirty-five, she had thought that her days of hiding away and trying to escape the mistakes she was making in her life were behind her, and yet here she was, spending the last hour of the year snivelling into a scrunched up tissue in a toilet cubicle.

Fuck that.

She blew her nose inelegantly and threw the tissue into the grey water, letting the flush take it down. She took some deep breaths. Composed herself. Gave herself a quick once over in the small mirror, fixing the smears of eyeliner under each eye.

And then, taking another big breath, she opened the door.

The very last person she expected to see was Jamie, arms crossed, leaning against the textured stone of the corridor, his eyes alight.

The way he was looking at her almost scared her. She couldn't be completely sure what the look in his eyes was, but it looked a lot like fury.

'What did Joe say to you?'

Was it an accusation? She didn't know. His voice was angry, that she was certain of. But why?

She met the fire of his gaze with a withering look. How dare he be angry with her, when he was the one kissing someone else. 'Only that you're on a date with the woman of your dreams. And you know, just all about how perfect you are together.'

She fired it as a shot, right into him. *Your move.*

'He's right,' Jamie shot back, the muscle in his jaw flexing the way it always had when he was angry.

His shot connected, right into the crumbling remnants of Rae's pitiful heart, and she felt the sting of tears threaten her eyes again. 'Ok, so...' She tried to disguise the tremor in her voice. '...congratulations for that, I guess.'

She moved to duck past him, to end the conversation, but he stepped aside, blocking her, his body so close to hers that she could feel the warmth coming from him. He looked down at her, his eyes holding her there as effectively as if he had his hands on her, and she couldn't move, or think, or *breathe* with him this close.

'So what does that tell you?' His voice was low, barely above a whisper, and the grit of it stirred her up somewhere inside.

'This is really none of my business, Jamie.' She stood tall, straightening to her full height. She didn't want to fight with him, but she couldn't allow him to break her without one. 'I barely even know you anymore.'

He didn't flinch, didn't move, just kept his eyes on her and carried on speaking. 'I mean, I'm here tonight with literally the most attractive woman I've ever seen. I mean, really, have you seen her?' He laughed humourlessly. 'It's just ridiculous. And Joe's 100% right, she is perfect for me. And yet somehow, when I'm talking to her, when I'm *kissing* her, even, the only damn thing I can think about is you.'

He looked away for the first time, a look on his face somewhere between a smirk and a snarl. 'I mean really, what the hell is that about?'

Rae felt as if he'd punched her in the stomach. 'Wow. Don't hold back, Jamie, Jesus Christ.' She threw her hands up in surrender. 'Why not tell me what you really think?'

'You're not hearing me,' he gritted out, his voice louder now, but still barely audible over the clatter of glasses and laughter.

Rae shook her head, looking down, and all of a sudden she felt the air shift towards her, and then the grip of Jamie's fingers around her waist as he pulled her into him in one decisive movement.

He looked down at her, his eyes darkening. 'Fuck's sake, Rachel. I said the *only thing* I can think about is *you*.'

There was a flare of something, then, and it all happened in what felt like slow motion, like a bomb going off. One second Jamie was grabbing her arm, a little more firmly than was comfortable, and the next they were both pushing through the fire door to the side and out into the cold of Roy's courtyard.

It was a small yard, enclosed on every side by walls and outbuildings, and they fell together against the rough brick of the pub wall. And when Jamie's hands found the back of her neck and brought her lips to his there wasn't a damn thing she could do about it. There wasn't a damn thing she *wanted* to do about it, except kiss him back with every last thing that she had.

Somewhere, in what seemed like the far distance, she vaguely registered a countdown.

Ten...

The kiss deepened, tongues dancing, the intensity making her head spin as he marked her, claimed her, trapping her against the hard, cold brick with a hardness of his own which made her gasp a little into his open mouth.

Nine...

He broke away, eyes searching hers, his breath coming in pants which sent flumes of white into the frozen night. 'Stop me, Rae.' His voice was thick, quiet against the sounds of the crowd inside. 'Just tell me to stop and I'll stop.'

Eight...

But she didn't stop him. Her hands snaked around his waist, finding the gap where she could feel his bare skin under her fingers, the contact alive with a buzz of electricity. His eyes closed with a groan as his mouth crashed back against hers, fingers gripping her waist with a bruising pressure that was equal parts pleasure and pain.

Seven...

'Stop yourself if you want to stop,' she breathed into his mouth, sliding her hands around to the warm skin of his back, and then lower, her fingertips just sneaking below the band of his underwear, pulling him harder against her. Wanting him so badly she couldn't think straight. Needing the weight of his body on hers.

Six...

'I don't want to stop,' he muttered, his lips leaving hers and kissing a sweet trail down her neck and into the soft dip behind her collarbone, sending a cascade of shivers through her as raw heat began to pool in her belly. She must have dreamed about kissing him a hundred times before, but it had never been like this. *Fuck*, his breath on her neck. She could hardly breathe.

Five...

She moaned, pressing into his touch, and he responded, gathering her up against him, his mouth back on hers, nipping at her lower lip with a possessiveness that set her whole body on fire.

Four...

She hadn't even noticed her body moving, grinding, pushing against him until he matched her movements, pulling her closer, his hands marking her skin like he was branding her.

Three...

He pulled back slightly, looking at her from under hooded lids. Desire had turned his eyes to molten fire, his lips warm and wet with promises she wasn't sure she cared if he could keep or not.

Two...

His thumb traced the outline of her lower lip, and when he kissed her again it was softer, filled with longing and with relief. And when he touched her face it was with a reverence which took her breath away.

One...

She wanted to speak, to acknowledge this feeling thundering through her, but she was falling, speechless and aflame, back into him. Further into him. Harder against him. More, she wanted so much more. She needed so much more...

HAPPY NEW YEAR!

'Fuck!' He jumped away from her with a start, the cold air rushing into the space where their bodies had been touching.

And then as unexpectedly as he had appeared, he vanished, leaving Rae standing alone against the sound of muffled cheering and a bastardised version of Auld Lang Syne with nothing but swollen lips and the rumbling remains of her desire.

And so it happened that Rae started the new year with the taste of Jamie Stamford's lips on hers, the memory of his hands in her hair, and the crushing feeling that after that moment everything and nothing would be the same.

13

THEN – April 1974

T he Monday after Easter was a day which had always
rubbed Zosia up the wrong way, because it was
Śmigus-Dyngus – the old Polish tradition of throwing
water over each other to mark the end of Lent, and Zosia *hated*
getting wet with a passion. It was a throwback perhaps from
her youth, from having to run out to the shared ablution
blocks in the camp in all weathers. She couldn't be sure.
Either way, the morning of Easter Monday never failed to
make her very grumpy indeed.

Even now, she could feel a faint stab of paranoia grip her as
she padded through the quiet flat which she had just moved
into with Danusia. Her sister went by *Nush* now, and at first
the subtle anglicisation had annoyed Zosia immensely. But
that was until she first time she'd heard Ray say it.

Ah, *Ray*. Zosia sighed to herself, as dreamily as were
possible for her. She'd had a thing for him since the moment
she first saw him. He didn't seem handsome at first glance, but
there was something about him, an understated charm, some
vital warmth which poured out of him and had absolutely

captured Zosia in its spell.

She'd pushed it away, at first, quite sure that he was in love with her sister. Everyone always was, though most of the time Nush was oblivious to it. Ray had even asked Zosia, once, if she thought her sister would be interested in him, so Zosia was surprised and uncharacteristically delighted, a few weeks after that, when Ray had asked her out instead.

There was still a small thread of doubt running through her, but she pushed it away, seduced by the much louder roar of joy at the idea that she might have found her future in him.

Because Zosia had always longed to start a family.

Growing up with only her sister had taken its toll on the young Zosia. Though the girls had always been taken care of, they had never quite settled anywhere. There was Pani Krysia, the first to take them in, though she never seemed at all happy about it. Then gentle old Pani Genia who opened her home to them when Pan Kazik died and Pani Krysia was too mournful to bear the brightness of young girls around her.

Then, when Zosia was eight, the camp closed, and they moved to the city with Pani Grażyna, Pan Leszek and their four younger boys. They were a warm family, so loving, and Pan Leszek in particular went out of his way to make the girls feel welcome, but Zosia could never open herself completely. She could never *allow* herself to be cared for by them.

This is not your family, the voice in her head would remind her, and she longed for that connection, for a family of her own. When she looked at Ray, when he'd kissed her softly outside the small café where she worked, she had seen, for the first time, a flash forward to her future. She saw herself, older, with Ray and their beautiful hazel-eyed children and

107

the feeling took her quite by surprise. The feeling, she thought, of completeness. At last.

Her dreaming was interrupted then by another surprise; by the shock of cold droplets on the back of her neck, and she shrieked and spun, meeting the mischief in her sister's eyes with fury in her own.

'Śmigus-Dyngus' Nush sing-songed, and Zosia rolled her eyes. Nush was her opposite in so many ways. *Of course* she would love this stupid tradition.

'I didn't know you were up.' Zosia felt her voice come almost as a snarl, but it only made Nush laugh harder.

'We're meeting Ray in town,' Nush said, twisting her long, wild curls up absentmindedly. 'He said he'll buy the food if we're quick.' She raised one eyebrow.

Zosia huffed. 'Fine. I'm ready, anyway.' She pulled her handbag onto her shoulder and slipped on a pair of pumps, and the two sisters headed out.

As they reached the ground floor of the house which made up the flats, Zosia swung through the main door into the blinding sun of the mild April day and was immediately met by a sudden rush of cold that took her breath away.

She couldn't help the scream which escaped from her, and she looked up, dripping wet, to see her sister, soaked through and laughing so hard she was making herself cough. They both turned at the same time to see a red-faced Ray clutching an empty bucket.

'*Shmingus stingus,*' he offered sheepishly, his soft Edinburgh accent making his pronunciation of the Polish even more ridiculous.

Nush swatted him playfully, still giggling, but Zosia was frozen, furious. Her sister's laughter stirred a feeling somewhere inside her, that uneasy feeling of being the outsider which she had always hated so deeply.

'You bastard.' Zosia spoke slowly, deliberately, with the faint chatter of teeth from the cool breeze on her damp skin. But Ray just laughed, pulling her into a warm hug, and holding her tightly until she had all but forgotten that she was even angry in the first place.

And to her surprise, she found that the uneasy feeling, for then at least, was gone.

14

Everything and Nothing

Winter blew into Blackston Bay like the snow it brought with it, twirling and dancing on the frigid January winds, hiding the whole of the village under a fresh covering of white.

Rae was hiding too, and despite Nush's increasingly creative schemes to get her up and out of the house, she hadn't ventured far from the safety of the mill since New Year.

She'd nipped out twice to Mr Cramer's shop, her heart in her throat the whole time, once for an extremely brief and bracing walk along the beach, and once even to church, if only craving the peace she imagined sitting in the pews would buy her. Her plan had turned out to be flawed, though, and when Father Kevin had asked her twice how she was getting on before she'd been there five minutes, she decided that going out anywhere was a ridiculous idea and one she should probably abandon forever.

She was sulking, and she would have rather preferred to be left well alone to do it.

Nush had never asked directly what had happened on that

night. When a ruffled Jamie had run back into the main bar of the pub just after the stroke of midnight, Rae imagined that most of the residents would have been too busy cheering and kissing and singing to notice, but Nush wouldn't have missed it. Nor would she have missed Rae's absence from the celebrations.

But she hadn't said a word about it as Rae had quietly excused herself and headed back to the mill alone, blaming the sudden onset of some kind of mysterious ailment. And she hadn't said a word since, only asked in the vaguest of senses if everything was ok.

If there was one thing Danusia Nowak was good at, it was knowing when to leave the hell alone.

Her patience was not unlimited, though, and one particular morning when Nush came to set a perfectly sweetened cup of lemon tea on Rae's bedside table, she didn't duck out of the bedroom with a gentle smile as she had been doing. Instead she motioned for Rae to move her legs out of the way, and plopped down onto the end of her bed, making the bed springs creak and curse.

It was almost four weeks into the new year now, and whether Rae was ready or not, Nush was going to talk.

'Kwiatuszku, this moping is making you sick.' She tucked a strand of wild, grey hair behind one ear as she spoke.

Rae's smile was flat. 'I'm not moping, I'm writing.'

'And there is a difference?' Nush laughed lightly, not unkindly.

At that, Rae's smile grew more genuine, but it still didn't reach her eyes. 'I guess there probably isn't.'

Nush picked up her own tea from where she'd put the two mugs down and sipped it cautiously. 'It's been weeks. *Weeks* where all you have done is write and sleep.' She blew the steam from the top of the mug contemplatively. 'You either need to show me the masterpiece you've been producing, or you need to leave the house.'

Rae sighed, closing the lid of her laptop, but not moving it from her lap. In truth it hadn't been one masterpiece she'd been working on, but an endless string of failures, chapter after chapter written and deleted until she'd started to question why she was even trying.

'It's rubbish,' she said quietly, looking down at the computer on her knees and not at her aunt. 'Total rubbish. I keep getting to the same point in different stories and when I read them back, they're always terrible.' She shook her head in defeat. 'What if I'm just not a writer, Ciocia?' She inhaled, a shake in her shoulders, her voice small. 'What if I'm just not good enough.'

Nush's face softened, and she grabbed her niece's hand in both of hers. 'Maybe you need to stop chasing the words?' She squeezed Rae's hand gently. 'Let the story come to you.' The double meaning in her words was clear.

'I don't want to talk about Jamie.'

Nush brought her hands to her chest in mock innocence. 'Who was talking about Jamie?' She laughed lightly. 'I was talking about writing.'

Rae's mouth twisted into a smile. 'Fine. I'll let the story come to me.' She was also definitely not just talking about the words. 'But what if it never does?'

Nush's expression grew serious then, and Rae knew she was thinking about something else. Something deeper than words, or illicit kisses in pub courtyards.

'Kochanie, sometimes it doesn't. But still life continues.'

For a second the look on Nush's face was so lost, so mournful that Rae could hardly bear it. Her eyes shone, swimming with a lifetime of regret, with the bitter sting of resignation.

Her ghost, Rae was sure of it.

She grabbed Nush's hand back and smiled, wanting only to chase away this darkness that she had so rarely seen before. 'Have you ever noticed that you get more Polish when you feel like you're dispensing priceless life advice?'

There was a quick flash of something which looked like gratefulness before Nush's lips pursed together, eyebrows raised. 'It isn't something I keep track of.'

Rae nodded slowly, a twinkle in her eye. 'Like a latter day Yoda.'

Nush snorted. 'I have half a mind to send you back to your mama.'

Rae's laugh was genuine that time. She set her laptop aside and picked up her cooling tea, downing half in one long gulp. 'Come on Nush, why don't we go for a walk?'

'A walk? I don't believe it!' Nush raised her hands to the sky dramatically. 'She leaves the house, *mój Boże!*'

Rae rolled her eyes but couldn't fully hide her amusement. It was the first time she'd genuinely smiled in almost four weeks. And she knew exactly where she wanted to go.

It was around an hour later when they finally climbed up the rocky promontory jutting proudly out into the sea. Black Rock was the village's namesake and Rae's favourite place in the world. The dark stone smoothed to a flat plateau on top before dipping down sharply a little way at the cliff edge and then sloping gently down into the sea. Over time, the elements had worn away parts of the dip to form a perfect, sheltered cove, and it was there that a much younger Rae had gone when she needed to right herself, to get away from the noise of life. There had been many times she had screamed her frustrations to the sea and the sky, her pain shattering against the rocks below and crumbling to pieces.

There was only one other person in the world who she had ever shared the cove with. Today she was ready to make it two.

'What is this place?' Nush took Rae's hand as she offered it, stepping down from the exposed top of Black Rock into the welcome shelter of the cove. 'I have lived here as long as you have been alive and I never even knew this was here.' She adjusted her hat, smoothing her wind-blown curls underneath it, before shaking her head in disbelief. 'I must have walked on the top of this rock a thousand times. How can that even be?'

Rae smiled. 'You never went far enough. People don't.' She pulled one glove off, trailing her fingers along the smooth stone inside the cove. It looks as if you're at the edge, that the rock just falls away to nothing.' She shrugged. 'Once you get here, you realise that the drop isn't as sheer as it looks, but no one wants to get that close to the edge. They're too afraid to fall.'

Nush looked at her with a curious expression. 'But you weren't?'

'I was,' Rae said, looking out to sea, the waves cold and calm against the palest blue of the sky's gradient. 'I didn't used to let that stop me.'

'I remember well!' Nush laughed heartily, the sound reverberating about the cove, spilling out eventually to the waves, which made her laugh again, this time in delight.

Watching her, Rae felt the gnawing of something which had been with her for a long time, the merest hint of a feeling tugging at her. The last time she had brought another person here it had been her dad, just after his diagnosis. She'd associated the cove with that feeling of loss ever since, and she desperately wanted to turn it back into the sanctuary she had relied on so often in her younger years.

'I want to show you something,' Rae said, only just loud enough to hear over the sharp snap of the sea breeze blowing past. She took Nush's hand and led her to the edge of the cove, where the wind was stronger. Speaking louder now, Rae turned to face her. 'If you've got something to get off your chest, stand right up here and yell it as loud as you can. You can barely hear yourself. I used to think it was the wind taking my problems away.' She chuckled to herself. 'Ok, fine, I didn't understand physics, whatever. But try it. It helps.' She took another step, until her toes were right up against the raised ridge of the cove edge, and glanced quickly at Nush. 'Watch.'

Rae filled her lungs with icy sea air and shouted as loudly as she could.

'MY BOOOOK IS REALLY SHIIIIIIIITT.'

And just as she had described, the sound was whipped away from her, taking her truth away with it, and out to sea forever.

Nush turned to look at her, and for a second Rae expected to be scolded for swearing, until Nush's chin creased with the slightest dimple and both women exploded into laughter.

After a few moments, Nush wiped her eyes and took a deep breath in.

'MY NIECE IS A FINANCIAL DRAIN'

115

'Woah!' Rae laughed in mock hurt. 'This isn't about me, it's about you. If you want the sea to take your problems, you have to offer them to it.'

She turned to face back out.

'JAMIE STAMFORD KISSED ME AND THEN HE RAN AWAY.'

When Rae turned back to face Nush, her eyes were wide with interest, but she said nothing. Just raised one eyebrow slowly, which made Rae roll her eyes and laugh to herself.

After a beat, Nush's face pulled into a frown, as if she were working through the events of that night in her head, and she fixed Rae with a serious look before turning back out to the sea again. Understanding that the stakes had been raised, Nush stood motionless, closing her eyes against the wind. It was a few minutes before she took another deep breath, yelling one simple truth out into the wind.

'I MISS YOU.'

Silently, and without turning to look at her, Rae took Nush's hand and stepped up beside her at the ridge, breathing in the scent of the saltwater a few times before she yelled her final truth.

'I MISS YOU.'

She shouted to Jamie, to the younger man who had stolen her heart so many times as much as the Jamie from the other night who'd kissed her like his life depended on it.

To her dad, to that day they had stood here together, each taking it in turns to yell 'FUCK CANCER' into a dark and stormy sea.

And to herself, to a different version of herself who seemed long gone now.

They stood there for a while, looking out to the horizon,

each deep in thought. And when they stepped back from the ridge, Nush's face seemed lighter, with no sign of the sadness which had been lining her eyes.

Rae studied her aunt carefully for a moment.

'Tell me your ghost story, Nush, and I'll tell you mine.'

But Nush just smiled enigmatically, pushing her glasses back up her nose. 'Another day.' She gestured out to the mouth of the cove. '*Dziękuję*. Thank you for this.'

Rae nodded in understanding.

'Dobra,' Nush pulled her hat down over her ears, bracing for the short walk back into Blackston. 'Now let's go get something warm to drink.'

They walked back up the limestone path which crossed the scrubland between the village and the coast, marvelling in silence at the crisp beauty of the winter morning. What the sun lacked in warmth it made up for in brightness, and the intense blue of the sky cast long shadows from the bare branches of Blackston's trees. They walked past the sea front cottages, mostly let to tourists these days, past the mill and up to the small stone building of Jan's cafe.

A few years older than Nush, Jan Jowett had lived her whole life in the village, and was Nush's oldest and dearest friend.

The cafe was empty when they went in, and Jan was sitting at a table in one of the bay windows, thumbing through a trashy magazine.

'Ladies!' She stood as she heard the bell over the door, brushing imaginary dust from her apron. 'What can I get you?'

Jan was a short, stout woman, with a shock of dyed ruby hair which waved and curled around her shoulders and sharp green eyes, which like Nush's, missed nothing, and all but disappeared into the deep creases of her face as she smiled.

Nush ordered a fancy coffee, dealer's choice, while Rae went for a hot chocolate with everything. 'Everything' varied from day to day, depending what Jan had left over from the desserts of the previous day, but could always be relied upon to provide a serious sugar hit in times of dire need.

'Ooh, good choice,' Jan cooed, shuffling into the kitchen. 'It'll be a good one today.'

Her voice faded as she brushed through the bead curtain which separated the kitchen area from the main room of the cafe. The decor had barely been updated in here since the late seventies, and that was just how the residents of the village liked it. Jan's no-frills menu drew a steady stream of passing truckers and tourists, too, at the right time of year, but on this January morning there were none of either to be seen.

The two women took the table which Jan had been sitting at. It was the best table in the place, with the large bay window giving a perfect view over the bridge to the mill, and beyond to the sea, or the other way up the hill into the village, past Mr Cramer's shop and straight up the lane to the church. Jan spent many an hour behind the secrecy of her voiles, keeping a sentinel's watch on the comings and goings of the villagers.

Nush settled into the watcher's spot which Jan had freed up, while Rae sat across from her, feeling the welcome warmth of the sun through the glass of the window. They said nothing for a long while, sitting together in a comfortable silence, rubbing their frozen fingers to warm them, and gradually stripping off their winter layers.

Nush spoke first, seeing Mr Harper the vet and his wife climbing into their immaculate white Range Rover.

'They clean that car inside and out every evening.' Nush

had a tone in her voice that Rae knew well. Her eyes always softened too, when she was gossiping, now focused on a faraway point. 'It can look as spotless as it does now, and they will still get that jet wash out every evening, seven on the dot.' She loosened the scarf from around her neck and began to pull it off. 'What the hell are they doing in that car that they need to clean it every single day?'

'Dogging?' Jan offered, putting a tray with their drinks down on the table, along with a mug of tea she'd made for herself and a small bowl of biscuits.

Rae laughed, the sound escaping as a snort, and Jan hooted along with her.

Nush smiled, looking back towards the other two with an animated expression. 'I think they're killing people.'

At this Rae laughed louder, but Jan was quiet, as if pondering the possibility. She pulled a third chair up to the table and set the bowl and the drinks down before she sat, reaching to put the empty tray on the table behind her.

'Cappuccino for you, my lovely.' She beamed at her old friend. 'And a hot chocolate for the young 'un.'

Rae smiled in thanks. She loved the way the older generation of Blackston spoke of hers - as though they were still children, even though there were a fair few residents her age who now had children of their own.

She remembered the time Nush had told her about the return of *young Jamie Stamford* and her heart clenched in her chest.

She wrapped her fingers round her drink, the heat thawing them quickly, and took a sip. The whipped cream on top was peppered with fragments of meringue and cinder toffee, with small curls of white chocolate here and there. Her eyes closed a little with the pleasure. 'Amazing everything today, Jan.' She lifted the cup slightly, almost a *cheers*, causing the other woman to beam back at her.

Nush carried on regardless. 'I'm serious. I've been thinking. about this for a long time. Ever since they moved in, really.'

The Harpers were relative newcomers to the village, arriving five years ago in a cloud of designer fragrance and sharply-cut clothes which had made the older residents altogether suspicious from the outset. They had bought the big detached house which sat just over the river from the mill. It had belonged to old Stan Swift, been in his family for generations. But when he was forced into assisted living because of his advancing Parkinson's, it had to go. Old Man Stan, as they'd called him, was a second grandfather to most of Rae's peers, playing Santa Claus in the village Christmas event for as long as anyone could remember, and his sudden replacement with the odious pomp of the Harpers didn't sit at all well with the villagers.

'They bought a pure white car, which honestly I thought was a weird choice from the get-go, and they clean it completely every single day.' Nush looked at her niece with wide eyes. 'Misia, you really don't think that's a strange thing?'

'I think it's strange that they can be bothered,' Rae answered with a shrug. She'd owned her car for four years and in that time had cleaned it exactly once.

'Even the interior is cream leather. And they clean that every day, too,' Nush continued, not indulging her niece's cynicism. 'I mean... cream? He's a vet!' She paused dramatically for a beat. 'You'd think that his profession would come with a certain amount of, you know...' Her hands gesticulated a non-specific shape. '...I don't know, cow pat and things?' She shrugged. 'It just seems like a strange choice.'

Rae smirked. 'Maybe it's the cow pat and things that he's cleaning off?'

'Well it looks clean to me!' Nush huffed. 'That's why I think it's so suspicious that they clean it so often. It looks as if there is nothing there to clean!'

'Also, wait, you think he's murdering people every day?' Rae cocked her head. 'Where are these 365 people a year coming from? Has no one noticed they're missing?'

'He has access to medical supplies, of course. He's a vet.' Nush continued, ignoring Rae's logic completely and, stirring her coffee with a thoughtful sigh. 'And an incinerator, I'm guessing.' She waved a conspiratorial finger at no one in particular.

Jan pulled her chair a little closer, starting to invest in the story. The two had been firm friends ever since Nush's arrival in the village three decades ago. 'I've always thought there was something fishy about those two, you know, but I could never put my finger on exactly what.' She took a big gulp of tea and Rae could almost see the cogs turning in her head. 'You know, I did always walk past their garden and wonder how they're maintaining those beautiful rhododendrons.' She picked a bourbon out of the bowl and bit the end off, brandishing the rest like a weapon. When she spoke again, it was through a mouthful of biscuit. 'They won't grow in my garden. Soil's too chalky.'

Rae stifled a laugh. 'Ok, so are they incinerating the bodies, or are they burying them under the rhododendrons?'

'Who knows,' Nush continued. 'Maybe both?'

Jan's eyebrows shot up. 'Maybe they're fertilising the soil with the ashes!'

Nush shrugged lightly, as if that were something she'd already considered.

Rae picked a jam cream from the biscuit bowl. Her favourite. 'So, the Harpers are murdering people, burning them in a veterinary incinerator and spreading the ashes on their garden, before clearing that giant car inside and out, and they're doing this every single day?' She nibbled the edge of her biscuit. 'While both holding down full-time jobs?'

Nush and Jan shared a look, then both half-nodded, half-shrugged.

'People find time for things if they need to,' Nush said, slipping back into the Polish lilt which affected her voice when she made what she believed to be important statements.

Rae smiled broadly, not believing a single word of it, but loving every second. 'I'm just saying I admire their time management skills, that's all.' She popped the rest of the biscuit into her mouth.

The Harpers' Range Rover pulled onto the main road then, and drove up the hill and out of sight. They all watched it go.

Jan broke the silence after a few beats. 'So, Penny was in yesterday, telling me all about the craft club she's been trying to set up.'

Rae wrinkled her nose, trying to locate the memory. 'Which one's Penny, again?'

'Sleeping with the priest!' Nush and Jan blurted in unison, before sharing a look and giggling to themselves.

Nush blew a quick breath to stop from laughing, shaking her head. 'Myszko, we've been through this.'

'I get her confused with Pauline,' Rae said with a chuckle. 'So, it's Penny with the art gallery?'

Jan nodded. 'That's the one.' She swiped a stray biscuit

crumb from the side of her lips. 'Anyway, she was trying to get a craft club set up at the gallery, but she wasn't getting many people signing up.' She picked up another biscuit. 'It's cold in there, you know, and I'm always a bit scared I'll break something, aren't you? Some priceless piece of art or something.'

A small smile touched Rae's lips as she nodded. Penny's art gallery was filled with pieces by local artists. It was hardly the Louvre.

Jan carried on. 'So, I suggested she move it here. What do you think?' Her hands adjusted her apron as she spoke. 'We could do Tuesdays at seven. We'll learn different crafts, I'll make snacks.' She threw her hands up in excitement. 'I mean, it's warm in here, I have chairs. And I can make people whatever drinks they like. What do you think?'

'Will there be hot chocolate with everything?' Rae finished the last dregs of her mug and raised it in a question.

Jan lit up. 'Always!'

'Then count me in.'

Nush nodded enthusiastically. 'Definitely.'

And the three women chatted animatedly about all the crafts they'd like to learn until their ideas had them giddy with excitement, and Rae didn't even realise she'd stopped thinking about Jamie Stamford's hands in her hair for the first time in weeks.

15

A Better Man

The second good thing that Jamie Stamford did was under his own steam.

He took it upon himself as a penance, not for kissing Rae while he was on a date with Nina, but for *enjoying* kissing Rae while he was on a date with Nina.

He hadn't meant to kiss her, *Jesus*. He was enjoying a perfectly pleasant date with the hottest woman he'd ever seen in real life, and she was nice, really nice, and funny, too, and smart. And interesting. And, most importantly, interested in him.

And he was an idiot.

He couldn't say for sure why he'd even followed Rae in the first place. He'd watched her talking with Joe, seen her look his way, then watch her expression crumble as if Joe had physically hurt her.

He'd seen it all unfold on her face - the initial impact of whatever it was that Joe had said, fading into the numbing haze of shock before the pain began to spread.

Had he been asked, he would probably have been able to

pinpoint the very second her heart broke.

He didn't choose to go after her, either. He saw her hand on Nush's shoulder, and he saw her disappear, and he'd looked away at that point, turned his attention back to the conversation that Nina and Allie were having. For a few minutes he'd even convinced himself that he didn't care, and he joined in while the girls reminisced about chocolate bars from their youth.

But his thoughts were drawn away time and time again, lost to Rae's gravity, which pulled them into orbit around her.

And, like gravity, he could feel the force of her attraction and was powerless to resist.

He hadn't thought about any of it, really. Not consciously. One minute his worry for her had grown so profound that it had turned almost to anger, and the next he was pulling her out of a fire door and kissing her with such intensity that every last inch of his body had felt like it was screaming for more.

Her lips, God he'd dreamed about those lips, so warm and wet and humming with the sound of those little fucking moans which connected like a direct line to both his heart and his cock. And the warmth of her hands on his skin, exploring, lighting small fires in their wake.

He'd told her to make him stop, given her an out, but she hadn't taken it and he'd succumbed to her in a heartbeat.

Until the muffled sounds of the crowded pub yelling HAPPY NEW YEAR hit him like a gunshot and all at once he'd realised what he was doing - pouring his whole heart and soul into Rae Logan while another woman waited for him in the bar. Not to mention that this was not the first time he'd tried to give his everything to Rae, and it hadn't ended well that time either.

He'd bolted almost as an instinct, the adrenaline racing through his veins turning from fight to flight in an instant, and he was on the other side of the fire door before he'd even really had time to think about it.

He'd fumbled an excuse as he got back to their table, before his brain had had anywhere near enough time to process what had just happened.

'Sorry, I was on the toilet,' he'd blurted awkwardly. 'It took longer than I expected.'

All to much hilarity from Joe, of course, whose Happy Poo Year jokes ended up taking weeks to die down.

But Nina had just smiled kindly, mistaking his clear guilt for the flush of embarrassment, and pulling him in for a New Year kiss of her own.

At that point, Jamie had taken the only course of action he felt was prudent, and asked Nina on another date. She'd accepted happily. And that second date had led to a third, then on to a fourth, and before he knew it she'd referred to him as her boyfriend and he hadn't corrected her.

It was the tug in his chest at the mere mention of Rae's name, plus the distinct lack of small fires on his skin during his perfectly satisfying sex with Nina that led him back to Father Kevin. He remembered the pride he'd felt for Joe after watching him leave the posy of snowdrops for Norma Grey, and he wondered if he could find a way to capture that feeling for himself.

At the very least, he wanted to make a good choice for once.

The priest looked up with a smile as Jamie pushed through the double doors of the church hall. 'Jamie.'

He didn't say *I've been expecting you*, but Jamie wanted

him to. Instead he stood from behind the small desk and strode forwards to shake Jamie's hand firmly. Jamie wondered vaguely where Penny was until he heard the tinkle of a teaspoon hitting china in the small kitchenette.

Jamie hadn't spoken to either of them since he was in the hall last with Joe, filling out forms and signing his consent to a background check.

'You can't be too careful these days,' Penny had said with a sad smile.

'Your check came back clear,' the priest said, brightly. 'Not that we weren't expecting it to, of course.'

He half laughed, and Jamie smiled politely.

'Anyway, it's come back at a good time,' Father Kevin continued, 'because we have a small job which needs doing for Edie Dunham.'

He picked up a stack of papers and shuffled them, searching for one in particular.

'Ah yes,' he said with a small smile. 'This is an easy one.'

Jamie nodded.

'Edie Dunham's gravel path all but washed away in those bad rains we had, and she has a terrible time getting from her house to the car on all the mud.' Father Kevin eyed Jamie carefully. 'She has a stack of flagstones piled up behind her garage, she just needs someone to haul them out and lay them into a workable path.'

Jamie nodded again. 'I can do that.'

And even by the simple act of agreeing, he already felt like a better person.

The next day dawned bright but brisk, and Jamie was thankful for the physical labour. The burning in his muscles as he hauled up the flagstones was a welcome distraction from the relentless churn of his mind.

By the time he'd moved the whole stack from behind Edie Dunham's shed and started arranging them into a solid path, he'd almost stopping thinking about the conversation he'd had with Nina the night before about his plans for Valentine's Day. There had been something about the light in her eyes when she asked the question which suddenly made him feel like the biggest arsehole alive.

'Oh,' he'd said. 'I haven't even thought about it.'

But as he'd watched her visibly deflate in front of his eyes, he'd quickly added, 'Where we should go, I mean.' He'd kissed her lightly, trying to think quickly. 'Or maybe it's a surprise?' He'd added a comedy wink for effect.

You absolute shit.

She'd smiled warmly in relief. Lovely Nina, so happy and kind and objectively sexy, and not even the slightest bit suspicious of any of the things Jamie had said or done. Thoroughly oblivious to the inner turmoil racing through his veins.

She really was the perfect woman. And he didn't have the slightest clue why that wasn't enough for him.

He turned his attention back to the job in hand for a moment. The stones were heavy, and the slip of sweat on his hands did nothing for his grip. He set the stone he was holding down by his feet and paused a minute, massaging the cramp out of the base of his thumb.

He saw movement out of the corner of his eye and noticed Edie watching him from behind the window, her face alight with gratitude, and he felt a small swell of pride as he raised his hand to wave at her. She beamed as she waved back, gently tapping her fingers on the glass.

He got it, then. Father Kevin's whole thing. This would take an hour out of his day, maybe less. That's all it would take to turn him from Jamie who makes bad decisions to Jamie who makes bad decisions but does good things for people. It was something.

Spurred on by the thought, he laid the last of the path in no time, and when he knocked on the red gloss of Edie's front door he couldn't fight his smile.

She answered quickly, holding his face in the soft warmth of her age-worn hands, and telling him over and over what a good boy he was, as if he were a golden retriever rather than a full-grown man.

She offered to pay him, of course, but Jamie would have none of it.

'I don't want your money, Edie.' He'd laughed, as she tried to force a note into his hands. He took the note and purse from her, put the money back inside and set the purse down on the sideboard. 'Just save some of those macaroons for me at the next church fayre,' he said, with a wink, feeling the warmth of her chuckle thaw out his cold edges.

Then he kissed her lightly on the cheek and skipped off along the path he'd created, taking a left out of her gate to head down the hill to Jan's cafe. All that work had given him the taste for a good breakfast butty, and Jan's were the best.

He felt the buzz of his phone and reached into his pocket to check it. Two texts from Nina.

NINA: Hey, hot stuff. Been thinking about you all morning.

NINA: Can't wait for my surprise xx

'Ah shit,' he said aloud, stuffing the phone back into his pocket. The warm buzz of pride slowly faded back to guilt and sat heavy in his stomach. He wasn't all in with Nina and he knew it. He knew he owed it to her to be honest.

But breaking up with her a couple of days before Valentine's Day, wow. Surely he was better than that.

Wasn't he?

He ran through all the possible scenarios of ending things in his head as he strode down to Jan's. It had brightened into a fine day, and if it weren't for the sharp nip at his ears he might have believed it were much later in the year. A different month where he didn't have to worry about this nonsense at all.

His mind wandered to Romilly and he winced. Hadn't he promised himself that he wouldn't fall into the same trap again? And yet here he was, only a few weeks into a fresh relationship and already feeling suffocated by indifference. He wondered what Mills was doing for Valentine's Day for a few moments before shaking his head.

For God's sake, man, stop doing this, the voice in his head said. *You don't love Mills and you don't give any size of shit about bloody Valentine's Day!*

He breathed a long breath out, looking down at his muddied feet as he stepped into Jan's cafe, and then up, straight into the startled eyes of Rae Logan.

His breath caught in his throat. He hadn't seen her since he hotfooted it away from her in Roy's courtyard, and the feelings of that night rushed back into him all at once. He coughed them away.

Rae's eyes darted away from him quickly, and it was only then that Jamie noticed that she wasn't alone. She was sitting across from a man who was looking straight at him, wearing an expression like the cat that got the cream. Jamie's eyes narrowed involuntarily.

Wait, was she... on a *date*? His heart dropped like a stone at the thought.

He nodded, a vague hello, and walked up to the counter awkwardly, where Jan greeted him with a grin.

'The usual, please Jan,' he said, through a smile he hoped looked genuine.

'Absolutely,' she replied, jovially. 'Just for you today?'

Jamie heard the light sound of a cough being smothered behind him but didn't turn to look.

'Please.' He tried to make his voice sound normal. 'I'll take that to go, too, if you could?'

Jan nodded, dropping the coins Jamie handed over into the register before turning energetically on her heel, disappearing behind the bead curtain into the kitchen area. Jamie dropped onto the chair closest to the counter with a light sigh, trying his level best to look completely enthralled in his phone screen and resisting all temptation to look back at Rae.

Who was that guy she was with? He was artsy like her and about her age, and he could hear them giggling together in hushed tones. Was it their first date? Second? Fifth?

He wondered with a bitter taste in his mouth if she lit little fires on *his* skin, and huffed the thought away quickly. He had no claim to her. She'd actually never been his at all, save for those ten perfect seconds in the icy air of Roy's courtyard.

But then, he had been the one to run away.

His hand gripped the back of his neck, pinching out the tension. He set his phone on the table in front of him, unlocking it to read Nina's message again, this time with an edge of fire in his veins. If Rae could go on a date, well then so the fuck could he.

He tapped in a number he knew by heart and pressed call.

'Mick?... it's Jamie... Yeah, good thanks, how are you?... Yeah, I'd like to book a table for two, please?... This Sunday... yeah, the 14th...Dunno, about seven thirty?... Brilliant. Thanks, mate.'

He hung up with a flourish, firing a shot.

And when Jan appeared back at the counter a few seconds later with a paper bag in her hands, he took it and walked straight to the door, not looking at Rae or her mystery date even once, but feeling the burn of her eyes on his skin the whole way.

16

Word Gets Around

Penny's craft club hadn't taken long to become a regular fixture in Rae Logan's life.

The first meeting had been modest, just Rae, Nush and Jan, and Penny had got them relief printing, carving simple shapes out of potatoes. They'd scoffed at first, especially Nush - *I'm Polish, dear, and I can tell you that potatoes are for eating, not for painting* - but by the end of the session they were laughing aloud while they printed repeat patterns on to brown paper and calico.

By the second session, word had spread, and nine of them crammed round a small table as Penny demonstrated needle felting.

Rae stabbed herself with the felting needle eight times, each time swearing a little louder and more furiously, while Nush tutted at her with the hint of a smile at the corners of her mouth.

Afterwards Rae had stayed to help Penny clear away the wisps of fleece peppering every surface of the cafe.

'If you need any help,' she'd said, 'I'd love to get involved.

I'm not much of a crafter, but I have got a lot of time on my hands.'

Penny had smiled broadly. 'That would be wonderful!' And she'd assigned Rae the task of finding people who might want to come in and teach a class as a guest.

That was how Rae had met Kieran Quinn.

Kieran was a paper artist who she'd found through a message board in the art supply shop in the next town. He'd replied to her message almost immediately, bubbling with enthusiasm at the idea of teaching his craft, and they'd arranged to meet in Jan's cafe the following day.

He breezed in to the cafe and into Rae's life that morning like a breath of fresh air, a tall, handsome stranger with art in his soul and joy in his heart. Funny, charming and as gay as the day is long.

Rae loved him on sight.

'Rachel?' His voice was deep and warm, like someone draping a blanket around her shoulders.

She nodded quickly. 'You must be Kieran.' She stood to offer him her hand, but he used it to pull her into a hug and rock gently for a few seconds. She felt her heart lift at his enthusiasm.

He stood back, assessing her. 'That's me, beautiful.' His smile was dazzling. 'I hear you want to talk about art?'

Rae nodded, beaming back at him. 'I do.' She gestured to the table by the window, Jan's watching table. 'Come on, let's sit. Can I get you something to drink?'

Kieran pulled out the chair and started unwinding his wool scarf. 'That would be marvellous.' He hung his coat on the back of the chair, combing his wild russet mane back into place with his fingers. 'What's good?'

'I'm a big fan of hot chocolate with everything,' Rae said with a wry grin.

Kieran widened his eyes dramatically. 'Everything?'

Rae nodded, slowly. *'Everything.'* She enunciated every syllable, dragging the word out while her hand gestured vaguely, fingers spread.

Kieran threw his head back and laughed with abandon and in that moment Rae knew that he was someone she wanted to keep around. The friends that she'd had in the city were very much friends that she'd shared with Simon, and she hadn't been much interested in a custody battle.

But Kieran, with his unkempt curls and beautiful, dimpled smile, felt like someone she'd known forever.

Rae ordered their drinks and at once they set about getting to know each other. Kieran told Rae about his art, the stationery shop that he'd poured his whole life into, and about the handsome and brilliant Croatian boy, Ezra, that he planned to marry.

Rae told Kieran about her failed engagement, her new life living with Nush, and about the many terrible false starts of the novel she was struggling to write.

Kieran took a long sip of his hot chocolate as Jan set it down, today featuring hazelnut brittle and a swirl of chocolate sauce. 'Books start in the heart, don't they? Maybe you just need a little action?'

Rae said nothing, concentrating instead on ignoring the rough thump in her chest.

Kieran's eyebrows shot up.

'Wait,' he exclaimed, throwing both hands up. 'I saw that look. There *is* someone!' He chuckled lightly. 'You dark horse! I thought you'd only just split up with Sean!'

'Simon,' Rae corrected.

'Whatever.' Kieran waved his hands dismissively. 'Cheating arsehole, name begins with S. That's all I committed to memory.' He took another slurp of his drink, pointing down at the mug. 'This is amazing, by the way.'

Rae smiled. 'Told you so.' She ran a teaspoon along the cream on the top of hers and then licked it off slowly.

'Don't feel like you got away with that.' His dark eyes danced as he licked a smear of chocolate off his top lip. 'I made one little throwaway comment about getting some action and you nearly jumped out of your chair.'

Rae rolled her eyes. 'I barely moved.'

Kieran ignored her and carried on. 'Which can mean one of two things.' He stroked his chin in thought, like a Dickensian detective. 'Either you've been getting some action, or you're thinking about getting some action.' He smacked his hands lightly on the table. 'So which is it, Logan? Spill...'

Rae sighed in defeat. 'There's nothing to spill. Not really.' She ran her hands through her hair, raking out the waves. Calming her racing thoughts.

Kieran scoffed. 'There is definitely something. *Someone?*' He leaned in on his elbows, lowering his voice so that only the two of them could hear. 'Man? Woman?'

Rae's breath escaped in a sigh. 'Man.'

'Excellent, my favourite subject.' He clapped his hands together with a knowing smile. 'Continue.'

Rae barely knew this man but he had a quality about him that made her want to spill all her secrets. 'Ok, fine. There's a guy I've known since I was a kid. We used to be friends, way back when.' She sipped her chocolate, ignoring Kieran's frantic gestures to hurry her up. 'He moved away from

Blackston for a long time, but when I came to stay with Nush he was back here. He kissed me on New Year's Eve and it was all kinds of amazing and then he ran away and I haven't seen him since.' She wiped some stray cream off the side of her mug with a finger and licked it off. 'Happy?'

Kieran studied her for a second. 'Have you tried? To see him, I mean.'

Rae shook her head. 'I've kind of been hiding out in Nush's house ever since.' Her nose crinkled in embarrassment. 'You know, on account of my utter mortification.'

Kieran blew a breath out of his nose, sitting back in his chair. 'Don't you be embarrassed, petal. *He* kissed you. And then *he* was a dick about it. *Him.* You haven't got a single thing to be embarrassed about.'

Rae smiled at him, but she couldn't shake the shame dragging her down, and she felt it begin to nip at the back of her eyes. Her throat tightened and she coughed it away.

'Now,' said Kieran, with a change of subject so timely she could have kissed him. 'What's to be done about this craft club of yours?'

Rae relaxed then, and they discussed arrangements for the craft night. Kieran would teach them paper marbling, and then later, decoupage. They swapped numbers and Rae was just about to get up and pay for their drinks when she saw a familiar character walking over the road towards the cafe.

She stiffened in her seat.

'It's him, isn't it?' Kieran asked in a low voice, and she barely had time to nod before the door swung open and there he was, every bit as captivating as he had been the last time that she saw him. And probably every bit as unavailable, she reminded herself.

137

Jamie's face was flushed, dark curls of hair clinging to his temples, which had the slightest sheen of sweat despite the nip in the air. His eyes, warm and sweet like pots of melted caramel, met hers for a second and blinked once, not enough for her to get a read on what he was thinking, before they moved to Kieran and narrowed.

Jamie looked away then, striding past them to Jan's counter to order his food.

Rae's heart, which she could have sworn had stopped beating entirely, thudded and skipped in her chest as she watched him speak to Jan and then sit at the table nearest the counter. He wasn't just not looking at her, he was deliberately making an effort to look anywhere *but* at her, and the thought clawed at her throat.

'Oh, mate,' Kieran whispered, leaning into her. 'I'm not surprised you're all torn up about him running out on you. Put my name down for *that*.'

Rae half glared at him, eyes wide, trying to suppress the shocked giggle bubbling out of her.

'Good God,' he continued, waving away Rae's attempts to shut him up. 'I would legitimately sell a part of my body to get a go on a man like that, I'm not even joking.' He brought his hand to his chest. 'Don't tell Ezra.' He fanned himself, eyes fluttering dramatically. 'I mean, *damn*.'

Rae shushed him, her held-in laugh beginning to shake her at the shoulders.

Kieran smirked at her, miming a slow clap. 'Bravo... ...just bravo.'

Jamie spoke, then, stunning them both into silence, and it was a moment before Rae realised he was on the phone. Speaking to Mick Doherty, by the sound of it, owner of the best restaurant in the area. Rae's stomach turned over as she heard him book a table for two, on Valentine's Day, and the small flame of possibility which had been licking at the pit of her chest since the kiss burned away to nothing. There was her answer.

Jamie stood, then, taking his food from Jan's waiting hands and heading for the door without looking even for a second in Rae's direction.

Kieran let the door settle back into place behind Jamie before he spoke. 'That table isn't for you, is it?'

Rae's smile was slight, lifeless. 'Nope.'

'You missed something out of the story, didn't you?'

She nodded. 'Yep.'

Kieran's eyes narrowed in thought. 'He was with someone else, wasn't he?'

Rae's sigh was almost imperceptible. 'Yep.'

He smiled kindly at her, reaching across the table to gently take her hand. 'You going to start giving me more than one-word answers?'

She smiled then, genuinely. 'Nope.'

He grinned broadly, this man. He was a single step from being a stranger, and yet she felt a comfort from being with him. It was if they were meeting again rather than meeting for the first time.

'Well, let me tell you something,' Kieran said, his deep, velvet voice low and serious. 'I don't know you all that well, and I don't know your devastatingly handsome mystery man even slightly, but I know one thing for absolute certain.' He leaned in. 'I watched his face change as he saw you here with me, and I would bet everything I own that he's torn up about you, too.'

He sat back in his chair, grabbing his scarf and wrapping it around his neck, not losing eye contact with her. 'So, beautiful, I will see *you* here for our date next Tuesday.' He winked, jokingly, and when Rae offered him her hand to shake, he kissed it with a flourish.

And then he was gone.

The days passed, as days do, so slowly that Rae couldn't fathom the speed at which the end of the week came.

Rae was spending her Saturday morning in the least glamorous of ways - waiting for the garage in town to call about her car's MOT. Nush had gone for one of her walks and Rae was making the most of the empty house by sitting with her laptop in the warm stream of sunlight across the kitchen table.

She was on her seventh or eighth incarnation of chapter one and it was no better than her first.

She huffed to herself, starting to read, as she always did, from the beginning. Her plot was clumsy, her characters stilted. She was fighting for every word, and second guessing herself in a way that left her tired and her ego torn to shreds.

She really should have given up a long time ago, but there was something in her, a small voice deep inside herself which led her back to the keyboard every time, a stubbornness which refused to let her give in.

One day, it whispered. *One day you'll find the right words.*

Today was not going to be that day, though. She inhaled deeply before sighing hard and deleting the entire thing. She typed *Chapter* out one more time and was about to write *One*, too, but was interrupted by the sound of her phone buzzing.

She grabbed it. 'Hello?'

'Car's ready, love.' Phil Molloy was the only mechanic Nush

trusted and she wouldn't hear of Rae going anywhere else, even if it meant a trip to town.

'Thanks, Phil.' She braced herself. 'What's the damage?'

'Passed first time.' Phil was the very definition of no-nonsense. He could find no use for any words in a sentence other than those which were absolutely necessary. 'Thirty-five quid, whenever you're ready.'

God love the trusty old heap of shit.

'Amazing, thank you. Can I come now.'

'Aye, love,' Phil said, and he hung up, abruptly but somehow not impolitely.

Rae looked at the large station clock on Nush's kitchen wall. Eleven fifteen. The bus to town came every two hours on a Saturday, and if she left now she'd be just in time to catch it.

She pulled her coat and scarf on, laced her feet into her boots and grabbed her bag, hot-footing it down to the stop just in time to see the bus appear over the top of the hill.

Saturday had brought with it another beautiful winter day, the brightness of the sun trying hard to mask the fierce nip in the air, and she pulled her coat tighter around herself as the edges of the wind crept in through the seams.

The bus pulled up and she paid her fare and got on, taking a seat by the window. She sat with her handbag on her knee and was just putting the change back in the zipped pocket of her purse when she heard a familiar voice.

She looked up, her heart thumping a rhythm in her ears as her eyes met Jamie's. He looked less shocked than she felt, perhaps he had seen her getting on the bus in front of him. He looked down at the floor after a moment, and she turned her eyes down too, finishing up with her purse and winding her handbag strap around her fingers.

She didn't look at him again until he sat down next to her and her heart immediately kicked up a notch, hammering involuntarily against her ribcage. She looked at him and he offered a small smile, almost sheepish.

'Hi.' A peace offering.

She took it. 'Hi.' Her voice was soft, small and unsure.

'Taking the bus now?' A smile played at the edges of his mouth.

'Picking my car up.' She held his gaze a second, then smiled back, looking away. 'MOT.'

He nodded. 'Oh, right.'

'What about you?'

'I was out last night. We'd had a few, had to leave my car.' The *we* caught at Rae as he said it. Did he mean *we* him and Joe? Did he mean *we* him and Miss Universe?

She huffed the thought away. 'Ah, ok.'

Rae turned, then, drawing shapes in the condensation on the window with a pad of her finger. His proximity made her whole body hum, suddenly acutely aware of the edge of her thigh which occasionally brushed his as he fidgeted in his seat. The draft from the window changed as they stopped and started, bringing his scent her way in waves, and she breathed in each one deeply. He smelt fresh, something like cut leaves on a spring day, with an undertone of masculine warmth, and she felt the familiar tug of desire in the pit of her stomach. She blew a breath out of her mouth, suddenly very still.

'Look,' he said, soft and sincere. A pause. 'I'm sorry about everything.'

She looked up at that, straight into those honey-gold eyes. 'Everything?' Her brow furrowed. It was a challenge.

He knew it. 'Come on, you know what I mean.' He

looked away, rolling his bus ticket into a small tube, then straightening it again, his hands nervous. 'New Year's Eve. Leaving you like that.' He rubbed his scruff of beard, blowing a breath out. 'I just wanted to say I know it wasn't ok and I'm sorry.' He looked forward, not at her.

'Are you sorry for ignoring me for a month afterwards?' She didn't intend the edge in her voice, but it found its way in regardless.

The sound he made was almost a laugh. 'I literally didn't see you anywhere for a month afterwards.'

She turned to him, although he was still looking straight ahead. 'And for glaring at me the other day at Jan's.'

'I didn't *glare* at you,' he said, indignantly. 'You took me by surprise is all.'

She didn't say anything, but she didn't look away either, and he must have been able to see her still studying him because he turned back to her, and the force of their eyes meeting again felt like electricity, a charge in the air.

'Ok, fine.' Almost a smile. 'I'm sorry for glaring at you at Jan's.' He looked down then, as if there was something he wasn't saying.

'You're forgiven,' she said, softly.

Their silence was more comfortable that time, although still Rae was aware of his every movement. Of the quiet rasp of him clearing his throat. Of the subtle heat of his thigh next to hers. She didn't look anywhere in particular when she next spoke.

'You know, tomorrow would have been my wedding day.'

She heard his breathing change a little, the pattern shift. 'Valentine's Day?'

'Cheesy, I know.' She smiled by way of explanation. 'But

Simon was into all of that. He thought it was important.' Her fingers moved more quickly in her bag strap, deftly winding it around in one direction and then in the other.

They both sat with the weight of their silence then, Rae running through a million scenarios in her head before she finally spoke.

'He was cheating on me.'

Jamie huffed, a soft breath out, and when he spoke his voice was careful, laced with a tenderness she hadn't often heard in him. 'I heard.'

'Word gets around, right?' She turned to him, a slow smile starting to creep over her face.

'Something like that.' He smiled back.

She'd forgotten what it was like to see him from this distance, and she took in all the details of his face which hadn't been there when they were younger. The corners of his eyes which creased softly at the edges as he smiled, and how the light picked out the peppering of grey in his stubble. And how it all came together all at once and made need swell in her chest, her whole body suddenly alive. It overwhelmed her, consumed her, and she looked down at the floor, retreating to safety.

In her periphery she noticed that he hadn't looked away. 'Do you miss him?'

Rae shrugged lightly. 'I miss having someone.' Her finger traced a line down the hard plastic of the seat in front. 'I miss not feeling like I've run out of time, you know?' Her laugh was barely a laugh at all. 'But no, I don't miss him.'

'You have time.'

His voice was gruff, edged with something she couldn't make out, and she looked back up at him then, into his eyes, now darkened and trained on her. His gaze darted down to her lips and after a beat he coughed and looked away, twisting his hands together as her heart thumped a crazed beat in her throat.

Had he been about to kiss her?

She shook the thought away, watching out of the window as the bus pulled onto the section of dual carriageway which told her she wasn't far from Molloy's garage.

She reached past him to press the bell, feeling the soft heat of his breath on her hand. 'Anyway, this is me.' She told herself to stop there, but her mouth paid no heed, and carried on. 'Enjoy your date tomorrow.'

He smirked. Of course he would have known she'd been listening. 'Yeah, thanks. I will.' His eyes narrowed slightly, a flicker of a challenge in them. 'And I suppose you'll be out with Ol' Handsomeface from Jan's the other day?'

'What, Kieran?' She bit her lip, trying to hold in her grin. 'I dunno, I imagine he'll probably want to spend the evening with his husband-to-be.'

She watched as his face changed, realisation dawning slowly through his features, chased by a faint hint of embarrassment.

Rae stood, and as Jamie stood to let her pass she was so close she could smell him, a warm scent of soap and mint which took her right back to the courtyard. Heat knotted deep in her belly as she paused slightly, almost touching him while she passed.

'He'll be *delighted* to hear that you think he's handsome, though.' She smiled, less awkwardly now, bolstered by the subtle shift of power. 'See you around, Jamie.'

And she strode down the aisle and off the bus, feeling for the first time that she had the upper hand with him. Had he been jealous of Kieran? The thought made her chest tighten. But it didn't change the fact that he was taking another woman out to dinner tomorrow, and she couldn't get tangled up in that.

She stepped down onto the pavement, wrapping her coat tightly around her, and turned to look back up at the bus window. Jamie sat where she had just moments before, his brows knitted together, lips parted slightly, and his thoughts what looked like a million miles away.

In that moment he was breathtaking, and it took every last ounce of her strength to pull her eyes away from him.

17

The Bridge

" The packhorse bridge over the River Stam must have been a fine sight in Victorian Blackston. The proud structure crossed from the mill side to the houses on the west bank, allowing access from the centre of the village to the coastal path without having to navigate the variable conditions of the ford crossing,

The original stone structure of the bridge was destroyed by flooding in 1919, and, spurred on by the growing popularity of motorcars and a need for a more consistent route across the river, a new bridge was constructed. The new design was engineered to fit the village aesthetic while being able to accommodate the heavy vehicles which were now relied upon to transport grain and other goods across the river, paving the way for Blackston's flourishing economy, and ultimately a more united village."

- F.W. Merryfield, *A Brief History of Blackston Bay*

18

The Craft Club

By the time Rae Logan got to Jan's cafe that Tuesday evening, the good ladies of the craft club had already fallen completely in love with Kieran Quinn.

He and Penny were busying themselves organising the supplies that Kieran had brought, while the others sat in varying degrees of enthralled, watching them.

All except Jan, who was cleaning down tables. She looked up as Rae closed the door behind her. 'Evening, lovely. You didn't come up with Nush today?'

Rae shook her head, shrugging out of her coat. 'I had a bit of work to finish.'

'You're working now?' Jan stopped wiping down the table top. 'That's great news, pet.'

'I'm just doing a bit of freelancing for a web content company.' Rae added her coat to the rack which Jan had moved out into the cafe. 'Blogs, and stuff. You know what I mean.'

Jan laughed, her eyes crinkling to nothing. 'I really don't know what you mean. At all. But it sounds lovely.'

At that, Rae laughed too, but it was a small sound compared to the noise inside her - the roar of celebration. She had never quite felt that she belonged anywhere, and she definitely hadn't fit into the bustle of the city, but here in Blackston she was beginning to find her feet.

She looked over at Kieran, who was now helping Nush to pick some paint colours, and he winked back at her. He was chatting to Nush like they were dear old friends, talking through the selection of blues very seriously.

On another table, Penny was demonstrating a simpler method. She sprayed shaving foam into a baking tray, dropped in small blobs of food colouring and used a toothpick to swirl and form them into shapes, the colours mixing and combining into stunning patterns in the soft peaks of the foam. She then pressed a sheet of paper into the foam, picking up the colours and setting it aside to sink in. After a few minutes, she carefully scraped the foam off to leave a riot of colour exploding every which way. The ladies clapped in delight.

'It's like alchemy!' Edie Dunham exclaimed, clasping her hand together in delight. 'Just magical.'

Rae watched the ladies take turns, marvelling one by one in the simple joy in their faces as their papers were revealed.

'Come on, petal.' Kieran's deep voice shook her from her thoughts. 'Let's get you marbling.'

They chatted easily as Rae pondered her options, thumbing the tubes of colour, grouping them together in her hands to see the swatches next to each other.

She settled on a deep cobalt, cerulean and a warm gold ochre, the colours of twilight, and let Kieran guide her as she dropped the pigment into the carrageenan bath and began to swirl it with a thin rod. He hummed in appreciation as the colours mixed and pooled, spreading out before their eyes.

'That's beautiful, mate,' he said gently, so as not to startle her. 'Like the evening sky.'

'That's exactly what I was going for,' she gushed, proud of herself.

He showed her how to carefully dip in her pre-prepared paper, letting the sheet pick up the colours, replicating the pattern she'd created perfectly.

She let out a little squeal. 'You're a magician!'

He threw his head back, his laugh raucous, contagious. Totally out of proportion to the humour of the situation, which Rae loved.

'Actually...' He lowered his voice to a stage whisper. 'I prefer wizard.'

He carried on, speaking casually, as if he were talking about nothing in particular. 'On an unrelated matter, did you forget, when you told me the story about Jamie the other day...'

Rae tensed at the mention of his name.

Kieran continued. '...to mention the small matter of you *being in love with him forever*.' He half closed one eye at her in mock accusation.

She laughed, too quickly. Defensive. 'That's not even true. Who've you been talking to?' She looked around at the others. Nush, prime suspect, was totally engrossed in swirling a shock of colour into a tray of shaving foam. 'We were just friends.'

He raised one eyebrow, unbelieving.

'It was nothing.'

He raised the other eyebrow. 'You won't tell your old pal Kieran the truth?'

'This is literally only the second time we've met.' She rolled her eyes jokingly. 'I mean, what even is love? Who are any of us?' The corner of her mouth tipped in a smile. 'Why are we here?'

He didn't miss a beat. 'I feel like you're being an arsehole about this, babycakes.'

She chuckled, punching him lightly in the shoulder. 'You stick to making pretty pictures, mate. I get enough of the psychoanalysis from Nush.'

Kieran nodded, eyes still narrowed. 'Ok, fine. But don't think for a second this is the last we're going to speak of this.'

He was quite right. It wasn't.

After the last sheet was laid out to dry, they pulled chairs around one of the empty tables and Jan set about making everyone a warm drink. It was dark outside, the wind howling and screaming past the buildings, but it only made the light and warmth of the cafe feel cosier.

'It was lovely to meet you, ladies,' Kieran beamed at them, and Rae felt the warmth of every person in the room smiling back at him with genuine affection.

'You're a lovely young man,' Iris Atkins said, taking a delicate sip of her tea. 'Rachel, he's lovely, isn't he? Maybe *he* could take you out?' She raised one sparse eyebrow, suggestively.

Rae laughed. 'I don't think I'm his type.'

'You're what, dear?' Now in her eighty-second year, Iris was getting progressively more deaf with every one that passed. She reached behind her ear, fiddling with a dial on her hearing aid.

'He likes boys, Iris,' Rae said loudly, making young Flora blush shyly and hide behind her hair.

'Well, don't we all,' Iris chuckled, bumping shoulders lightly with Edie Dunham, who leaned into her in reply, and they giggled together like much younger women.

Edie coughed away her laughter. 'I always thought you'd end up with the Stamford boy.' She lowered her voice, almost to a whisper. 'The good one.' Her smile turned mischievous. 'He's good looking now.'

Rae shook her head in disbelief. 'You as well, Edie?' She smiled, but with an edge of exasperation. 'You'd think there wasn't a single other thing happening in the whole village.'

Iris was having none of it. 'Well, you'd do well to listen, young lady. Even old fools like us could see he was in love with you.'

'Don't give us any of that crap about being friends, either,' Edie chimed in. 'We're old, not blind. I know what *friends* looks like. I've had friends my entire life. And none of them have ever looked at me like that.'

Rae opened her mouth to argue, but the sound didn't reach her mouth. Memories flitted in and out of her mind's eye. She tried to remember even a single time where Jamie had looked at her with indifference in his eyes and came up short. Whether they'd been laughing together or fighting, every last memory was alive with the spark which had always hung between them.

With nothing to say in response, Rae looked up to see Kieran watching her from across the room, chin propped on a loosely clasped fist. And as their eyes met, his mouth slowly quirked into a smile which was thoroughly, unbearably smug.

It was after nine when Rae and Nush left Jan's. They stepped out into the howl of the winter night and Rae braced herself against it, fisting her hands into the deepest, warmest part of her pockets and shrugging her shoulders up to close the gaps where the icy wind nipped at her neck.

It was a short walk from the cafe to the mill, a few hundred yards or so, and neither woman spoke as they marched, heads down, toward the bridge.

Neither of them noticed the shadowy figure lurking over the other side of the river until he stepped out into their path, making both women shriek, instinctively reaching for each other.

The man's familiar eyes widened in the dark, suddenly embarrassed. 'Oh shit, I'm so sorry. It's me. It's just me.'

Rae would have known the gruff of that voice anywhere.

The idiot.

'Jesus Christ, Jamie!' She swiped at him with a gloved hand. 'You scared the life out of me!'

Nush's relief spilled out of her in giggle, and she clung to Rae's arm, squeezing it tight.

Jamie's head dropped a little. 'Sorry. I didn't mean to jump out on you like that. I just saw you coming out of Jan's.' He pointed vaguely in the direction they'd just come from. 'I was walking back home and I...' The rambling was unlike him and it put her on edge. 'Listen, can we talk?'

'What, now?'

'Ideally.' He shoved his hands in his jeans pockets and swung back on his heels, the action making him look younger - just like the awkward teenager she remembered. Her heart leapt, but was then tempered by suspicion, and the slightest scent of scotch in the night air.

'Are you drunk?' She wasn't angry, but the adrenaline still rushing through her bloodstream cut her words off short.

His face was indignant. 'No!'

She raised an eyebrow.

'Ok, a little.' He ran a hand through his hair, tugging at the strands. 'But only enough to be able to say what I need to.'

She crossed her arms in front of her. A habit. Shielding against the sting of whatever harsh words he might throw her way. 'So say it.'

He shook his head. 'Not here. Come to the cottage with me.'

She laughed at that, a short sharp breath of incredulity. 'Seriously?'

'I just want to talk.' She noticed his eyes flick to Nush, who she had completely forgotten was there. 'I'll walk you home after, I promise.'

She took a deep breath. 'Fine.'

She turned to Nush, who was looking at her with the slightest trace of a smile on her lips, and something much bigger swimming in her eyes.

Nush kissed her lightly on the cheek. 'Go. I'll see you when you get in.' She patted her gloved hand on Rae's cheek. An instruction.

Rae nodded, and turned to watch as Nush walked the final few steps to the mill, before nodding again at Jamie, falling into step beside him as they walked the few hundred yards in the other direction, along the ridge of the hill to his cottage.

Neither spoke as they walked, Rae's mind alive with a million thoughts about what it was that he had to say, what was so important that he had to jump her in the middle of the night.

It only took a couple of minutes before they were at the cottage door.

Jamie unlocked it, letting Rae in ahead of him, out of the cold of the night, and then he pulled it shut behind him.

Rae had spent a lot of time in the cottage in her younger years, and she wasted no time reacquainting herself with it. Jamie put the fire on in the main room and she gravitated towards it, welcoming the light burn of the heat on her legs as she edged closer.

The room had barely changed since she had last been there. Don Stamford, Jamie's grandfather, was not a man who believed in mod cons, and she remembered the cottage had looked dated even fifteen years ago. The passage of time had not helped any.

There were new things too, though, among the memories, quiet hints here and there of a Jamie she had to keep reminding herself she didn't know anymore. A small flat-screen TV on Don's old sideboard. A phone charger. Car keys.

The smell was different, too. Don's house had always smelled *old,* like biscuit tins and pipe tobacco, but the cottage smelled like Jamie now, like washing powder and cut grass and his aftershave and she breathed it in deeply.

She didn't turn to look at him as she spoke, absentmindedly running a finger along Don's brass carriage clock. 'What was it you wanted to say?'

'I wanted to talk about New Year.' His voice was low, serious, with an edge to it that made hot fury rise in her body.

She huffed. 'Now you want to talk? Are you serious?' She turned to face him, eyes narrowed. 'You know when would have been a good time to talk about this? New Year's Day. That would have been a good time.'

He at least had the good grace to look sheepish. 'You're mad.'

'Yeah, I'm a little mad.' She laughed humourlessly. 'You think I shouldn't be?'

'Because I was with Nina?'

'Because you ran away!' She took a step towards him, anger breaking down her boundaries, and she said the next thing on her mind without really thinking about it. 'I waited twenty years for you to kiss me like that and you ruined it!'

He had opened his mouth to reply, fire burning behind his eyes, but her words stopped him in his tracks. He stared at her, brows drawn together, mouth parted, as her heart thumped a crazed rhythm in her chest.

When he spoke, it was slowly, his voice thick. 'You... what?' He didn't take his eyes off her. 'You wanted to kiss me?'

She looked away, the whisper of a smile tugging at the corners of her mouth. 'Apparently I didn't fully realise it until quite recently, but yes.' She looked back up. He hadn't moved even an inch and she could feel the heat of his gaze, moving from her eyes to her lips.

Her heart swelled for a moment before she remembered that this man, this beautiful man who was standing in front of her saying things she'd wanted to hear him say forever, was not hers to take.

'Anyway, then you ran away and now you're going on fancy Valentine's Day dates with the world's most beautiful woman, so that's that, isn't it?' Her voice caught in her throat towards the end and she looked away, blinking away the sharp threat of tears which burned behind her eyes.

He was silent for a moment before she heard him take a step forward.

'I called it off.' He spoke quietly, barely audible over the rush of blood to her ears.

'The date?' She didn't look up.

He paused, clearing his throat. 'The everything.'

She looked at him then, ablaze with an anger that she couldn't be sure wasn't masking another feeling. 'What the hell? Why?' She thought about the perfect specimen of woman she'd seen him with that night. 'Have you got eyes?'

'Because of you!' His mouth twisted in confusion, his voice rising. 'Why are you angry with me about this?'

Her voice rose too. 'What do you mean because of me?

'Because I've been in love with you for half my life, obviously,' he blurted, defensive now.

The admission hit like a fire arrow in her chest, flame catching and spreading until the whole of her was alight. 'What?'

His chin tipped up. 'You heard.' He took another step, within reaching distance now. 'And I was ok with it. I was dealing with it. Until that night.' He shook his head, smiling slighting. 'God, kissing you, I could have stayed there forever.'

'But you didn't.' She'd meant it as an accusation, but all the air had been sucked out of her lungs and so when she spoke it was breathy and quiet. She saw his eyes darken, pupils dilating.

'No. I didn't. I heard everyone cheering and I imagined Nina sitting by herself wondering where I was while everyone else was kissing and celebrating, and I suddenly felt like the biggest dick alive.' He shrugged. 'I had to go.'

He took another step, so close now that she could smell the faint sweetness of whiskey on his breath. 'But obviously, by that point, all the blood had left my head for my, y'know... ...*other* head, and my decision-making skills kind of went out of the window.'

Rae's mind jumped back to the feeling of him pushing against her that night and her body flushed with warmth at the memory of how much he'd wanted her.

'Ever since then I haven't been able to get a single second of that kiss out of my head. Even when I *was* going on fancy dates with the world's most beautiful woman.' He smiled then, open and warm. 'Thanks for ruining me for all other women, by the way.'

Her pulse jumped, his smile doing things to her insides, but her voice stayed steady, teasing. 'You call this an apology?'

He raised an eyebrow, smirking. 'You need to hear the words?'

She nodded, all at once giddy and breathless. She needed to hear him say it. To spell it out. She didn't want to leave even an inch of room for interpretation.

He straightened, steeling himself. 'I'm sorry.' His voice was thick, rough with emotion and the sound hit her somewhere deep inside her body. 'I'm sorry I ran away.' His head tilted to the side, suddenly serious. 'I'm sorry if I made you feel even for a second like it was because of something you'd done. And God...' He paused a beat, eyes half closed with regret. '...I'm so fucking sorry I'd never kissed you until that night.'

He looked away, blowing a steady breath out and she heard the shake in his body as he did it. She was suddenly overwhelmed by his fragility, by the rawness etched clearly on his face, and it broke her heart and made it whole all at once.

'Jamie?'

He looked up, eyes narrowed a little, as if they were hiding a million thoughts. 'Yeah?'

'You get to me.' She didn't look away now. She could look at nothing but him. Her hands went to her scarf and she began to unwind it, slowly, before pulling it all the way off and laying it over the arm of the sofa. Her fingers found her coat buttons and began unbuttoning, not breaking eye contact.

'Yeah?'

'Yeah.' She nodded for emphasis, biting down on her lip. She shrugged out of her coat and laid that down, too.

He made a small sound somewhere deep in his throat. 'You get to me, too.'

And in a single stride he'd closed the gap between them, gathering her up in his arms and pulling her in close, before finally, deliciously, bringing his mouth to hers.

He kissed her slowly, at first, writing in promises and apologies and all the things in between, while one hand settled on her waist and the other fisted in her hair. It was so different from the last time, but so familiar too, with the faintest taste of whiskey and the soft tickle of his scruff on her face. And the way his mouth moved with hers, slowly, softly at first, and then deeper, as the need grew in both of them and rippled outwards in all directions like small waves in a pond.

And then she was moving, pressing into him, feeling his heartbeat hammering through his clothes, her hands finding the soft hair at the nape of his neck. She felt her barriers weaken, crumbling to dust all around her as the man she had loved from afar for so long made her his. And there was not a single thing she wanted to do about it.

'Jamie?' she half-whispered against his lips.

'Yeah?' His voice was gruff, a rumble against her chest where it touched his.

'What is this?' His mouth had moved back down her neck, kissing over her collarbone, and her eyes closed in response. 'What are we doing?'

His words came out as a grumble between kisses. 'I don't

know.'

'You don't have a plan?' She sighed as his lips found a certain spot at the base of her neck, sending a riot of shivers through her body.

'Oh, I had a plan.' He pulled back slightly, looking her straight in the eye. 'I planned to apologise and then I planned to kiss you again. That worked out pretty well. I didn't really have a plan beyond that.' He trailed a finger gently down her cheek, his eyes alight. 'Honestly I was half convinced you were going to tell me to fuck right off.'

She laughed, the sound bubbling out of her as she grinned at him cheekily. 'Honestly, I considered it.'

He laughed too, then, and pulled her back into him, their kiss light and soft this time, as something unspoken passed between them.

'Come on, you know what Nush is like, she'll have half the village talking.' He grinned. 'Word on the street will be either that I've kidnapped you or married you by the time we get up tomorrow.' He moved to grab her coat and scarf from where she'd draped them over the arm of his sofa. 'Let's take you home.'

And a thought had settled in her head before she really had any time to think about it.

I am home.

19

Neighbourhood Watch

Rae Logan floated through much of the next day in a daze, somewhere between the replay of the previous night playing over and over in her head, and the bones of the new plot-line which had slowly begun weaving its way into her skull.

She had written and deleted three chapters before lunchtime, and with Nush at school and the cupboards bare, she was torn between a trip to town to do the shopping and finding someone who would make food for her. Through laziness, or perhaps because it was her birthday, she chose the latter.

Jan's cafe was half empty when she arrived, and she plopped down onto her favourite table, got her laptop out and thumbed through the paper specials menu propped between the salt and pepper shakers. Jan loved a rummage around all the good farmers' markets in the area, and when she had specials on they were usually worth a punt.

Jan finished with the customer she'd been serving and pulled up a chair next to Rae as she read. 'Lovely girl, nice to see you again so soon!' She smiled at Rae with genuine affection. 'You writing?'

'Trying to,' Rae replied, returning her smile. 'I was getting nowhere looking at the same four walls at the mill. Thought I'd try a change of scenery.' She nodded towards the specials menu. 'What's good today?'

'They're all good, of course!' Jan laughed, her eyes vanishing into the soft creases of her face. 'If it were me, though, I'd give the winter veg hot pot a try. It's real writing food.' She pointed it out on the menu, a habit. 'I'll even make you extra dumplings.'

Rae nodded. 'Sounds good to me. Thanks, Jan.'

'And the usual to drink?' Jan asked, standing and smoothing her apron back down into place.

'Perfect.'

'Coming right up. And it's on the house.' Jan smiled broadly. 'Happy birthday, lovely.'

And she was off, swishing through the bead curtain before Rae even had the time to thank her.

Rae smiled after her, opening her laptop and pulling out her notepad and the pen Nush got her for Christmas, the barrel soon warming in her hand as she scribbled out notes as fast as they tumbled into her head. It wasn't long before she had the bare bones of a story sketched out in front of her, and as she absentmindedly doodled flower shapes in the margins, her phone buzzed with a message.

She knew who it was before she picked the phone up. She smiled to herself as she remembered the walk home, their last kiss, pressed against the stone wall of the mill, just out of sight of Nush's watching window. He'd handed over his phone, asked her to put her number in, given her his. He'd be away until the weekend, he'd said. Just going out of town for work. Some conference in London. Worst timing ever, he'd said, and he'd kissed her again and vanished off into the night.

She'd barely said goodnight to Nush when the message had popped up on her screen.

JAMIE: Goodnight beautiful xx

And she'd smiled to herself like an idiot as she read the message over and over, two simple words which had made her heart flutter like a swarm of butterflies in her chest.

She picked up her phone to read today's message.

JAMIE: I think we should go on a date.

Her face crumpled in a confused smile and she smiled wider as she wrote back.

RACHEL: Isn't it a bit late for that? Pretty sure we got to first base last night.

JAMIE: I'm hoping to get to at least second base after I take you out properly.

RACHEL: Confident, eh?

JAMIE: In a respectful way.

RACHEL: Of course.

JAMIE: Leave Saturday free. I've got something in mind.

RACHEL: Works for me. Do I need to bring anything?

JAMIE: Handcuffs, and your passport.

RACHEL: WHAT?

She'd laughed out loud before she could stop herself, hunching back over her notepad in embarrassment.

'Well, someone's having a whale of a time,' the deep, familiar voice said from behind her, and she read Jamie's reply quickly, before she turned around.

JAMIE: Kidding, obviously. Just bring you xx

Kieran stood behind her, sharply dressed in a wool peacoat and a scarf the colour of spring leaves which made his auburn hair pop.

'It's chartreuse,' he said, noticing her eyes on it, and she laughed at the endearing charm of his pomposity.

'It's fabulous,' she said, with a smile.

'And this,' he began, grandly, gesturing to the tall, slender man beside him. '...is my lovely fiancé. Ezra... Rachel. Rachel... Ezra. You can call her Rae.' He gestured between them. 'Rae, you can call him Ezra. Or The Future Mr Quinn. Or Sugarpuff.'

Ezra rolled his eyes jokingly. 'Ezra is fine.' His English was perfect, his voice laced only with the slightest hint of his mother tongue. 'It's really nice to meet you.'

He offered his hand and Rae shook it, smiling up at him. He was taller than Kieran, easily six two or three, and slight, with a wave of dark blond hair flopping forward onto his face, half hiding his eyes, which were the clearest shade of green Rae had ever seen. They made a stunning couple.

'What are you doing in Blackston on a Wednesday?' Rae turned back to Kieran, who was now starting to unbutton his coat. 'Isn't the shop open today?' She gestured to the table, gathering her notebook and pen together and sliding them into her bag. 'Come, sit with me.'

'Got my assistant covering it.' Kieran stroked his chin smugly. 'I was telling Ezra about the magic of Blackston and I mentioned Jan's hot chocolates. He absolutely had to try one.'

Rae's eyes twinkled. 'You have an assistant? Get you! Business must be booming.'

'I do ok, yeah.' He grinned modestly. 'I have to make it up a bit with the courses I teach. Do the occasional hen party and what have you, you know.'

A little chuckle shot out of Rae, her eyes wide. 'Hen party? You strip?'

'I'd pay for that,' Ezra quipped.

Jan appeared from behind the counter and set Rae's drink down on the table. 'Wouldn't we all!'

Kieran threw his head back in the theatrical laugh which Rae was quickly learning was just exactly *him*. 'No petal, I do a craft workshop with them. It's for the classy ones, you know. No dick straws or anything.' He stage-whispered the last bit.

Ezra laughed lightly, the slightest hint of crow's feet lining his eyes. 'I'm not paying if there are no dick straws.'

They all laughed, especially Jan, who reached behind her onto an empty table to swipe a cutlery set wrapped in a forest green napkin, putting it in front of Rae.

Kieran continued, his fingers combing his auburn hair back off his face as he spoke. 'Minimal dick in general, actually. Just mine.'

'On balance, I'm still in.' Ezra winked at him, and Rae's nose crinkled at the corners as she smiled at them.

'God, look at the two of you.' She took a small sip of her hot chocolate, today topped with fudge pieces and salted caramel cream. 'It's kind of a shame you'll need someone else's genetic material to make a baby, your kids would be ridiculously beautiful.'

'Maybe it'd be too much, though.' There was a chuckle in Jan's voice as she spoke. 'Like the sun. You'd need to use special glasses to look directly at them.' There was a beeping in the kitchen and she hurried off, swishing through the bead curtain which separated the kitchen from the cafe.

165

'She's right, you know.' Rae looked between them, her mouth twitching into a smirk. 'I'm happy to donate you my eggs if you want to, y'know, dumb it down a bit.'

Kieran chortled. 'You keep hold of those eggs for now, sweet pea. You might be needing them yourself.'

She smiled, in what she hoped was a lighthearted kind of way.

'Woah, that was a look!' He eyed her with suspicion. 'Who's been having a go at your eggs, babes?'

'Oh leave her, K,' Ezra chastised him, a dance of light in his eyes. 'A lady's eggs are her own business. How would you like it if we were all sitting around discussing your sperm?' He pointed a long, slender finger at Kieran before throwing his hands up. 'Actually, you don't need to answer that. I've known you long enough to know you'll happily talk about your swimmers with anyone who'll listen.'

'Sharing is caring,' Kieran sing-songed, a deep chuckle bubbling out of him. 'And I'm a sharing kind of guy.'

Ezra looked at Rae and rolled his eyes dramatically, but when he turned back to Kieran they shone with nothing but love. They shared a smile before Ezra turned back to Rae, his manners impeccable.

'So anyway, tell me more about you, Rae.' His dirty blond hair fell forward into his eyes as he spoke and he nodded his head to the side to flick it away in a practiced gesture. 'K tells me you're writing a book?'

'Trying to.' Rae smiled, nodding to the laptop in her bag.

'What's it about?'

'God, what is it about?' Rae always struggled to explain what her plots were about, and she didn't really consider that it could be because they weren't really about anything. 'Love, loss, betrayal, death. Set against the backdrop of the miner's strikes in the eighties.'

Ezra's eyes widened, and he nodded encouragingly. 'Sounds...' He paused for a beat, thinking. '...gutsy.'

Rae's nose wrinkled. 'Gutsy bad?'

'Gutsy *gutsy*,' Ezra continued, his smile warm and genuine. 'I like it.' He gestured to her, palms up. 'I mean, obviously I have literally only just met you, but I think you can pull it off.'

Rae returned his smile. 'Thanks, mate.' She was less sure that she could. 'So, what do you do, Ezra?'

'He's a photographer,' Kieran gushed, his eyes lighting up with pride.

Ezra laughed, sneaking a quick look at him. 'It's generally not as exciting as it sounds. I take portraits when I'm working on my own stuff, but that doesn't pay the bills.' His smile was a little lopsided, quirking up more on the side his hair was the floppiest. 'Most of my time is spent freelancing for small companies. Product shots, marketing stuff, you know?'

She knew all too well. 'Same story here.'

'I am working on an interesting project at the moment though,' he continued, one hand moving to scratch the light stubble on his chin as he spoke. 'It's for a local historian who's writing a book about Blackston through the ages. He wants me to take photos of the village as it is now, so he can compare and contrast with the photos he already has from other eras.'

'Is it old Frank?' Rae asked, with a barely-concealed smirk. Frank Merryfield's magnum opus was well known in the village. Ironically titled 'A Brief History of Blackston Bay', word was that it was now over four hundred pages long and still barely nearing completion.

Ezra smiled brightly. 'It is! You know Frank?'

She nodded. 'He's a bit of a local legend.'

'He's a lovely man. Just so...' He paused, searching for the words. '...kind.' The *kind* was hesitant, almost a question.

Kieran huffed loudly, throwing up his hands theatrically. 'He's the most boring man I've ever met!' He turned to Rae. 'Ez left me with him once while he popped out to buy a new memory card and I am not exaggerating when I say that he talked to me about the many breeds of bird noted in the Blackston area for a full forty-five minutes. FORTY-FIVE MINUTES.' His voice slowed at the last part, enunciating every syllable. 'I honestly didn't know that many different types of bird existed in the world.'

Rae laughed. She had been the victim of one of those stories more times than she could count. Frank Merryfield's heart knew no bounds; he would do anything for anyone, but he was, unfortunately, as dull as dishwater. Duller, perhaps. Even Nush, who found merit in the company of most people, could not bear to be left alone with him.

Ezra clucked his tongue in disapproval. 'Well there are worse things a person can be than boring. He's been good to me.'

Rae smiled gently at him. 'To me, too.' She leaned in, lowering her voice conspiratorially. 'I definitely don't want to read that book though.'

'God, me neither,' Ezra said, with a chuckle. 'Maybe just look at the pictures?'

And they laughed together until Rae felt, as she had with Kieran, as if she had known Ezra forever.

She made him promise to take her author portrait if she ever got published. He made her promise she'd help him write all the blurb for his website when he got it up and running, and by the time they parted they were all hooting together like old friends.

Nush was sitting at the kitchen table with a mug of tea when Rae got back to the mill that afternoon, and the whole house smelled warm, like honey and spices.

She looked up with a smile as Rae walked in. 'Happy birthday, *Słoneczko!* I made walnut cake.' She nodded to the counter behind her. 'It's just come out.'

'Thank you,' she said, smiling back. 'It smells amazing!' It was Rae's favourite.

Nush nodded. She knew that, of course. 'And when it cools down, you'll sit with your old ciocia and have a slice.'

'Sounds good,' Rae set her laptop down on the table, pulling up a chair beside her aunt.

'And you can tell me what happened last night that has put that spring in your step.' Nush's eyes twinkled, excitement burning behind them.

Rae stood to make herself a drink, noticing that Nush had left a mug out for her with a tea bag in. She flicked the kettle back on. 'What makes you so sure something happened?'

Nush made an exasperated sound. 'Oh, come on, please.' She adjusted her glasses on her nose. 'Because I know you. And obviously because I was *there* when you went with him, and when you came back you were not the same Rachel.' She sipped her tea, one eyebrow raised. Waiting.

Rae couldn't resist teasing her just a little more. 'Sounds ominous.'

'In a good way, Żabko!' Nush huffed. 'You left me all surly and dark, and you have returned to me as a beautiful ray of sunshine.'

Rae chuckled, hand going to her chest in mock hurt. 'Aw, Nush. Are you saying I wasn't always a beautiful ray of sunshine?'

Nush raised one warning eyebrow. 'Don't change the subject.'

'Ok, fine.' The kettle boiled and clicked off, and Rae poured the steaming water into her mug. 'We talked. He isn't seeing that otherworldly beauty any more. He apologised for *the incident.*' She shrugged, as if it were nothing, but for the slight speed in her pulse. 'And we might have kissed.'

Nush threw up her hands in delight. 'Oh *Gołąbeczko!* I have never been so proud!'

'Really, never?' Rae laughed lightly. 'Not when I walked for the first time? Not when I *graduated*?'

Nush took a long sip of her tea, eyeing Rae the whole time. 'You are impossible. Ok, I have occasionally been prouder.' She stood, retrieving the knife she'd left on the counter. 'But he lights you up and it's a wonderful thing to see.' She tapped the top of the cake lightly with one finger before beginning to slice. 'You know, really the only thing I want for you in your life is that you are happy.'

'I am.' No teasing. 'I'm happy here.'

And it was true.

Nush beamed. 'I know. Let's drink to that.'

Rae finished brewing her tea and the two women sat beside each other in a comfortable silence, enjoying Nush's signature walnut cake.

When Nush spoke again, it was in her slight Polish lilt, and Rae knew what was coming.

'Myszko, I have been keeping an eye on the end terrace over the road and I'm a bit worried.'

Rae snorted. 'Keeping an eye on it?' Her fingers mimed the inverted commas. 'You mean you've been spying?

'Pssshhh, I have only been watching.' Nush sipped her tea, her eyes staring into the far distance thoughtfully. 'We're a community, you know, and a community sticks together. What do you think Neighbourhood Watch is for?'

Rae couldn't hold in her smirk. 'Definitely not for this.'

Nush gave her a withering look. 'Would you like me to tell my story or not?'

'Yes, sorry,' Rae laughed. 'Go on.'

'So, there is a young woman who is living there.' Nush's gaze rested on the little house she was talking about. 'She's about your age, has two young boys. Beautiful blond-haired things.'

Rae held in her smile, knowing from experience that *about your age* could mean anything from young adulthood to retirement.

Nush continued. 'Anyway, I've noticed that she often has visitors. Male visitors, usually.' She stretched out *male* for effect, labouring on the first half.

'Right.'

'I've counted them.' Nush finished the last of her tea, putting the cup on the table, and pinched the last crumbs of her cake between forefinger and thumb, popping them into her mouth delicately.

'Of course you have.'

'And there are seven different men who come to the house. All at different times.' She looked up then, straight at Rae. Making her case. 'They stay for an hour each, except for the younger-looking one who stays two hours, always at the same time.' She ended on a flourish, as if waiting for applause

Rae was confused, 'And you think....'

'...She is selling herself, of course!' The way Nush said it was almost a punchline. 'One time I even saw one of them giving her money at the door!'

'Damning evidence.' Rae was laughing now. 'I bet you had your binoculars out and everything, didn't you?'

Nush pushed her glasses back up her nose. 'You are laughing but I *would* like some binoculars. My eyes are not what they were.'

'You seem to do ok with them.'

'I see what I need to see.' Nush smiled a little, the lines around her eyes beginning to crease and fold. 'I would see more with binoculars.'

'And God help the good people of Blackston then!' Rae laughed to herself, and she looked down as her phone buzzed with another text.

JAMIE: Green or blue?

Her heart skipped a little at the sight of his name, at the ease with which he was communicating now. She smiled to herself, feeling the weight of Nush's gaze following her, but not caring even a little bit. She was beginning to see flashes of the old Jamie appearing, rediscovering that carefree boy she had wanted so badly to notice her, and she didn't care if Nush knew it. She wanted Nush to know it. She damn near wanted to shout it from the rooftops.

RACHEL: Depends what.
JAMIE: Don't think too hard, just answer.
RACHEL: Green.
JAMIE: Green it is.
RACHEL: What is.
JAMIE: Your surprise.

JAMIE: I mean, don't worry about it. Forget I said anything.
RACHEL: Tease.
JAMIE: You have no idea.
JAMIE: Oh, and one more thing.
RACHEL: Yes?
JAMIE: Happy birthday, Rachel xx

She looked up then, as Nush pretended to be staring off into the middle distance, hiding the huge smile on her face as best she could, about as subtle as a house brick or ten through a window.

Rae's mouth twisted into a small smile.

'Don't read my texts.' She couldn't even pretend to be mad.

Nush's smile was soft, her whole face alight with happiness and with pride.

'Wouldn't dream of it, Żabciu.'

Rae's chest swelled a little then, a mixture of residual heat from the implication of Jamie's messages and the warm contentment of this place, this curious, beautiful place that she was beginning to call home.

When she'd said she was happy earlier, she couldn't have meant it more. It was a far cry from the sharp lines of the city where she'd felt so constricted, so suffocated by every last aspect of her daily routine. So numb to the motions that she was going through. And so quietened, so completely diminished by pretending that her heart was ever free to give away to Simon Collins.

The nip of Blackston's sea air was unravelling the tight knot of her old life like a long-held breath released and, between them, Nush and the craft club and Jamie Stamford were starting to put her back together.

20

THEN – March 1978

It was the sixteenth month in a row which Zosia, now officially Mrs Zofia Logan, had prayed for a baby.

It was also the fourth month in a row that Zosia, now desperately tracking the days of her cycle on her calendar, had prayed for a miracle.

That morning, like so many others, it seemed her prayers had gone unanswered. She had almost convinced herself, as she did every month, that she felt different this time. Was that a strange heaviness in her pelvis? The flutter of sensitivity beginning in her breasts? The slightest feeling of sickness beginning to churn deep in her belly?

By the time she noticed she was bleeding, she'd all but sworn she was pregnant this time. But, like all the months that came before, she suddenly, demonstrably, wasn't. She wiped the tears from her cheeks with the backs of her hands, sniffing ungracefully as she sat on the toilet and it wasn't long before she was snorting out sobs into the stillness of the tiled bathroom.

But she was supposed to be meeting Nush in half an hour, and she needed to get herself together. So, she let herself cry for only as long as she needed to be sure she could swallow down the rest of her hurt and hide it away from the world.

By the time she breezed into the classroom of the small Catholic infant school where Nush taught, no one would have been able to tell there was anything bothering her at all.

No one except her sister, of course.

Nush looked up at her gently as she walked in, and it was all Zosia could do not to burst into tears on the spot. But Nush nodded once, understanding, and turned back to her class, smiling brightly.

'Children, this is Mrs Logan. She's come to help us decorate the eggs for Easter, and then we'll take them down to the church to be blessed.'

The children squealed and chattered in delight – even more so when Zosia pulled out the package she'd stashed in her bag. Pani Grażyna had dropped off the small parcel that morning, filled to bursting with brightly-coloured egg dyes and transfers from her cousin back in Kraków.

The sisters had decorated eggs together during Easter week for as long as either of them could remember, and when Zosia had suggested that Nush could do it as an activity with the children in her class, Nush had absolutely insisted that Zosia come in to help.

Zosia had agreed at the time, but her reluctance soon grew, first at the idea of spending time with a class full of children when she was seemingly unable to have any children of her own, and now again at the easy manner which her sister had with her pupils. Without warning, a knot of pain tightened in Zosia's gut.

175

She would make a much better mother than me, the voice in her head said, not for the first time, and she braced herself against the familiar ache which gnawed at her ribcage.

She took a deep breath and blew it out steadily, looking back up into an unfamiliar pair of eyes. An unfamiliar pair of warm blue eyes on a face, Zosia couldn't help but notice, which was very handsome indeed. She cleared her throat and smiled, tucking a few loose strands of her dyed red hair behind her ear.

'Can I help you?'

The man's smile made his whole face light up, and his eyes darted to Nush for a moment before he looked back at Zosia, holding a hand out with a big grin.

'You must be Zosia,' he said, his deep voice gravelly and thick. 'Nush talks about you all the time. I'm Graham. I teach the next class.'

Zosia was not nearly as attuned to the small clues in people's behavior as Nush was, but even she couldn't fail to notice the softness in his voice at her sister's name. He obviously felt something for her, and as Nush turned to look at the two of them, Zosia raised her eyebrows in a question. But Nush only smiled enigmatically, turning back to her class.

Zosia had long suspected that her sister was harbouring secret feelings for someone, but until now she had been at a total loss as to who it could be.

Was this the mystery man in Nush's life?

She broached the subject later on as the sisters walked with their basket of eggs down to the Polish church to have them blessed.

'Graham is nice,' Zosia started, in a manner she thought was very subtle indeed.

Nush didn't look at her, but her cheeks stained with a blush which reached part-way down her neck, and the start of an awkward smile tugged at the corners of her mouth. 'He is nice.'

Zosia ploughed on. 'I think he likes you.'

But Nush only shook her head. 'I don't know. There's something not quite…'

'Your standards are too high, Kochanie.' Zosia half-shrugged with a frown, cutting her sister off. 'You need to start lowering them or you will be alone forever.' She darted her eyes down, trying not to cry as a wave of sadness hit her out of nowhere. Her voice quietened almost to nothing as she said, 'And what will become of our family then?'

Nush stopped dead on the church path, turning to her sister and taking her hand gently. 'It will happen for you, *Siostrzyczka*, I know it.' Her smile was warm and gentle, and it soothed Zosia, just as it had when they were small. 'You will get your child.'

But as they stood together in the house of God, each clutching a basket of beautifully decorated eggs, Zosia wasn't so sure that was the truth.

21

Better Than Lemons

Time slowed almost to a standstill as the weekend approached and by Friday afternoon Rae Logan had just about given up on passing the time productively. Nush was working and so Rae was making the most of having the mill entirely to herself, having finished all her work for the week the previous day. By eleven twenty-six she'd finished all her housework jobs and baked a banana loaf, and she had the choice between working on her book idea or watching Columbo while eating ice cream out of the tub.

She made the obvious choice.

She was on her fourth episode when she heard a knock on the door, and she scuttled to answer it with her TV-watching blanket still draped around her shoulders. Not expecting anyone, she'd dressed in leggings and an oversized sweatshirt with her hair scraped back and not a scrap of makeup on and it didn't occur to her to care until she opened the door to find Jamie standing on the front step.

Her heart skidded to a full stop in her chest. 'Wait, you're here?'

'Apparently so.' He scanned her, taking in the details, landing back on her eyes with a smirk.

'I'm busy today,' her mouth blurted before her brain had the time to engage.

His smile grew. 'Yeah, you look busy.'

'Fine, I'm not even slightly busy.' She smiled back, suddenly self-conscious. 'But I'm not ready for our date.'

He laughed lightly. 'Good job this isn't our date.'

'You know what I mean.' She lowered her voice, even though there was no-one around to hear. 'I haven't shaved my legs.'

He stifled a smile. 'Steady on, lass. What kind of man do you take me for?'

'I dunno,' she said, with a teasing edge. 'The kind of man who drags women into pub courtyards to kiss them?'

'Touché.' His eyes roamed over her face for a few seconds, and when he looked back in her eyes, there was an expression in them that she couldn't place.

'Why are you looking at me like that?' She frowned. 'I look like shit, don't I.'

He shook his head. 'You look beautiful. In an... off duty kind of way.' His eyes danced with humour.

'Shut up.'

He laughed. 'I still would, if that helps any?

She felt the flush in her cheeks. 'Yeah, it helps a little.'

'Good.' His eyes held hers, pulling her in. He was all windswept curls and brooding stare, and she felt a rush of warmth through her body at the idea that he was here for her. His hand went to his face, smoothed over the light scruff of his beard. 'Anyway, what I was going to say, if you'd let me finish, was that I got back from London early and I didn't want to have to wait until tomorrow to see you.' He paused for a beat, his eyes growing deeper. 'So, put your bloody ice cream down and let me kiss you.'

She reached behind her to put the tub down, without breaking eye contact even for a moment. He reached for her, but she was faster, and she sighed as she lifted her face up to his. His lips were warm and wet, soft against the light scratch of his stubble, and she fell into them willingly, grasping for him.

The pad of his thumb skated along her jawline, setting off a cascade of shivers which rushed and sparked through her.

'Balls to waiting for tomorrow,' she whispered into him. 'Let's go out tonight.'

He kissed her again before he said, 'I'm busy tonight.'

'Sod off, you're not.' She broke away, looked up at him from under her furrowed brow.

'I am!' He nodded, his thumb lightly stroking the side of her neck. 'I'm seeing Joe.'

Her eyes closed slightly. God, she didn't ever want him to stop touching her 'Sack him off.'

'No way, it's prearranged.' He kissed her lightly, little more than his lips grazing hers. A goodbye. 'Anyway, you know what they say, bros before...'

'Don't you dare,' she cut him off.

And with a cheeky kiss and a wink he was gone.

She felt the chill of his absence immediately, and she pulled her TV-watching blanket around herself, retreating back into the warmth of the mill. She put the ice cream away and was almost all the way back to the sofa before her phone beeped.

JAMIE: And sort those legs out.

'Cheeky shit,' she laughed to herself, although she felt a

flicker of something awaken in her as she imagined the feel of his hands on her bare skin. All the time she'd watched those hands, imagining them touching her. Her pulse roared in her ears. *Bloody Joe.*

She heard movement behind the door again and her heart leapt, before abruptly crashing back down as a leaflet appeared through the letterbox. It floated to the floor like a feather before she grabbed it, her face cracking a smile as a realisation dawned upon her.

Nush didn't get back from school until after five, and by then Rae had done all the dishes and was just finishing dinner when she heard the click of the lock. She followed the sounds of Nush's routine - shoes together by the door, coat hung, scarf hung, keys in the bowl - and when Nush walked into the kitchen, Rae was waiting for her.

'The end terrace over the road.' Rae phrased it almost as a question, but it wasn't one.

Nush smiled, though her eyes narrowed in confusion. 'Yes?'

'The woman about my age,' Rae continued, a dramatic pause to her voice. 'With the beautiful boys? You know, the one you're painting as a call girl?'

Nush nodded.

Rae help up the small, colourful leaflet between her first two fingers. 'She's a piano teacher.'

Nush stepped towards her at that, took the leaflet and read the whole thing carefully. When she finished, she handed the leaflet back to Rae and after a beat she exploded into giggles.

'Melody McGuire,' Rae said with a smile. 'Isn't that the most perfect name for a music teacher that you ever heard?'

Nush wiped her eyes and blew a long breath out. 'Oh Kotku,

that's amazing.' She wiped a stray tear from one eye, adjusting her glasses afterwards. 'I'm not always right about everything, you see.'

And the two women sat together, eating the pasta and homemade garlic bread which Rae had made, laughing about Nush's stories until they were both quite exhausted.

The following day dawned bright and brisk, and Rae was following the directions Jamie had sent her the previous night. She followed the limestone path down to the beach, but instead of heading right towards Black Rock, she took a left, walking the path along the low cliff top towards the breakwater at the far end of the village.

Spring was beginning to just edge its way into the landscape, with crocuses and daffodils blooming along the edge of the path, splashes of colour against the hard grey-green of the coastal terrain. Her feet slapped lightly against the smooth stone of the path as she walked, beating a rhythm which took her all the way to the end of the bay.

She felt Jamie's eyes on her before she saw him, tucked away on the bench in the curve of the sea wall. She walked over to him and he stood, walking the three strides to meet her.

'Hey,' he said gently, his eyes alight.

She smiled. 'Hey.' Her hand gestured vaguely to herself. 'Better?'

He didn't answer, but smiled down at her, pressing a kiss right at the corner of her mouth. The innocence of the gesture caught her by surprise, her heart speeding a little.

'So what's the plan?' She adjusted her scarf around her neck, the sea breeze a little stronger here than further up in the village.

Jamie smiled at her, his happiness etched in fine lines around his eyes. 'We're going on a walk.'

Her brows knotted. 'A walk?'

'Down Memory Lane.'

'Oh, smooth.'

'It sounded cooler in my head,' he shrugged, with an awkward smile. He rocked back on his heels, fists shoved in his pockets, and for a second or two he looked like a much younger man, suddenly unsure of himself. 'It's just... I guess I've got some wrongs to right.'

Rae felt warmth rise in her chest, and she nodded.

He took her gloved hands and walked her back the few steps to the bench. They sat together, the ache of the cold stone gnawing at Rae's legs through her jeans.

'We were sitting on this bench the day you told me that you'd never kissed a boy before.' He looked out to sea, pensive for a second. 'I was literally about to grab hold of you and kiss you and then you said you were going to get Liam Hurley to do it. I was crushed.'

She thought back to that day. Remembered that she'd used Liam to try and make Jamie jealous, but he hadn't seemed at all bothered by it. She'd been so put out by his rejection that she'd marched right over to Liam, grabbed him by a handful of t-shirt and kissed him, there and then.

'I remember,' she said quietly, her hand finding his.

He was still focusing on the waves cresting in the bay. 'He was nearly a full year older than me, I didn't think I could compete with that kind of maturity.' He smirked, but when he looked back at her, his smile was laced with the faint traces of sadness. 'This is what I should have done.'

He leaned in towards her then, kissing her light and fast,

barely more than a peck.

She looked up at him, confused. He chuckled.

'How was that?'

'Bit of an anticlimax, to be honest.'

He laughed, his thumb tracing small circles on the knuckle of her first finger. 'Oh, it would have been.' His eyes were clear now, warm and bright. No trace of the sadness or awkwardness which had ghosted through them earlier on. 'Teenage me had zero game. I just wanted you to have an authentic experience.'

She went to speak, but he jumped up from the bench, pulling her with him, and set off back along the cliff path.

'Come on, we've got more to get through and it's arctic out here.' He grinned at her as they walked, hair flopping down over his forehead, whipping in the breeze. 'This seemed like a better idea in my head.'

'It's perfect.'

He flushed in response, the confident lines of his face softening as he glanced across at her, the low winter sun illuminating him from behind like a vision, and for a few moments she forgot that she was cold at all.

In another few strides they were at the foot of Black Rock, and he led her around the bottom edge, around the scrub which it backed on to, and down on to the sand on the other side. This was the more sheltered part of the beach, flatter and sandier and, most importantly, largely hidden from the prying eyes of the good people of Blackston. They had spent a lot of time playing on this beach as teenagers, making the most of the shelter afforded by the loom of the rock as they got up to things their parents definitely wouldn't have approved of.

Jamie stopped by the part of the rock where the stone was smooth, worn into a perpendicular wall, and he leaned against it, pulling Rae with him so that she rested against him, their chests touching. He linked his hands casually behind her back.

'I remember standing right here one day. It was that really long, hot summer, do you remember? You weren't in Blackston at the start of the summer holidays and I didn't know why.' His body was warm against hers and she leaned into him for comfort. 'I was way too shy to ask Nush what was going on, so I just assumed you weren't coming.' He laughed softly at the memory. 'Then, on that day, I was standing right here when a girl I didn't recognise skipped right past me wearing this amazing red bikini. She was all tanned and she had these curves, man...' His eyes deepened. 'All the right parts were in all the right places, let me put it that way. And when she turned to look at me I just...' He trailed off, blowing out a sharp breath. 'It was you.'

Rae nodded, remembering. 'It was the year my dad published his first book. He took us away for a couple of weeks, down to Cornwall. It was the only proper family holiday we ever had. Before that they never had any money, and after he was always too busy.' Her voice caught a little at the thought. 'Mama bitched about it the whole time, of course, but I didn't care. My dad let me get a proper haircut and bought me some new clothes. I felt like a film star.'

'I always thought you were pretty, but that day, Jesus. You blew me away.' His body tensed a little, the smallest of movements. 'I was standing right here. I should have called you over. Talked to you. Done this...'

He dipped his head down, his lips light and sweet on hers. He pulled away for a moment, just a fleeting second, then

185

kissed her harder, pulling her body into his with the lascivious enthusiasm of a teenager. When he pulled away the second time she laughed.

'Only remember we were only in our swimmers,' he said, his voice breathy. 'So, I would have been fully erect.'

She swatted him, giggling, and he kissed her, gently again. He released her and his hand slipped back into hers, leading her away.

'Come on.' He led her back around the base of the promontory, back over the stones to the path. 'I'd love to spend more time *reminiscing* down here, but we need to carry on.'

'Yeah, you seemed pretty enthusiastic about reminiscing.' She smirked, her eyes meeting his as a spark passed between them.

'Oh I am.' His eyes darkened, pupils growing. 'But right now I'm just rattling through them cause I'm cold as all hell. We need to get to the inside ones.'

Her nose wrinkled. 'Can't we skip and go straight to the inside ones?'

'Patience, beautiful.' His smile was a beacon, a flare of warmth against the winter wind. 'We're nearly there.'

They walked back up the limestone path into the heart of the village, over the bridge and up to Mr Cramer's shop. He stopped her outside, turning to face her on the pavement.

'Then there was that day before Christmas that I ran into you right here. I didn't see you coming at all.' His hand reached up to rub his chin. 'You were like a sledgehammer to my perfectly dull life.'

Her mind wandered back to that day. The rush of blood to her cheeks. Her heart in her ears. 'You made me drop my lemons.'

'I'll buy you new lemons right now.' His eyes didn't leave hers.

She fought a smile. 'The moment's gone.'

He raised an eyebrow. 'I'll buy you something better than lemons...' His palms came together in thought, fingertips against his lips. 'Melons?'

She laughed, the sound coming easily. He smiled in response, reaching for her hands, their fingers intertwining.

His face was suddenly serious. 'Anyway, we were standing here, right here where we are now.' His brows pulled together. 'I didn't tell you that I'd missed you, and I should have.' His smile seemed almost shy. 'This is the abridged version, by the way. I'm freezing my knackers off.'

She laughed. 'Noted.'

'Now let's get our arses to The White House.' He moved to leave, dropping one of her hands, but keeping the contact in the other, and the warmth of their connection made her smile against the wind.

'Good God yes,' she said, falling into step beside him.

They pushed through the doors into the warmth of the pub and Rae welcomed the burn of heated air on her face. It was busy, but the booth nearest the door was empty and he pulled her to it.

'Hungry?' He grabbed the menu from its holder.

She shuffled up close to him so she could see it better. 'Always.'

She scanned the menu, although it was just for show. She always had Roy's signature chicken pie. Jamie strode off to the bar to order, and Rae didn't even feel bad about watching him every step of the way.

When he slid back into the booth, he sat on the same side

as her, and he didn't look at her as he spoke. 'I was sitting at this table when I had my first date with Nina.'

Her eyes widened jokingly. 'Wow, we're going there?'

He grinned, cautiously, reaching for her hand as he spoke. 'Don't be weird about it, this is an important bit.'

'I'm not being weird, it's just...' Rae looked away. Gathered her thoughts. '...she's just really pretty, is all.'

He didn't miss a beat. 'You're really pretty.'

She huffed. 'Oh, you know what I mean. I'm ok if you get me at a good angle.' She didn't look up at him 'She was undeniably stunning. Like probably not even human stunning. Even I wanted to sleep with her.'

'It takes more for me.' His voice was quiet.

She looked up at him then, one eyebrow raised in disbelief.

'Ok fine. I mean I *forced* myself.' His eyes sparkled, lit with mischief. 'But my world was kind of un-rocked.' His eyes went to their hands, joined together on the table. 'Don't get me wrong, it was nice. But who wants their first time with someone to be *nice*?'

Her laugh was equal amounts uncomfortable and amused 'Is it weird that we're talking about your sex with your ex on our first date?'

'You started it.' His mouth edged up at the corners. 'All I wanted to say is that I tried really hard to get that same feeling that I had kissing you in the courtyard, like my whole body was turning inside out, but I couldn't. Nina was the perfect woman. *Should* have been the perfect woman. But it wasn't enough.'

Am I enough, she wanted to ask, but she said nothing. He was still looking at their joined hands, eyes soft, and she watched him silently as his thumb traced circles on her skin. She hadn't been enough for Simon, she thought, and it nagged at her, nipping at her throat before she forced it down.

She studied Jamie, tried to remind herself of the differences between the two men. Jamie's hair fell forward onto his forehead, baby curls licking at his temples, a week's worth of stubble softening his sharp edges. He was wild and beautiful there, and when he looked back up at her it made her chest tighten and squeeze.

She kissed him lightly on the scruff of his cheek, excused herself and headed off down the long corridor to the toilets, offering Roy a small wave on her way past.

She pushed back out of the door to find Jamie leaning against the wall, in just the same spot as he had been on New Year's Eve. When he took her arm and pushed her through the fire door this time she was all in.

He kissed her immediately, his mouth warm and firm on hers, hands gripping her waist, pulling her into him. She heard him groan into her, a small noise that sent flickers of heat rushing through her bloodstream, and she deepened the kiss in response.

Her fingers, as if reliving the memory, found the space between his clothes again, and her fingers slipped over the warmth of his body, trailing a path up his sides.

He smiled against her mouth. 'I'm not running away this time.'

'Don't,' she said, almost a whisper as his mouth found her neck, back to that secret spot which had damn near made her lose her mind.

'We'll pick this back up later.' His voice was rough.

She smiled. 'We'd better.'

'Don't you worry, I've thought of very little else since the last time we were here.'

By the time they slid back into the booth, their food was waiting for them and Roy was looking over with a knowing smile. Rae blushed.

Then she tucked into her pie happily, closing her eyes as she savoured the flavour of the rich sauce against the buttery pastry, and she wasn't sure she'd ever been happier in her whole life. At least until they finished their meals and Jamie led her on to Jan's cafe, where over a hot chocolate with everything they reminisced about old times in Blackston until Rae was laughing so hard she couldn't breathe.

It was late in the afternoon by the time they got back to the cottage, and the winter light was beginning to fade, darkness falling and settling over Blackston like a fog. Jamie drew the curtains, turning on the lamp in the corner which cast the whole room in a tungsten glow.

Rae moved to the sofa, sitting tentatively, looking back up at him. 'Any regrets in here?'

He didn't speak at first, ran a hand through his hair and then looked up, straight at her, shaking his head gently as a slow smile spread across his face. He moved over to the sofa, sat beside her, rubbing his palms down the thighs of his jean a couple of times before he turned to face her. And as his eyes lowered to her lips for a beat she felt the roar of need awakening in her belly.

His eyes shot back up to meet hers and it only took one word, a single finger on a trigger firing a spark which spread through her body like wildfire.

'Hi.' His voice was soft, barely audible. Heavy with want,

with need, his eyes loaded with a lifetime of untaken chances.

She moved to him, so close she could feel his breath on her face. 'Hi.'

The kiss was easy at first, deliciously slow and unhurried, and she fell into him like a trance, eyes falling shut, skin on fire. She felt the soft pads of his fingers under her chin, stroking gently, moving down her neck, taking her in, and when his mouth joined them, she couldn't stop the moan which fell from her lips.

It was like a rubber band snapping then, tension building, building and then all at once the give, mouths hurrying together, her hands in his hair. A charge in the air that neither one of them could resist.

He sat back on the sofa, pulling her with him, and she twisted to sit astride him, the new intimacy of the position making her breath catch. She felt the vibration of his groan through his chest, the pitch hitting her somewhere deep inside. She couldn't get close enough to him. Couldn't resist. Couldn't wait.

She nipped at his lower lip with her teeth and he broke away for a second, pupils dilating, eyes alive with desire. He opened his mouth as if to say something, only exhaling heavily after a moment.

When he kissed her again it was demanding, his fingers almost bruising around her hips as he pulled her body into his. She could feel him, a heartbeat through his clothes, wild and alive and entirely at her mercy and the thought sent a scatter of goosebumps over her skin.

She sat back a moment, pulled her jumper over her head, flung it blindly somewhere. Her fingers moved to the buttons on his shirt, her eyes never moving from his as she undid them, one by one, pushing the soft cotton back and off his shoulders.

She drew in her breath with a small noise as she saw the man that the Jamie she'd known had grown into - broad and toned, with a smattering of dark hair covering his chest and disappearing down beyond the waistband of his jeans.

He half closed his eyes with a sigh as her fingers found his skin, explored the planes of his chest, trailed the softer skin of his belly before moving back to take her own t-shirt off. He bit down on his lip, brow furrowed as his eyes moved further down, lower and lower, before dragging back up the length of her and settling on her lips.

He kissed her with hunger and with reverence and she abandoned herself to him without a second thought. There was no game playing as there had been with Simon, no pretence. Their bond was honest, with a rawness she felt in every last inch of her body.

She would have given her whole self to him in a heartbeat, but he stopped her, his hand covering hers as she reached for the buckle of his belt.

'Not today.' His voice was heavy, breathy and thick, and it sent shivers through her. 'I want to, God I want to.' He trailed a gentle line up the centre of her body with one finger, from the waistband of her jeans, up over her belly, then higher, up her breastbone and up to the small hollow between her collarbones. 'I've imagined this for years, I just...' He sighed heavily, a war in his eyes. '...I just don't want to take it all at once, you know?' His smile was small, an apology.

But she simply kissed him, her lips light and sweet. 'I know. It's ok.' She smiled against him. 'You did promise me second base though.'

He laughed at that, the sound bright and warm, the tone a melody of happiness. Then nodded, his fingers slipping effortlessly around her back to unhook her bra, a gasp on his lips as it fell away from her in one smooth movement.

'You're beautiful.'

There was a quiet wonder in his voice, an edge of something that she'd never heard before. He trailed a finger lightly over the softness of her skin, his lips finding hers again, less hurried now.

She felt the energy change in the room as he shifted to lie on the sofa, moving her so they were stretched out side by side, his hand lazily exploring the contours of her skin as he kissed her without a care in the world.

She could wait, if he wanted to. She would have done anything for him in that moment. She wanted him more than she'd ever wanted a single thing in her life, but she could take what she wanted in pieces.

And as she lay on the soft, old velour of Jamie Stamford's sofa, their bodies touching, skin on skin, the connection between them was alive with a heady combination of familiarity and the bright spark of something new.

22

The Notebook

Spring blossomed into Blackston Bay like the first tender shoots of a new relationship, and it was in the sprawling shade of the old cherry blossom tree in town that Jamie Stamford had first happened upon the idea for the notebook.

He'd been on his lunch break, eating a steak sandwich on the bench under the tree and enjoying one of the first warm days of the year when he first noticed the sign. It had sparked something, the beginning of a tumble of ideas which eventually led to a plan.

At first he did nothing at all except sit and ponder, working up the courage to go into the shop. It was called Paper Crane, the fascia painted duck egg blue with the writing in a darker blue, the font simple and elegant. The window display was a riot of colour, showcasing a rainbow of notebooks piled next to quirky stationery, pens in pots, and small gifts here and there, while a canopy of tiny paper cranes were draped down from the top like a curtain of colour, floating above the display as if by magic.

Rae would absolutely love this, he thought to himself, the idea that he could share his discovery with her sitting well with him.

But it was the sign in the window that he was particularly interested in, sitting in the corner of the display, simply printed on pale yellow paper. It read:

Notebook embossing available here.

It had drawn Jamie's attention straight away. He'd bought Rae a small notebook while he was staying in London. He hadn't given it to her as soon as he came home, though, instead squirrelling it away in a drawer in the old desk his grandfather had used in the cottage's study. He'd been waiting, but he hadn't known why. Not until the second he saw the sign.

If he'd have been a bolder man he'd have gone into the shop as soon as he saw it, but if there was one thing Jamie Stamford wasn't, it was hasty.

He liked to bide his time, to ponder and research, to really know what he was getting into before he made any kind of commitment.

It had been a few days though, a glorious few days of the weather turning, of springtime beginning to edge into the air, and it was on the fourth day that he felt ready.

The bell over the door of the shop rang with a satisfying clatter as he went in, drawing the attention of the figure sitting behind the counter. There was something familiar about him, the shade of his hair sparking a memory he couldn't quite place, and it wasn't until the man stood to his full height and looked straight at Jamie that he realised where he'd seen him before.

'Kieran Quinn,' the auburn-haired man offered with a collected smile, extending his hand.

195

Jamie took it, shaking firmly. 'Jamie Stamford.' He hesitated for a moment, suddenly awkward. 'Listen, I'm sorry about that day in the cafe.' He looked to the ceiling, his gaze tripping awkwardly. 'I just... there was a lot going on.' He smiled hesitantly. 'Rae's told me a lot about you. She's very fond of you.'

'She's a good girl,' Kieran said with a smile. A peace offering. Jamie took it. 'She is.'

A pause, each man considering the other.

It was Kieran who spoke first. 'So, what can I do you for?' The double entendre was casual, conversational.

'I'm actually looking to get something embossed.' Jamie's hand went to his hair, as it always did when he felt a little out of his depth, and he tugged lightly at it. 'A leather notebook,' he explained. 'It's a present.'

Kieran's eyebrows drew together as he studied the other man. 'For Rae?'

Jamie nodded, his mouth twisting into a smile.

Kieran studied for a beat longer. 'You really like her.'

It wasn't a question, but Jamie nodded again.

Kieran's face changed, then, his eyes creasing into a smile and Jamie could almost feel the shift of energy in the room.

'Oh honey,' he said, with an affectation he seemed to save only for his most dramatic statements. 'Then it looks like we are going to be spending quite a lot of time together.'

Jamie laughed lightly. 'Looks like we are.'

'Come on then, champ.' Kieran leaned his weight on the counter in front of him, splaying his fingers. 'Let's have a little look at this notebook.'

Jamie nodded once, decisively, and reached into his work bag for the small paper package he'd retrieved from the desk drawer that morning. He'd been walking past the stall in the makers' market when it had caught his eye, the colourful hides an oasis in the sea of bath bombs and drudgery, and something about the pile of books particularly had drawn him in.

They're hand-stitched, the stall holder had said, her small features worn and softened with age. *Books shouldn't be made by machines. They should have a soul.*

And in that moment it was inconceivable that he would leave without buying one for Rae. He'd pored over the rainbow of colours, digging deep in his memory for any time she'd mentioned her favourite colour, but the only thing which he remembered was when she had once said she loved something because it was the colour of the sea.

Blue, he thought at first, before quickly realising that the sea at Blackston was more of a jade green. *Blue or green*, he'd wondered, and in the end he'd had to let her decide.

He'd walked away from the stall holding that paper-wrapped parcel as if it were the Crown Jewels, and he had kept it under lock and key ever since.

He laid the package on the counter and unwrapped it carefully.

'Oh, she's a stunner,' Kieran beamed, reaching a finger out to touch the buttery soft leather. 'That colour!' He brought his hands to his chest. 'She'll love it.'

'I hope so,' Jamie said quietly.

'I know so,' Kieran replied with a flourish, a kind smile touching his lips for the shortest time, before his voice turned serious as he took Jamie through the embossing service, how it worked, how long it would take. Jamie could hear the love that he had for his business in every word that he spoke.

'So all you need to do is tell me what you want it to say,' Kieran finished, pushing his hair off his face with a practiced flick.

Jamie smiled. 'I think I've finally figured that out.'

By the time Jamie reached the church hall that night he was practically singing to himself. Between his plans with the notebook and the cheeky texts from Rae which had blood rushing everywhere in his body except where it ought to be, he was in a rather chirpy mood.

Father Kevin looked up with a smile at the creak of the door opening.

'Jamie!' He stood, hands moving to a prayer position. A habit. 'I'm really glad you've come. There's something I'd like to discuss with you.'

Jamie lifted an eyebrow with interest, but some reservation. Those words historically had not had the best outcome for him, but he trusted Father Kevin, and there was a positive tone to his voice which allayed the panic beginning to creep in around his ribcage.

'Come and have a seat,' the older man said, moving around the desk to sit at one of the two chairs there.

'Hi, Jamie!' Penny's voice carried from across the hall, and he noticed for the first time the half of her body protruding from a cupboard.

He laughed easily. 'Hey, Penny.'

Father Kevin cleared his throat, adjusting his collar. 'We've had a request come in which doesn't really fit with our...' He paused to think, fingers smoothing his short beard '...well, our *usual* way of doing things.' He spoke slowly, taking great care over his choice of words. 'I was going to politely decline the request. It felt like something which called for something in the way of a longer-term commitment.' His eyes moved to Penny's backside, still protruding from the cupboard as she searched busily for whatever the hell it was they kept in there. 'But Penny talked some sense into me.' His face softened, his affection for Penny written all over his expression. 'She told me that one good thing is still one thing even if it takes a bit longer to do. And this may not be the easiest of things to do. But I feel... no, I *know*, that you are the right man to do it.'

'Ok,' Jamie said carefully. 'What is it?'

'How are your reading skills, Jamie?' Penny had disentangled herself from the cupboard, and pulled up another chair to join them, setting a stack of books on the desk behind her.

'They're... good?' It shouldn't have been a question, but it sounded like one, the confusion lifting his intonation as he spoke.

Penny clapped her hands together. 'Wonderful!' She looked between the two men. Her smile was bright, but there was a faint tinge of sadness lining her eyes. 'I knew you were the right man for the job.'

'Do you remember Old Martha Brannigan?' Father Kevin's voice was soft, serious.

Jamie nodded. 'I haven't seen her around since I've been back.' His voice lowered. 'Did she...?'

'No,' said Penny, quickly. 'But she's very ill. She's bed bound now, they say she only had weeks left.'

'Her daughter died a few years back,' Father Kevin picked up. 'They'd never had the easiest of relationships, but no mother should have to bury their child.' He paused a moment, a silent prayer on his lips. 'Cancer it was. Very quick *God rest her soul.*'

Penny glanced over at Father Kevin in awe at the last

199

statement, as if he had a direct line to heaven. 'She only has her granddaughter left now.'

'Gemma,' Father Kevin interjected. 'You remember Gemma Brannigan? She's around your age, I'm sure.'

Jamie *did* remember Gemma Brannigan, and the words he would use to describe her were not fit for use anywhere near a church. So, he said the only thing he could think to. 'Yeah, I remember Gemma.'

'She has...' The older man paused, searching for the right words. '...*repented* somewhat in recent months.' His tone was diplomatic, his face even.

With good reason, Jamie thought. Gemma Brannigan had been the bad apple of Blackston, all eyeliner and cigarettes and underage tattoos. They'd been in the same year at school, not that Jamie had ever seen her actually go to school all that often.

'She's a good girl,' Penny said kindly. 'She works hard, and she looks after Martha with such care.'

'Her mother died.' Father Kevin adjusted his collar. 'Her father was long gone.' He looked up, eyes meeting Jamie's in earnest. 'She changed her life, Jamie. She's trying her hardest.' He shrugged. 'She has only her grandmother now, and she'll likely die too. She needs help.'

Jamie's mind swum with the possibility of what they were going to ask him for. 'I'm not a carer,' he said, his voice kind but firm. 'I can't take care of a dying woman.'

Penny smiled, her eyes kind. 'We would never ask you to. Gemma takes good care of her. She has a nurse come in from town twice a week, and Gemma does all the rest.' Her hand went to her heart. 'She must be exhausted, poor girl.'

'So...' Jamie's confusion spilled into his voice, the words

slow. '...you want me to...?'

'Read to her,' Father Kevin said, decisively. 'She was a poet, did you know that?' His hands moved back to his praying position. 'She published many anthologies of poetry in her years.' He smiled, sadly. 'She lost her husband as a young mother, it wasn't long after the war, and she has some letters which he wrote to her while he was serving over in France. A shoebox full of these letters.' He smoothed his beard, fingers moving in a rhythm. 'Her dying wish is to hear her husband's words again before she leaves this earth to join him.'

Jamie looked between them, his eyes serious. 'And Gemma can't...'

'She can't read, Jamie.' Penny looked at him, her face almost stern, although it softened after a second. 'Not properly. Can you imagine what that feels like for a girl her age?' She shook her head. 'She was almost too embarrassed to ask, the poor thing.'

Father Kevin cleared his throat again, looking Jamie straight in the eye. 'She asked us if there were anyone who would be able to visit her, a couple of times a week maybe, to read the letters to her grandmother.' His eyes searched Jamie's. A plea. 'It's all she has left.'

It felt like a lot, but not so much as losing the last member of your family. Jamie cleared his throat. 'I mean, sure.'

Both Penny and the priest smiled then, small smiles filled with gratitude and a touch of sadness, and Penny bent to pick out her diary and arrange a time for him to go around and meet with Gemma.

'Just one thing, Jamie,' Penny said gently, as he moved to leave. 'Don't tell anyone about Gemma and the reading situation. She felt so ashamed, the poor thing.'

Jamie nodded quickly and left. He wouldn't tell anyone that Gemma couldn't read, of course he wouldn't. And the easiest way to do that, he told himself, was to not tell anyone about any of it at all.

It was over a week before Jamie finally worked up the courage to give Rae the notebook. When Kieran had sent him the message that it was ready, he'd rushed straight back to the shop, running his fingers lightly over the newly embossed leather with a small smile. It was perfect.

He'd thanked Kieran, their eyes meeting as a look which wordlessly spoke of their mutual affection for Rae passed between them, and they'd parted ways with a firm handshake.

His confidence dipped before he was even back home, his mind racing and churning, absurdly unsure of himself.

It's just Rae, he told himself. It's only a small present. It doesn't matter if she doesn't like it.

But the small gesture felt like something greater, in a way that he couldn't quite put his finger on.

Jamie's heart was thumping a beat as he knocked on the mill door later that same day. Warm air spilled out of the door as Rae swung it open and it hit him at the same time as the sight of her, leaving him hot and breathless.

Her hair fell in loose waves around her face, eyes rimmed with a smudged line of black which made them all he could see as he caught her face lightly in his fingers and brought her lips to his.

'Hi.' His voice was barely more than a whisper.

She smiled up at him, cheeks flushed. 'Hi.'

And as she shouted a quick goodbye to Nush he slipped his fingers through hers and led her wordlessly on the short journey to the cottage.

It wasn't long before they reached the wooden front door, and Jamie turned to close it behind them, pushing Rae back against it with his hips, her breath warm and sweet against him as she laughed out loud, the sound catching him right behind the breastbone. He blew out a steadying breath, running his hands up her sides, collecting his thoughts, slowing himself. He'd spent hours the previous night thinking of a plan to present her with the notebook, but the details were fading now against the roar of blood in his ears.

And when he opened his eyes he saw Rae looking back at him with an expression so raw, so vulnerable, that the last threads of his master plan were lost to the all-consuming need to be with her. Just that. He'd figure the rest out later.

He felt the knot of her hands in the hair at the back of his head as he leant down into her again, and with it the small flame in his belly leapt and grew, the heat licking up into his chest as he kissed her. The kiss was at once tender and urgent and fierce and reverent and it wasn't long until every single part of his body was aflame.

Her small hands were on him, seeking out skin, grabbing and stroking and pulling, and when she breathed out a small moan, barely even a sound at all, he could do nothing except gather her up in his arms and carry her to his bedroom.

His eyes met hers as they crossed the threshold, a question, and when she nodded once in reply he laid her down on his bed, her hair wild around her, her eyes burning. He wasn't sure he'd ever seen anything more beautiful in his entire life, and the thought stilled him, just for a second, until she slowly began to unbutton her shirt, sliding it off her shoulders and flinging it lightly away.

His mouth quirked into a slow smile and instead of going back to her, his hands went to his own shirt, pulling it over his head, moving to his belt buckle as his eyes stayed on her.

She returned his stare as she shuffled out of her jeans, only breaking eye contact to drop her gaze pointedly to his belt before snapping it back up, one eyebrow raised.

He chuckled and stepped out of his jeans. Mimicking her, he dropped his eyes first to the soft teal lace of her bra, and then lower, to her underwear, before dragging them back up to hers, his gaze now heavy with want.

She blinked once, slowly, her breaths quick and shallow, her neck flushed, and she didn't take her eyes off him even for a second as she unhooked her bra, letting it fall aside as her fingers moved to the cotton and lace of her underwear.

Dispensing with them swiftly, she leaned back against the soft grey flannel of his bed sheets, dipping her eyes for a final time to his underwear and pulling them back up, slowly, agonisingly, shamelessly taking in every detail of his body on the way.

Her smile was so small he could have missed it, but he didn't miss the heat in her eyes, nor the quick flash of her teeth as she bit her lip.

And as he kicked off his underwear, all that existed was the beautiful sight of Rae Logan naked in his bed after all the times he'd imagined it. But this wasn't the younger Rae of his fantasies. This woman was warmer, her body softened by age, with all the years that had passed written on her skin like stories.

And he longed to explore every word.

He rushed back to her, lips searching out lips as his eyelids grew heavy, his fingers closing around her hips, pulling her close, close, closer. And then there was nothing but lips hurrying down necks, across collarbones. Skin touching skin, muscles flexing, moving, mouths soft and warm and wet.

And with a rush of breath, the graze of fingernails on thighs and the sweet sound of his name on her lips, he abandoned himself to her completely.

Afterwards they lay together, her finger lazily tracing a trail through the dark hair on his chest.

'We should have done that a long time ago,' she said, her voice warm and rough.

He laughed lightly. 'Hey, I tried.'

'You didn't try very hard.'

He couldn't see her face, but he could tell she was smiling. He snorted. 'I'll give you *very hard*.'

And as he pulled her back onto his chest and she squealed and laughed between kisses, he forgot about the notebook entirely.

23

The New Road

"Construction on the New Road began in the latter months of the twentieth century, a reaction to the apparent lack of affordable housing in the Blackston Bay area. It marked the first building work in the village for over fifty years, save for maintenance works on existing structures.

The residents at first protested vociferously, particularly to the selling off of the 936m of farm track which was necessary to accommodate the new development; a track which comprised the final section of a popular circular walk around the village.

Though they were largely appeased by the decision to move the site 65 metres to the west, thus preserving the route of the woodland footpath which follows the river inland, the road remains, for some, a bone of contention and a sure sign that change is afoot in Blackston."

- F.W. Merryfield, *A Brief History of Blackston Bay*

24

Busted

There were few things Danusia Nowak enjoyed more than a brisk walk on a bright spring day. She was especially pleased by such an outing if the position of the sun in the sky afforded her the opportunity to wear the fake designer sunglasses that Rae had bought her from the local market the previous summer. Not only did she think herself very dapper indeed when wearing the thick tortoiseshell and gold frames, but the dark tint of the lenses allowed her gaze to linger for much longer than usual on the good people of Blackston going about their business.

Business, of course, that Nush was always very interested in watching.

She crossed the river and headed down the coastal path to the edge of the private estate on the beachfront, then headed inland, taking her favourite route down the farm road. This occasionally allowed her to exchange pleasantries with Ted Garratt, the farmer. And if Ted were in a particularly jovial mood as she passed, it wasn't unusual for him to gift Nush a pint or two of the very freshest milk, a gift that she enjoyed very much.

There was no sign of Ted today though, and as Nush followed the rubble track behind the barn and past the garage building, she noted that Ted's Land Rover was there, but his old maroon hatchback was missing, meaning he'd probably taken a trip into town.

She wondered briefly what business he had in town as the path turned from rubble to tarmac under her feet, and before she knew it she'd reached the crossroads. She took a left at that point, across the new road and down the small stone steps which led to the wooded river path. Nush wasn't a fan of the new road, nor its residents, who tended to conduct their business out in the street. It was all much too frank for her liking. She much preferred to speculate on business conducted indoors.

It was cool and dark and damp in the woods at this time of year, with the smell of wild garlic just starting to hang in the air, thick beside the sweetness of early bluebells. Nush slid her sunglasses up onto her head, closing her eyes a moment to help them adjust, while she took in the bubbling sounds of the river and the faint melody of birdsong.

It wasn't until she heard the knocking that she opened her eyes again.

It had been close by, a knock only loud enough to get the attention of whoever was inside, but with a subtlety which piqued Nush's curiosity immediately.

She stepped behind a tree, shielding herself so she was able to have a good look.

She saw him then, a familiar figure in a forest green sweater and jeans with his dark hair curling around his face. But what was Jamie Stamford doing at the old Brannigan house?

Nush slid her glasses back down, craning her neck so that she could watch him more closely. She watched with interest as young Gemma Brannigan opened the door, and then with an increasing heaviness in the pit of her stomach as she watched Jamie look over his shoulder, in one direction and then the other, before quickly following Gemma inside.

He didn't scan the woods behind the house, and if he had have done, he may not even have seen Nush's jaw drop from her hiding place behind the tree trunk.

Nush stood for a minute, barely breathing. What *was* Jamie doing with Gemma Brannigan? Her lip curled at the idea that something untoward might be going on, at even the thought that Jamie might be entertaining Gemma when he had Rae. *Her* Rae. Her stomach turned over.

She walked home quickly, along the path by the river, not noticing any of the sounds of nature that she normally revelled in. By the time she walked up the slope which brought her out by the bridge a few minutes later, she had more questions than answers.

Why had he looked so suspicious? She couldn't stop thinking about the quiet hesitancy of his knock, nor the careful way he'd looked over both shoulders before hurrying into the house. She knew one thing for certain though - that boy had not wanted to be seen. Her brows knotted into a tight frown.

Rae was sitting at the kitchen table when Nush got back to the mill, and she looked up with a bright smile as she heard the door open.

'I made lunch if you want some?' Rae gestured to the lurid bowl of soup in front of her. 'It's carrot and coriander. And I got some of the Jewish bread from Mr Cramer. Did you know he's started stocking it now?'

Nush shook her head.

'Is... reaaally good with... soup,' Rae said between mouthfuls, pausing only to blow lightly on the steaming spoonful while she brandished a thickly buttered slice of bread in her other hand.

Nush made no move to sit. 'I thought you'd be having dinner with Jamie today?' She hoped the question sounded natural, although she wasn't able to stop the slight shake in her voice.

Rae paused, spoon aloft. 'I'm meeting him later. He just had an errand to run with Joe this morning, but I'm going to meet him after lunch.'

Nush froze at that. The combination of the unabashed joy which crossed Rae's face and the quiet horror of catching Jamie in a lie made her feel sick to her stomach. She blew out a slow breath and reached for the back of a chair to steady herself.

'Ciocia, are you ok?' Rae had stopped eating and was looking at her aunt with concern. 'God, you look grey!' She stood up, moving to help, but Nush shook her head.

'I don't feel too good, that's all,' Nush lied, thoughts spiralling in her head. 'Just a bit of a headache. I'm going to have a lie down, that will help.' She patted Rae's face lightly and headed to her bedroom, crawling under her sheets and cocooning herself in them.

Her head, which had actually been perfectly fine only a few moments ago, now whirled and thumped with thoughts.

Was Jamie cheating on Rae? Surely not.

With Gemma Brannigan? Really Jamie?

Should she tell Rae? It would surely break her heart. How could she do that to her so soon after all the mess with Simon?

How could *Jamie* do that to her at all?

Nush fancied herself as rather a good judge of character, and she wasn't at all sure how to deal with the possibility that she'd been entirely wrong about him. She'd seen the way he looked at Rae and she couldn't fathom how someone could hold that weight of love for another person in their eyes and not be completely committed to them.

But then she had been wrong about such things before.

Eventually she fell into a fitful sleep and woke to a quiet, dark house. Rae must have gone out, she thought to herself, feeling a sharp pang of sadness as she remembered what she'd seen.

She padded to the kettle, flicking it on and rooting about in the cupboard for her favourite mug, and she pondered her next move as she retrieved it and dropped in a teabag.

She needed more evidence, she decided. Maybe her eyes were deceiving her. Maybe she had just jumped to an unfair conclusion. Jamie could have been at the house for any reason, she hadn't even seen them touch for God's sake.

She decided that she would take the same walk again the next day, just to see what she could see. So, the next day she did exactly that.

And when she didn't see even a single sign of Jamie anywhere near the Brannigan house, she took the same walk the following day. And the day after.

But then, on the fifth day, just as she was walking back up the slope to cross the river, she was stopped in her tracks by white and blue police tape cordoning off the road by the Harpers' house, a flurry of activity behind it.

Blue lights blinked frenetically, reflecting off the crisp fabric of the forensic suits and Mags Harper's immaculate white

Range Rover. Patrol cars and vans lined the main street, the volume of which Nush had never seen in her life, much less all at once and all in Blackston.

She stayed for a few minutes, surreptitiously registering as much information on the scene as she could without drawing too much attention, and then hot-footed it up the street to Jan's cafe.

The cafe was empty but for Jan sitting at their favourite table, and as Nush burst through the door Jan looked up, her eyes wide.

They stared at each other for a beat, speechless, before Jan smoothed her hands down the front of her apron and scooted over on to the next chair to allow Nush to sit and share her vantage point.

'Do we know what's happening?' Nush's voice was pitched higher than normal, a strange combination of anxiety and dark excitement flooding her body.

Jan shook her head. 'I haven't heard anything definite.' She pressed her palms together, tapping the point of her fingers lightly against her chin. 'It's big though. Whatever it is.' She squinted out of the window. 'You don't get the best part of North Yorkshire Police in your front garden for nothing.'

Nush took a deep breath. 'You don't think...'

'You called it, Nush.' Jan's brightly coloured lips pressed into a flat line. 'You always had your suspicions about them.'

Nush nodded quietly. If she was right about this, then maybe she was right about Jamie, too. She closed her eyes against the thought, just as the bell over Nush's shop rang, startling them both.

Rae rushed in, phone in hand, eyes just as wild as Jan's had been.

'Have you seen?' She dropped the phone on the table in front of the two older women, scrolling to a news story. Nush didn't have her glasses on, but as she squinted at the screen, she saw the headline come into focus and she gasped.

Yorkshire Vet and Wife Arrested on Suspicion of Murder.

'We told you!' Jan threw her hands up dramatically. 'Didn't we tell her, Nush?'

Nush nodded again, but she didn't speak.

'It's the plants,' Jan continued. 'I told you there was something fishy about those plants. How on earth else would they have got them to grow in this godforsaken soil?'

Rae laughed quietly, humourlessly. 'I've got to admit, I thought the two of you were off your rockers, but you were right on the money. I thought they were nice people.'

'Maybe that's your problem, *Pszczółko*,' Nush said, before she could stop herself. 'You are too trusting. Not everyone deserves your trust, you know.'

In a split second, she watched Rae's face change and instantly regretted her words.

Rae's eyebrows pulled together in confusion. 'What do you mean?'

Nush shook her head quickly, forcing all her thoughts on Jamie away. 'Nothing, no no. Forget it.'

Rae's frown deepened. 'No, come on, tell me. Who shouldn't I trust?'

'Forget it, Kochanie,' Nush sighed, her guilt at worrying Rae a stranglehold around her neck. 'I just mean like with Simon, but that's all in the past now.' Her heart clenched in her chest with the lie. 'Forgive me, it's been a strange day. My mind is everywhere.'

And with that, Rae softened, touching Nush's arm gently.

'Will tea help?'

Nush smiled and nodded, and they both looked towards Jan, who jumped to her feet immediately with a grin, rushing off to make tea and leaving Nush making uncharacteristically awkward small talk with Rae and hoping to hell she was wrong about Jamie.

The following day, after somewhat of an internal battle, Nush set off on her walk again. Part of her had wanted to drop it, to head off in a different direction and shake off the whole idea. But a small voice in her head had convinced her to see the week out, to walk the same route for seven days and if she had seen nothing else suspicious in a full week, she'd chalk it down to something harmless, maybe an errand.

That day's walk passed without incident, and she smiled at the police officers still guarding the threshold of the Harpers' land as she passed. They nodded back politely.

On the seventh day, Ted Garratt was in his smallest paddock as she passed, and he shouted to her as he heard the clap of her soles against the cattle grid.

'Nush!'

Ted was a stocky little man, with hips several times too wide for the length of his legs. He waddled across the small field, smiling broadly at Nush.

She stopped as she saw him, absentmindedly kicking the dirt off her boots as she waited for him to close the gap between them.

'Nush, my old girl,' Ted beamed. He had always talked to her as if she were one of his dairy herd and Nush was rather fond of it. 'What's all this commotion up your end?' He lowered his voice a little, even though they could both clearly see that there

214

was no one around. 'I've seen the headlines of course.' He took off his cap, shaking his head and scratching his greying hair thoughtfully.

'You know, I'd always thought it about them,' Nush said quietly. 'I have my theories about everyone.' She spoke slowly, choosing every word with precision, the faint hint of accent creeping in. 'But I'm never sure whether I'm happier when I'm proven right, or when I'm proven wrong.'

Ted nodded solemnly. *'Murder?'*

His voice was incredulous, but Nush could hear the thread of vulnerability running through it. It was something that the whole of Blackston felt. The news of the Harpers' arrests had set the villagers on edge, and when they'd been charged the following day it were as if a cold knife had been plunged into the very heart of Blackston. In a place where everyone knew everyone, a threat to any of them was a threat to all of them.

Nush smiled at Ted, but there was no humour there, and she could almost feel the weight of the last week pulling downwards on the corners of her mouth. 'Murder.'

The word felt foreign on her lips and it sent a cold chill pricking at the back of her neck. She had been right all along. Her mind jumped to the image of Jamie sneaking into the Brannigan house and it made her feel nauseous.

'How will we get over this, Ted?' Her question seemed simple, but it was loaded with the secrets and struggles of a half-century and she blew a heavy breath out as Ted smiled kindly at her.

'Ah, lass,' he said gently, again using a term of endearment he used for his cows. 'The same as we always do.' His smile widened, creasing the weather-worn skin around his eyes. 'We'll just keep going.'

215

Nush's smile was genuine now. 'It's all we can do.'

'It is.' Ted tapped his cap, which he had been spinning thoughtfully in his fingers through the whole exchange, and put it back onto his head as punctuation. 'Let me get you a pint or two, lass, while you're passing.'

And before Nush could even reply he was striding off toward the outbuilding where they kept the fridges, returning with a bottle of his freshest milk which he handed to Nush as if it were his firstborn child. She smiled widely and thanked him, before setting off on the last half-mile of her walk with a spring in her step but a million thoughts on her mind.

She had bent down to look at a flower by the river bank when she heard the door close, and as she turned to look she realised that she was at the Brannigan house already and had not even thought to investigate. There was Jamie, clear as day, a genuine smile on his face for Gemma, and Nush's heart clenched.

Part of her had really believed that the first visit she'd seen had been a one-off. She was so fond of Jamie, so easily able to see the good in him, the clear affection in his eyes when he looked at Rae. Yet here he was, in front of her very eyes, leaving another woman's home.

Nush watched, her stomach rolling, as the two of them stood talking for a second. She was too far away to be able to hear what they were saying, but she could see that this was not lighthearted chitchat. They didn't embrace as a goodbye, but Jamie touched Gemma's arm gently before he turned to leave, lighting the first few sparks of rage in Nush's belly.

She waited until he was out of sight and then hurried to Jan's cafe on burning feet.

'Good morning!' Jan yelled from the back room of the

cafe as Nush burst through the door, even though it was past noon already and the force at which Nush's door opening had struck the bell should have signified to Jan that this was not a good anything.

Nush took a moment to steady her breathing, and when Jan emerged from the back holding a pot of coffee her face dropped at once.

'Nush, what is it?' The almost imperceptible tremor in Jan's voice mirrored the feeling Nush had in her gut. 'What happened?'

The two women moved to their table, and Nush sat, taking a deep, steadying breath before starting to speak.

'I saw...' She was uncharacteristically hesitant, her confusion clear in her voice. 'I think Jamie might be cheating on Rae.'

Jan's eyes widened. 'What? With who?' She quickly scanned the cafe, but there was only a thin crowd of regulars. No one was interested much in their gossiping.

Nush lowered her voice regardless. 'With the Brannigan girl.'

'The bad one?'

Nush nodded reluctantly. She of all people was not one to judge people on the actions of their past, and in different circumstances she was quite sure she would have had an amount of sympathy for Gemma. But not like this. 'I saw him going into her house a week ago. When I asked Rae where he was she said he'd gone to see Joe. And then just now I caught him leaving.' She paused. Normally at this point she would have paused to add the necessary dramatic weight to her story, but there was no pleasure in this gossip. She just felt empty. 'I didn't actually see anything happen, but the way he looked at her, the way they were together... I don't know. There was a tenderness there.' She took a moment, the memory making the anger and shock mix and churn in her stomach. 'They weren't speaking like strangers.'

Jan nodded slowly and shifted her chair an inch closer to Nush's. 'I saw him there too, a few evenings ago. I thought my eyes were deceiving me, that it must have been some other boy, but I was so sure it was Jamie. That hair, you know?' Her eyes searched Nush's, her skin paling. 'He looked like he didn't want to be seen, too. Pretty shifty.'

'Same when I saw him!' Her fury was beginning to overtake her nausea. 'He looked like he was definitely hiding something.'

Jan shook her head in sympathy. 'And the Brannigan girl. Gemma, isn't it? I mean, of all people.' Her voice was a harsh whisper. 'She's not a good girl, Nush.'

Nush's fingers went to her lips, her thoughts racing. 'Do I tell Rae.'

Jan shrugged. 'Do you want her to find out from someone else?' Her eyes were kind. Rae was like family to Jan. 'Or even worse, not find out at all?'

Nush shook her head, sadness suddenly flooding into her chest. 'I have to protect her, Jan.'

Jan nodded, her hand reaching to gently pat Nush's arm. 'Then tell her.'

'It'll break her heart. After Simon and everything.' Her voice dropped almost to a whisper. 'It'll break her heart.'

Jan's brows pulled together, her shared hurt palpable. 'She deserves to know.'

Nush's eyes closed, her breath escaping in heavy bursts as she realised Jan was right.

Rae needed to hear it, and there was only one person who

could tell her.

'I know.'

25

Small Grenades

Rae Logan was not a woman with a fondness for cleaning, but when the mood did happen upon her from time to time, she undertook the task with great fervour and unsociably loud show tunes.

She'd borrowed one of Nush's old scarves and used it to keep her unbrushed hair off her face as she worked, tidying and sorting, mopping and scrubbing, singing to herself the whole time. Occasionally, during a particularly dramatic solo, she would use whatever bottle or brush or sponge she was holding as a microphone and sing along so loudly that her throat was raw.

She was in the middle of wiping down the shower when her phone rang the first time. She squinted over the bathroom to where she'd rested her phone on the shelf over the sink. She couldn't make out a name, but she knew exactly who was calling by the assigned photo she'd never got around to deleting.

Simon.

She huffed to herself.

What the hell does he want?

She frowned, suddenly annoyed by her task, until the music kicked back in with the opening to Don't Rain on my Parade, and by a few bars in, she was back to singing along.

'Don't bring around a clooouuud... to rain on my paraaaaade... Yeah, you tell him, Fanny,' she said to no one in particular, singing into the shower head before turning it on and giving the inside of the shower a good rinse.

She was in a wonderful mood, and there was absolutely no way that she was going to let Simon Bloody Collins have any influence on that at all. The spring sun was shining, the birds were singing, and she was still on a high from the perfect evening she'd spent with Jamie the previous day.

He'd gone to fetch food from the good Chinese takeaway in town, and they'd eaten it off a blanket in front of the old bay window in Jamie's bedroom which just happened to have a near-perfect view of the sun setting over the cliffs at this time of year.

After they'd eaten, he'd presented her with a shabbily-wrapped gift, his face painted with a curious mixture of pride and abject fear, and she'd laughed and gently peeled back the worn layers of tissue to reveal a butter-soft leather notebook in the most beautiful shade of sea green she'd ever seen. Her fingers had gone to her mouth in awe, before reaching to run along the small embossed words which sat unobtrusively in the bottom right hand corner.

This is your story, Rachel. All you need to do is write it.

She'd drawn a breath in, heart singing and eyes burning, before looking up to meet Jamie's eyes. He'd been studying her, so vulnerable and expectant in that second that she could do nothing but reach for him.

'I believe in you,' he'd said quietly, his hands moving to stroke her cheeks.

Her heart had swelled. 'Thank you.' Her voice had been a whisper, and he'd stolen the last of it with a kiss which she'd felt all the way to her bones.

She smiled to herself, replacing the shower head and moving on to wipe down the sink, singing both parts of the ballad that was currently playing. She didn't stop smiling until her phone rang a second time. She looked at it in annoyance, as if simple will would silence it. This wasn't a mistake. Simon had intended to call her. It was the first contact they'd had since the break up, which even then was just a few hurried texts to sort out who would cancel the wedding arrangements. She hadn't actually *spoken* to him since the day she'd left.

She frowned. She was happy with Jamie. Whole. He was thoughtful and funny and the sex with him was so good she sometimes thought she might just lay down and die. She felt like a completely different person than the shell of a woman who'd walked out on Simon that day. She didn't know what he wanted, but she was quite sure she didn't want to hear it.

She switched her phone to silent and pushed it into her back pocket.

'That's enough from you,' she said aloud. 'This house ain't going to clean itself.'

And she scrubbed and wiped and swept and sorted until Simon was a distant memory and the whole house was sparkling.

When Nush arrived home just after six, there was only the kitchen left to do, and Rae was polishing the hob and singing a Les Mis medley.

She looked up into Nush's confused eyes and laughed. 'I'm

222

cleaning.'

Nush nodded, still incredulous. 'I can see that.' She looked Rae up and down. 'You look like a babushka.'

'That was the look I was going for,' Rae quipped, not breaking pace with her scrubbing.

Normally Nush would have laughed warmly at that, but she'd been uncharacteristically quiet for a few days now, and today was no exception.

'Make tea when you've finished, Kotku.' There was an edge to Nush's voice. 'We need to talk.'

Rae wiped off the last of the hob, throwing her sponge into the sink. 'I've finished now. What's up?' She washed her hands quickly, before filling the kettle and flicking the switch on.

'Where's Jamie today?' Nush's tone was flat, not at all her usual warm sing-song.

Rae frowned, confused. 'He just had to stop by Joe's after work.' She pulled the headscarf off her head, running her hands through her hair to tame it. 'I'm going to his at seven.'

'I think he's cheating on you,' Nush said all at once, the words spilling out of her in a rush and falling like tiny grenades around them.

Rae's voice was quiet when she eventually spoke. 'What? What do you mean?' A feeling of dread began to creep up her body, curling around her spine and setting deep fingers into her ribcage.

'The times he's said to you that he's at Joe's.' Nush took care with her words, the rhythm of them slowing as she spoke. 'He isn't. He's with Gemma Brannigan.'

Rae drew in a breath, recoiling as if she'd been punched in the face. 'Why would you even say that?'

Nush took off her glasses, cleaning them on the hem of her blouse. 'I saw him going into her house a week ago. Yesterday I saw him leave.' She slid her glasses back on, adjusting them to sit perfectly before looking Rae straight in the eye. 'He told you he was at Joe's house both of those times, but I am telling you that I saw him with my own eyes, and both of those times he was at the Brannigan house. Jan's seen him there too.'

The air seemed to still around Rae as the words sunk in. Maybe there was an explanation. Something perfectly innocuous. And she'd ask Jamie about it, and he'd explain, and they'd laugh about it together over dinner.

Jamie was not that kind of guy. Jamie would never hurt her. *Would he?*

'Nush...' She began.

'I know you like him, Kurczaczku,' her aunt interrupted. 'I like him too.' She reached a hand out to take Rae's, the skin of her palm smooth and warm. 'But I am telling you that he is lying to you about where he is, so who knows what else he is lying to you about?'

'Maybe there's an explanation?' Rae said, more to herself than anything, a quiet prayer grasping at the last strands of hope which were beginning to flicker and fade inside her chest.

'I hope there is.' Nush nodded slowly, her eyes never leaving her niece. 'I so hope that there is.' Her grey eyes were soft, lined with a sadness so consuming that it was almost enough to break Rae's heart. 'But Misia, you need to find out.'

Rae nodded slowly, her pulse thundering like a freight train, slow breaths doing little to calm it. Nush was right, of course. Nush was always right. She needed to know, and there was only one way to find out.

Her heart was in her throat as she knocked on the cottage door later that evening. She could see the flicker of the lights behind the glass, hear the low sound of Jamie humming to himself as he moved behind the door, and when he opened it wide and smiled broadly, her heart felt as if it had skidded to a stop.

He reached for her, pulling her in for a kiss, but she turned her face at the last second and his lips fell on her cheek.

He pulled away, brow knotting with confusion, looking at her so earnestly that it immediately made tears well in her eyes.

'Rae?'

The familiar way he said her name cut into her in this new context, and a hollow dread began to gnaw at the pit of her stomach. He was looking at her, waiting for her to say something. His eyes fixed on her, searching hers with a rawness which tugged at her skin.

In that moment he had never looked more beautiful to her, and she had never been more afraid of him.

She took a deep breath, steadying herself, and when she spoke it felt as if the words were coming from someone else's mouth.

'I'm going to ask you a question and I need you to be honest with me.' She couldn't have stopped her voice from shaking if she tried.

His frown deepened, the bewilderment clear. 'Ok?'

'Where were you just now?'

'I told you,' he said, and she didn't miss how slowly he spoke, nor the care he took over every word. 'I had to stop by Joe's house.'

Even if she hadn't already known it was a lie, the small

twitch in his face would have given him away. The small embers of hope that Rae had clung on to, the small chance that this was all a misunderstanding, slowly began to dim and burn out.

'Right.' There was an edge in her voice this time. 'So, if I give Joe a call right now, he'll confirm that, will he?'

'What?'

A flicker of panic crossed Jamie's face, a nearly imperceptible shift in his expression. She could almost see the cogs beginning to turn, and anger began to creep in alongside her fear.

'You were at Joe's,' she continued, carried now almost entirely by adrenaline. 'So, if I call Joe and ask him if you were just at his house, he'll say yes, right?'

Jamie's eyes narrowed, defensively. 'Of course.'

'So, there's no problem here.'

He nodded. 'There is no problem.' He looked at her for a beat, eyes holding hers with a silent plea, before clouding, muddying. 'Wait, what are you saying?' His voice was rough. 'Don't you trust me?'

Rae's laugh was hollow. 'I think we're both beginning to see that the answer to that is no.'

'What's going on here, Rae?'

He moved back towards her, his hand reaching for her upper arms, and she snatched them out of his grasp, feeling a wave of fury swell within her.

'Don't touch me. Just...' She blew a breath out. 'Just don't.' Gritted her teeth. 'You're telling me that you've been going to Joe's a couple of times a week. Helping him out with something or other.'

He nodded, although it hadn't been a question.

'So, I'll just quickly call and confirm that and then everything will be ok, won't it?'

She found her phone, thumbed through her contacts until she found Joe, heard the catch in Jamie's breathing a split second before he spoke.

'Wait, stop!' He sighed. 'Don't.' His voice seemed small, far away, heavy with a tone which she recognised.

She looked him straight in the eye. 'That look on your face. I've seen it before.' She rubbed one temple, her head beginning to spin. 'It's guilt. You're *lying* to me, Jamie.' She shrank away from him, her arms pulling in of their own accord. 'You're telling me that you're going to see your brother when people have *seen* you going into Gemma Brannigan's house.'

'Shit.' The word flew out of him like an admission. Another grenade thrown in.

'Yeah, shit is right.' She couldn't look at him.

'Look, it's not what you think.' There was something in his voice that she couldn't place. 'I was helping her with something.'

She snorted. 'Yeah, I bet you were.'

'Rachel.' A plea.

'Don't. Don't bother.' There was a tremble to her voice which she felt all through her body. 'I've heard it all before. I won't be lied to again, Jamie. I can't…'

Even if she had known how to finish that sentence, she would have been cut off, as her phone, still in her hand from when she'd searched for Joe's number, began to ring. They both looked down at it at the same time, and from the change in his breathing she could tell the exact moment when Jamie realised who was calling.

When she looked back up, his eyes were on fire.

'Really, Rae? Simon?' He was hurt, his voice betrayed that much. He was also furious.

'Ah, he only started ringing me today. I didn't even answer it.' She shook her head. 'Wait, why am I defending myself on this?'

He took a full step away from her, his glare slicing clean through her. 'Looks like I'm not the only one in question here.'

She laughed humourlessly. 'You've got to be kidding me.'

He said nothing, but she could feel him mounting his defences against her, as every barrier he had lowered to her began to raise back up.

'You're surely not comparing me missing a few calls from my ex with you lying about going to see Joe so you can sneak off to another woman's house?'

'I told you I'm helping her!' His hand went to grab his jaw in frustration, his voice straining with anger now.

But she knew a thing or two about anger herself, and she would not be made a fool of. Not this time.

'And I told you I don't want to hear it, Jamie!' She took a small step back. 'If I can't trust you we should forget this whole thing.' She looked up, holding his gaze defiantly, even though she could feel her heart begin to shatter at the mere suggestion.

He didn't miss a beat. 'If that's how you feel then we should.' His eyes were dark, narrowed. She had never seen him like this before. 'Then maybe the next time Simon rings you can pick up?' He aimed the last part at her as if it were a weapon, and she felt it connect, ripping through her body and bringing the burn of fresh tears to her eyes.

'How could you?' She felt her voice break. 'I... after

everything. How could you?'

As she turned to leave, the look on his face was the pull of the pin from the final grenade. And with that, the words which had fallen around them began to blow small holes in Rae's foundations as she ran back to the mill, until she found herself there on the doorstep - cold, alone, and entirely decimated.

26

Repentance

Gemma Brannigan had never been one for religion, but she appreciated the cool silence of an empty church as much as anyone.

She came down to St. Teresa's twice a week, Tuesdays and Fridays, when the respite carers visited Nana Martha. She slid wordlessly into the smooth wood of the pews and just sat, hands knotted. Reflecting. Repenting.

That was how she'd met Father Kevin.

And it hadn't taken a whole lot more than five minutes in the confessional box for the kindly priest to absolve her of all her sins.

Eager for the chance to clear her head, she'd tried going for walks when she first arrived back in the village, but she hadn't counted on the stares and whispers which followed her. She was saddened, but she wasn't surprised by it all. She had burned one too many bridges in Blackston.

These days she barely left the house, unless she was going to the shop or to church. Mr Cramer and Father Kevin were the only two people in the village who looked at her with kindness in their eyes, and she craved the sanctuary they each provided.

Bill Cramer, as it happened, was a big believer in second chances, and Gemma was more in need of one than most.

She had a lot of names. The Bad Apple of Blackston. That Brannigan Girl. Trouble. She'd heard them all.

And it was difficult to argue with them, especially when her skin was branded by the bad times like a warning. The gnarled scar snaking up her forearm from the razor wire which had sliced through her as she tried to run from a warehouse robbery. The faint shadows of track marks in the crooks of her elbows. A decade of cheap tattoos littering her body, her hands, her neck.

She'd arrived back in Blackston a year ago, newly sober and completely broke, and Nana Martha had taken her in without question. She could still remember the way the old woman's eyes had widened in recognition as she'd opened the door, before clutching her granddaughter tightly against her ample chest, just as she had when Gemma was a child. Nana Martha had worn the same cloying lavender perfume for forty years, and Gemma had breathed it in deeply, unable to stop the rambling apology which tumbled out of her as she sobbed in her grandmother's arms.

She'd been a sight back then, six stone seven if that, with sharp hollows in her cheeks and shadows the colour of bruises around her eyes. Martha had run one thumb tenderly along the jut of her cheekbone before smiling gently at her granddaughter, grabbing the bags she'd brought and pulling them into her house.

She hadn't made even a single comment on what Gemma looked like, how thin she was, the shake in her stride. She'd dropped the bags at the foot of the stairs and simply said, 'Let's eat,' as if Gemma had been away for a weekend and not a decade.

Martha cooked all her granddaughter's favourite childhood meals, always taking care to give her the bigger portion. By the time they celebrated six months of Gemma's sobriety, she was strong and healthy again.

Two weeks later, Martha was diagnosed with cancer.

Gemma had been devastated, but she'd tried her best to hide it. In another life she would have turned immediately to drugs to numb her from the pain, but the old woman had taken such good care of her when she was at her most vulnerable that it was inconceivable to her that she wouldn't return the favour.

I can fall apart, she thought to herself, *when she's gone. I can't let her see all her love go to waste.*

The doctors said it had started in her lungs, and then it had spread to her bones, and to her brain, growing in a place that was making her slowly lose her vision. The treatment was gruelling, but Gemma was there for all of it. She sat with the nurses as they went through her care, learning which tablets to give her by the size and colour. Big white ones twice a day, small orange ones with her lunch. The tiny white ones, two at a time, only when the pain was unbearable.

She gently rubbed lotion into Martha's skin as it split and bled from the treatment, and helped clean her up with such care when she had accidents. She couldn't drive, but the women took the bus to appointments together, and later on Gemma would sit beside her grandmother in the ambulance, never complaining.

She was there through it all, and she was there on the day that, solemn-faced, the doctor called the two of them in for an urgent consultation.

We've come to a crossroads, the doctor had said. *You can choose to continue with treatment. It may give you a little more time. Or we can help make you comfortable, and let nature take its course.*

The doctor was a tall man, with dark skin and kindly eyes, and well-spoken in a way which implied a privileged education. He went to great lengths to explain his prognosis, and Gemma didn't understand a lot of the words the doctor used, but she got the gist.

Nana Martha was dying.

The old woman sat for a moment in silence, head nodding gently, before she turned to her granddaughter with a small smile and a misting of tears in her eyes.

'I'm old, and I'm tired,' she said slowly, her voice roughened by the toll of the treatment. 'But I'll keep going if you want me to.'

Gemma had spent enough time on the streets to recognise a hopeless fight when she saw one. And she wouldn't put her grandmother through that. Not after everything Martha had done for her.

She reached out to take Martha's hand, noticing not for the first time how it was little more than thin skin stretched over bone now. Her heart clenched, the prick of tears filling her eyes.

'I just want you to stop hurting,' she said in a quiet voice, and it was the truth. Never in Gemma's life had she cared more about another person's needs than about her own. She'd spent a lifetime running away from the things which hurt her, and yet here she was, faced with losing the only person she'd ever loved, and though the very thought of it brought her to her knees there wasn't a single part of her that wanted to run.

Martha squeezed her hand gently in return, and though neither of them said a word, it felt as if the old woman could hear every thought screaming through Gemma's head.

Thank you.

I love you.

I'm here for you.

You're all I have.

I'll never stop missing you.

She coughed her emotion away and turned back to the doctor. 'If we stop the treatment... how long...?' She couldn't finish the sentence.

He shrugged lightly. 'Weeks.' His voice was kind, but matter-of-fact. 'Maybe six weeks. It can be hard to say exactly.'

A small strangled noise rose in Gemma's throat and she tried to disguise it as a cough. Six weeks. Her vision blurred and swam. It wasn't enough.

'And I can go home?' Martha asked, evenly, but with a scratch in her voice. 'I don't want to die in a hospital.'

It was the following week that Martha had first mentioned the letters.

She'd shuffled off one day with the determination of someone about to do something their body wasn't capable of anymore, and as she always did, Gemma gave her the illusion of a head start before following her to help.

She'd found Martha on her knees by the side of her bed, grasping blindly for something underneath.

'Here,' Gemma said gently. 'I'll do it.' She laid a hand on her grandmother's shoulder, flinching slightly at how far her hand closed, how thin she was now. 'What is it you need?'

Martha sat back on her heels, her cough a rumble which ripped right through her. 'There's a shoebox under there. I can't see well enough to find it. It's green, with a shoelace tied around it. See if you can reach it.'

Gemma ducked down until she could see under the bed, eventually finding the shoebox tucked away behind stacks of books and piles of papers wrapped in bin bags. She pulled it out, sniffing and coughing at the dust she stirred in the process.

She looked back at Martha to find her eyes were filled with tears and a strange faraway look.

Gemma's brow knitted in concern. 'Nana, what is it?'

Wordlessly, Martha took the box, her frail fingers fumbling with the lace for a few moments before it came undone. She lifted the lid, running her fingers gently over the mountains of paper tucked inside, navigating mostly by touch.

The box was full of letters, each still in their envelopes, with only the ragged top edges giving away that they had even been opened at all. Their true age was betrayed by the fading of the ink and the darkening of the paper, but they had been kept with such care as to otherwise look almost brand new.

Martha pulled the first letter out of the box and handed it to Gemma as carefully as if it had been a bullion of pure gold. 'Open it.'

Gemma nodded, pulling the thin paper letter out of the envelope and smoothing it out, carefully. The delicate, looping cursive flickered and swam before her eyes.

'They were from your grandad.' Martha's voice was hoarse and small. 'While he was in France.'

Gemma knew precious little about her grandfather other than that he had fought in the war and that he'd died when her mother was a baby, but she could tell by the change in her grandmother's voice that these letters were a thing of great importance to her.

She swallowed back the lurch in her throat, the choking feeling which followed her around. She'd learnt to read when she was younger, but as soon as the text in her books shrank, her problem grew. The letters started to melt together, move and swirl and flash so much that she didn't know where one word finished and another began.

She'd started acting up, then. Playing the fool. Trying to distract people long enough for them to not question why she was falling behind. By the time she was in high school, the shame had grown and swelled in her like a sickness. And as shame often does, it attracted more shame, and joined by doubt and fear, shifted her into a version of herself that even she didn't recognise.

She almost whispered it: *I can't read, Nana.*

Martha's chuckle was soft and kind. 'I know that, my lovely. Gosh, I may be old, but I'm not stupid.' She smiled up at her granddaughter, misty eyes focusing on Gemma's face, but not quite meeting her gaze. 'These things happen. I only wish I'd have known when you were small, so I could have helped you. By the time I saw what was happening you wouldn't have accepted my help anyway.'

Gemma looked up at that, and the failing eyes looking back at her were edged in something she barely recognised. It wasn't judgement, or pity. It was understanding.

She felt a pang of something in her chest. Guilt, perhaps, or maybe regret.

Martha held her arms out and Gemma steadily helped her to her feet, walking them both back over to the ageing brocade sofa in the living room and easing Martha's tired body down gently before sitting down beside her, the shoebox on her knee.

They were both silent for a beat before Martha spoke again. 'I just want you to have them.' She paused again as another cough rattled through her. 'The love in this box has kept me going for a lifetime. Anytime I felt sad, or scared, I had his words to comfort me.' She smiled wistfully, her hand reaching out toward the box. 'It's been my safety. My sanctuary. I want that for you.' The corners of her mouth quirked up in a lopsided smile. 'Maybe one day you'll find someone who'll read them to you?'

Gemma laughed lightly past the lump in her throat. 'Maybe.'

'How we both could do with that now,' Martha said, with such sadness that Gemma almost couldn't stand it. It was the first time she'd shown anything other than quiet acceptance of her fate, and the longing in her voice now was palpable.

All at once, Gemma knew what she had to do.

It was a few days later when the knock on the door came.

Jamie Stamford was like a breath of fresh air on the doorstep that day, all wild curls and intense amber eyes, as Gemma opened the door to the full six-foot-whatever of him leaning lightly against the low wall of the porch.

She recognised him from school, of course. *Shit*, she'd made his life such a misery And she'd seen him once or twice in the village since she'd been back in Blackston, but up close he was not the awkward boy she had tortured back then. She could still see shyness in the slight hunch of his shoulders and his arms slung across his chest, but this man in front of her was tall, broad and just the right amount of handsome. And his voice, when he spoke, was warm and deep and made her breath catch in her throat.

'Gemma?'

She nodded, hot and unsteady all of a sudden. 'Yes, I... um. Jamie.' She took a deep breath, her residual guilt making her fingers knot and twist together. 'You're Jamie, I mean. I remember you.'

There was an openness in his smile as he studied her, and she appreciated his clemency.

'Look,' he started, simply, 'We have history, I know. But what's in the past is in the past. Let's start again.'

Her voice was small. 'I was awful to you.' She picked at her fingers, a nervous habit.

'You were obviously going through some stuff.' He shrugged and ran his fingers through his hair, pushing it away from his face. 'I survived. It's not a big deal.'

Gemma could do nothing but stare at him, dumbfounded. When she'd spoken to Father Kevin about his One Good Thing program she had requested something for Martha, but this forgiveness, this *acceptance* that Jamie was offering felt like a kindness for her, too.

He held out his hand, smiling brightly at her.

'Hi, I'm Jamie Stamford. Pleased to meet you.

27

THEN – July 1980

It had been raining for thirteen days straight and Zosia was most put out. After the beautiful weather they'd had all spring, the near-constant humidity of midsummer was doing nothing at all for her hair and even less for her foul mood.

Married now for three years, Zosia had still not been blessed with a baby, and the sharp feelings of loss and inadequacy were tearing through her each time she thought about it. It was straining her love for Ray, testing her relationship with her sister. And most of all, making her angry with herself, feeling there must be something missing, something she was doing wrong.

She shook the rain from her hair in a huff as she hurried into Nush's flat without knocking. It was the same flat that the sisters had shared, before Zosia and Ray married, and the door was rarely locked.

Something was different today, though.

She wasn't sure what it was, at first. Zosia had never been one for reading subtleties, but she could tell, beyond all doubt, that something was happening, and it made her feel uneasy.

'Nusia?' She ventured tentatively into the still air of the flat. Nothing.

Until... was that a groan? Zosia strained her ears. Then a mumbled response, another groan, and a pained retch.

Zosia wrinkled her nose in disgust, hovering hesitantly outside the small bathroom.

'Nusia, are you ill?'

'Mmm... I'm okay.' Nush's voice was heavy, even through the thin wood of the door. 'Be out in a second.'

Another cough, then running water. And when the door opened, Nush looked almost grey.

'Oh, you do not look well,' Zosia shrieked, taking a step back. 'No, don't give it to me!'

Nush laughed weakly, heading over to the sink to fill up the glass she was holding. 'Don't worry, I'm not contagious.' The action looked smooth. Practiced. And a horrible thought gripped Zosia and tugged, the mere idea sending her heart plummeting to her feet.

'Kochanie,' Zosia started, almost a whisper. 'Are you... pregnant?'

And the look on Nush's face then was answer enough.

Zosia would remember that moment for the rest of her life. That split second when her aching heart cracked and broke, the pain spreading through her body like a burning fire.

'Whose is it?' Zosia's voice was clipped – the demanding tone of a spurned lover moreso than a sister.

Nush didn't look at her. 'It was a mistake. We were only together one time.' Her voice dropped to a whisper. *'O Boże!'*

The fury rose and grew in Zosia like a fever. She believed unwaveringly in God, but that didn't stop her occasionally being very cross with Him indeed. How *dare* He bless her sister with a child from one poorly-judged act of passion when she had done *everything* right and still she was barren?

And who on earth could the father be?

Zosia frowned, before her mind took her back to that day at Nush's school. The handsome teacher. The softness in his eyes when he had spoken of her sister. Now, what was his name?

'Graham?' Zosia blurted, suddenly remembering. 'Was it Graham?'

Nush didn't say anything, but she looked around at her sister then, the expression on her face at once mournful and mortified.

Zosia took that as a *yes*.

'We need to go, anyway,' Zosia said, her tone short. 'Mass is at eleven.'

It was a tradition the sisters had. Zosia didn't like to celebrate the anniversary of their mother's death, so every year they celebrated her *imieniny*, her name day, instead. They'd go to morning mass and then stop off for lunch at the Polish centre afterwards, each saying their own silent prayers to her over *gołąbki* and lemon tea.

This year the mood at lunch was sullen, and Nush picked at her food, still a little green around the edges, while Zosia stabbed her forkfuls with barely concealed rage.

"Will you keep it?" Zosia all but hissed.

Nush's eyes filled with tears. "I don't know.' Her voice was a whisper. 'Can I? Would you help?'

Zosia huffed out a humourless laugh. 'Do I have a choice?'

Nush's gaze softened. 'Always.'

Zosia swallowed down the anger which rose in her throat as best she could. 'Well you can't get rid of it.'

Nush gasped. 'Don't speak of that here.'

'I mean, you can,' Zosia continued, her eyes holding her sister's in a challenge. 'If you want to burn in hell for all eternity.'

'Zosia!' Nush's voice was small, strangled.

'Of course, who's to say you won't burn in hell anyway for having a child outside of wedlock.'

'Zosia...' Nush said again, her tone more insistent.

But Zosia would have none of it. 'I know it's hard to hear, but it's the truth, Danusia.'

At that, Nush reached for her arm, squeezing urgently. 'Zosia, I think I'm bleeding.'

And despite her anger, the panic and sadness written through her sister's voice caught Zosia deep in the chest. It was a sadness she was only too familiar with, and as they hurried down the short path to the local hospital, Zosia reached for her sister's hand, wondering as she did if she had somehow caused this.

Had the depth of her despair been enough to tear the tiny life out of her sister?

And at that moment, had Zosia believed in such silly things, she might have wondered if there was a possibility that their family was cursed, their bloodline damned to disappear from history for all eternity.

28

Fourteen Missed Calls

Rae Logan was not ordinarily a woman who was at peace with her emotions, but she was a writer after all, and as such there was one emotion she could pull off particularly well.

Despair.

She'd spent the first few days after the fight almost entirely holed up in her room, emerging only for toast and tea and listening constantly to the drone of an especially melancholy singer-songwriter's album she'd accidentally stolen from Simon.

God, *Simon*. He had tried to call her thirteen more times since *that* time, and left her four separate voicemail messages. She hadn't listened to a single one.

By the seventh day, she'd taken to singing along with the droning, occasionally punctuated by a dramatic sob.

By the twelfth day, Nush had had quite enough.

'I know you're hurting, Gołąbeczku.' The gentle Polish lilt was Rae's only warning that she was about to be told off. 'But if I have to hear that racket for even one more day I will be hurting too, because I will have pulled my own ears clean off.' The corners of her slate-coloured eyes crinkled into a gentle smile. 'There is feeling pain, and there is causing pain, and somehow you are managing to do both at once.'

Rae pouted. 'Haven't you ever had your heart shattered into pieces so small you feared you'd never be able to gather them all together again?'

'Of course I have.' Nush's expression changed for a split second, pulling in tightly, before relaxing again just as quickly. 'And yet I managed not to take it out on the hearing of everybody around me.'

'Sorry,' Rae mumbled, her voice rough, worn to gravel by her sadness.

But Nush didn't need an apology. She pulled her niece into a tight hug.

Rae's tears returned at the intimacy, and she sniffed back a sob. 'Nush, how could he?'

Nush clucked her tongue in disapproval. 'He's a fool.'

On the nineteenth day, Nush was speaking to someone on the phone when Rae trudged into the kitchen, and from the ridiculous animation in her voice, Rae guessed that it was Kieran. The two were fast friends now.

Nush looked up at her as she walked it. 'She's here right now, actually.'

Rae harrumphed. 'Pretend I'm not.'

'No, she looks a bit better today.'

'I'm not better, my soul is slowly crumbling to dust.'

'She says she's feeling much better.'

Rae looked up at her aunt with a frown.

'I don't know, maybe you could take her out for lunch today

and find out?' Nush raised both eyebrows as a question.

'Absolutely not under any circumstances.'

Nush squealed. 'She says she'd love to! How about Jan's at twelve thirty?'

Rae huffed. 'I definitely do not consent to this.'

'Perfect! It's a date.'

And that was how, against her better judgement, Nush finally convinced Rae to leave the house.

It was a mild day in Blackston. The year was finally in full swing, gardens blooming in swathes of colour atop the vibrant green of new leaves as the sun beamed down from high in the sky. On another day, Rae would have stopped to appreciate it all, the contrast of pure, white blossom against sepia bark and branches, sitting just so against the cerulean sky. And she would have breathed in the thick scent of pollen and cut grass which hung in the air and appreciated how it all came together to make the perfect spring day.

But on this day she had her mind on one thing only, and that was getting from the mill to Jan's cafe and back without catching even a glimpse of Jamie Stamford.

Kieran was already at a table when Rae pushed gingerly through the door, and he bounded out of his seat with a squeal when he saw her.

'Oh sweetie!' He bundled her in a warm hug and she breathed in the now-familiar scent of him, of paint and designer aftershave.

'I missed you,' she mumbled, voice distorted by the press of her face against his broad chest, and she felt the vibration of his chuckle rumble through him.

'I missed you too, beautiful.' He broke the hug to smile

warmly at her, raising his hand to guide her to the table.

She sat, shrugging out of her jacket and scanning the room quickly. There was no sign of Jamie, and she felt her anxiety drop a notch.

'I'm glad you came,' Kieran said, almost carefully.

'I didn't want to.' Rae's lips twisted. 'Nush made me.'

'I know.' He smirked. 'I heard every word.'

Rae nodded. 'The two of you are a dangerous combination.'

At that, Kieran threw his head back and laughed heartily for a moment, before smiling brightly at her over the small table. 'She's like the mother I never had.'

'Wait.' Rae's brow furrowed. 'You don't have a mother?'

'Ok, I *do* have a mother.' Kieran's voice changed then, his eyes gazing off into the middle distance. 'But she's disowned me.'

'You're not serious,' Rae said, even though she could tell from the sudden change in him that he was.

Kieran didn't look at her. 'Yeah, she didn't much fancy a gay son.'

He said it simply, matter-of-fact, but there was an edge of something else, the nag of pain in his voice which caught Rae right in the chest.

She drew a breath in and reached out to touch his arm gently. 'I didn't know that.'

'Yep.'

His face tensed, just for a moment, as if he allowed himself only that brief second of self pity before he swallowed it back down, and his body language snapped back to the Kieran she recognised.

'Spoiler alert, babes.' He looked back at her for the first time since he'd mentioned his mother, now with just the faintest trace of sadness left in his bright eyes. 'Life's a bitch and people are arseholes.'

Rae's huff was softer that time, filled with understanding. 'Amen to that.'

Kieran grinned at her. 'So, what are you having? My treat. Hot chocolate with everything?'

'Not today.' Her mind played a montage of 'drinking at Jan's with Jamie' scenes like some low budget TV drama. ''Everything' feels too grand. Maybe hot chocolate with some things.' She breathed a dramatic breath out. 'Small things.'

Kieran couldn't hide his smirk. 'Oh petal, you are feeling all your feelings today, aren't you?'

'Don't laugh at me.' Rae's pout was more comical that time.

Kieran's smirk grew into a wide smile. 'Wouldn't dream of it.' He winked at her. 'Fancy back-to-backing three slices of cake with me? It's lemon drizzle.'

'Yes,' Rae said quickly. Then, 'No.' She sighed. 'Not in public anyway, maybe at home later. You know, because I'm a lady.'

'Sorry, you're what?' Kieran made a big thing of pretending not to hear and she rolled her eyes at his histrionics.

'A lady.'

'Ah, I thought you said because you're lardy.' The corner of his mouth quirked up in a smile.

Rae stared at him for a beat. 'I hate you.'

His smile grew. 'You *love* me.'

'Fine.' She huffed, but she was almost smiling.

Jan came over to take their order then - soup, a hot chocolate with everything for Kieran, and a hot chocolate with only some things for Rae, along with only one slice of Jan's homemade lemon drizzle cake each.

Jan smiled at Rae with the warmth of an old aunt as she

quickly scribbled down their order and left.

'So,' Kieran started, drawing out the vowel sound with theatrical flair. 'Jamie Stamford turned out to be a bit of a snake, eh?'

Rae ignored the sharp pain which ran through her body at the mention of his name. 'Looks that way.'

Kieran's brows pulled together thoughtfully, and he ran a hand through the mess of his auburn hair. 'You know I never saw that coming.' He played with a single curl which was hanging down into his eyes. 'I'm normally pretty good at reading people, you know? I dunno, he just seemed like a genuine guy.'

Rae pressed her lips together. 'Any chance we could not dwell too much on how wrong we all were?'

Kieran nodded seriously. 'So wrong.'

'You're still doing it!'

He shrugged. 'I really feel like I'm helping.'

Rae raised an eyebrow. 'I really feel like you're not.'

Kieran raised an eyebrow right back. 'Ok, fine. Let's talk about something else.' He made a show of adjusting himself in his chair. 'Tell me what you've been up to lately.'

Rae blew a quick breath through her nose. 'Moping and writing, mostly.' She half shrugged. 'I suppose at least all of this has given me some time to work on my book.'

Kieran brightened at that. 'Oh yeah? How's that going?'

'I dunno.' She looked down, fingers fidgeting. 'It's getting pretty dark. Maybe I should avoid the whole broken-hearted author cliché?'

Jan arrived with their order, and Rae was simultaneously both annoyed and delighted to see that her hot chocolate had been made with more everything than usual. Jan threw her a wink over her shoulder as she walked off.

Kieran wrapped his large hands around his mug. 'Isn't that what writers are supposed to do? Turn your pain into poetry and all that?'

'Maybe.' Rae paused to lick whipped cream off her spoon. 'But I'm pretty sure what I'm doing is just turning my pain into more pain. Only with really awkward metaphors.'

Kieran grinned. 'Well who doesn't love a really awkward metaphor?'

Rae opened her mouth to reply but was silenced by the rattle of her phone on the table.

They both watched in silence as the phone vibrated a pattern before the display switched to read: *Simon Collins - missed call (14).*

Kieran looked up at her pointedly. 'Looks like *someone's* trying to get hold of you.'

Rae widened her eyes in exasperation. 'Urgh Simon. What do you think he wants?'

He rolled his eyes dramatically. 'Um, you?'

Rae couldn't stop herself from snorting out a humourless laugh. 'Don't be daft. The last time I saw him he was balls deep in our super-glamorous neighbour.' She shook her head and gestured vaguely to her face. 'He wouldn't come back for all of this.'

'Well, honestly you've looked better...' Kieran started.

Rae cut him off with a snort. 'You're a good friend.'

He widened his eyes at her in mock frustration. 'But *yes he would* come back. Babycakes, they always do. A lot of people would kill for all of this.' He gestured vaguely to the same area as she had.

She huffed out a breath. 'Oh, like you'd know.'

He cocked his head to one side in confusion.

Rae continued. 'You know, with you being more of a hot dog guy than a... burger guy.'

Kieran reared back in horror. 'Rachel, no!' His face crumpled in disgust. '*Burger* guy? Really?'

She tried very hard not to smile. 'I thought it was a pretty good metaphor.'

'If that's what your think is a good metaphor then no wonder your book is where it is.' He shook his head, before catching her gaze as his tone turned serious. 'Honey, I may not want to buy what you're selling, but I know a good deal when I see one.'

This time Rae couldn't hold back her grin.

Kieran sat back in his chair with a flourish. 'Oh, good lord, was that a smile?'

Rae rolled her eyes.

'Eye rolling! Even better.' He raised his fork in triumph. 'Ladies and gentlemen, we are back in business!'

Rae hated to admit it, but Nush had been absolutely right. A couple of hours with Kieran had done her the world of good. She still felt the raw sting of Jamie's betrayal in every cell of her body, but she felt calmer now, filled with a quiet determination to carry on.

She said her goodbyes to Jan and to Kieran, who were now busy working out some details for craft club the following night, and stepped out into the brightness of the early afternoon sun. She squinted against it for a few moments, before she turned to walk back to the mill and collided with a very solid, very familiar body.

It took all the air out of her lungs for a moment.

'Rachel,' the familiar voice said, sounding as relieved as he was shocked.

Simon.

Her eyes finally adjusted to the light, and she looked up at him, still a little winded and more than a little confused. His face seemed familiar and jarring all at once. She noticed that his dark hair had grown out a little and couldn't help but think it looked good on him, although she would have died before telling him that.

'I've been trying to get hold of you.'

His hands moved to grasp her upper arms gently, and she shied away from his touch.

He didn't seem to notice her evasion, or if he did, it didn't deter him. 'I've called loads.'

Rae held her phone up, the missed call notification still visible on her screen. 'Yeah, I've been ignoring them.'

His sharp blue eyes bored into her. 'You won't want to ignore this.'

She had a sudden flashback to the moment she'd seen him in the kitchen with Carla. She wanted to be filled with rage, but for the life of her could muster little more than mild disinterest.

She raised an eyebrow. 'Does that line work for you?'

'Dammit, Rae, it wasn't a line.' His eyes were intense, filled with an emotion she couldn't put her finger on. 'I'm serious.' He took a steadying breath, ran a hand through his hair. 'Can we go somewhere and talk. I've... got something I need to show you.'

Rae rolled her eyes. 'I swear to God, Simon, if it's your penis I'm going to pull the damn thing clean off your body.'

'It's not... fuck's sake Rae!' His eyes widened in exasperation.

'This is important.' And there was something, some strange tension in his posture, some tone in his voice which told her that was the truth.

'Ok, fine.' She looked up at him, the relief clear in his face. 'You've got one chance. Any funny business and I'm out.'

He nodded.

She pulled her bag tighter on her shoulder. 'We can go to the mill, it's just up there.'

'Not the mill.' Simon's voice was tight.

Rae eyed him with suspicion. 'Fine. It's a nice day. We can sit on the bench that looks over Black Rock.'

They walked the short journey together in silence, and by the time they reached the bench, Simon's face was pale. She could see him working up to something.

God, she hoped it wasn't a declaration of love.

'Ok, so. The wedding...'

Rae braced herself.

'Remember when we went to apply for the licence, and we couldn't do it because you didn't have a passport?'

She crinkled her nose, confused. 'Yeah?'

Simon looked earnestly. 'So, you had to apply for your replacement birth certificate, cause you didn't have one of those, either.' It was a statement, but the intonation of his voice made it sound like a question. 'We had all that trouble getting it, do you remember? And we were going to go pick it up just after Christmas and sort everything out with the registrar, only I...'

'You fucked someone else,' Rae finished for him, matter-of-factly. The sting had long since gone from those words for her, but Simon visibly winced.

His blue eyes swam with remorse, but not with regret. 'Yeah, sorry about that.'

She shrugged. 'It's fine. If it hadn't been for that I guess we'd be married now, so I should be thanking you.'

'I guess so.' His smile was tight. 'Anyway, this came in the post a couple of weeks ago.' He reached into his inside coat pocket and pulled out an envelope addressed to *Mr R Collins*. The top edge had been opened roughly. 'I just read it as Mr Collins, so I opened it. We must have left both of our names and confused them.' He handed her the envelope. 'This is definitely for you though.'

She took it off him, reading over the address slowly while her brows pulled together in confusion. Her fingers found the paper inside and pulled it out.

Certified Copy of an Entry, the red text declared, and she noticed her own name and date of birth at the top.

She looked up at Simon. 'So, it's a copy of my birth certificate? This was 14 calls worth of urgent?' She laughed a little to herself before looking back at him. 'Maybe that's fair, I will need it for the next idiot I agree to marry.'

His eyes held hers steadily. 'Read it.'

She scanned the rest of the text.

Father: Raymond Joseph Logan, born 14th September 1949

Ok.

Mother: Danusia Magdalena Nowak, born 8th June 1950

Wait.

Rae's heart leapt into her throat. She read it again, slowly, pausing after every word to be sure her eyes weren't playing tricks on her.

Mother: Danusia Magdalena Nowak, born 8th June 1950

'This is a mistake, right?' She spoke out loud, more to herself than anything. 'I mean, they couldn't even get the name on the address right.'

'I doubt it,' Simon said gently. 'That's an official document.'

She turned back to Simon, eyes wild, heart hammering like a freight train.

'Nush is my mum?'

29

THEN – June 1980

There were few things in Danusia Nowak's life she handled well, but drink was one of them.

It had been a sticky-hot start to the summer, the air hanging humid and thick around the city, so when Zosia had suggested a trip to the coast to celebrate their birthday, Nush couldn't think of many reasons to disagree.

Just one reason, really.

Ray Logan.

The love of her life.

And her sister's husband.

He hadn't been her sister's husband when she fell for him, of course, but life seemed to have a plan for her which included shitting on her from a great height, and here she found herself; a trip to the beach on the eve of her thirtieth birthday, with her baby sister and the man she loved with all her heart but could never have. Happy birthday, indeed.

Born on the same day four years apart, the sisters had always been thick as thieves.

Their early lives had not been easy.

Refugees. Orphans. Foreigners.

As children they were like chalk and cheese, but once they emerged from of the safety of the camp, they soon found they had more in common with each other than either of them had with anyone else.

It had tested them, caused their emotions to flare like fire, but once the flame died down, a bond remained, tempered by all the bad in their lives and so strong as to be unbreakable.

Or so they thought.

Nush had met Ray first. They'd been at the same teacher-training college, Nush studying to teach Primary, Ray Secondary English.

He'd been standing at the bar of the student union one night in her first year when she'd popped in for a drink. He didn't have the most handsome face in the room, nor the loudest voice, and his plain-knit sweater and ageing jeans wouldn't have caught anyone's eye at first glance.

But Nush didn't just glance once. She could feel the pull of him from across the room, an unseen force which caught her gaze in its weight, pulling her back time and time again.

When she went to the bar, she felt him next to her before he spoke. He was a scent, an energy which drew her in, and when he opened his mouth, the deep timbre of his Edinburgh accent set permanent roots into her heart.

'Hey,' he said simply, and when she turned towards him, she was met with a smile which shattered her. 'I'm Ray. Ray Logan.' He held out his hand.

'Nush Nowak,' she smiled back, taking his hand and shaking it warmly.

And so began a friendship which should have lasted a lifetime.

The years passed, slowly at first, and then quicker and quicker, and before she knew it, Nush had been in love with her best friend for five years, and she hadn't breathed a single word about it. Not even to Zosia, who now joined them a lot of the time.

There were days when she would have bet her life on him returning her feelings. There was a heat in his eyes sometimes, a lingering glance. An edge in his voice when she talked about other men she was interested in. But it was so subtle. *Too* subtle.

If she had been braver, maybe if she had been surer, she might have gathered her courage. Talked to him. Been clear about how she felt. But Nush liked to be certain about things before she acted on them, and with Ray, certainty was in short supply.

But although there was a piece of her which longed for more from Ray, Nush was truly happy with their curious little trio.

Until that day one spring when Ray pulled the rug out from under her feet.

'I want to take your sister out,' he'd said, out of the blue.

They'd been sitting on the low wall outside the little cafe where Zosia worked, waiting for her to finish her shift.

Nush had felt her heart fall to her feet. When she replied, her voice was small. 'Oh. Ok…'

She'd kicked at the dirt under the wall, suddenly feeling very much younger than her twenty-five years.

Ray had paused for a beat, and then spoken again with a careful tone in his voice. 'Unless… there's a reason you're not ok with that?'

Nush had been blindsided. Speechless.

It had been all she could do not to cry right there at the side

257

of the road. She'd shaken her head quietly just as the bell over the cafe door opened and an exuberant Zosia had bounded out.

'Let me know if you think of anything,' Ray had said quietly, his gentle Scottish lilt doing nothing to soothe the churn of her insides. And he'd pushed himself away from the wall and gone to greet Zosia.

Nush never did give him a reason why not. She couldn't bring herself to.

Not two weeks later when Ray took Zosia out on their first date, and not three years after that, when the priest asked, at their wedding, if anyone present knew of any good reason why they should not be wed.

Her heart had been screaming the whole time, but her voice never uttered a sound.

And that was how she'd ended up alone on the beach at North Landing on the eve of her thirtieth birthday, soaking up the burning rays of the late spring sun.

They'd been drinking since lunchtime, sitting at the bar of the small guest house they'd found a mile inland, and as usual, Zosia and Nush had ended up arguing. It was over something and nothing. Fuelled by drink, Zosia had taken aim at Nush and fired, and ever the stoic older sister, Nush had simply taken it and walked away.

Literally walked away, a mile and a half down the road, until she'd happened across the perfect cove, and felt altogether very smug that she'd thought to grab her beach bag on the way out.

It was late in the afternoon, but the sun was still oppressively hot, and she welcomed the prickle of sweat starting to bead on her skin. She breathed a deep breath out, blew out all her anger, felt it catch and lift on the wind. And then it was only her, alone, lost in the sounds of the waves for what felt like hours.

Until she wasn't alone.

As was usual, she felt Ray there before she saw him, smelled the cut of the alcohol on his breath, heard the weight of his body thump into the sand next to her.

She opened an eye to squint at him, just in time to see his eyes snap up back to hers, dark and intense. It was an expression she hadn't seen on him before, and it sliced into her.

'Where's Zosia?' Her voice was thick.

'Drunk,' he said, the hint of laughter in his voice. 'She went to bed.'

Nush opened her other eye. 'You're drunk too.'

Ray smiled. 'A little.'

'A lot a little.' She smiled back at him, pushing her sunglasses up on her head and squinting against the glare of the light.

His speaking voice was deep and smooth, but when he laughed there was such a different sound, such a boyish chuckle which burst out of him that it caught her off guard every time. The sound hit her like a spark, warming, spreading through her body like an inferno.

She cleared her throat and drew her blouse back around her, suddenly ashamed.

He reached out, touched her arm gently. 'Don't.'

Her face flushed crimson. 'But I'm basically naked.'

'I've seen you in a bikini before.' His smile undid her. 'Don't be embarrassed. It's just me.'

She huffed out a small breath. 'You and all these people.'

She followed his gaze as he turned to look around the

small cove. There were a couple of young families, an older couple sitting on deckchairs further up the sand. No one to be concerned about, really.

No one except the man sitting next to her.

'Don't worry about them.' He turned back to her. 'They're not looking.'

She met his eyes. 'But you are.'

His eyes burned into her for a moment. Just a split second, but she felt it in every part of her. Then he coughed and looked away.

His voice was rough when he spoke again. 'Look, I'm sorry about Zosh. What she said... she...'

'It's ok,' she interrupted gently. 'You don't need to speak for her. I know very well what she's like.'

He nodded, and opened his mouth to speak again, but Nush silenced him with a small wave.

'Forget it.'

He smiled, offering out his hand. 'Deal.'

She took it, jumping slightly as she always did at the passing contact, his skin hot against hers.

Then he pulled off his shirt, using it as a pillow as he laid down in the sand next to her, arms behind his head, eyes closed. She pulled her sunglasses back down over her eyes and tried hard not to study every detail of his body as her curls whipped and snapped in the sea breeze.

They stayed like that, in a comfortable silence, and his breathing grew so rhythmic and steady that she had thought he was asleep. Up until the point that he spoke.

'That felt like rain.'

She frowned at the sky, just as a big droplet fell right on her nose and she squealed in glee. It was such a welcome feeling -

cool and refreshing against the unrelenting heat of the day.

Then all of a sudden the sky was the colour of slate and the rain was hammering down. The other people on the beach fled, and it was just the two of them; drunk, soaked to their skins and giggling like small children.

Nush packed her towel back into her small bag and skipped about happily on the beach, face to the sky, feeling as free as she could ever remember feeling in her life.

She saw the flash when it came, and before she could turn to see where it had come from, Ray's hand was in hers and he was pulling her, guiding her into one of the small tunnels in the rocky edge of the cove.

'I was dancing,' Nush started to object as he pulled her deeper into the rock, before the tunnel opened out into a small cave.

He spun back around to face her, breathing hard. 'Well, you won't be dancing if you get struck by lightning, Nush, and I can't…'

He didn't finish his sentence. His breaths still came heavily, sandy hair messily pushed back from his face and dripping rivulets of water down onto his shoulders, down his chest and then further, eventually disappearing into the fabric of his running shorts, which were soaked through and plastered to every inch of him.

Every. Inch.

She couldn't stop herself staring. Couldn't stop the heat rushing through her body, the heartbeat thundering in her ears. He hadn't let go of her hand, and she couldn't move, or think, or breathe with him so close.

'Ray, I…' She didn't even know what she wanted to say.

His eyes dropped to her lips, just for a second, then back up, boring into her with such ferocity that she could barely stand it. She didn't know who moved first, but all at once it was like the touchpaper had been lit and from there everything happened in flashes.

His mouth on hers, soft at first and then harder, deeper. The warmth of his skin underneath her fingers. The fresh smell of sweat and the sweetness of whiskey on his breath. The roughness of his sandy hands on her body. The absolute lack, for that time, of any appearance from her conscience.

He was just Ray, and she was just Nush, and in that moment there was just the two of them, and everything unspoken in the years which had passed. Like the thunderstorm, there was a charge in the air that they were both powerless to resist.

His hands were around her hips, pulling her into him urgently, and he was hot and wet and hard against her as he whispered words she couldn't remember while he looked at her in a way she could never forget.

He kissed her like his life depended on it.

She kissed him back like it was the only chance she'd ever get.

When he reached for her bikini bottoms, she didn't stop him, only wriggled her hips to make it easier to get the damp fabric off. And then her hands were at his waistband, fumbling, grasping. Pulling his shorts to his knees as her breath caught in her throat at the sight of him.

And when he pushed inside her there was a second, just a small moment of time, when absolutely nothing existed outside of the two of them.

Her conscience showed up later, as he held her, their breathing starting to slow. And when it came it crashed over her like a wave, heavy and immediate, drowning her in regret as she lay in the arms of the man she loved. The man who, before God, had promised his life to her sister.

'Nush,' he said, his voice raw, something about the intonation strange, as if he had more to say. But he didn't say anything else.

She turned away from him, pulling free from his arms, with her heart sinking like a stone in her chest and her eyes burning with tears. She pulled her bikini back into place, scrabbled around in her bag for her clothes, covered herself.

When she looked back, Ray had his shorts back on and was watching her, his expression somewhere between shell shock and some kind of relief.

Her voice was small when she spoke. 'What did I do?'

He reached out for her. 'It was both of us.'

'I can't…' she started, pulling away.

He cleared his throat. 'We have to tell Zosia'

Her heart dropped to the pit of her stomach. 'We can never tell her. *O Boże! O Jezu!*' She felt sick. 'How could I betray her like this? She's my sister.' She looked back up at him and the look on his face tore her in two.

'But…'

She closed her eyes against the guilt twisting up into her guts. 'Seriously, just erase every last detail from your mind. Imagine it never happened.'

Something changed in him at that, some imperceptible shift. 'We can't just forget it.' His eyes were dark. He spoke slowly. 'I can't just forget it.'

She recognised the expression on his face. It was an emotion she had seen a lot of in her life. He was hurting. She had hurt him.

She went to him. Took his hand in hers. 'Please.' Her voice

263

was soft. Her other hand went to his face, stroked the soft hair on his cheek.

And, like a reflex, he reached for her in return, his fingers gently cradling her face as he rested his forehead against hers.

She blew an unsteady breath out. 'When my mama died...' she started, feeling his fingers tense a little against her cheeks at the words, '...one of the last things she asked of me was to take care of Zosia.' A small sob rose in her throat. 'I'm the only family she has. She needs me.'

'And what about you, Nush?' His voice was low. 'What about what *you* need?'

She swallowed down another sob, her voice almost a whisper. 'If you care even a little bit about either one of us, please don't tell her.'

He looked at her for a beat, and then he brought his lips to hers. The kiss was different that time; soft and slow, filled with a rawness and a longing which brought her to her knees.

She should have pulled away. She would have pulled away, but in the moment she recognised it for what it was.

He was kissing her goodbye.

'Please,' she whispered again after their lips parted, and they stood as they had been, foreheads still touching, for a long time.

'Aye,' he said, eventually, and after that he said nothing.

She felt every step of their silent walk back to the guest house. Felt her heart shatter into a million pieces as Ray let himself into the room he was sharing with Zosia, and when she went separately to her room, she flopped down on her bed and cried until her throat was raw.

And as the three of them sat down to their subdued breakfast the following morning, Nush knew with absolute certainty that nothing would ever be the same again.

30

She Knows

It was past four by the time Nush heard the familiar sound of the mill door opening.

She'd expected Rae back two hours before, as she'd caught sight of Kieran leaving Jan's and walking back up the hill to the car park. When there was no sign of Rae by three, she wracked her brain for ideas of where she could be. She even conjured up fantasies of some kind of reunion with Jamie, but then she saw him walking, alone, across the village and into Jan's a little afterwards. And she knew Rae wasn't at Jan's, because she'd called Jan three times to check.

By the time Nush heard Rae's key in the door and the heavy thump of her kicking off her boots, she was positively bubbling over with excitement.

That is, until she saw the look on Rae's face, red-rimmed eyes stark against the pallor of her skin. Nush had become quite used to Rae's varying expressions of anguish over the last couple of weeks, but there was something different about her now which caused a small surge of panic to swell behind her ribcage.

'Oh Myszko! Nush could feel the shake in her voice. 'You look as if you've seen a ghost.'

Rae laughed a little, barely more than an exhale, and there was no humour behind it. 'I do want to talk about ghosts, actually.' She moved towards Nush, but kept her eyes down, fixed on something she was holding in her hand. 'About your ghost, specifically.'

'What...?' Nush's panic amplified, screaming up into her throat as her words deserted her and she felt the tug of long-held secrets beginning to twist and loosen in her grasp.

She knows.

Rae looked up, their eyes meeting for the first time since she walked in.

'It was my dad, wasn't it?'

And in that second, Nush felt as if the ground had been pulled from under her, like the earth beneath her feet was crumbling and she was falling much too far and too fast to stop.

She said nothing. What could she say?

'There's something else, too, isn't there?' Rae's voice was low, even. She gently pulled a document out of the envelope she'd been clutching and held it up between two fingers.

Nush couldn't make out much, just the distinctive contrast of the red print again cream paper. She had the original copy of that document, hidden away so carefully that she probably would have been dead before anyone found it. Her breath caught in her throat. She had longed for this moment almost as much as she'd dreaded it.

'What do you want to know?' Her voice was almost a whisper.

Rae held her gaze for a beat. 'Just the truth.'

Nush took a deep breath. 'It looks like you've already found that.'

'So, it's true?' Rae's voice was edged in anger, but underneath that there was something else, and although Nush didn't quite dare to believe it, it sounded a lot like hopefulness. 'I'm your daughter?'

It was the first time Nush had ever heard the words out loud, and they pulled every last bit of air from her lungs, her heart all at once as full and as empty as it had ever been. It felt as if it were someone else's voice when she finally replied. 'You are.'

Rae's breathing faltered. Her eyes brimmed with tears, but they didn't fall. Her inhale, when it came, was shaky, catching along the way with the enormity of her discovery.

Very slowly, very carefully, she put the certificate back into the envelope and set it down on the table before she looked back up. 'Were you ever going to tell me?'

'Honestly? No. I wasn't.' She felt an apologetic tug of emotion somewhere in her chest, but she couldn't lie. Not about this. 'Your dad, he wanted to. But I couldn't. It would have broken your mama's heart.' She flinched as she thought of Zosia. This would still break her heart.

'Didn't you think I deserved to know?' Rae's voice was even. It wasn't an accusation.

'Would it have changed anything?'

'It would have changed *everything*.'

Nush felt her own tears then, biting at the back of her eyes. So many times over the years she'd swallowed them down, put on a brave face as her heart splintered in her chest. It was almost a relief to let them fall. Her voice caught in her throat and broke as she said the only thing she could think to say.

'I'm sorry.'

And she stood there in her kitchen, motionless for a moment but for the bobbing of her throat and the small clenching and unclenching of her fists. Her sobs came in waves then, a tidal wave of grief which swept away all the small details of her life and laid bare all the things she had lost. All the things she had given up.

It felt impossible. *Insurmountable.*

Until she felt a warm hand take hers and squeeze softly. When she opened her eyes, Rae was standing with her, Nush's pain reflected clearly in her eyes. And it soothed her, a little. Just enough to stop the raw sting of her pain from cutting right through her.

'Tell me now,' Rae said, simply, her hazel eyes warm and open.

Ray's eyes, Nush thought, and the loss gripped her, as it always did. She breathed through it. 'What?'

'Tell me the story now.'

Nush huffed gently. 'Where do I start?'

Rae shrugged lightly, her face soft with understanding. With forgiveness. With love.

'At the beginning,' she said, the light back in her voice at last. And her smile then was the sweetest sight Nush thought she had ever seen.

Nush nodded and went to the kettle, fell easily back into that comforting routine, and over steaming mugs of lemon tea she told her daughter everything.

About how she'd met Ray, how she fell for him. How she'd never been sure enough to act on it. How she'd watched him marry her sister and not been able to say a single word to stop him. About the day on the beach, and how Ray hadn't looked her in the eye for weeks afterwards. How everything had changed that day, in so many ways.

She told Rae about the day she'd found out she was pregnant. How desperately alone she'd felt. About the look on Ray's face when she'd told him. How, overcome with emotion, he'd turned up at the hospital when they'd thought she was losing the baby and blurted everything to Zosia, and how that had torn the sisters' relationship irreparably into tiny pieces of what it once was.

How angry she'd been when Ray had first come to her with the idea that Zosia could adopt the baby. How hollow she'd felt when she realised that keeping her would mean she would end up absolutely alone. How desperately she'd hoped the act of selflessness would repair her relationship with her sister.

She told Rae about the brutally cold February night that she was born, how Ray made it to the hospital but Zosia had visited a friend in the next town and ended up snowed in. About how it was just the two of them again, for that one night, and how, through all the pain of labour, Ray never left her side. How they had both cried when a tiny, squawking Rae had been bundled up and laid gently in Nush's arms, and how Nush had cried again, alone, when a nurse brought in the adoption papers the following day.

She told Rae how she'd ended up running away to Blackston then, only a few months after the adoption was finalised, completely alone after all, but much too late to do anything about it.

And most importantly of all, Nush told her daughter how she never, not even for a single second, stopped loving her with every ounce of her being.

And when Nush had told Rae everything she felt so much

better, as if she'd let out a breath she'd been holding for three decades. She had needed this so badly and not even known it.

'I can only hope, Kwiatuszku,' Nush said, now nursing her second cup of tea, 'that you find some way to learn from the mistakes I have made.'

Rae regarded her with careful eyes. 'But it wasn't just a mistake, was it?' She took a thoughtful sip. 'You were in love with him.'

Nush nodded slowly, her eyes bright with tears, her smile soft and sad.

'But he didn't love you?'

'Maybe in some way he did. I don't know.'

Rae's brows drew together. 'You never asked?'

Nush's smile only reached one corner of her mouth. 'Never.'

'And now...' Rae started, more to herself, before realising and quickly stopping herself.

Nush's heart seized in her chest, but she smiled through it. 'Now I'll never know.'

'Nush...' Rae's eyes were a plea, an apology.

'You don't have to sugarcoat it for me, Kochanie.' Her voice was steady. 'I remind myself of this every day.'

Rae smiled gently, and the two women sat in easy silence for a while, each entirely lost to separate thoughts of what could have been.

It was Rae who finally spoke. 'Remember when I was small and I used to tell you that I wished you were my mum?'

Nush nodded. She remembered every single time. Each had been a sharp blade straight through her heart.

Rae's eyes were soft. Contemplative. 'I mean, I didn't know.' Her fingers toyed with the slim handle of her mug. 'I'm just saying maybe, in some way, I did.'

271

Nush's brows pulled together. 'What do you mean?'

Rae smiled, the merest hint of tears in her eyes. 'Because you've always felt like home.'

And with that one sentence, it was as if she had taken all the small fragments of Nush's broken heart and slowly begun to piece them back together.

31

The Black Rock

"Black Rock gets its striking colour from the rich black of the jet and igneous rock which makes up its composition, which local geologists have estimated dates back around 200 million years. Jet is often found in seams of shale on this section of the North Yorkshire Jurassic coastline, and the geology of Blackston in no different, but over time, the softer sedimentary rock of the cliffs to each side have worn back to leave the proud structure of Black Rock jutting out into the North Sea.

In past times, the seams of jet have been mined to varying degrees, but the issuing of a protection order in 1992 put a stop to all mining activity so that the prized namesake of the village could be preserved in its entirety.

Black Rock stands today as a constant, a landmark, a muse. A shelter where, out of sight of their parents, the youth of the village are afforded the freedom to frolic as they wish on the sheltered shores of the southernmost section of Blackston Bay. The author can only wonder how many secrets Black Rock has known over the years."

- F.W. Merryfield, *A Brief History of Blackston Bay*

32

It's Not Rational

I t had only been two weeks since the last craft club, but when Rae Logan stepped through the door of Jan's cafe the following Tuesday, it felt like a homecoming.

'You've got me again today, ladies,' Kieran's warm voice boomed from somewhere at the back of the cafe. 'Penny's helping Father Kevin out with an errand at the moment. She'll pop along later.'

Nush turned to raise a single eyebrow. Rae giggled and shushed her, although she'd be very surprised if the others had even noticed over the much louder sound of them swooning over Kieran as he effortlessly brushed his russet mop out of his face.

He winked at Rae as he caught her eye and she felt a small bloom of warmth in her chest. However single and alone she felt, however wronged, she had never felt less lonely. She'd found her place here in Blackston, found her *family*, and she couldn't imagine ever wanting to leave.

They sat around two tables as Kieran began to explain the evening's project.

'This evening I will be teaching you the fine art of decoupage,' Kieran said with a flourish, dragging out the last syllable dramatically. 'I have brought you each one of these very, very plain terracotta plant pots, and you are going to make them very, very beautiful.'

And the ladies oohed and ahhed around him as he spread out his vast array of delicately patterned papers and coordinating paint colours and carefully explained the whole process.

Rae picked out a sunny yellow colour and a paper with pretty botanical illustrations on, and set to work carefully sponging on a layer of paint as Kieran had showed them, her brow furrowed in concentration. Beside her, Nush was tearing a bright, tropical-print paper into long strips.

'We missed you last week, Rachel,' Iris Atkins chirped, cheerfully painting her pot rose pink.

Edie Dunham snorted cordially. 'Off gallivanting with her fancyman, no doubt!'

She smiled across the table and Rae could almost feel Nush and Kieran stiffen in defence.

Rae cleared her throat. Braced herself. 'He's not my fancyman anymore, Edie.' She forced a smile. 'Not so fancy, it turns out.'

Three faces looked up at her with expressions of surprise and sympathy while Edie's face fell. 'Oh, sweet pea, I'm so sorry, I didn't know.'

'It's ok. I guess it just wasn't meant to be.' It wasn't like Rae to dispense such platitudes, but heartbreak was wearing down her eloquence.

She felt a small wave of sadness begin to rise in the pit of her belly, but then, from the corner of her eye, she saw Nush raise another eyebrow, and she turned to see her slate grey eyes crinkle into a smile. As always, it was as if Nush could read her thoughts.

Jan brushed through the beaded curtain of the kitchen, setting a tray full of drinks in the middle of the table before taking her mug and sitting back down in her chair, smoothing her apron over her knees the way she always did. She paused for a few moments before speaking again.

'Did you hear about the Harpers?' She stirred her coffee and took a long sip. 'They've been sentenced.'

Rae felt Nush's energy change next to her. Nush loved a bit of gossip, and this was *big*. News from the Harper case was all over the village at the moment.

'I didn't know they'd reached a verdict,' Rae said, concentrating on her second layer of paint.

'Guilty,' Nush declared with a flourish. 'It was unanimous. The evidence was overwhelming.'

'I haven't really been following it,' Caroline Connolly said from the other table. She was a newcomer to craft club, but Caroline had quickly become one of the family. No one was really a stranger in Blackston. Not for long.

Jan blew out a dramatic breath, her brightly painted lips quirking into a grin. 'Have you been living under a rock?'

Caroline laughed softly. 'I've got a fifteen-year-old and a full-time job. I've got a lot on!'

'They were killing people.' Nush put her paper strips down on the table and picked up her pot as she spoke. 'Hired hits, you know?'

Jan didn't even feign interest in her pot as she chimed in. 'Mags used her estate agency to lure them in. She'd ring the victims to set up a viewing, spin them some yarn about how the house was a once in a lifetime deal, wouldn't be on the market long, you know, so they needed to go see it the same day.'

'Less chance they'd tell someone where they were going, then,' Nush added dramatically.

Rae smiled to herself. She had always loved Nush and Jan as a double act.

Jan nodded emphatically. 'So, she'd drive them out to see these properties, and offer them something to drink while she drove, only the drinks were poisoned with something or other.'

'Jeremy was a vet, you know.' Nush set her pot down, surrendering entirely to the account. 'He had access to *all manner* of substances'

'Yes!' Jan smiled broadly at her friend. The rest of the craft club were enthralled. 'So, she'd drive around with them in the car until she could be sure they were either dead or well on the way, and then under cover of darkness, she'd drive back to the vet hospital where she'd meet Jeremy, and together the two of them would throw the poor bugger into the incinerator.'

Rae laughed a little to herself. 'Wow.'

Jan carried on, regardless. 'Those things can turn a full cow to charcoal in a few hours.'

Kieran's laugh erupted from him like a gun firing, a single *HA!* which immediately gave Rae the giggles. He caught her eye and, widening his, mimed zipping his lips closed, which only made her want to laugh more. She coughed the urge away as best she could.

'And the reason they washed their car every day,' Nush concluded theatrically, 'was so that it didn't look suspicious when they actually did need to clean any evidence away. So, the neighbours were so used to it they wouldn't bat an eyelid.'

Rae actually did laugh at that. 'Except the neighbour they chose to move next to obviously batted several eyelids. You two had them all figured out, didn't you?'

Kieran snorted. 'Ever thought about fighting crime together?'

'Jowett and Nowak, I love it!' Rae chuckled, smiling warmly at them both. She mimicked Jan's brash voice. 'It was all in the rhododendrons, Sir!'

Jan shook her head gravely. 'Oh, they weren't putting the ashes on the plants. Apparently that would hinder their growth. Jeremy was just buying really good fertiliser.'

There was a moment of silence then, an interim before Kieran's laughter burst out again into the quiet of the cafe and before long every one of them was laughing.

'It's not funny,' Iris said, wiping at her eyes as she spoke through her laughter. 'People died.'

But that only made them laugh harder.

And, as was usual, for craft club, once the mirth had died down, they all felt the subtle peace of their outside worries fading. It wasn't until Flora Dunham spoke that the chuckles stopped completely.

'Why, though? Why did they do it?' Flora, Edie's great-granddaughter, was the youngest of the group by some way. She was a shy scrap of a thing, with a pretty face and long, poker-straight hair which hung over her face, shielding her from the rest of the world.

'Why does anyone do what they do?' Iris didn't lift her eyes from the delicate bird motif she was cutting out. It wasn't even a question.

Edie smiled sadly at her great-granddaughter. 'There are

good people in the world, Flora, but there are some bad ones too. There's no telling why people do the things that they do.'

'It's money, normally,' Jan declared confidently. 'Money or love.' She picked her pot up at that point, but only to use it as punctuation. 'Even when people have it, they just want more. When it comes to those two things, people go a little crazy.'

Rae huffed quietly. 'Don't they just?'

The bell over the door rang then, and Penny shuffled into the cafe with a small smile and a wave, dumping the cardboard box she was holding on one of the free tables and pulling up the spare chair next to Flora. The others smiled at her quickly, looking up from their projects, before Edie spoke again.

'I'll tell you a crazy story. Or a love story. They're the same thing, aren't they?' The corners of her dark eyes creased and folded as she smiled a little to herself, remembering. 'It was the summer of 1952, the year the Queen came to the throne. I started seeing a man around the village, a very handsome man. Put together, you know?' Her wisps of eyebrows quirked into a frown momentarily as she paused to brush paste over the strip of paper she'd just added to her pot. 'Well, he swept me off my feet, I might say. He was all talk of the future, full of stories for where we'd marry, how our life would be. He was so handsome, it was all I could do not to stare at him all day. I was so in love with him I didn't know what to do with myself.'

Edie paused and looked up at the others, all now enthralled by the story, frozen in suspense with whispers of smiles touching their faces. But when she smiled back Rae didn't miss the edge of something else. Some long-buried heartbreak behind her eyes.

'Then one day I told him I was carrying his baby.' Her face fell, the hurt in her expression palpable. 'Well, that was that.

He left town the same day and I never saw him again.'

The room was shocked into silence. Someone gasped.

'Are you serious?' Caroline's voice seemed smaller than usual.

Edie shrugged lightly, barely a movement, as her lips pressed into a humourless smile. 'As serious as I've ever been.'

'What happened?'

'Oh, I was devastated. Not to mention the shame. Things are different now, but can you imagine the shame I felt then? An unmarried girl, expecting a child.' She shook her head.

Rae felt Nush stiffen beside her.

'But then I met my Arthur.' Edie's eyes changed then, warmed and lifted, and she looked up at the others. 'I met him one day walking by the beach and I just *knew*. He'd just moved here, so I assumed he didn't know my story. I was so worried to tell him about the baby, I avoided it for weeks. Then one day we were out for a walk and I fainted! Right there on the side of the road like some kind of Victorian gentlewoman. I was so embarrassed, you can imagine, and I just blurted it out by accident. I was so scared, positive he'd have nothing at all to do with me.'

Every face in the room was turned towards her as she spoke, hands unmoving on their projects.

Edie continued. 'Well, it turned out he knew the whole time. We married just before the baby was born and he raised her as if she were his own.' She looked up then, eyes seeking them all out in turn, before resting on her great-granddaughter. 'He was a good man, God rest his soul.'

Flora nodded back, her eyes glinting with tears. 'Sounds like a fairytale, Nanny.'

Iris huffed, stabbing her brush into the leaf green paint she'd chosen with all the elegance of a caged hog. 'Marriage isn't always a fairytale, Flora. I wouldn't get your hopes up.'

The mood in the room changed then, all at once, with the group wearing expressions which ranged from shock to amusement. Kieran caught Rae's eye and smirked, and it was all Rae could do not to laugh out loud.

Iris seemed oblivious to the reaction she'd caused. 'Don't get me wrong, it's fine. But my Ernie's neither use nor ornament these days.' The sound she made was almost a snort. 'When we're alone in the house I sometimes turn my hearing aid off so I don't have to listen to him talking.'

Rae couldn't help but chuckle to herself that time, setting off a ripple of laughter through the room.

Caroline took a deep breath, calming her giggles. 'You know, I'd settle for fine. Spencer's dad left us when he was five. Turned out he was sleeping with his son's reception teacher.'

'No he wasn't!' Jan exclaimed, almost dropping her pot.

Caroline nodded sadly, and the collective intake of breath nearly sucked all the air out of the room.

'What did you do?' Nush's voice was gentle.

'What could I do?' Her voice was calm, resigned. 'I ran away. Came back to Blackston to be near my parents.' She paused, scissors in hand, and looked up at the group. 'That was ten years ago and I haven't been on a single date since.'

Rae could almost hear the cogs whirring in the ladies' minds as they catalogued any potential suitors they might know. If there was anything the ladies of Blackston loved as much as gossip, it was matchmaking. She smiled to herself. Caroline was in for a real treat.

The room fell quiet for a while, punctuated only by the

sounds of snipping and dabbing and the faraway sound of a dog barking when Flora's small voice carried over them all.

'I've never been on a date at all.'

Everyone looked up at her with a start, her cheeks flushing deep red. She looked as if she were about to cry, or to run away, but she did neither. She took a deep breath and spoke again. 'There's a boy at school, in my art class. The way he looks at me I sometimes think...' Her soft laugh held no humour. 'Anyway, what if I'm wrong about it and he laughs at me? Or, worse, we're not friends anymore?'

'What if you're right about it?' Kieran's deep voice piped up from the other side of the cafe. He fixed his gaze on Flora, his eyes soft and kind and steady.

'It's scary.' Her nerves were evident in the subtle shake of her words, but she didn't break eye contact with him.

'Yeah. It is.' Kieran nodded, sweeping his hair artfully back, out of his eyes. 'And I wish I could tell you you'll never have your heart broken, but you will. Probably more than once.' His smile was wide, with no trace of the sadness which edged into his voice. 'Flora, I've had my heart ground totally to dust more times than I can count.'

Flora blushed again at the sound of Kieran saying her name, her mouth twisting into a shy smile. But she didn't stop looking at him.

He smiled back at her as he carried on. 'But I've loved so hard with it. And you know, the good bits... well...'

'The good bits make up for the bad,' Rae finished for him, shocking herself as much as anyone.

Every pair of eyes in the room moved from Flora to Rae, the weight of their questions hanging heavy in the room. It was Caroline who put them into words.

'What happened with Jamie?'

'Something's happened with Jamie?' Penny asked from across the room.

Rae braced herself, saying only as much as she felt could without losing her cool. 'It was going great. I *thought* it was going great. But he's been sneaking around with another girl.' She blew a quick breath out of her nose. 'I confronted him about it and he lied to my face.'

Penny's expression changed at that, and there was something in her eyes which Rae couldn't place. Some small shift which registered somewhere. 'Wow, what? I honestly didn't think he was the type.'

Jan snorted, one painted eyebrow raised. 'They're *all* the type!'

'I don't know. I don't think that's true.' Penny shrugged. 'I like to believe that people are mostly good.' She didn't say anything for a minute or two, but she didn't move either, a motionless hunch over the pot she was painting. When she spoke again, it was with a caution which sounded foreign on her lips.

'I was married once, you know. While we're sharing.' She laughed, but there was no sound to it.

Rae looked at her curiously. 'Was?'

'He left one day. We'd been married ten years.' She pulled her gaze away, over-concentrated on her task. 'Just said he couldn't do it anymore and moved out the next day and that was that.' Her voice was hollow, nothing at all like her usual energetic chirp. 'We didn't have any children, that made it easier. The worst part of it all was that when I really thought about it, when I looked back over all the time we spent together, I knew that he was right to do it. We weren't happy together. We just weren't a good fit. How could I not have known until then?'

She looked up, eyes rimmed with sorrow, and there was a catch in her voice when she spoke again, though she tried to hide it with a smile. 'Oh, I'm being all silly over nothing now. He was a good man, and I don't blame him for doing what he did. I just wasn't ready for it to be over.'

Rae smiled back at her, nodding lightly in recognition before picking her pot up and tapping the paint lightly, testing.

'I left my husband for a woman.'

Jan's statement cut through Rae's concentration, her head flying up in shock.

'Whaaat?!'

'High five!' Kieran mimed the action from across the room and Jan reciprocated with a giggle.

'Met her when I was working in a restaurant in town. She was the chef and I was the head waitress.' Jan spoke with the same pace and drama that she had when recounting the details of the Harper case. 'This was the eighties, you didn't get a lot of lady chefs then, and I was completely in awe of her. No one had ever been able to put me in my place before, but she could.' Her eyes drifted off in thought, her features wistful.

Iris all but gasped. 'Jan, I never knew you were a...a...'

'A lesbian, Iris?' Kieran asked with a smirk. 'It's ok, you can say it.'

Iris flushed crimson with embarrassment and she firmly concentrated her gaze back on her plant pot.

Jan's eyes vanished into her laugh. 'I don't know that I am. I've only been with men since. There was just something about her, wow.' She shook her head, a nostalgic smile tugging at the corners of her mouth. 'She hit me like a ton of bricks, and I never really got back up. We didn't work out, of course. Ah, we tried to make it work for years and it just never quite did, but I don't know. I keep looking for someone who makes me feel like she did, but it's been thirty years now, and no one's even come close. I think she might have been my one.'

Edie nodded sagely. 'The one that got away.'

Rae's voice was almost a whisper as she looked over at Nush. 'Your ghost.'

And Nush, with a sad smile, could only reply, 'I know a thing or two about those.'

Something changed in the room then. Some frequency, a feeling. Most of the craft club members had never heard Nush speak about her past before, and the air was tense with wonder at how much of her life she would share. They all listened attentively as Nush set down her pot and papers.

'I spent most of my life loving my best friend, and I never told him. And now he's dead.' Her voice was unrecognisable, high and tight without the faintest trace of an accent. She reached for her tea before she carried on with her story, stirring gently before taking a sip.

'I didn't want to be the one to make the first move in the beginning, you know? I was never sure about how he felt. He was never *clear*. And then it got complicated, and I *couldn't* tell him.' She spoke slowly and cautiously, as if deliberating each word. 'That man was the centre of my universe for forty years and he never knew it.'

She took another sip of her tea, looking up at the faces watching her, but not quite meeting their eyes. 'There wasn't anyone else. I didn't have space in my heart for anybody else. Even now he's gone, even though he was really never even mine, I can't imagine ever feeling that for someone else. It doesn't make any sense. It's...'

'It's not rational,' Penny finished for her, her voice soft with understanding.

Nush looked straight at Penny for a beat before her face softened and she nodded gently. 'That's it.' She tilted her head to the side, eyes still on Penny, and something in her expression changed. 'Do you have someone now?'

Rae tried to hide her smirk. That was so *Nush*. Trying to dig for gossip in the midst of a heartfelt moment. She caught Nush's eye momentarily, lifting one eyebrow, but Nush just smiled innocently back, before turning her attention back to Penny, who was winding up to tell a story.

'No. Well, yes. I mean... no, not really.' Penny's hesitancy piqued Rae's interest. There was a story there. 'I mean, there is someone. But he doesn't know and he never will.'

She flushed with embarrassment, hands moving to fidget with the chain around her neck, and she had to catch her breath before speaking again.

'I have feelings for someone, all kinds of crazy feelings that I didn't even have with my husband, but I've already come to terms with the fact that being with him isn't a possibility.' She laughed quietly, an undertone of longing colouring the sound. 'Ah, at my age I may as well just put myself out to pasture and be done with it.'

Rae laughed. 'I might join you.'

'Oh, please,' Jan scoffed. 'You've got your whole life left. So, you've had a bad run. So what?' Rae couldn't see Jan from where she was sitting, but she sounded as if she had her hands on her hips. 'Not every man is going to run off to the Gemma Brannigans of this world.'

At that, Penny drew in a sharp intake of breath. 'Wait, what?' She pointed at nothing in particular before bringing the finger back to her lips thoughtfully. 'Jamie's sneaking was with *Gemma Brannigan.*'

Jan snorted in derision at the mention of her name.

Rae looked over at Penny, her smile sad, resigned. 'Yep. Nush saw him going into her house a few times, looking shifty as anything. Jan did, too. Then I asked him where he was and he lied about it.' He heart twisted in her chest at the memory. 'It doesn't take a genius to figure out what was going on.'

Penny looked at her with an expression Rae couldn't read. Was it pity? Or sympathy? It didn't look like either.

A pause, then Penny's voice again.

'Have you heard about Father Kevin's One Good Thing programme?'

Penny was speaking to everyone, but she was looking at Rae.

Rae shook her head. 'I think I saw a poster once? I didn't really know what it was.'

Penny's reaction was somewhere between a nod and a shrug. 'I help him with it, every evening. Just for half an hour or so. Anyway, the idea is that we match up people who are searching for repentance with people who are in need of a little helping hand.'

Helping people. Not sleeping with the priest.

Rae shot a pointed look at Nush, who at least had the decency to shrug sheepishly back.

'It started as something for people who felt lost,' Penny continued. 'Or maybe they felt overwhelmed by their problems, or they'd done a bad thing and felt swallowed up by it. These people, they had nothing, you know? We'd ask them to name one good thing about themselves, just one. And they couldn't.'

Her smile was sad, laced with empathy. With understanding. 'On the other hand, we had a lot of people locally who needed a little bit of help. Just small things. Father Kevin's idea was to match the two groups up. People who need help with people who are able to give it. And when they do give it, when they take time out of their day to help another person, *that's* their one good thing.'

'Anyway, Jamie...' Penny smiled to herself, the fondness clear in her eyes. 'Well, Jamie has done more than just one good thing. He's one of our regulars.'

Rae's eyebrows pulled together in confusion. 'Jamie's been... doing things for people?'

Jan snorted, as if she were about to make another comment, but Penny shot her a look and she quietened.

'He has.' Penny smiled broadly. 'And it's funny, because he doesn't really have anything to repent for. He's one of the good ones. He's helped people all over this village.'

'He laid my new path for me,' Edie chirped up with a loaded smile, and Penny smiled back at her.

The confusion swirled and grew in Rae's belly like a cyclone. These things Penny was saying - they were things she'd thought about Jamie. Right up until she didn't.

'Ok...' Rae's voice was thick, hesitant. 'But why are you...?

There was uncertainty in Penny's expression, a nervous shake to her hands as she smoothed them over her lap. 'Gemma...wow, I really shouldn't be telling you this...'

Rae's eyes widened, her heart stuttering in her chest as something, some tiny seed of hope began to sprout somewhere deep within her. In that second, she knew what Penny was going to say before she said it.

'Gemma is one of the people he's been helping.'

'What? Helping with what?' The voice was so distant that Rae didn't even recognise it as her own.

Penny took a breath. 'Her grandmother's dying. Gemma's been caring for her pretty much alone, but there were a couple of things she couldn't manage to do, and when she approached us for help, I knew that there was one person I could rely on.'

'Jamie,' Jan and Nush cooed in unison.

Penny smiled, nodding gently.

God, Rae so wanted to believe this version of events. The possibility tugged at the very fabric of her being, a whisper of promise making her heart skip and flutter.

But hadn't this naivety been her downfall before?

She frowned. 'Why would he lie?'

Penny shrugged. 'We did ask him to keep it to himself. I mean I didn't intend for him to take it to the *grave*, but Gemma was so embarrassed about having to ask for help. She doesn't have the greatest of reputations around here.'

'I don't know...'

'I'm just saying maybe you should give him another chance to explain before you write him off completely.' Penny's lips pressed into a lopsided smile. 'So you don't end up sitting around a table in thirty years' time telling stories about the one who got away.'

'Ok,' Rae said, only she couldn't be completely sure what she meant by that. At that moment, the fear of trusting Jamie and the fear of not trusting him held equal weight.

She picked her plant pot back up and got to work cutting out floral motifs to paste on. The room fell quiet then, but for the occasional sound of cutting and ripping, underscored by Edie humming lightly to herself as she worked.

Rae's mind worked and whirled, replaying Penny's words over and over. Was she wrong not to have believed Jamie on this? Had she jumped to conclusions?

She remembered the look on his face, though. It was guilt, she could have sworn it. He'd been caught out.

Hadn't he?

She threw herself into decorating her pot, trying to drown her thoughts out completely. It wasn't until Penny spoke again that she was pulled from her trance.

'Nush?' There was something in Penny's voice. A note of hesitancy, maybe. She took a deep breath before she asked the next question.

'Do you wish you'd have told your ghost that you loved him?'

Nush looked up from her work, her face a picture of loss and longing. 'Of course.' Her mouth tugged into a sad smile. 'If you love someone like that, you give a piece of yourself to them. And it's theirs whether they know it or not, but if they don't know it, that piece of you goes to waste.' She put her pot down and turned, giving Penny her full attention. 'I didn't have an agenda. I knew we could never be together. But I loved that man for half my life and he died without ever knowing it.' Her smile fell then, her eyes darkening. 'So yes. I say if you love someone you should tell them. While you still can. Even if it doesn't change anything.'

Penny paused for a beat, before replying in a small voice. 'Even if it *can't* change anything?'

Nush nodded emphatically. '*Especially* if it can't change anything. This part of you, it's a gift, but you aren't giving it away, you're holding on to it. It's taking up space in here.' She patted her own chest lightly, over her heart. 'If you keep it to yourself, it will only weigh you down. Set it free.'

Rae listened intently, all at once completely sure of one single thing.

She was in love with Jamie Stamford.

Blood rushed to her ears, her hands suddenly trembling, her heart in her throat. She could still hear talking, but it wasn't until she looked up that she realised Nush was now speaking to her.

'People don't *have* to love you back. A lot of the time they *don't* love you back. That's the thing.' Her slate eyes fixed on Rae's, her smile creasing into crow's feet around them. 'It happens, we see, in books, in films, they always do, but in life mostly that is not how it is.' She paused for a minute, gathered herself, and when she looked back up she was as serious as Rae had ever seen her.

'And if they *do* love you back it's a rare and beautiful thing. So don't throw it away!'

Rae's breath was ragged when she inhaled, and her heart thumped a riot in her chest.

Nush was right.

She was an *idiot*.

She looked up at the seven faces staring hopefully at her. 'I've ballsed this whole thing up, haven't I?'

'Yup.' Kieran nodded slowly, the faintest smile touching his lips.

'He loves me, doesn't he?' She could barely get the words out.

'Yup.' Only Kieran spoke, but all the ladies nodded emphatically behind him.

'Are you going to stop giving me one-word answers?'

'Nope.' He smiled widely, taking the half-finished flowerpot from her claw grip and setting it down on the table before leaning in to whisper in her ear. 'It's your story, Rachel. Re-write it.'

She laughed, tears springing from nowhere. 'Have you been talking to Nush?'

He took her hands, pulling her to her feet, before his hands moved to her shoulders and he leaned in close to talk to her.

But Rae only heard him say one thing.

'Go. Find him.'

33

Take Tonight

Rae Logan wasn't sure she'd ever moved so fast in her life as she did on the four-hundred-yard dash from Jan's cafe to Jamie's cottage.

Her heart was pounding like a drumbeat, her brain conjuring stirring montages of their impending make up scene, where she'd burst through his front door and collapse in a heap of underskirts and apologies like some Romantic era heroine.

It took her no time at all to reach the solid wood of the cottage door and she hammered on it like a maniac, her body alive, possibility humming through her veins like an electrical current.

C'mon, c'mon, she whispered to herself, a bundle of nerves suddenly gripping her as she stood back away from the door, tapping nervous fingers against her thoughts.

And then... absolutely nothing.

No noise, no movement. No sign at all of Jamie being home. *Dammit.*

Her heart dropped like a stone. She hadn't, not even for a

second, entertained the idea that he wouldn't be home. She put the palms of both hands against the smooth wood of the door, willing ideas into her head. Where would he spend his evenings? With her, until a few weeks ago. Occasionally at the pub, but probably not on a Tuesday. Or with...

Joe! Of course. They were always so close. He must spend a lot more time with Joe now. She thumbed to Joe's number in her phone, heart going ten to the dozen. It only rang twice before he picked up, confusion clear as a bell in his *hello?*

'Hey.' She cleared her throat. Tried to calm the tremor in her voice. 'Look, I know it's a bit weird that I'm calling you.'

Joe huffed amicably.

'Is Jamie with you?'

The second of silence that followed felt like a lifetime.

'No, sorry kid,' Joe said, simply. *Too* simply?

'Is he actually not, or has he just told you to say that cause he's avoiding me?'

He laughed. Such a similar laugh to Jamie, she noticed, and the thought ripped right through her. 'Sorry kid, it's just me and Allie tonight. I'm sure he'll turn up, though.'

The last part had an edge to it. She couldn't tell if it was a peace offering, or a drawn dagger.

'I just really need to talk to him,' she said, her voice small. 'He's not at home.'

'Well,' Joe started, and she could hear the deep breath he took. 'He's pretty much always either here, there or with you. Until you shredded his heart into tiny pieces, of course.'

Another blow straight to the chest. But she couldn't afford to lose this fight.

'Joe, please. It's important.'

He paused for a beat, and when he next spoke the tone of

his voice had softened. 'Sorry. I genuinely don't know... wait, what time is it?'

'A little after half seven.'

He hummed lightly. 'Have you tried the church hall? He sometimes helps out with a project which is based there.'

One Good Thing.

She felt a pang of guilt. How had she not known about this side of him? He was a better man than she'd given him credit for.

'Ok, thanks. I'll try that.'

Her march up the hill to the church was just as fast and twice as brutal on her lungs as her sprint across from the cafe. By the time she arrived she was almost wheezing with the effort, and Father Kevin looked up at her with a start as she tumbled through the double doors and all but collapsed on the parquet floor.

'Rachel?' His brows tugged into a quizzical frown.

She smiled apologetically, holding up one finger while she caught her breath and Father Kevin nodded in return.

'I'm looking,' she managed between breaths, 'for Jamie. Have you seen him, Father?'

He smiled then, the edges of it soft with understanding, like a piece of something fitting back into place, and he started towards her.

'Sorry, Rachel, he hasn't been in at all tonight.'

'I've looked everywhere.' It was barely more than a whisper.

He stopped short a couple of feet from her, his smile touched with surprising affinity for a man who had been celibate his entire life.

Rae looked up at him. 'He was doing jobs for you?'

'Kindnesses.' The priest nodded.

'I'm sorry?'

He brought his hands together like a habit. 'I don't like to think of them as jobs. Feels like such a negative word, doesn't it?' His smile was slight, a punctuating gesture. 'They are more small kindnesses which we can send out into the world. Paying it forward, I suppose. I've heard people say that a lot. 'He paused, searching her eyes. 'You'll let me know if you're ever looking to join us, won't you?'

'I will, Father.' She smiled, almost sheepishly. 'But right now, I have to find someone.'

His laugh was light and pure, exactly how Rae imagined a priest should laugh.

'Why not take tonight?' he asked, gently. 'Try again tomorrow. You know, some things are worth the wait.'

And although she knew that his advice was sound, Rae had absolutely no intention of taking it.

She spilled back out onto the street, her mind racing and she scanned the village at the foot of the hill, her eyes skipping from place to place as she puzzled over where Jamie could be. And then her breath caught in her throat as she realised where he could be. The one place she had no business looking for him.

Could he be at Gemma Brannigan's house?

The thought hit her all at once, along with Father Kevin's words playing over and over in her mind.

Take tonight. Try again tomorrow.

Obviously the priest would know if Jamie was there. Was that it? Was that what he'd been trying to tell her? Now she knew at least part of the truth, she couldn't even be angry with him for being there.

She blanched, stock still on the path of the church as the sky paled to an almost grey. Her eyes didn't move from the village, still searching for another explanation. A quiet desperation flooded her like adrenaline, pumping through her veins as she started back down the hill to the village.

She passed the school house and the old post office and was just passing The White House when she about turned and pushed through the heavy doors of the pub.

Roy was part-way through pulling a pint for Bill Cramer, who was sitting at the bar, spinning a beer mat idly between his fingers. They both looked up as they heard the door.

Rae waved awkwardly, before scanning the pub. It was quiet, probably more so than normal for a Tuesday night. A gaggle of students sat in one corner, nursing what little alcohol they could afford to buy. Ernie Atkins chatted to Iris's brother on their usual table near the door. Beyond that she could see only a couple she didn't recognise poring over a table full of tourism leaflets.

No sign of Jamie.

She sighed, shrugging out of her coat and heading over to the bar, where Roy and Mr Cramer greeted her warmly.

'Now then, lass,' Mr Cramer said with a wide grin, the warmth of his accent comforting against the rough beat of her heart in her ears. 'How's tha been?'

She could never help but to smile back at him, with his outdated moustache and wrinkles in all the places which spoke of happiness.

'Hi Mr Cramer.' She pulled up a stool next to him. 'Hi Roy.'

'Rachel,' Roy nodded in greeting, setting Mr Cramer's pint down on the mat he'd now laid flat on the bar. He looked up at her with a smile. 'Looking for someone?'

Her lips pressed into a grin. Roy didn't miss much. She'd

hazard a guess that he already knew exactly who she was looking for and why she was looking for him, but she found herself explaining anyway.

'I'm looking for Jamie. We had a fight... I'm sure you know that already.'

Roy raised a single eyebrow in response, barely even a movement.

'I need to talk to him.' She pulled herself up on the barstool next to Mr Cramer. 'I've... well, I was wrong about something, really wrong about something, and I need to tell him I'm sorry.'

Roy nodded again, sagely. 'And have your whole 'doing the making up' thing, as the young people say.'

Rae smirked. 'Not sure any young people say that, Roy.'

And the three of them laughed, Roy's face creasing and crumpling along his laughter lines.

'Anyway,' she said, smile fading. 'I'm pretty sure I've cooked my goose on that front.'

Mr Cramer looked at her over his glasses. 'What's tha on about?'

'I've burned my bridges.' Her smile was sad that time. 'You know, blown my chance.'

The wiry shopkeeper considered her for a long while, smoothing his moustache with thumb and forefinger. 'Lass, ah know what tha's sayin'. Ah just canny understand why tha's sayin' it.'

Her brow furrowed. 'That ship has sailed.' She could feel the rush of new tears, the subtle shake in her voice. 'I'm trying to shut the stable door, but the horse has bolted.'

Without missing a beat, Roy handed her a tissue.

The two men looked at her curiously, the way men do when trying to solve a problem. Mr Cramer's fingers went back to his moustache, Roy's to the bar top, fingers splayed on the varnished oak.

'Yer daft in the 'ed,' Bill Cramer finally said, softly.

Roy nodded conspiratorially. 'He's barely been in since he's not been with you.'

'Because I messed everything up!' Rae exclaimed, blowing her nose like a foghorn. 'I'm a ruiner. I ruined him and I ruined the chance I had of having anything with him.'

Mr Cramer's smile twisted to the side, barely visible beneath the short brush of hair. 'Ah, not this again. Tha's talking in riddles, lass. Mekin' things complicated when they really ought not to be.'

'I mean, they're idioms. But ok.' Rae smiled through her tears. 'It is what it is. I missed the boat. I'm too late.'

'Aye, ah know,' Mr Cramer said. 'Tha keeps on sayin'.' He downed the remnants of his pint in one long gulp and set the empty glass back on the bar, sliding it back over to Roy. 'But if tha never listens to owt else ah say, listen to this. That lad looks at thee t'same way our Roy looks at a fine Scotch.'

Roy thought for a brief moment before nodding with a half-shrug. 'Looks pretty simple from where I'm standing.'

'None of this is simple,' Rae said quietly, working the tissue into a hard ball in her hands.

Mr Cramer rose from his stool, patting her shoulder with an age-worn hand. 'Wi' love,' he said, the corners of his kind eyes crinkling into a smile, 'it never is.' His hand went to her shoulder, squeezing lightly. And then, nodding his farewell to the two of them, he strode out of the pub.

Roy's clear blue eyes stayed trained on the door until after it had slammed shut. He'd been a handsome man in his prime, and Rae could still see the blueprints of it in the curve of his jaw and the bow of his lips, his once-dark hair now shot through with thick streaks of silver.

He turned back to her with his trademark smirk just touching the corner of his lips. 'What can I get you? It's on the house.'

She held a finger up, shaking her head. 'No, nothing. Thank you, though.' She blew a long breath out, puffing her cheeks out and feeling a little tension leave her as she did. 'I really did just come in here to find Jamie.'

'Ok,' Roy said simply, although his tone implied he had more to say on the matter.

Rae raised one eyebrow. 'Just say it, Roy. I can see you thinking it.'

Roy's grin had an edge of sheepishness, but it fell as he met her gaze, serious eyes boring into her. 'It's just...' he started, his hesitation burning away before her eyes. 'It's just that if we only ever got one chance at things in this life, the whole damn lot of us would be buggered.'

Warmth spread through her like an embrace. She'd never felt more like part of a family as she did in this funny little village.

She felt the tightness in her chest before she heard it in her voice. 'What if I can't fix it?'

There was a knowing twinkle in his eyes. 'You can.'

Her brows pulled together. 'What do I do until then?'

He shrugged. 'Whatever helps.'

She nodded then, an idea coming to her all in a rush and she hopped off the stool, thanked Roy for everything, and pushed through the heavy wooden door.

She looked up as she stepped out onto the coarse stone of the path outside. In that moment there was something about

Blackston which gripped her, holding her with a permanency she felt in every bone in her body.

It was beautiful then, this tiny village she'd chosen to call home.

She walked down the path to the river, past Jan's cafe, which was still lit with the buzz of the craft club. She could just make out the deep rumble of Kieran's laugh as she passed, could see the shadow of Nush gesticulating wildly about something or another, and she smiled quietly to herself.

She padded over the bridge, remembering the time Jamie had scared the living daylights out of her and Nush there. Remembering the heat of his kiss that same night.

Then she was on the path to the beach.

The darkness of Black Rock loomed out in front of her, the late evening sky pastel and scarred here and there with the last remains of passing planes. The sea was calm, despite the breeze which whipped at her as she clambered up on the rock.

The twist and hop down into the cove at the end was just muscle memory, and as her feet hit the ground she straightened, looking out to sea, her face turned to the breeze, eyes half-closing with preemptive relief. She breathed in deeply, filling her lungs completely with the fresh salt of the sea air.

'FUCK', she screamed out into the dark turquoise waves.

It was then that she heard a low cough behind her and she spun in surprise, her heart in her throat, hands beginning to curl into fists instinctively. In all the years she'd been coming to the cove she had never once come across anyone else in it.

So, the very last thing she expected to see there in the pink light of the setting sun was Jamie Stamford.

He was leaning lightly against the smooth rock of the cove

walls, arms crossed defensively across his chest. He didn't meet her gaze as she turned to face him, and she could almost feel the forcefield he'd pulled up around himself.

'God, I didn't know anyone else knew about this place.' She wasn't too far off a shout, yet her voice seemed quiet against the crash of the waves. 'I've been looking everywhere for you.'

His eyes didn't move from the floor. 'You found me.'

His voice was rough, weighted with anger, or maybe with hurt. She studied him, the lines of him which had grown so familiar somehow now at odds. The smudge of dark shadows under his eyes. The knot of tension in his shoulders. The light in his eyes, that light which made her heart swell and skip, now nowhere to be seen. Guilt sat heavy in her stomach like a bad meal.

'I wanted to tell you I'm sorry,' she offered.

He nodded, a slight movement. But he didn't move. Didn't look at her.

She continued. 'Penny told me about Gemma. That you're helping her out.'

He frowned, a flicker of a reaction starting through his body, but still he didn't speak.

'Look,' she said, walking towards him, stopping just short. 'I didn't trust you and I should have. I believed rumours over you. And I know that was a shitty thing to do.'

'Yep,' he muttered, so quietly that she would have missed it had she not been standing so close to him.

She took a breath. She had something to say and she was going to say it. 'I walked in on my last boyfriend, the man I was going to *marry*, while he was fucking someone else in our kitchen. You've got to understand why I might have reacted badly. You know, I've spent my whole life feeling like I'm not quite enough. It wasn't such a stretch for me to believe I wasn't quite enough for you.'

She saw something in him then, some subtle shift in his posture. A release. Though he kept the barrier of his arms up and his eyes down, she knew in that moment that he was hearing her.

'Jamie,' her voice thinned, almost breaking. 'I'm saying I was wrong. I'm saying that I'm sorry.'

He nodded again, more definitely this time, but still he didn't look at her. He pushed around her, walking to the edge of the cove, and for a moment she half-thought he was going to clamber out and leave her there, but he stopped at the edge, looking out to sea.

They stood silent for a few minutes, watching the roll of the waves, shimmering and golden in the last light of the day. Then Jamie began to speak.

'I found this place the summer I thought you weren't coming to Blackston. I don't think I'd realised before then how much I was looking forward to seeing you again. Not really.' His brow creased. 'And then all of a sudden summer was there, but you weren't.'

His lips pressed together, the tension visible in his jaw. 'I walked up close to the edge, maybe a bit *too* close, and I was bracing myself against the wind when I saw it.'

'You weren't afraid to fall?' she heard herself asking, although by the time it reached her lips it sounded more like a statement.

'I was.' He huffed out a short breath. 'I still am.'

And she knew then he was talking about more than just the rocks. She took another step towards him, standing beside him at the edge of the cove and she felt his body react to her proximity.

He cleared his throat. 'I loved you, you know.'

'I know.' Her smile was at once wistful and expectant. 'I wish you'd have told me that at the time.'

'What would you have done if you knew?' he asked, eyes meeting hers for the first time.

'I don't know,' she answered honestly. 'But I'm here now.'

He nodded again, the corners of his mouth turning up slightly, almost a smile, and her heart soared at the sight. Maybe it wasn't forgiveness, but it was a start.

He shifted, turned so that he was facing her, one hip resting against the low front wall of the cove. 'I should have told you about Gemma.'

She turned too, mirroring him. 'Penny said they asked you not to.'

'They asked me not to share it with everyone.' He shrugged. 'You're not everyone.' One hand reached for hers, the union sending small fires racing through her, warm fingers of flame reaching into her chest. 'Maybe we both should have trusted a little more.'

'I'm sorry,' she said again, her eyebrows pinching together.

His eyes lit. 'I know.'

'I love you.'

'I know that, too.'

And his face broke out into the most magnificent smile, a smile she felt in every last cell of her body.

He tugged lightly on her hand, pulling her in towards him, and his other hand went to her face, tracing the line of her jaw, the slope of her neck. His eyes studied hers, alive now, the warm embers of his irises almost glowing in the golden hue of the evening light.

'Not going to say it back?' She couldn't hide her smirk. 'God, Jamie, way to keep a girl hanging.'

But he said nothing, only slipped his hand into her hair and brought his mouth to hers in a kiss which spoke to the very core of her, his lips soft and warm and wet, full of promise, and of longing, and of love.

As he broke away, the smile that was left on his face was breathtaking.

'Of course I love you, you idiot.' His forehead rested against hers, their lips barely apart. 'I've loved you for twenty years.'

And her chest swelled then with a joy, a completeness which she hadn't known was possible. It made her laugh out loud, the sea swallowing the sound in the crash of its waves.

She swatted him lightly. 'You're the idiot, you idiot.'

He laughed too, the sound bright and warm, a rumble in his chest which she could feel racing right through her. And then his lips were back on hers all of a sudden, kissing her with a softness which turned slowly to heat as he breathed her in as if she were something vital. Something he needed to survive.

'Rachel,' he whispered roughly against her lips as he broke away a second time. 'You *are* enough. You're everything.'

She smiled, eyes closed against the wave of feeling which sparked and flamed deep inside her, and she kissed him until she was breathless.

When she opened her eyes again, twilight had begun to fall over the crisp salt air of their secret cove and Jamie had entwined his fingers in hers.

'C'mon old girl. Let's go home.'

And as he helped her clamber out of the cove and led her wordlessly back up the limestone path towards the cottage, Rae knew one thing to be absolutely true.

Blackston was her home.
Jamie Stamford was her home.

34

Dearest Martha

Rae Logan had never truly considered herself to be a
writer.

She was a person who wrote, a person who enjoyed
writing, certainly, but until the day she put the final full stop
after the final word of her manuscript, she had never thought
herself worthy of the title.

The book was born from her need to tell her family's story.
Bolstered by the new truths she had to tell, ideas had poured
into her so quickly she could barely keep up. Within two
months she'd written a full draft.

Between writing, she'd been helping with old Martha
Brannigan's letters. Sometimes she and Jamie went together
to read, sometimes they went alone. But for Rae especially,
the letters felt like a gift.

She'd known Martha had been a poet in her younger years.
Nush had always had few books of her work knocking about
at the mill, but she'd never really thought about the woman
behind the words. And the romance documented in the fading
letters was a tale of fierce, fleeting love, told with a depth of

emotion so strong that Rae couldn't help but be moved by every word she read.

Gemma, too, seemed to be changed by the letters. The first time Rae had gone with Jamie to see them, she'd been struck by the shy, thin character nibbling on her fingers and hiding behind her hair. Such a change from the brash girl she remembered. If it hadn't been for the dark vines of ageing tattoos peeking out from under her clothes, Rae wouldn't have believed she was looking at the same Gemma Brannigan.

As Martha gradually deteriorated, Gemma seemed to do the opposite. Caring for her grandmother had been the making of her, and it was written all over her. Her face had filled back out, the colour long since returned to her cheeks, and there was a new light in her eyes which might never have been there, not even in the before.

Martha had been given six weeks to live at the beginning of the year, but with the care and love that Gemma had given her, she'd lived months longer than anyone had expected.

It was July now, and the dry heat of midsummer had Blackston in its grip, pulling weekend tourists from the cities. The weather left its mark scorched on the landscape, turning the earth to dust, the grass fading from lush green to straw.

Martha too, was fading, but there was one letter left to read, one final message from another life before she left this one. She had been growing weaker before their eyes these last few days, sleeping more than she was awake, shivering against the stifling heat of the old cottage.

She was close to the end, and Rae could see it etched into Gemma's face as she opened the cottage door.

'Hey,' Gemma said, smiling weakly. The dark shadows under her eyes which had all but left were beginning to sneak back, but her face this time was laced with worry rather that with sickness.

Rae pulled her into a hug. 'Hey.'

After a shaky start, the two women had quickly become friends. Much like Jamie, Rae cared little about the Gemma she'd known as a teenager, and had found a lot to like about this new version.

'How is she?' Jamie asked, stepping from behind Rae to give Gemma a quick hug of his own.

Gemma visibly winced. 'She woke up this morning and she seems on top of the world.' She tried to smile, but the edges of her mouth tugged down rather than up. 'I called the nurse, and she said she's rallying. That this happens a lot and we should make the most of it, but that it normally means that the end is close.' Her eyes filled with tears, and as she quickly tried to sniff them away. 'That it could be any time.'

Rae felt the familiar ache growing behind her breastbone. She had been here, once. Not knowing when. Watching her father slip away in slow motion as the disease silently conquered him, piece by piece, and then all at once, submerging, pulling him down like quicksand.

She took a steadying breath and rested one arm around Gemma's shoulders.

'Come on, lovely. Let's put the kettle on.'

It had only taken a couple of visits to the mill before Gemma understood the healing powers of Nush's magical lemon tea. Like Nush, she didn't sweeten hers, preferring the bite of the lemon to come through, and as Rae made tea for all of them, she dug the little extra she'd brought out of her bag. Nush's signature walnut cake was her go-to when things could not be remedied with tea alone.

When Rae padded back into the other room, Jamie had found the final letter and was busying tidying all the others back into the box. They'd agreed he would read the last letter. He'd read the first, and so he should read the last.

He turned the aged envelope over in his hands. 'This one's addressed to you in hospital, Martha? Delivered by hand?'

Martha smiled, her eyes aimlessly searching for Jamie. 'Ah, yes. This one's from a few years later, after the war.' Her hand went to the gold locket she always wore around her neck and she touched it absentmindedly. 'It was when I had Gemma's mother, Janet. The fathers weren't allowed to stay in the hospital then, you see. It was all very businesslike. They could visit quickly, then they were hurried away again. I stayed in for ten days after the birth, on very strict bed rest.

'Tommy wrote that letter on the ninth day. He'd come in the previous afternoon to visit us, to make plans for us to come home. On the tenth day I was due to be discharged, he was so excited. Telling me all about the crib he'd built, about the blankets the neighbourhood ladies had made for little Janet.'

She paused then, and caught her breath before she continued. 'That was the last letter he ever wrote to me. He walked to the hospital to deliver it, and on his walk back, he was hit by a car.'

Rae and Jamie gasped in unison.

'Oh Martha, that's awful,' Rae said quietly, carefully squeezing her hand, barely more than skin and bone in her grasp. But the old woman only squeezed back lightly, the faintest trace of a smile on her face.

'They said he had terrible injuries. That it would have been very quick.' Her voice stumbled on the *quick*, the pain written through her. 'I never saw him again, his family sorted everything out. Because of the baby, you know? His brother went to identify him, his father sorted all the arrangements. I went to the funeral, of course, but the casket was closed, so...' She trailed off, catching her breath again, the rattle in her cough shaking her whole body. 'He was there and then he wasn't. And I had a baby, but I didn't have a family.'

'That must have been really hard,' Jamie said, gently.

'It was,' she conceded, but lightly, as if she were skimming over all the bad parts. 'But we made it work. His family were a great help and they all doted on Janet. We muddled through.'

Rae sipped her tea. 'But you never married again?'

Martha's smile was broader that time, so wide that it stretched out the thin skin of her face. 'I just never met anyone who made me feel like he did.' She looked up, eyes seeming to fix on a point on the ceiling. 'But it's ok, I'll be seeing him soon.'

She turned back to Jamie. 'You need to get on and read the letter though. I don't have long left, you know.'

Sorry, Martha,' he said, with a low chuckle, and he cleared his throat and began to read.

Dearest Martha,

Words can't explain the pride I feel when I see you with our beautiful daughter. I thought my life was full before, but now I can't even imagine how I used to feel before I knew her. I have absolutely no doubt that you will make a wonderful mother, as you have made such a wonderful wife.

I know it's only one day until we will be together as a family. But I couldn't wait another second to tell you that I will love the two of you with every beat of my heart and far beyond.

Yours always,

Your loving husband, Tommy

Jamie's voice caught at the end, his breath a little ragged, and when Rae looked up she could see traces of tears in his eyes. Gemma was crying quietly too, and Rae could feel tears on her own cheeks.

The only person who wasn't crying was Martha. Sitting back against the nest of pillows Gemma had arranged for her, the old woman's face fell into a relaxed smile, one hand on her gold locket and her expression one of gentle joy and, Rae thought, of absolute peace.

Jamie put the letter away carefully, as had become their habit, and Gemma took the box from him and padded off up the stairs to stow it away safely.

It was a few moments before Martha spoke, but when she did, her tone was steady. 'Thank you, both of you, for everything you've done.'

And then more quietly, 'I can go now.'

Jamie blew out a long breath, wiping his eyes delicately on the heel of his hand. 'How can you be so ok with dying?'

Martha's chuckle was as light as her failing lungs allowed. 'You're young, so you don't understand. But one day you will.' She reached blindly for his hand, and he moved it to hers. 'It's like being at a party. Imagine your taxi arrived as you were sitting down to eat. You wouldn't want to leave at all. You're just getting started, and you think of everything you'll miss out on and you don't want to go. That is how death feels when you're a young person.

'But I'm not a young person. I'm eighty-nine. For me, it's the end of the party. I'm cold, I'm tired, I've had much too much to drink, and my feet are sore from the beautiful shoes

313

I've been wearing all night.'

She turned, almost as if she were meeting his eyes, although her sight had been almost completely gone for months now. 'I have loved this party dearly, although it hasn't always been easy. But it's time now. I'm ready to go home.'

Something in the energy of the room changed then, and Rae felt it. Like the flick of a switch, some force turning off, or maybe turning on. An inevitability.

Jamie's nod was slight, barely a movement at all, but it spoke volumes. 'I get it.'

'You're a good boy.' Martha reached for him and he guided her hand until it was at his cheek, which she patted lightly. 'I can't begin to thank you for what you've done for us. For Gemma. But I need to ask you for one more thing.'

Something in her face changed then. It was a flicker of tension, worry which twisted and seized her features. 'You must look out for her after I'm gone. I'm so afraid she'll have no one. I can't find my peace until I know she'll be ok.'

Rae's chest tightened. 'She'll be ok,' she said, gently. 'There are no strangers at the mill. Nush makes sure of it.'

Martha's face lit brightly for a moment. 'Oh, dear Nush. She has such a big heart.' Her gaze tripped and searched, and for a second Rae could have sworn Martha looked her dead in the eyes.' You get that from her.'

Rae's heart stopped dead in her chest. 'How did you...?'

'I've always known.'

'She told you?'

Martha laughed lightly, shaking her head. 'She didn't have to. To a mother, some things are obvious.'

Both women smiled at the same time, a silent understanding passing between them. Then they heard a noise upstairs, a dull thud and a crash, and then what sounded like a lot of swearing.

Jamie looked over at Rae with a chuckle. 'I'll go.'

And he kissed her lightly on the cheek and rushed off up the stairs to check on Gemma.

Rae watched Martha, now a little dimmer than she had been, laying back weakly against the carefully arranged pillows, and she couldn't help but think of her dad. She wondered if he'd had this peace at the end. Wondered if he knew she hadn't been there. Wondered if he'd chosen that moment on purpose.

A thick lump formed in her throat and she swallowed around it, rising from her chair and busying herself collecting up the empty mugs. She was just grabbing the last one, over the other side of the bed, when she felt Martha studying her, following her with her ears more than her eyes.

'Are you going to marry him?' she asked suddenly, catching Rae off guard.

'Jamie?' Rae's brows drew together and she answered automatically, 'I don't know.'

Then more quietly, more honestly, 'I hope so.'

'I knew. With Tommy, I mean.' Martha's voice was weaker now, the rattle of her breathing slowly beginning to creep back in. 'The second I met him I knew he was the one. And when he died...'

She tailed off, anguish lining her fragile face at the memory. 'I was angry, for a long time. I was hurting so much that I sometimes wished I had never met him at all. But you know, there's nothing like your own impending death to make you see the truths in your life.' She laughed, but there was little humour in it, and the effort made her wheeze and splutter, before steadying herself, speaking slowly.

'And the truth was that I loved that boy with every last thing that I had and if I had to do it all again, even knowing how things would end, I would *still* choose him. Over and over again.'

She smiled wistfully, but there was something else in her expression now. Determination, maybe?

She took another careful breath and carried on. 'I'm going to give you some advice. Writer to writer.' She laughed at herself again, and again the wheeze gripped her lungs, but she didn't stop smiling. 'Gosh, I've always wanted to bestow my worldly wisdom on someone on my deathbed.'

Rae's throat was thick now, but she laughed through her tears, reaching out for Martha's hand, which gripped hers back with surprising strength.

'So, I'll just tell you this.' Martha's smile was clear and bright, then. Her eyes tried to search for Rae's face out of habit. Her cool hand squeezed Rae's lightly. 'Love as long as you have life left in you. Love honestly and fiercely and let that be enough. Because you never really know what's around the corner. You might have a lifetime with the people you love or you might lose them that same day. These moments you have with people, they're not unlimited.'

Rae blew out a small laugh, wiping tears with the back of her free hand. 'So basically you're saying don't mess it up?'

Martha's laugh was as much a cough. 'I'm saying just love him. The rest will work itself out.'

'Have you always been this wise?' Rae laughed again, still wiping tears, and holding on like crazy to this dying woman, a woman she had barely known before the last few weeks. 'I should have come to you about more stuff.'

Martha cough-laughed again, squeezing Rae's hand with

316

both hers, now visibly shaking from the effort. 'What is wisdom really, other than learning from our own mistakes?' She smiled weakly. 'Maybe I've just made a lot of mistakes?'

Rae smiled too, squeezing her hand back, and when she felt it slacken against hers, she arranged Martha's arms carefully by her sides as she used to do with her dad, smoothing the covers around her to make her comfortable.

Then Martha's breathing slowed as her eyelids began to droop and close, letting sleep creep up on her, and the room was quiet against the faint sound of vacuuming somewhere upstairs.

'Martha?' Rae said, gently.

Her eyelids flickered, but they didn't open. 'Yes?'

Rae leaned in towards her, speaking clearly and slowly. 'We'll take care of her. You don't need to worry.'

And Martha's voice was barely audible when she replied, 'Thank you.' And as she did, the very edges of her mouth quirked in the faintest hint of a smile before sleep washed over her like a wave, dragging her down. Claiming her.

When Jamie and Gemma came back in, Rae was sitting quietly, watching the steady rise and fall of the crisp cotton sheets covering the tiny body in the bed. Thinking about the words she'd said. Words which had affected her somewhere, deep in her ribcage, in the very marrow of her bones.

Just love him.

She could do that.

Gemma drew her breath in sharply as she stepped back in 'Oh God, is she...?'

Rae shook her head, putting one hand lightly on Gemma's arm. 'Just sleeping, I think.'

Gemma nodded at that, a glint of fresh tears welling in her

eyes, and walked around to her chair on the other side of the bed, picking up her grandmother's lifeless hand and stroking it gently.

Rae remembered very well the feeling written all over Gemma's face. The sorrow, the helplessness. The waiting. The knot of grief tightened inside her.

'It's scary, I know,' she said out loud, before she even realised she was speaking. Jamie and Gemma both looked up at her. 'Being here, not knowing. I mean, death is scary as hell. But when my dad died...' She tailed off. Breathed away her tears.

'I wasn't there. I was too late. And now I'd give anything to go back to that day and just say goodbye one last time, but...' She shook her head. 'It feels hard now, but in time you'll look back and see that this was a gift.'

Gemma nodded gratefully, the smile on her face tight, but genuine.

'Gemma?' Jamie said, a tenderness in his voice.

She looked up at him in response.

'Call us if you need us. If anything happens. You don't have to do this by yourself.'

'Thank you.' Her voice was a whisper, but her face showed something else. Something more.

Through the heartache written all through her expression there was a new strength emerging in her, like the first green shoots pushing through tough spring ground. She was not the same woman who had arrived in Blackston last year.

She had asked for one good thing, but she had been given something more. She had been given a second chance.

As Rae took Jamie's hand and they waved goodbye, leaving the walnut cake on the side and stepping out though the still house, she could hear the quiet sound of Gemma talking softly to her grandmother and she smiled to herself.

Somehow, through hardship and pain, through the threat of losing the only person in the world she thought she had left, this tiny scrap of a woman had found her calling.

The rest will work itself out.

And it was three days after that, on a perfectly clement Tuesday, that Martha Brannigan took her final breath.

35

A Ghost Story

Danusia Nowak was practiced in many things, but
none so much as mourning

Through her lifetime grief had gripped her in
various waves. First the loss of her parents, a longing for the
homeland she never knew, and then later for the relationship
she had lost with her sister and, of course, for the love of her
life. But if there was one thing she could always rely on to
help, it was finding a connection.

That was why, in the dry heat of early August, she was sitting
alone on the beach at North Landing, burying her toes into
the scorched sand and finding comfort in the sting of the sun
on her cheeks.

She'd made the trip back to the cove every year since Rae
was born. At first she would come on the eve of her birthday,
but after Ray's death five years ago she'd begun to make her
visits on the anniversary of that date instead. She had never
once visited his grave in the city, instead gravitating to the
place she had felt closest to him while he was alive.

In the dark, cool depths of the caves she had known him,

really *known* him, and the memory of his fingers under her chin and his breath on her face had stayed with her for a lifetime.

Her routine was always the same.

She would sit on the beach for an hour or more, gathering her thoughts. Then, only when she felt as if she were ready, she would venture into the darkness of the cave for her annual conversation with Ray.

She would tell him about her life in Blackston, about the progress she was making on the mill, about the time that she spent with Rae. Sometimes she would cry in there, hidden from the judgement of the wider world, sometimes she wouldn't. Either way, by the time she emerged from the cave and walked back up the stone steps to the cliff, she would find herself lighter, stronger, freed from the weight of her silence for another year.

And in the moments after that, when she'd stand on the cliff top, bracing herself against the push of the sea breeze, there was a window of time when she felt absolutely at peace.

The swoop of a seagull pecking at her sandals pulled her from her thoughts, then, and she smiled to herself, brushing the sand from her linen trousers as she stood, gathering her things into her small beach bag.

She could have found the entrance to the cave with her eyes shut now, the temperature at once changing as she pushed further into the sanctuary of the stone. It was just as she remembered, always. The smooth jut of the rock as her fingers trailed the walls. The give of damp sand under her feet. Even the smell was the same, the crisp salt of the sea air sharp in her chest as she breathed it in.

She reached the rock where she had been together with Ray,

and, as she always did, pulled herself up to sit on it, the stone a welcome coolness on the backs of her burning legs.

'Hey,' she said quietly out into the silence, her voice warped and changed by the strange acoustics of the cave. 'It's me.'

And, as always, she was soon overcome by the compulsion to speak, to tell the memory of her lost love all her troubles, all her hopes, everything she wished she had been able to say to him while he was alive, and more. Things she could barely admit to herself.

She spoke about Rae, about the ways that the emerging truth of her conception had freed the both of them. About the craft club, this new network which was ebbing and growing in the village that she loved. She spoke about the murders, about the rumours, and about all the trouble she had inadvertently caused.

And, most importantly, she told Ray how their daughter, before her eyes, had blossomed at last into the woman Nush had always known she could be, and how the handsome young Jamie Stamford had found a lot to love in her.

'He looks at her,' Nush started, her voice suddenly flooding with emotion, 'the way I always hoped you would look at me.'

And she cleared her throat and pressed one palm flat against the smooth rock beneath her, feeling it ground her, feeling the hurt flow out of her all at once into the silence of the cave. She felt the tears fall, and she didn't stop them, just sat for a while, just her and her ghost and the cool stillness of *their* place; sharing her pain, making it smaller, easier.

She didn't know how long she sat there, but when she emerged back into the stifling heat of the late afternoon the sun was lower in the sky, and she had to squint against it as she walked back up the beach towards the stone steps.

She didn't notice the figure at the top of the cliff until she was almost all the way to the steps, and it startled her at first. There was often a crowd of people on the beach, especially through the weeks of the school holidays, but there was something about the figure which caught her attention straight away, a familiarity which knocked at her ribcage as she began to climb the steps. The figure looked like...

It couldn't be.

But when she reached the top, the sudden exposure gripped her almost as tightly as the shock of meeting her sister's eyes. Eyes she had not looked into for thirty-five eyes.

They stood, frozen, each silently contemplating the other for a few minutes before Zosia's face softened and the corner of her mouth hitched slightly into an almost imperceptible smile.

'Nusia.'

Zosia held out the childhood pet name like a peace offering. It was just one word, but it felt like more, a gesture so grand that it caught Nush's breath before the rush of the wind could. She didn't know what to say, so she said, 'How did you know I'd be here?'

'Rachel.' Zosia spoke in Polish, holding her sister's gaze. 'She told me you come here every year. On his anniversary.'

Nush nodded, still awkward. It had been so long. Her little sister was an older woman now, her hair still dyed the lurid red shade she'd always liked, but cropped short around her shoulders, her thinning lips still lined in her favourite shade of cerise.

'Since the book,' Zosia continued, a hint of apology on her lips, or maybe forgiveness, 'I speak with her every week. I don't know that we've ever got on better.'

Nush blew a steadying breath out, her face beginning to soften into the idea of a smile. When Rae had come to her with her idea for the book, Nush hadn't been sure at all how it would sit with Zosia, and she found an uncharacteristic amount of satisfaction in being proven wrong.

'I want to tell your story,' Rae had said to her, carefully, her eyes pleading a preemptive apology while she handed over a hot mug of lemon tea. 'The whole thing. From the camp, my Babcia, everything with my dad, then me...' She'd hesitated, just for a moment, suddenly unsure. 'But I want to tell it through Mama's eyes.'

She hadn't stopped referring to Zosia as her mama, but somehow it cut against Nush less now the truth was out, and the bond between Rae and Nush had only grown stronger.

Rae and Zosia, too, had made great strides in their relationship. While Zosia had been blindsided when Rae first approached her, shocked to her core that she knew everything, the process of telling her story had been so cathartic, so *healing* that by the time the story was finished she had felt almost like a different person.

'You know,' Zosia plucked the sunglasses from their perch on top of her head and settled them into place against the glare of the sun. 'All her life I was so worried that one day she would find out, that she would finally learn that she wasn't really mine, and that she would want nothing more to do with me.' Her smile then was as genuine as Nush thought she had ever seen on her sister, though edged somewhat in regret. 'Maybe I even tried to keep her at a distance so that it would hurt less when it happened. But it didn't happen at all.' Her laugh escaped as a single breath. 'It was strange at first, you know? But I think she understands me more now than she ever did. I mean, I can be an arsehole sometimes.' Her pink lips twisted into a smirk. 'But it's better. *We're* better.'

Nush nodded slowly, quiet for a minute, still gripped by the shock of seeing her sister after all these years, and even more by the mercy in her voice, the like of which Nush had not imagined she would ever hear again.

When she did speak, her voice was quiet against the roll of the waves below. 'She's a good girl.'

Zosia smiled, nodding gently. 'She is.'

Nush looked up, straight into her sister's eyes, the same grey-green as her own. 'Thank you for raising her.'

'Thank you for trusting me to.' At once Zosia's face softened into an expression that Nush had not seen on her since their childhood. 'It was difficult for you, I know. It was difficult for me too. And I said a lot of things back then.' Her voice weakened, stuttered to a stop before she regarded Nush carefully, cleared her throat and continued. 'But I don't think I ever said thank you. What you gave me. It was a gift.'

Nush nodded a *you're welcome* and it didn't seem like enough. But then none of her words would have come close either.

They stood, the two sisters, four feet apart, a strange tension still hanging between them, but with words spoken slowly beginning to outweigh words unsaid. It was then that Zosia spoke again, in English this time, and the mood changed in a heartbeat.

'Rachel told me that you loved him.'

Nush stiffened at first, the habit of hiding her secret still woven into her, before the tension dropped a notch and she nodded.

'He loved you too, I think.' Zosia shrugged lightly, the movement resigned. 'There was a part of him that was always yours.'

Nush's brows tugged together. 'He told you?'

Zosia shook her head. 'He asked me if you liked him, once. It wasn't long before he first took me out. We were talking and he asked me if I thought you would ever want to be with him. I said no. I said that you loved him like a brother. That's what you always told me.'

Nush's heart clenched in her chest as she thought of all the times the sisters had gossiped about Ray, and all the times she had assured Zosia she wasn't interested.

The regret crashed into her like a wave.

Zosia regarded her carefully before she spoke again. 'But I knew you were lying.'

Nush's stomach jumped into her throat. 'What?'

'I knew you liked him. It was so obvious.' Zosia's lips pressed together, her focus jumping away from Nush, out to sea. 'But I was jealous. I liked him too, of course. But I was so scared, Nusia, that you would marry and I would be left with no one.'

A million thoughts swirled in Nush's mind, lost chances and regret and validation all meeting and blurring into a riot of feeling which rushed up her throat all at once.

How things would have been different, she thought.

It's too late, she thought.

He loved me, she thought.

And she looked back up into the repentant eyes of her sister, who spoke two words in English, her voice steady and without the slightest trace of an accent.

'I'm sorry.'

'Me too.' Nush nodded, softly.

Zosia eyes filled with tears, but they didn't fall. 'I miss you.'

Nush nodded again. 'Me too.'

And as she reached for her little sister's hand, Nush let out the breath she'd been holding, releasing the knot of long-held anger deep inside herself and letting the ghost of what could have been fly away on the salt of the sea air.

36

The Future

"It goes without saying that the preservation of the area remains of paramount importance to the residents of the village, but there has been a particular focus in recent decades on measures to curb coastal erosion. The construction of the concrete sea wall and breakwater at the northernmost point of the bay was completed by the end of the 1990s, and though the rate of erosion has measurably slowed since then, there is still a concern that the coastal footpath could fall into the sea within the next hundred years if no further action is taken.

The young people of the village must come together now to help celebrate and preserve this area of outstanding natural beauty which they are lucky to be able to call their home, so that future generations are able to enjoy it as they have. The author will be long gone by then, but can't help but to pose one question; what will the future hold for the young residents of Blackston?"

- F.W. Merryfield, *A Brief History of Blackston Bay*

37

How the Story Ends

Autumn snuck up on Blackston Bay like the first smudges of ruby red on the leaves of the cherry trees, and a fresh sea breeze was making the craft club's handmade bunting flail and snap.

They'd spent the last six sessions making it, as well as a few extra evening sessions and one very late night for Rae and Penny mainlining Nush's double-strength tea while they stitched it all together. It stretched from St Teresa's at the top of the hill right down to the mill, zig-zagging to and fro across the street. It was a haphazard mix, triangles cut from any spare fabric people had lying around, as well as a fair few items of clothing which had ended up being sacrificed for the greater good of the bunting project. Many of the triangles had been decorated before they were stitched in - some painted, some printed, and a few just bearing messages of goodwill scrawled on with a permanent marker.

It had been an epic project, but the final result was breath-taking. Not that anyone had minded putting in the effort, of course. It wasn't every day that Blackston hosted a wedding.

It was a bright day, unseasonably warm for late September, and the birds in the trees were having a celebration of their own, chirping and tweeting a melody while the steady crack of the bunting held the beat.

Inside the mill, Rae was doing some chirping of her own, trying to keep her cool while Jan's stylish niece, Maya, attacked her with heated styling appliances on what felt like the hottest day of the year.

Nush giggled from her seat over the kitchen table, and Rae tried her best to give her a sideways glare without moving her head even an inch.

'Don't laugh, you're next.'

Nush hooted even louder. 'That's fine, Słoneczko. I am cool like cucumbers.' From the corner of her eye, Rae could see her lip lift into a smirk. 'A little cooler, maybe'

Rae huffed. 'It's not funny, I'm sweating.'

'Don't worry, I brought industrial strength deodorant,' Gemma yelled from the hallway, where she was searching for her shoes among all the wedding paraphernalia dumped there.

'You, my lovely, are a saviour,' Rae yelled back. She shot another glare at Nush. 'And I have nothing to say to *you*.'

Nush laughed again. 'It will all be worth it when you look like an angel.'

'A sweaty angel,' Rae muttered under her breath.

Maya stepped back, rearranged a few strands, then clasped her hands together with glee. 'Ok, you're all done! Go have a look.'

Rae jumped up, grateful for the breeze the movement afforded her, and shimmered to the hall mirror in a wave of blush chiffon and hairspray. When she saw her reflection, her jaw dropped.

'Woah, you *do* look like an angel.' Gemma appeared behind her, now slightly taller than Rae, which Rae assumed meant she must have found her shoes.

'I do,' Rae whispered quietly, in awe of the ethereal beauty staring back at her in the mirror. 'Maya is a wizard. Is this even me?'

Her wild hair had been curled into smoother ringlets, then twisted up carefully into a delicate topknot, with odd strands curling down on to her face. Her makeup was flawless too, natural and glowing, with an elegant flick of black eyeliner and the merest hint of deep pink on her lips.

'It's you, but like... way better,' Maya said from the kitchen, where she had now moved on to torturing Nush.

'*Way* better,' Gemma agreed with a nod, and the two of them stood together for a few moments, admiring this strange and beautiful new version of Rae Logan.

It was only then that Rae really looked at Gemma. 'Woah, look at you - you look amazing!'

And she did. When Gemma's first wage came in from the factory job Rae had helped her to get, the two of them went to have their hair done by one of Kieran's friends, who also turned out to have magical powers, because he transformed Gemma's hair from a bird's nest of cheap, grown-out dye to a long, blunt-cut bob in a bold shade of copper. She was wearing it wavy today, and with her dramatic makeup she looked like some kind of retro starlet. Her emerald green wiggle dress had a top layer of corded lace which covered her from her neck to her knees and made her look much less conscious of herself, and altogether completely stunning.

Gemma blushed modestly under Rae's stare. 'I feel good.'

'You should,' Rae said with a nod. Her perfectly painted lips twisted up into a smile. 'We scrub up all right, don't we?'

And they smiled at each other, these fast new friends who came together under the strangest and saddest of circumstances.

When Nush came trotting down the hall a little while later, they were even more taken aback.

'Nush, look at you!' Gemma exclaimed with a low whistle. 'Hubba hubba.'

Rae stood back with her hands on her hips and a broad smile on her face. 'Whoa, who knew all of *that* was under there?'

Nush's normally wild salt and pepper hair had been blow dried straight into a smooth style which framed her face, along with carefully-applied makeup which made her glow in the warm light of the mill. Her dress was simple and elegant, a large-scale monochrome floral which seemed to take years off her.

Nush beamed. 'I look pretty.'

Rae felt a small rush of pride, and she couldn't keep the smile off her face. 'You do!'

She smiled back, almost bashful. 'Well, I've never walked anybody down the aisle before. I thought I should probably make an effort.'

'Well it paid off,' Gemma added.

And the three of them linked hands, taking in the moment together.

As soon as Nush heard that Martha had died, she'd cleared the spare bedroom at the mill and insisted on Gemma staying with her any time she felt a little lost. Feeling she needed to atone somewhat for the trouble her rumour and speculation had caused, she'd gone the extra mile to ease Gemma's grief, and it wasn't long before she was staying at the mill more often than not. Ever the collector of waifs and strays, Nush was delighted to have her, referring collectively to Rae and Gemma as 'my girls' to anyone who'd listen.

Checking the old clock next to the mill door, Rae straightened, clearing her throat. 'Ok ladies, let's do this.'

The wedding was to be held in the grounds of The White House, and Roy had done a magnificent job of transforming it from a country pub beer garden to a magical haven, pulling the wooden picnic tables to the side and adorning them with white ribbon and wildflowers. An extra length of bunting hung between two trees at the back, made up of the best and most important triangles the club had decorated.

There was a white marquee at the side of the pub for shelter, with two more on standby in case there was any rain, although looking at the clear blue sky there seemed little chance of that.

Rae drew in a breath as she saw it, and again as she picked out, one by one, all the guests filing into the white chairs lined up in neat rows.

Roy was darting about making last-minute tweaks to his set up, looking dashing in a slim grey suit. Edie and Iris sat with the long-suffering Ernie, and behind them Caroline and her son, sitting beside young Flora Dunham and her date, who she'd finally found the courage to talk to, to the craft club's collective delight. Near them, Penny and Father Kevin sat, making plans for their next goodwill project.

Bill Cramer, who was helping Jan with the catering, stood by the pub's open doors, reeling numbers off to Jan, who was dressed to the nines and ordering trays of canapés about like a drill sergeant.

Even Martha was there, embroidered into one of the bunting flags and flying free in the breeze.

And then Jamie, of course, beautiful Jamie leaning lightly against the garden wall and wearing the hell out of a slim-cut navy suit. His dark curls had been tamed somewhat, his beard trimmed, and his warm amber eyes sparkled and creased as they met hers, the angles of his face folding into a dazzling smile as he noticed her.

Rae's heart jumped and skipped as he walked to meet her, pressing a chaste kiss to her lips.

'You make a beautiful bridesmaid,' he whispered softly, kissing her again high on her cheekbone before pulling back and smiling brightly at Gemma.

'And this stunner is my date, I guess?' His eyes twinkled as Rae swatted him with a manicured hand.

'Try it and see what happens,' Rae said sweetly, the warning in her eyes only a half-joke, as he chuckled to himself and offered Gemma the crook of his elbow.

She took it, leaning in to stage whisper to Rae as she did. 'Don't worry, mate. He's not my type.'

And the girls shared a conspiratorial smile as Jamie led Gemma to their seats and Rae could faintly hear Gemma laughing as Jamie tried to convince her that he was everyone's type.

Ezra bounded up behind them, a ball of energy, kissing Nush's cheek and then Rae's. Ezra always looked put together, but his herringbone suit was something else, paired with a navy bow tie and smart chestnut brogues, as well as a single white rose pinned to his lapel.

He looked as if he'd walked straight out of a fashion

magazine.

'Are you ready, ladies?' he asked, a note of something in his voice. Excitement, maybe anxiety.

'Are *you* ready? Nush replied, chuckling to herself.

'Always,' he chirped, with a wink and a grin, skipping down the aisle to take his seat at the front.

'Come on, Myszko,' Nush said, one hand lightly brushing Rae's shoulder. 'Let's go find our guy.'

They found Kieran inside the pub, leaning lightly against the bar and talking food with Jan. He was a vision in a deep cobalt three-piece suit, the russet red tie and pocket square matching the fiery hues of his wavy hair perfectly.

They both looked up as the two women walked in.

Jan hopped up with a grin. 'I guess that's my cue to go sit down?'

Nush nodded.

Kieran stood too, straightening his tie. 'Hurry up, Jan. You don't want to miss my grand entrance.' He fluttered his eyelashes at her.

She laughed, scrunching her nose at him before smoothing her ruby red skirt over her knees as if it were her apron and swinging through the pub door.

Rae turned back to Kieran. 'Hey, how did you decide which one of you would walk down the aisle?'

He shrugged casually. 'I've got a better walk.'

Nush patted him on both shoulders with a wide smile. 'Come on then, let's see it.'

He nodded once, definitively.

Nush didn't move her hands. 'You nervous?'

'Nope.' His deep voice was steady.

Rae couldn't help but smile. 'Then let's get you two cats

335

married.'

'Please never say 'cats' again.' Kieran deadpanned, raising one eyebrow theatrically. 'Unless you mean *literal cats.'*

Rae smirked. 'I can't promise anything.'

His eye roll was even more dramatic, but his eyes were sparkling. Behind the buzz of anticipation, Rae had never seen him so happy.

'Ready?'

He nodded, surely, before reaching behind him and depositing a small posy of white roses in Rae's hands. 'Ready.'

And Rae clutched them tightly in her hands, heart full, knowing of no greater honour than leading the way for her best friend to marry the man of his dreams.

It was a beautiful ceremony.

Nush cried first, almost before they had rounded the corner. When both of Kieran's parents had declined his tentative invitation to the wedding, he'd asked Nush if she would do him the honour of walking him down the aisle and Rae thought for a minute that Nush might actually burst with pride.

This time last year, she'd said, as they'd enjoyed a celebratory hot chocolate with everything at Jan's cafe, *I didn't have any children. And now I have three. Not to mention a handsome new son-in-law.*

She was positively beaming now as she walked steadily along with Kieran, holding the crook of his elbow with two hands, and when they reached the registrar, she kissed both of the men as if they were her own sons.

Rae watched them take their vows with awe, and with a vague flicker of something else. Something deeper. Her eyes sought Jamie's out in the rows of seats, and he smiled back at her as their eyes met.

And as the new Mr and Mr Quinn shared their first kiss as a married couple and the small audience erupted into a frenzy of cheers and whistles, Rae was humbled by the love and joy and acceptance which was woven into the very fibre of this curious little village. Even in old Ernie Atkins, though he had to be elbowed out of stony silence by his wife.

Rae saw in this place what Nush had all those years ago, and she knew without a single doubt what that feeling was.

Belonging.

The rest of the day passed quickly in a haze of food and laughter, as Rae cried like a baby at Kieran's speech, and then again at Ezra's. And as they danced under the stars on Roy's makeshift outdoor dance floor (which was originally intended to be Roy's temporary indoor dance floor), she pulled Jamie close, revelling in the heat of his body, of the low quiver of his voice as he hummed along to the song.

All of a sudden, she noticed that Gemma was dancing too, with someone she could have sworn was not at the wedding. 'Is that Joe?'

'Yup,' Jamie muttered without looking. 'He turned up an hour ago. Had a bust up with Allie, and I didn't want to ruin the day by asking too many questions.'

Rae watched them for a while. There was something about the way that they moved together which caught her attention, but she didn't miss the slump in Joe's shoulders, nor the clumsy grip of his hands around Gemma's waist.

'He's drunk.'

'Yeah.' There was an edge of resignation in Jamie's voice.

'But he's ok. He won't cause any trouble.'

'Ok,' she said, watching the two of them for a second more before nodding lightly, and settling back into Jamie, resting the side of her face against his chest she watched Penny and the priest talking seriously about something off the other side of the dancefloor.

They stayed like that almost through two songs, swaying like teenagers at a school dance. And as the second song was winding down, Jamie stopped humming and paused for a beat before he spoke, immediately capturing Rae's attention away from the goings on of the other guests.

'I want to do this with you.'

She sprung back like a reflex, looking up at him in shock.

He laughed. 'Doesn't have to be now. Just one day.' He leaned down again to stage whisper in her ear. 'Probably quite soon though, cause you're getting on a bit.'

She swatted him, laughing despite herself. 'Was that a proposal?'

'No,' he said, simply. 'It was a statement of intent. You'll know when I'm proposing to you.'

She raised a single eyebrow. 'Jamie, we're talking about you, here. I feel like I might not.'

He smiled, but said nothing, and she didn't miss the knowing look which crept into his eyes for the briefest of moments.

Her brows tugged together. 'What's that look for?'

He shrugged enigmatically. 'Haven't you ever wondered how the story ends?'

Her brows knotted even more. 'What do you mean?'

But he just smiled and pulled her in close, swaying gently to the beat of the song.

'Jamie!' She protested for a second, before thinking better of it and relaxing back into the slow dance, turning her face back into him.

'You know what, never mind. Just don't do anything embarrassing,' she said against his chest, and she felt the low vibration in his breastbone as he chuckled quietly to himself.

She didn't think much more of the exchange the rest of the night. Not while they danced until the autumn night grew too cold and they headed into the pub for a nightcap. Not while they laughed at Bill Cramer and Jan telling funny stories from their own weddings. Not even as she said goodbye to the happy couple as they headed off to the fancy hotel room Nush had booked for them, throwing an arm around each of them and kissing their beautiful newlywed faces.

It wasn't until she was back at the mill, gathering a few things so she could stay over at the cottage that she saw the sea green cover of her notebook peeking out from under the stack of her manuscript, and Jamie's words came back to her in a flash.

Haven't you ever wondered how the story ends?

How the story ends.

God, she must have looked at the inscription on the front a hundred times, but she'd never even thought to look at the back. She picked the notebook up and turned it over in her hands.

Nothing on the outside.

She ran her hand over the buttery leather softly, a habit, before opening it on the back page.

There it was, clear as day, written in black ink at the bottom right-hand corner of the patterned endpaper.

Marry me, Rachel.

Her heart skipped and lurched. She looked over at him, mouth agape. He was leaning lightly against the doorframe - casually, like he hadn't a care in the world.

'It's been there the whole time.' The merest hint of a smile crept into the very corner of his mouth. 'I was just waiting for you to get there.'

This time it all happened in slow motion and she committed every second, every *detail* to her memory. The messy scrawl of Jamie's words on the page. The jump of her heart in her chest as she read them again, twice, three times. The smooth slap of her feet against the floorboards as she walked over to the doorway where Jamie was leaning. The shift in his weight as he straightened, briefly, and then took a knee, his eyes darkening as he looked up at her and began to speak.

She didn't think at all about sandwiches, or about the weather. Nothing else existed except the man on one knee before her, a man that she already knew to be her past, her present and her future.

And it was there, barefoot in a cloud of chiffon in the place she had found her home, that Rae Logan found herself answering the most important question of her life.

About the Author

Katy Dyers lives in the wilds of Yorkshire in the UK and loves to write stories about love, life and the kind of everyday heartbreak which makes us human.

When she's not writing you'll find her eating cake, swearing at her sewing machine or taking eight million photos of a really good sky out of her bathroom window.

You can connect with me on:
- https://twitter.com/katydyers
- https://www.instagram.com/katy.dyers

Printed in Great
Britain
by Amazon